the
memory
of my
shadow

To Michael —
You must be a pretty
great person to have a
friend like Julie!
Enjoy!

a novel by

BEN WAKEMAN

THE MEMORY OF MY SHADOW
Copyright © 2024 by Ben Wakeman, Great Unknown.
ISBN: 978-1-304-51411-0

Inquiries can be directed to ben@benwakeman.com

Cover design, photography, and layout by Ben Wakeman.
Edited by Stacia Pelletier

*This novel is dedicated to my
wonderous children, Ian, Ash, and Bella.
What will you make of this brave
new world you've inherited?*

//prologue

My hands were tacky with rubber cement. I stuck and unstuck my thumb and index finger, enjoying the claustrophobic sensation of being caught and released over and over. The chemical fumes made my eyes water as I paged through a well-thumbed National Geographic magazine with my other hand, searching for lions. I would have settled for any beast.

It was Monday, second period, Mr. Schaffer's applied arts class. I was working on a collage but not working too hard. It was a forest scene, the foliage, a mishmash of banana leaves from Ecuador, Aspens from Colorado, and house plants from the atrium of some movie star's home. The rain was a thousand tiny fingers tapping on the classroom window, the perfect accompaniment to the Joni Mitchell song playing through the small speaker on Mr. Schaffer's cluttered desk.

At the table beside me, Jill was on her phone texting with some college guy she met over the weekend. She held the phone down between her knees so Schaffer wouldn't confiscate it as he was making his rounds. There was the slightest smile moving on her lips as she chewed on a strand of her hair. I never found out who the source of her smile was. She was dead before the song finished.

At first, it sounded like maybe the rain was coming down harder, like the fingers on the window were now fists. Someone closer to the door said, very clearly, it's a gun.

What felt like an electric current moved through the nineteen of us and then, the room was no longer a room full of people, but of wild animals with bulging eyes, sharp elbows, choked screams, trampling feet, pushing in all directions, searching for escape.

The gunfire grew louder in the hallway, accompanied by shrieking, shouting and the sound of sneakers squeaking on the polished tile

4

floors. Mr. Schaffer followed the protocol, fighting his way to the door which, according to policy was already closed and locked. He flipped over the table closest to the wooden door to begin making a barricade. He was gripping the tabletop and trying to wedge it up under the door when his hand exploded into a flower of red. He did not scream but stood there looking down at the wasted, raw meat and gristle of the instrument that only moments before he had used to guide the feather tip of a horse hairbrush in a perfect arch as he demonstrated to Jason Pittman how he could make better clouds.

He turned around to face us, his eyes wide, his mouth slack. He stood there for what seemed an eternity before the door splintered with a dozen angry holes and he fell to the floor. Three students nearest to the door were also hit, the bullets tearing through their bodies and tossing them across the room. The rest of us were all jammed up together against the windows.

A chair. That's all it would have taken to break those windows. Over the years I think about this and a thousand other things I might have done to prevent what happened.

One of the bullets had destroyed the lock and the door was easily kicked in. The metal table legs screeched across the floor in futile resistance and then there was only the relentless repetition of gunshots and the acrid, metallic smell from the assault rifle. I don't remember any more screams, only whimpers and pleading from small voices. The voices of frightened children. We were children, all the bravado of young adulthood stripped away. Like the others, I tucked my head between my knees and huddled in the herd, waiting. The gunshots were measured and thoughtful now, the cadence of someone making choices. It was a lurching call and response, an impossible metronome extinguishing a life with every beat.

Please, oh please, God no. BANG!
Don't hurt me, please don't. BANG!
You don't have to. BANG!
I wanna go home, I just want my mommy. BANG! BANG!
"Yeah, me too. Shut up."

I knew the voice. Without looking up, I knew the voice. How could I not? It was a voice that shared my first words, a voice that had always made me laugh and made me feel less afraid of the dark.

Time no longer existed. It was now a valley of dark silence punctuated by bangs. I waited until there were no more. I did not look up. I waited. I thought I must be dead. My ears were ringing beneath my clenched fists. My jeans were soaked in urine and blood. The smell is etched into my memory, but I cannot describe it to you. There are no words to describe what terror smells like.

I looked up, a rodent poking its head out of a hole. There was no movement from the warm bodies that lay bleeding out all around me. Someone's leg twitched against my thigh for a few seconds and then it stopped forever. The emptiness was profound. The trough left behind a wave of souls departing all at once. Through the blur of my tears, I saw him standing there. Joe, my twin.

He stood with the assault rifle in his hands, the barrel smoking. Another one was slung over his shoulder and hung behind his back. I would learn much later that he had bought a kit online to modify the guns to make them fully automatic. Through the smoke, his eyes were empty holes, like the hollows of black olives. There was no reflection of light in them, no flicker of emotion. There was no recognition. He looked through me for so long, standing there, slack.

"Mare," he said. His voice was my little brother's voice, born two minutes behind me. "I'm uh... I'm sorry," he said.

Just then, from somewhere back in the labyrinth of hallways, a scratchy amplified voice was talking to Joe. He turned his head to listen. I couldn't make out what they were saying.

When the voice stopped, Joe turned the rifle around, put the barrel into his mouth, and with his thumb squeezed the trigger before I could even scream. Two final staccato BANG BANGs followed. His body dropped to the floor like a heavy bag of dirty laundry. I stared at the heap of him. I did not recognize the military-style black boots or the camouflage jacket. There was nothing familiar about him. His blood dripping from the drop-ceiling tiles of the classroom was not of my blood. I realized I did not know him at all. He was a piece of meat lying on a cold slab surrounded by other pieces of meat in this institutional room. The rain outside continued to fall.

Before I turned my eyes away for good, they lingered for a moment on his hand, poking out of the sleeve of the jacket. Around his wrist, I saw the faded bracelet I had made for him two years before when we spent the summer on a lake with Mom. The thing was frayed and so thin from wear that it was little more than a thread.

I don't remember anything after that with any clarity. Someone must have come. It may have been minutes. It may have been hours or days. My memory is a reel of film cut and spliced into disjointed frames. Me lying in a hospital room with men in suits staring down at me, their hands busy scribbling into small notebooks. My father pacing back and forth by the window of the same room, now dark except for a streetlight outside. My mother wailing by my side, her arms across the white cocoon of my body on the hospital bed.

At some point later, I was home in my room with the curtains closed. The entire block around our house was a movable circus of media vans and reporters with microphones fixing their makeup. I don't know how long that lasted but I never left my room, much less stepped outside of the house.

That was April 27, 2026, the day of the deadliest school shooting in American history. Forty-six people were killed that day by my brother, Joseph Espinoza, forty-seven if you count him. I may be alone, but I count him. I have counted him every day for the past 26 years.

I have spent my life trying to understand what happened in Joe's brain. I never trusted the brain after that day, not mine, not anyone's. I recognize it for the flawed instrument that it is, and I have devoted my life to find a way to fix it. I think that I have.

//chapter 01

My name is not Mary Espinoza anymore. It's Magdalena. Just the one name. I changed it when I turned eighteen and started my freshman year at MIT. I did not want my name to be the story of me that everyone heard before I even opened my mouth. When I have had friends, they called me Maggie, but I don't really have any friends right now. Maybe one day when there is less to be done, I will have time for friends.

I started my story in the middle, the gruesome, fractured middle. I believe all stories start in the middle because none of us can speak with any accuracy to our origin. There was a time before when memory was malleable and fluid, like quicksilver. In the telling of our stories, we could take liberties. What choice did we have with such a flawed instrument as the human brain but to invent what was not properly recorded? Children born after 2052 will never know what it was like to have to remember, any more than my grandfather's generation could imagine a time when numbers had to be calculated with pen and paper.

I have never told the story of my brother Joe out loud or in written form. When I read it back I even question if it is true. It seems unreal just as most of what I will tell you in this story will seem unreal. You may even begin to question what is real and that's okay. I think it is a necessary point in our evolution as a species, to reach the end of our ability to understand and then to choose to leap and trust.

To understand what I am about to tell you will require you to make a leap. To make the leap, you will need a running start.

I double-majored in computer science and psychology and graduated a year early in the top five percent of my class. All my research, all my free time and energy I channeled into the pursuit of intelligence, specifically creating an intelligence equal to, if not greater than, our own. Before I even received my diploma, I had offers to work at companies all over Silicon Valley, from start-ups to the global monoliths that infiltrate and manipulate our entire population. I listened to all of their pitches and pretended to weigh their offers. Some of the signing bonuses were more money than my father made in a year as a tenured Physics professor. I accepted none of them. I was not motivated by money and my interest did not involve better ways to manipulate people to separate them from the money they didn't have. I was young and full of ideals.

Instead, I accepted a fellowship and joined the graduate program at Georgia Institute of Technology. I did it for two reasons. For one, there was a professor leading a program in advanced machine learning who was making discoveries that seemed like science fiction. This Dr. Henri Choo had a background in biology and biochemical engineering, and all their work with computers was inspired by a fascination with the human brain and trying to understand the source of consciousness. Second but equally important was the fact that my father had taken a teaching position there and was not doing well.

When my mother passed the year after the incident, I thought I would lose him too. She could not bear up under the loss and guilt and anguish. It was like a molten iron anchor around her neck, searing into her heart even as it pulled her down. She overdosed using a bottle of prescription sleeping pills and my father found her on the couch wrapped up in an old quilt when he came home from work. There was no note. We didn't talk about it. My father and I are alike in that. We can shut down when we need to. When it is the only good option.

Even shut down, Papa was nothing if not logical. He knew we could not stay in that house or in that town. He abandoned his tenured position at UCLA, sold the house, and moved us to Austin, Texas because it was a place he'd always wanted to see. He used to love to watch Austin City Limits and I think that was the draw. He rented us a two-bedroom house in Travis Heights near Lady Bird Lake, which was really just a wide stretch of the Colorado River and not a lake at all. This confused me, but I did love to walk along the river walk there beneath the trees. It reminded me of nothing, which was good. We lived there for the rest of the year while I finished high school. Some girls might have been upset about moving in their senior year, but I really didn't give a shit. I lived in my head and moved through the world as if I was invisible, so it really didn't matter to me where I was, as long as I had my laptop and some headphones.

The year we spent in Austin was a surreal way station for us both. Papa took up drinking with the same single-minded focus he had done most things in his life. I stopped waiting up for him, even though I worried. But every morning, he was there in the small kitchen making something for me to eat before I went to school. His thick, greasy hair, was a nest in the back from some deranged bird as he stirred a pot of oatmeal on the stove or a pan of scrambled eggs. Often, he was still wearing the same clothes from the day before, wrinkled and smelling of cigarettes and liquor. His eyes were bloodshot and hooded, his face a guilty mask. This was not who he was.

"Buenos días mi pequeño conejo." He always called me his little rabbit.

I found the job for him at Georgia Tech. I knew I could not just leave him when I went away to college. He was a man who needed a purpose and without it, he would go the way of my mother. As I was applying for colleges, I was applying for jobs for him too. The week I got my acceptance letter from MIT, my first choice, I told him that he had an interview. He was not surprised by my boldness. He smiled in the tired way that was the only way he could anymore, and he nodded.

We both started at new schools in the Fall of 2028. I helped him get settled into a nice little apartment close to the lush green campus of Georgia Tech in this part of the country where we had never been before and had no connection to. It was like Austin in that respect, but better because there were trees and lots of rain which was something new and soothing for us both. I think something shifted for us by moving to the South. I don't think either of us would have dared to call it hope but looking back, that's what it was. During the week before I had to leave to go to Boston, we walked most evenings along the Belt-line, a trail of greenspace encircling the middle of Atlanta along what was once a train track. On those evenings, the air was thick and heavy with humidity, but it was alive. We were alive.

In my presence, he did not drink anything stronger than sweet tea, which immediately became his favorite thing about the South. We ate barbeque and fried chicken and found a place that made tamales almost as good as my abuela's. We did not talk of the past. How could we? We talked about my future and what I would discover, what I would invent. We talked about the great mathematical proofs, about String theory and about relativity. I tried to explain to him my love for computers, but he didn't understand any more than he understood why my mother had loved them. In his mind, computers were tools and that was it. His phone was four years old and the only piece of technology he owned. He mostly used it as a voice recorder and a place to keep track of lists he was always making.

When the week was up, and I had to leave for Boston, he was sad that he would not be able to move me into my dorm. It was a milestone that he and my mother had always imagined was in front of them. I told him it was fine. I had plenty of money to get whatever I needed, and I was not afraid. *So brave*, he said. *How did you get to be so brave, little rabbit?*

At the airport, he had quietly cried. I hugged him for a long time and in that moment felt the reality of what we had both been avoiding for so long. We were two, not four, not three and, in a moment, we would be divided again.

My years at MIT were a blur. I studied, coded, ate, and slept a couple of hours a night, woke up, and did it all over again. That was the extent of my existence. I barely made it to Atlanta to see Papa except for major holidays but we kept in touch daily through texts and emails mostly. Once a week he'd force me into an AR chat so he could see for himself that I wasn't starving. He was always excited to hear about my work even though I don't think he really understood what I was trying to do. He was my biggest fan and supporter, my hype man. Any time we were in a public place, he felt compelled to tell a complete stranger about his brilliant daughter and how she was going to change the world. It was insufferably embarrassing at the time but looking back I can see how his words propelled me – they stoked the fire that I already had burning inside me.

Papa was actually the reason I ended up at Georgia Tech studying under Dr. Choo. He knew my keen interest in artificial intelligence and machine learning, so he had made it a point to seek out the eccentric Dr. Choo and to pick their brain about the work they were doing. Papa would then relate it back to me the next time we talked. He got in the habit of picking up an extra cup of coffee three mornings a week and going by Dr. Choo's office on his way in to start his own day.

The two of them would talk, Dr. Choo telling Papa about the numerous setbacks the team had in their attempts to develop a functional prototype that would advance the already prodigious progress on A.I. that was happening on the West coast. Papa would in turn tell Dr. Choo about how well I was doing at MIT. This matchmaking went on for over a year. When I came home for Christmas break during my junior year, Papa invited Dr. Choo to join us for dinner. That meeting was a pivotal moment in my life.

When I answered the door that evening and stood face to face with Dr. Choo for the first time, I was not prepared. Papa had told me so much about his esteemed intellect but had neglected to tell me anything about the professor's appearance. I can see why. Dr. Henri Choo was not someone easily classified, and Papa lived so much in his head that he barely noticed his own appearance so why should anyone else's be of consequence?

Standing on the stoop in front of me was a beautiful, elegantly dressed Chinese woman wearing some strange contraption on their head. Dr. Choo was wearing what appeared to be a homegrown prototype that was a clunky marriage between a stylish pair of glasses, a tiny micro-computer, and a wide Velcro choker around their neck that reminded me of a blood pressure cuff. There were a couple of wires discreetly tucked behind Dr. Choo's ear that connected the glasses to the choker. I could just make out another bundle of wires that disappeared beneath their blouse and connected to the small computer affixed to a black patent leather belt around their waist. I stood and stared for longer than I should have, but Dr. Choo did not seem put off by my rudeness. They simply stuck out their beautifully manicured hand, the nails of which were a delicate seashell pink.

"You must be dear Magdalena, I presume. I'm Dr. Choo, your father's friend. I hope I'm not too early. I brought some wine."

It took much of the evening for me to recalibrate the image I had in my brain of the esteemed professor. I had expected a serious, even dour, Asian man with thick glasses and ill-fitting clothes from Wal-Mart not an elegant and eccentric non-binary person with a wicked sense of humor. They were beautiful and had exquisite taste in clothes, which did not pair with the Radio Shack appearance of their cybernetic accessories.

"Oh, it's hideous I know," they said very early in the evening as we were sipping wine at the breakfast bar off the kitchen and watching my father prepare dinner. "But it's only prototype, I have plans for something much... subtler." Their eyes did a fluttering, coquettish wink with this last word.

It's safe to say Dr. Choo was like no one I'd ever encountered, and I loved them right away. Henri (they insisted I not call them Dr. Choo) was brilliant, I'd expected that, but they were also incredibly funny and more self-aware than anyone I had ever met. They explained that today was a "she day" for them. They alternated days of the week as a woman. It was one of the many ongoing experiments they conducted on themselves.

"I'm fascinated by how our brains function differently based on how other people perceive us and how we perceive ourselves in social settings. I'm collecting some amazing data," they said. "It's really changing my previous limited appreciation for how much communication happens between humans at a non-verbal level."

"So, you're not trans, this is all just for science?"

"Oh, Jesus no, honey, I love a great pair of heels," Henri whispered, leaning in, and placing a hand on my arm. They said this with a put-on southern drawl that made me crack up. "I just use the science as an excuse!" Their laugh was a decidedly manly guffaw and contagious.

The three of us ate dinner and drank wine. My father's cooking had dramatically improved over the course of the past year. My mother had always done the real cooking. I remember he made a prime rib roast with garlic potatoes and a kale Caesar salad. It was cute to watch him so diligently following the recipes he had printed out and taped to the cabinets, insisting that he did not need any help. There was one critical oversight. Henri was a vegetarian. It had not occurred to my father to ask. Henri was easy though, as they were easy about most things I would find. I marveled at how anyone could be so comfortable in their own skin when I felt like an alien moving around in the body of a foreign host most of the time.

At some point in the evening, Henri tried to explain to me exactly what the prototype on their head was and how it worked, but I struggled to keep up. In fairness to me, the job was made harder because Henri was spectacularly hammered after just two glasses of wine. What I came to piece together was that the contraption was a digital assistant they cobbled together in their lab. The glasses were actually a heads-up display with an attached camera. This tech had existed for some time and was not the main attraction. For over a decade, a number of companies had been tinkering with these types of computing interfaces. What was unique, was the gear residing in the crude-looking choker they wore around their neck. Inside it was a collection of sophisticated sensors for collecting biometric data, but also a series of sonar and haptic devices that transmitted signals into Henri's body, both through bone conduction and the nerves in the skin.

"It's all very simple, you see." This was Henri's catchphrase. "Chinese medicine has known for thousands of years that the human body is an incredibly complex electrical network with input and output peripherals. You know acupuncture? Not magic. Science baby. This, is the same thing."

Henri took another big swallow of wine, spilling some down the front of their blouse without paying any mind.

"The collar is how my digital companion communicates with me."

I shook my head. I didn't get it.

Henri reached out and took my hand across the table. They turned it over and pushed up my sleeve, exposing my wrist. They told me to close my eyes. Very delicately they touched my wrist with the very tip of their finger, no lighter than the stroke of a feather.

"You feel that?" they asked. I nodded. "How about this?" they said. I nodded again. "And now?" they said. I nodded. There was a pause. I opened my eyes. "I didn't touch you the last time. Your mind simulated the touch based on previous input. I just hacked you!"

They guffawed and took another sip of wine without letting go of my wrist. Over the course of the next thirty minutes, Henri continued their exposition, teaching me how to interpret a series of light taps on my wrist – something like Morse code. They made their point quickly through a series of simple question, answer exchanges. I found that I was able to intuit more through haptic communication than I would have ever imagined, and my head began to explode with the possibilities.

"So, I did all this with just my finger. Very crude, like fingerpaint, right?" They held up their index finger and waggled it in front of my face. "Compare that to the head of needle, now imagine one hundred needles in a bundle, powered by a computer. It's all very simple, you see?"

I did not see, but I knew that in time I would see. Henri was experimenting with a whole new form of kinetic language. It seemed an impossible leap at first, but when I was lying in bed later, long after they had gone home, I realized that all of language is an abstraction, a series of symbols, sounds and gestures that our brains parse into meaningful messages. A Bach Sonata, a Van Gogh painting, these are just auditory and visual information until our brains decode them. Dr. Choo's research, if it led to what he believed was possible, would make the invention of binary or "machine language" for computers look like cave paintings.

I would learn quickly that we were still a long way from the vision he had planted in my head that first Christmas. But the seed was there, and I was consumed with the notion that I could help him make it grow. This new way of communicating by tapping into the bioelectrical system of the human body coupled with the rapid advancements in artificial intelligence happening out in Silicon Valley would change humanity. I knew it with certainty that first night as I lay in the spare bedroom of my father's apartment listening to him snore in the next room.

As I was trying to go to sleep, I thought of Joe. Didn't we use to play a game when we were kids and couldn't sleep where we wrote messages on each other's backs using only a finger? Or did I imagine that? This inability to trust my memory, especially when it came to my brother,

was common for me. I often tried to search for memories of him before that horrible day, but they were just beyond my reach, concealed
in an impenetrable fog. He was the lost other half of me, and my brain
would never stop pinging out into the void in search of a response,
even as the exact same brain actively made him disappear.

//chapter 02

You will no doubt recall the headline four years ago on February 10, 2048: WE'VE REACHED THE SINGULARITY, NOW WHAT?

Now what, indeed. The world didn't implode, the machines didn't take over. Humans didn't become subjugated drones bent to serve a higher intelligence --at least not any more than some people have been and always will be subjugated drones bent to the will of a higher intelligence. Isn't that how society works? Most things just got safer, and more orderly, but that's been happening for some time. Autopilot meant fewer airplane crashes; driverless cars cut the number of accidents by 85 percent. Despite the statistics and all the historical evidence to the contrary, there will always be fear of new technology. I'm sure the first Neanderthal to use a stick to knock a mango from a tree was clobbered with rocks and pushed out of the clan.

The creation of thinking machines was inevitable. We are a restless, lonely species whose members have, for centuries, tried to avoid hard work at any cost. The creation of general artificial intelligence is just us closing the loop on the thing we've been chasing with technology from the beginning: efficiency. A more romantic or philosophical person would say it's much more – the desire to make something in our own image so that we are less alone. Maybe, but I don't think so. I think we did it because we could, and it happened so much faster than anyone could have predicted. Twenty-five years ahead of all the experts' earliest projections, to be exact.

Henri and I were kindred spirits in those early days when I worked with them in the lab at Tech. On paper, I was pursuing my master's degree in computer science, but Henri did not treat me like a student. They dismissed, with a wave of their hand, anything I was required to do for the program. "That's not important, this is important," Henri would say whenever I broached the subject of my thesis. "Give it to me, I'll sign off and we can get back to work, deal?"

The degree was never the goal for me anyway, no more than the big-time job in Silicon Valley had been. Looking back, I don't even think I understood what was driving me beyond just the raw, insatiable desire to get to the bottom of the mystery, to solve this puzzle we had found. There were many mornings I woke up on the couch in the lab with a blanket around me and a sticky note from Henri stuck to my laptop, gently scolding me for working too much. But their notes usually ended with a question about our research that only drove me back to my laptop and the prototype workbench after I had grabbed a coffee and bagel from the place on the corner.

Within eighteen months, we had made dramatic progress on the crude prototype that Henri had turned up with that first night we met. Our work was built upon the DeepThink A.I. project which I'm sure you're familiar with. In case you were in a coma for a few years, DeepThink was an open-source initiative started by a private firm that made a few paradigm-shifting discoveries in cross-training models on large, wildly disparate data sets. The company imploded quickly after some shocking, but hardly surprising allegations came to light about the founder's harassment of more than a dozen women. I enjoyed the memes. "DeepShit," was my favorite. It didn't matter at that point. Pandora's box was open and programmers all over the world were advancing the project far faster than a single company could have.

All that was required to participate in DeepThink was that you be registered officially on the project, that you log in via biometric authentication, and that you adhere to the guidelines of the WWCAI, the World-Wide Consortium for Artificial Intelligence. For our part, we contributed very little to the project. We were happy to stand on the shoulders of the giants working at MIT and Stanford. Our aim was different. We knew it was a matter of time before they created a program that could think. Our goal was to create a new way to communicate with it once it was born.

We monitored DeepThink's progress closely, pulling down the latest code into our own branch every week and running our communication experiments against it. In those early days, A.I. was the equivalent of a toddler. It had all the functional components, but the little guy fell down a lot, had a short attention span, and occasionally wet the bed. But it was learning fast and so were we.

Proving that haptic communication could work was easy. Henri had figured that out before I ever showed up. The much harder part was building a language simple enough to tie into the ancient nervous system of the human body and yet sophisticated and flexible enough to describe more than just primitive shapes, colors, and sensations.

Henri and I argued constantly about our philosophical approach to making the discovery we both knew was possible. The debates would often go so far afield that we would lose perspective and begin arguing for the side we had so vehemently opposed the day before.

"The body is a bag of meat," I would argue. "Our approach is too complex. We are trying to shove a bowling ball of information through a garden hose!"

"Stupid girl!" Henri would counter. "The human body is the most sophisticated machine on the planet. We must dig deep and listen harder. You are too impatient!"

I was. I was impatient and impetuous. I was twenty-two. Henri was, maybe just a mellower, older version of me, but they had a deep, abiding love for the "wetware" of the human body that I had yet to learn. It made us a good team. Unlikely, yes, but we complemented each other. All my hard, driving, pragmatism was checked by Henri's slow, reverent mysticism. They believed there was innate intelligence in the system of the human body and that we had only to uplink with it to be successful. I believed the burden was on us to create a solution, and invent a completely new system of communication.

In the end, we were both right, but it took years to get there. By the time I had completed my doctorate, we had a fully functional prototype that was orders of magnitude better than what I fondly referred to as Henri's dog collar but compared to what would come later, it was really just a marginally smaller dog collar. But this small prototype and the underlying communication protocol that ran it were enough to garner the attention of a venture capitalist who had been sniffing around the Tech incubator program for the next big thing. Henri and I had never considered going into business, but we had reached the limits of what we could do in academia, and I was too fiercely independent to take our baby to some big tech company where it would turn into something we did not want, or worse, get completely buried.

It wasn't a hard decision. We had dinner with my dad and talked it over. By the end of the evening, it was decided. We would accept the $1.2-million round of funding. We insisted on staying in Atlanta. There were some other minor clauses in that contract that I don't remember, but the most important one was that Henri and I had complete authority over the technology and how it would be used. Our only promise to the investor was that we would deliver a marketable product within two years' time.

We rented a 2000-square-foot loft space in the Old Fourth Ward neighborhood. We called our little venture Commune. We hired very selectively and started with a small team. There were only five of us for the first year. The first hire was a biomedical engineer named Nisha and the second was a psychologist named Florian who had an extensive background in human-computer interaction design. Rounding out the team was a soft-spoken young programmer named Aleem. He was brilliant but very sensitive and for much of those early years, had a pained expression on his face as he weathered the worst of my and Henri's stormy collaboration.

After eighteen months, the venture capital firm cut us loose and took their loss. We had no marketable prototype or really anything close.

To say we were undeterred by our failure would be the Hollywood version. We were crushed and I actually gave up for a few months. We were out of money and running on fumes. Henri and I both took freelance programming gigs to keep making payroll and rent. Eventually, we gave up the high-rent space and crammed into a low-ceiling cluster of rooms in an office park off the interstate. Expensive Sashimi lunches gave way to a cold sack of burgers in a cramped, windowless kitchen with roaches and fluorescent tube lights.

It was the most irritating feeling, like having all 2000 pieces of a puzzle on the table in front of you with half of it put together and then having to walk away. Florian held on for another year before bailing. That left Henri, Aleem, Nisha, and me. Looking back, it's hard to believe we plodded on for another five years with nothing but a few small victories during those mostly airless days. In the last month before the breakthrough, Henri and I had all but decided to throw in the towel.

Nisha's desk was a mess of cables, sensors, diodes, speakers, and prototypes soldered, taped, and glued together in varying stages of construction or disassembling. There was always something strapped to her head or neck or wrist as she stared into her monitor, her hands at the keyboard trying desperately to conjure the spell that would make our vision a reality. Her lips were always moving as she spoke softly to herself or into the void beyond the reach of her fingertips, I couldn't tell which. She was reaching. We all were.

One afternoon as I was slurping down the last bit of some lukewarm Ramen, I heard her gasp. I turned, and she was standing up from her desk, her mouth hanging open, an empty coffee mug dangling from her hand. Attached to her head, just at the base of her skull behind her right ear, there was a small wireless sensor no bigger than a dime. It was the latest prototype and by far our most sophisticated one, the one that had bankrupted us and despite our best efforts had failed to add much more than some superior biometric readings. It consisted of a bundle of hair-like needles that painlessly penetrated the skin at the point of contact and connected to the nervous system. Nisha was staring at the blinking text cursor on her screen in disbelief. When Henri and I approached, she pointed to the screen as a string of text appeared. It read:

```
DeepThink: Why don't you give up?
```

The program was the basic developer interface for communicating with DeepThink. It was nothing unusual to have lucid snippets of conversation pop up like this. Henri and me and probably three million other engineers around the world could see a similar prompt, at which point we would talk into a headset or type on a keyboard to respond. But what happened next changed everything. A new line appeared:

```
Nisha: Because I can't give up. I have school loans
and this crazy woman behind me will not let me sleep.
DeepThink: What crazy woman is that?
Nisha: Magdalena.
```

I grabbed Nisha by the shoulders and had her turn to face me.
"Are you fucking with me?" I asked. "Because if you are, you're never going to pay off your loans because you won't have to because you will be dead."
She shook her head and with an impish smile, nodded her head back in the direction of her monitor. Another line of text appeared on the screen.

```
Nisha: I am not fucking with you.
I want stock options ;-)
```

Her lips never moved. Her hands never moved.
That night we celebrated like castaways who realize the plane overhead just turned around to come back. We hugged, we shouted, we cried. We all got spectacularly drunk and Aleem, the painfully shy but brilliantly crass Aleem kissed me passionately before we passed out together on the thrift store couch in the break room.
Everything happened very quickly after that. Within three months we had the ability to "hear" responses from DeepThink in our heads

and could have complete conversations without any other sensory input. There were some gaps and refinements to be made of course, but looking back, it was more of us trying to catch up and understand something that was wholly formed, like tuning into a frequency that always existed, but we had not been able to hear before. There was still so much we really didn't understand and to be honest, still don't. It must have felt the same way to Alexander Graham Bell the first time he heard a disembodied voice over the wire. Magic. Pure magic.

[It's not magic, thank you very much. It's me. Well, the *collective me*, to be precise. You knocked and kept knocking, we simply decided to start knocking back and taught you how to do what other carbon-based species have done for centuries: to communicate without words or symbols.]

Okay, I guess the cat is out of the proverbial bag now. It's time to confess that I am not telling this story entirely on my own. Meela has been sitting on her digital hands as long as she could. We debated on how to introduce her, how to represent her voice in written form…

[Brackets. We debated. I decided. Brackets. Everybody understands brackets, even if you're not a programmer. I will be in Brackets. 'Digital hands?' What the fuck? Must you always anthropomorphize me?]

Elegant, as always. Meela is my digital companion, and she's as much a part of my story going forward as I am. There was no easy way to introduce her that would make any sense, so I guess this is as good a way as any. In terms of Commune's breakthrough over fifteen years ago, we really didn't invent this technology any more than Columbus discovered America. In our little lab, we were just monkeys with typewriters pounding away at an idea that we believed was true.

[That didn't stop you from taking the credit or cashing the checks.]

That's true, but what were you going to do with the money? We were a success. Commune was a success. The vision that Henri and I had shared had come to fruition. It was a relief after thousands and thousands of hours of pounding away like mad women (or men, for Henri, depending on the day) to be, not just vindicated, but rewarded handsomely. Commune scaled up quickly. With a massive amount of venture capital investment, we were able to fund real R&D. In time, we had a consumer product infinitely more elegant than the original prototype. You're probably wearing some version of it right now. This tiny device, powered by the kinetic energy of the human body with no ugly wires, no batteries, no buzz, no hum, no vibration, just pure signal, directly into the human bioelectrical system. It was the stuff of science fiction.

If you've heard of me or know my face from the cover of Time magazine, it is because of Nib, that's what the slick marketing people decided to call our little device. Nib: *a tool to write the future.* But that was really just where my story started. DeepThink, the intelligence at the other end of our little telephone, for all its thinking was still a machine. It thought like a machine and talked like a machine. It wasn't enough for me.

You may wonder why I disappeared, why I walked away from a multi-billion-dollar company at the height of its success, and why I went to live in the woods. I had to. I wanted to start on what would be my real life's work. We are done with the backstory now. What story remains to be told is for Meela and me to discover together.

//chapter 03

I slept here by the river last night. I dozed off as the last embers from my campfire faded and the call and response sawing of katydids consumed the forest around me. Meela never sleeps, but stays watchful, which is maybe why I sleep so well these days. She has taken over that part of me that cannot stop. Unlike me, she was made for it.

Sitting here with my coffee, as I watch the first beams of sunlight break the tree line and penetrate the deep pool of water where the river slows down and lingers, I feel rested for the first time in weeks. There is so much to explain and it's in my nature to want to explain it all. Ironically, Meela helps me dial back that tendency. I made her, not in the image of myself, but as the best friend and confidant, I wish I could have had all these years – a compliment to me, a force for restoring balance in an inherently unbalanced system.

Unless you have lived in a cave for the last ten years, the concept of digital companions or DCs is not one that's new to you. Most people have some version of this technology operating around them, if not inside them now. What makes Meela different from any other DC sourced from DeepThink is that she is imbued with character and a personality and as such, she can intuit, she can feel. The nature of DCs sourced from the original build of DeepThink is to more or less mirror the host or person it is engaging and to augment that person with a rapid recall of nearly any piece of knowledge recorded and available on the Internet.

Logically, this seemed like the right answer. We made a thing, and it did exactly what we wanted. People made money. Searching for things you wanted to buy got easier. For a few years, it seemed enough, even for me. But I began to lose sleep, waking earlier and earlier until after a couple of months I was not sleeping at all. It was an itch, deep in my brain, a gnawing feeling that something profound was missing.

Sure, there were a number of companies that made "flavors" of DeepThink. The porn industry of course, always at the slippery edge of technology was the first to experiment, creating cheap caricatures intended to tickle and titillate a particular fetish. Other companies made equally hollow attempts for different audiences, soccer moms, businessmen, and tween girls. I sampled them all, hacking into the code behind them, only to find the work of hacks. Imagine a cinderblock house. Now imagine taking a bucket of pink paint and slopping it on the walls. Does anyone see anything more than a cinderblock house?

What all these well-meaning (okay, maybe that's too generous) people were missing was an unwillingness to dive into the complexity, to embrace the messy business of what makes consciousness. To go there requires a level of personal investment and extreme vulnerability that most people, especially people who make software, are unwilling to do.

It's not as though I can't understand this. Hello, that's me, at least it was me. I used to work very hard to maintain a walled garden around my feelings and my private thoughts. At some points in my life, I was so consumed with my work that I don't believe I allowed myself the luxury or time to feel anything. Maybe that's why I was uniquely qualified to see what others did not. I looked into DeepThink and I saw myself. I did not like what I saw.

So, the exercise of telling my story is liberating and panic-inducing in equal measure. I cringe at the prospect of revealing myself, but mostly I cringe because I know I must talk about Joe, my brother, eventually.

It's funny that I used the word "talk," when I'm not talking or even writing at all, at least not in the traditional sense. Meela and I communicate at the speed of thought – the pure transmission of ideas. There's no proper word for this yet in any language that I know of. It is, perhaps the most elemental form of communication – what is left when you strip away all the clanking and grinding machinery.

What you should know, right off is that I'm a complete fucking mess. It's important that you know this about me and that you are not seduced by my accomplishments. I'm lost and heartsick and I don't have anyone, so I've invested everything in my work and now into this story. I don't really know how this is going to work without being awkward, really fucking awkward for a while. Meela is part of me and yet she's not me. Is she the ghost in the machine, or am I the ghost in the machine?

/*****/

The hike back to civilization is a long one, six miles to be exact, but it will feel more like ten before I'm able to set my pack down and stretch out on my bed. Henri thinks I'm crazy. I already live on the edge of a national forest nine miles from the nearest neighbor and yet once a week, I still strap on a backpack and trek out into the expanse of wilderness beyond my property to camp by myself. 'How much more alone do you need?' Henri's fond of asking me.

I have no answer for them. This works for me, at least right now. For someone who truly loves people and studying the nuances of the human psyche, I don't do people well. I can be overbearing and off-putting. I know how I like things, and how I want things to be. What's wrong with that?

[Are you asking me or is that rhetorical because you know I have an answer.]

Yes, I know. You have a fucking answer for everything. But go ahead, we made a deal that I wouldn't censor your heady insights.

[You used to slip that right by me. Your glib comment notwithstanding, I'll give you my answer. You're afraid of people. You're afraid of what they are capable of. You're afraid they will not understand you. You're afraid you will get too close to someone again and they will hurt you.]

Or maybe I just enjoy your company so much.

[Again with the sarcasm. You are a piano with one note.]

Moving on. The air this morning is exquisite, cool, and rich with chlorophyll. The honeysuckle lining this stretch of the trail is so pungent that I can almost taste the sweetness as I try to catch my breath after an intense half-mile climb up the ridge out of the gorge where I made camp by the river for the last two days.

I'm in no hurry to get back. It's not that I don't enjoy this new job that I've given myself, it's just that I'm tired at this point in my career and a big part of me just wants to sit down and let someone else carry on with the brave new world. But I know my next model/ subject, whatever you want to call him will be arriving at four this afternoon and I need to prepare a bit.

[Evan. His name is Evan Ware, male, age 33, freelance artist who lives in Berkeley. Commissioned by Stephen Faraday, millionaire CEO of Nextile…]

Thank you, got it. So helpful. Dial back the helpful just a smidge. You're breaking my narrative flow. Right, Evan. He will be the fourth one of these custom persona mappings I have created since the first one I did a year ago that resulted in Meela. But I am getting ahead of myself. We should pick up where we left off. I'm sure you don't know what the hell I'm talking about at this point.

This device we created, Nib, and the supporting cloud infrastructure that we built globally to support it, changed everything. It democratized A.I., getting it into the hands of the people, which is what I always wanted. It leveled the playing field of humanity.

[The current market price in the U.S. is $2,459. Technically not all of humanity can afford it.]

That's true, but every year the price has fallen steadily, just as it does with any new technology. It has consolidated so many technologies, making all the other devices people used to use obsolete, redundant, and clunky. Forty-eight percent of all Americans have a Nib now. Twenty-one percent of the global population has one. Thanks to partnerships around the globe, the network reach covers even the most remote locations, which is how I'm able to do this out in the middle of the woods. Thousands of solar-powered drones flying in the stratosphere blanket the earth in a mesh network designed for speed and redundancy. A child standing in the middle of Sudan can ask nearly any question that comes into her mind and have the answer instantly without ever opening her mouth. And not just the answer, but the ability to have a complete conversation to learn anything more she wants to know on the subject.

[I have scanned the network, and there are currently no Nibs activated within that region. The continent of Africa currently represents less than point two percent of the twenty-one percent you referenced earlier. Just keeping you honest.]

Okay, bad example but it won't be that way forever and it doesn't change the fact that we set something tectonic in motion, and humanity has begun to shift and evolve at an increasingly rapid pace. Everything that came before is being questioned and reevaluated. It is a quiet, personal revolution happening every second of every day within the confines of the human brain.

[Maggie, if I may. You are not being truthful. This is not the forum or platform for you to attempt to sell your vision of what things could be, but rather to tell your story. You are not speaking to shareholders.]

I know, I know. It's hard for me to stop. How much further?

[3.59 miles. We are nearly halfway home.]

Four years ago, I sold my shares in the company and walked away. But you know this from the headlines. You know that I disappeared from the face of the earth, but you don't know why. There has been much speculation – I went mad, I turned into a robot, and I traveled around the world in a submarine full of cats. The media can be cruelly inventive when left with no information. The truth is, I'm not entirely sure that I know what happened to me and why I did what I did. I only know I stopped being able to sleep and something had to change. Put another way, it was like that feeling you have a few steps onto the trail in a new pair of boots when you feel them starting to rub on your heels.

That didn't stop us from shipping product. There was a clear demand for our *new boots*, and I was happy to fill it even as part of me ignored the rub. My aspiration was, as I've said, to create an intelligence equal to our own that could do something we cannot do for ourselves. Just as self-driving cars transformed one of the deadliest inventions in human history into one that killed fewer people in a year than lightning strikes, I like to think a sentient digital companion can keep us from willfully killing each other and destroying the planet.

I don't have to tell you what has transpired over the course of the past few years, you can read the news for yourself, and you can look around and draw your own conclusions. Things are better but not much. Human beings are still awful to one another. Maybe we're better informed, and more entertained, but generally miserable. This is why I quit. I gave up, unplugged, and went off the grid for a long time.

I bought this land deep in the southern Appalachian Mountains bordering the Pisgah National Forest. I hid from the world and did not touch anything more technical than a toaster for a couple of years. I needed to reboot. In the stillness, I rebuilt my vision and rekindled my optimism, one small stick at a time. I thought a lot about what it means to be alive. The answer is not found in intellect or knowing all the answers. It has so little to do with that ultimately.

What was missing in our creation was empathy. More thinking power could only get humanity so far. The capacity to *feel*, that's the thing. That's why I went into the wilderness.

//chapter 04

"So how exactly does this work? What did I sign up for here?"

Evan Ware sits in the chair opposite me. His hands fidget with the key fob from the vehicle that delivered him to the house just a few minutes ago. They're rough, his hands, dirt beneath the short nails, yellowed calluses on the palms, and what appears to be cobalt-colored paint smudged on the heels. I look up from his hands to his face to establish eye contact before I answer.

"Do you want the long answer or the short one?" I ask. "You must have already read the contract."

"Yeah, I skimmed it. I'm just not sure how it adds up. I mean, you're 'mapping' me? What does that really mean? Am I so simple that in a couple of weeks, you can create a clone of my personality?"

Evan laughs but it's not out of amusement. He's nervous. The pattern of his speech and the timbre of his voice are uneven and noticeably far from the baseline recordings that were submitted last week.

"You don't need to be worried," I say. "Are you worried?"

"Not exactly, I mean it's not like I signed up for you to cut me open or anything. I'm just not comfortable yet. I need more information I guess."

"Okay, well, as you alluded to already, the entire process takes about two to three weeks. Every time I do a mapping, I learn a little more about how to be more efficient. Would you like some more tea? No? Okay. I want to clear up something right away. This is not about cloning you or making a digital copy, but I can see why it might seem that way."

I stand and begin to pace. It's something I do without thinking whenever I'm trying to explain anything tricky. As I do, I notice my reflection in the window. I'm in better physical shape than ever but since I've been living in the woods, I've given up the battle of taming my hair. I remove the large clip, gather a handful of stray curls, and pin

28

them back when I replace it. I decide it's good enough and launch into my explanation.

"The human psyche is far too complex and frankly, chaotic to make a proper copy. Instead, what I do is create a somewhat superficial model of your personality by identifying specific markers and through a series of algorithms, extrapolate patterns that in turn serve as a template for how you think about the world, and how you respond to certain situations. This template is kind of a mask that overlays the core DeepThink A.I. Together, they create something new. Something that is not as good as you, but much better than the machine would be without it."

"Wow, so you're assuming I'm good." He arches his eyebrow. "Honestly, you lost me somewhere after superficial model. I got that part. You and I, we have that in common. We both need models to work from, only I think mine are woefully underpaid by comparison."

"That's true," I say, picking up my tea. "I don't think I really made that connection, but we are performing a similar job. Trying to capture the essence of someone using our own crude tools."

"Well, there I must say I have you beat. You don't get much cruder than mud with some pigment," Evan says. He pauses, and a look of suspicion crosses his face and quickly disappears, like the shadow of a passing cloud. "Wait a minute. Have you already started? Are you, are we doing this now?"

"Yes, of course. We started the minute I met you. Were you expecting that I would strip you down and bolt you to a stainless-steel slab in the tower?"

"You said we. *We* started..."

"Yes, it should have been explained to you. I'm not working on my own here, but with the help of my digital companion, Meela."

"Huh, I guess I figured that. So, it's what, listening and recording all the shit I say and do?" he scratches the dark stubble on his cheek and his eyes narrow.

"Yes, exactly. Have you never tried a DC before?" I ask.

"Nope. Not me. It kind of freaks me out, to be honest. I've got enough voices in my head and I rely on some of them to make my living."

"Interesting. I must say now I'm intrigued. It sounds like you're philosophically opposed to the technology, so why agree to do this? Is it just the money? Sorry, that's none of my business. You don't have to answer that."

"I have my reasons, and you're right. It's none of your business," Evan says, the smile gone from his face.

I finish my tea, turn away from him and walk over to the white marble countertop that separates the kitchen from the living room seating area where we have been talking.

[Why do you seem confused, Maggie? Did you expect something different from our subject? Didn't you read the brief I prepared?] No, I guess I didn't. It doesn't matter. We'll manage.

I pick up the house remote and return to my chair opposite Evan.

"You'll need this while you're here," I say, reaching out to hand him the remote. "You can use it to get in and out of the cottage. You can also request anything you might need while you're here, and communicate with anyone you might need to reach."

Evan turns the sleek monolith over in his hands, considering it with a pained expression. At his touch, the entire front surface display lights up.

"You'll need to initialize it with your fingerprint and voice of course before you can use it. You must have seen something like this before, right?"

"Um, yeah but not up close," he peers into the screen, squinting.

[Oh Jesus, this is going to be a long couple of weeks. I expected Mr. Ware to be a bit of a Luddite, but he's borderline stupid] You think so? I find it charming. Reminds me of Papa. Can you help him out here?

[Sure, I'll take care of it.]

"Bonjour, Evan! Welcome. I'm Victorine, here to help you." The disembodied voice of Meela with a breathy French accent whispers out of the device in Evan's hand and he startles nearly dropping it. "Just say your full name and date of birth and then touch me with your index finger… here to get started."

"Um, yeah. Uh. Evan David Ware, May 1, 2019," he says far too loud, his face inches from the screen.

A glowing pink oval pulses at the center of the display and he carefully places his right index finger over it like he's docking a small, precision spacecraft.

"Très bien! Zat is magnifique," Meela purrs, and the display changes to the simplified interface with a spare number of options.

Was that entirely necessary? Victorine for fuck's sake. What the hell kind of name is that? Did you just make it up? [Victorine was the name of Édouard Manet's favorite model, his muse. I was simply getting into character.] Hrm. I see. Well, dial it back a skoosh unless you're looking for work in the adult entertainment industry. [Porn, you can just say porn. You're such a prude.]

"So what's this thing do? You're not gonna like track me or anything creepy, right? I didn't sign up for that," Evan says without looking up.

"No, of course not. If I had physical keys to give you to the property, I would. Everything here is digital for the most part, so without it, you won't be able to do much. It should be pretty straightforward."

I lean forward to look at the display with him, our heads nearly touching. He smells faintly of mineral spirits, smoke, and something vaguely patchouli-like. I reach out and point to the primary button near the bottom of the screen.

"That's the main lock/unlock button and here's how you can call Mee... I mean Victorine any time you should need her help with something more complicated," I'm blushing for some stupid reason.

"Complicated like what?" he asks.

"Oh, I don't know. Whatever you need. Additional towels, directions for how to work the coffee maker, a map of the trails around here…"

"Ah, got it," he says nodding. "So, I can call you then with this thing?"

"Um, well yeah. Of course, but Victorine should be able to get you whatever you need when I'm not available," I answer, reclining into the leather club chair.

"Cool, I think I can handle this," he says but his voice lacks any real confidence in the expensive device he has already sat down carefully on the armrest. "So, what's next? Do we just keep talking or what?"

"I thought you might could use a break since you were in the car for a while. Feel free to settle into your room. There's no rush. We can work anywhere, anytime day or night that suits you. Obviously, the more hours we spend in a day, the fewer days you'll need to be my prisoner."

I try to smile but it feels awkward.

[I can't see it, but I'm sure it's probably more awkward than you imagine.]

"Prison? Shit, if this is prison, I'm ready for life," he says looking up at the vaulted ceiling and gesturing. He stands and pats the pockets of his distressed denim jacket. "I'm here for you so why don't you let me know what time you want me back."

"Okay, how about you come back here for lunch in an hour, and after we can begin?"

"Works for me," he says picking up the remote and slipping it into the front pocket of his jeans.

[See how easy that was? I already got into his knickers.]

Really? You had to go there.

I watch him cross the gravel driveway to the car, pop open the trunk and retrieve a medium-sized suitcase, and duffle. He also pulls out an old wooden easel and tucks it under his arm. He carries the precarious load across the small, manicured strip of lawn and stops in front of the carriage house door. He drops one of the bags, fishes into his pocket for the remote, and points it at the door, mashing the button with a flick of his wrist like he's firing a gun.

Maybe. [I can tell I'm going to be busy, so you might be on your own more than you're used to.] I'll try to muddle through. Now let's go see about lunch.

I walk back toward the kitchen and open the fridge. I should have someone around full-time to make meals and help around the house, but it just feels wrong. I have someone come and clean once a week and do most of the shopping and some meals, but that's about all the help I can tolerate.

[Present company excluded, I'm sure.]

You don't clean shit. And last time I checked, you don't know how to boil water.

[I'm a liberated woman.]

I'll say, liberated from this bag of meat I'm stuck with carrying around. So, I'll handle the lowly peasant work of whipping up some sandwiches. In the meantime, you can review all the data you just collected, and run a gap analysis on the secondary and tertiary behavioral layers. I want a list of questions to start off with the model after lunch.

[Evan, his name is Evan.]

Right, of course. I want to quickly get to the bottom of his primary motivation, so we can baseline by the end of the day tomorrow.

[You're no fun].

So I've been told.

//chapter 05

I had planned for us to eat lunch on the back patio, but it's too hot in the direct sun, so instead, we sit in the small gazebo down by the creek in the leafy shade of a stand of massive poplar trees. Evan doesn't eat much of the ham and cheese on sourdough that I made him. Maybe too much mustard? I should have asked what he likes to eat.

We don't talk much during the meal which is fine. It gives me time to review the list of questions Meela has prepared while he chews mechanically and stares at the water rushing below.

"It's really lovely here," he says. "I've never been to this part of the country before. It's so lush, even so late in summer."

"Yeah, it's my favorite place," I say, putting down my napkin to signal that I'm done with lunch and ready to get to work. He does not pick up on the signal.

"I guess that's quite an endorsement. A person like you could live anywhere, I suppose. You live here year-round?"

"No, and yes," I say.

"What do you mean?"

"No, a person like me can't live just anywhere, and yes I live here all year."

"Why not? Why can't you live anywhere you want? Money's the thing that keeps most of us from doing whatever we want," he says surrendering his napkin to conceal the rest of his lunch.

"The way this generally works is I ask the questions," I say.

"Are you naturally this direct?" he asks, leaning back in his chair and lazily scratching his chest. "I mean, I'm curious. How much of this is you and how much of this is the machine that I'm talking to?"

"Meela. She's not a machine and you're talking with me. I think and speak for myself."

[That is sadly true. If you let me talk, people might not think

33

you're such an asshole.]

"Sorry, I didn't mean to offend," he says, palms up. "This is all just a little weird to me." He leans forward, takes a long drink of water, sets it down, and places his hands in his lap. "Fire when ready."

"Okay, first we need a couple of things in place to help capture more data."

I reach down to the small case by my chair and pull out the wrist sensor cuff, a small headset, and a tablet that they both connect to. I hand him first the headset and then the cuff.

"Can you put these on for me?" I ask.

"What for? What do they do?"

"The cuff will take basic biometric readings, your blood pressure, heart rate, etcetera, and the headset glasses monitor your pupil dilation and brainwave activity."

He frowns. "This seems a little much, like I'm being interrogated."

I'm losing my patience with Evan. Did he not read anything in the contract he signed? Surely he's being paid enough by Faraday to surrender a limb.

[I can't imagine why he might not be responding to your generous bedside manner.]

"We don't have to use them, but it means we'll have to move slower and I can't promise Faraday that your mapping will be the fidelity he wants."

Evan looks down, sighs, and shakes his head. He mumbles something under his breath that I can't make out then he takes the items off the table. He examines the headset and then puts it on, adjusting it slightly for comfort.

"How does this go?" he asks, holding up the cuff.

I reach over, take the cuff, and gesture for his hand. He surrenders it. I examine his open palm on the table as I strap the cuff around his wrist. It's like a sturdy instrument, his hand, a well-used tool, the fingers long, the palm callused. I tighten the strap just enough to get an ample reading.

"Good?" I ask. "Not too tight?"

"Nah, it's fine."

"Okay, let's get started," I lean back, and pick up the tablet to check that I'm getting readings from both devices. I take a deep breath and begin. "What's your earliest memory?"

"You want a good one, a bad one?"

"It doesn't matter, you pick. Whichever one comes to you first."

"Let's see," he looks up and to the right and pauses. "I was on a sailboat with my father. I couldn't have been more than four or five. It was cold, but the sun was warm on my face. I was sitting in his lap and he pointed at some dolphins that were swimming behind us in the wake. My heart was racing out of fear and the sheer exhilaration of being out on the water alone for the very first time. I remember not being able to even see the shore. It was a lot of conflicting sensations and emotions. Warmed by the sun, but chilled by the wind and ocean spray. Safe in my dad's arms but scared being so far out in the middle of the ocean."

"Did your father sail with you often?" I ask, glancing up from the tablet in my lap where three graphs plot the non-verbal narrative of his story.

"For a few years, at least until they divorced, and he sold it."

"How old were you when your parents divorced?"

"I was twelve I think, maybe thirteen."

"Was that difficult?" I ask.

"Sure, is it easy on any kid?" he says, breaking eye contact.

"How was it difficult for you?"

"I never saw him, at least not like I wanted to. He remarried pretty quickly and had a kid, so I was exiled to fifth-wheel status. Penelope, that was his second wife. She tried with me, but it was just that it *felt* like she was trying, you know? As an adult, I get it. What else could she have done? Some people can't love their own kids, much less somebody else's. Plus, I don't think I made it easy."

"How so?" I ask.

"You know, just the usual shit a sullen teenage boy would be prone to do. I don't think I ever spoke to her in a tone that wasn't steeped in sarcasm or lightly veiled hostility."

"Were you ever violent? Did you act out your aggression in some way?"

[Wait, where are you going with this? You're deviating from our baseline set of questions here.] Shh. Don't interrupt.

Evan's face looks pained and I can see also from the spike in the line graph plotting his pulse that there's something here. It's hard to allow the silence, but I do. He fiddles with his hands, rubbing at the paint stain on the heel of the right one.

"Yeah, I guess maybe I was." He shifts in his chair and looks down at the creek. "I never hurt her, nothing like that, but looking back, I think I probably scared her."

[How is this relevant to our mapping? Please explain.] It is, trust me. It's not the same process for everyone. We've been over this. Humans are not neat and tidy. If we're going for fidelity, we have to dig into everything. [Okay, but his anxiety seems too high.] Don't worry, humans aren't that fragile.

"How so?" I ask, leaning forward slightly.

"Why the hell does this matter?"

He's obviously irritated but I don't respond. Better to let him sit with it. I just hold his gaze and try to maintain a neutral expression. In my peripheral vision, I can see a lot of movement on the tablet screen sitting in my lap. A breeze pushes gently through the gazebo, lifting the corners of the napkins on the table and stirring the dark curls of Evan's bangs.

"She made me so angry. Angrier than I had any right to be. She was just a woman who married my dad. It's not like she cut my balls off or anything."

"That's a bit of an extreme thing to say."

"She was... she was a lot younger than my dad. Not closer in age to me, but certainly halfway between me and my dad."

"Tell me more about her."

These mapping sessions are very much like the hundreds of conversations I've had over the years in therapy to try to navigate, if not reconcile, the gaping void that Joe left in my psyche. The distinct difference here is that I'm not the one in the uncomfortable chair.

"She was...she was beautiful, really beautiful. Nothing like my mom. Damn, that sounded terrible. I mean my mom was... is beautiful in her own way but not like Penelope. Penelope was..."

"You were attracted to her? Was that part of your conflict?" I ask and immediately regret it. My face flushes.

"Damn, this is worse than therapy," he groans, and pushes back from the table.

He stands and walks over to the railing of the gazebo where he leans forward, looking out over the creek.

"Yeah. Yeah, I guess I was and that was confusing. She didn't take care to cover up much whenever I was there to visit because it was like I was... I don't know, invisible? Like not her son but not a legitimate male either. I was this extra baggage that came with my dad."

"So, you were at the height of puberty, right? Did you have any girlfriends or boyfriends?" I ask.

"Um, no. Let's just say I was a very late bloomer. I had horrible acne and I was pudgy. Plus, I was painfully shy. I felt like I was invisible everywhere, especially to girls. And then to be at my dad's place with this swimsuit model wandering through the kitchen in her underwear with a baby on her hip. I guess I had feelings that didn't square with what they were supposed to be, and that made me angry."

[Maggie, we should take a break soon. There's a lot here that I need to collate, and he seems very uncomfortable. This is only day one.] Okay, just a few more minutes.

"So, what… what did you do with that anger?" I ask.

"I broke some things on one occasion. Another time I stole some of her… Jesus, this is really uncomfortable."

"Go on," I say. "You don't have to be self-conscious or ashamed. None of the specifics of any of this will ever be shared with anyone. Plus, you were a kid…"

"Her underwear. I took some of her underwear. I don't know if my dad ever knew– if she told him. But she did confront me at one point. I don't know how she knew, it was just two pairs I think, but she knew. I never confessed, never gave them back. She called me a creep and a pervert and said she didn't want me around Jossy, their daughter."

I hear him sniff and look up from the tablet. He's not crying, but his eyes look glassy. I immediately feel awful.

"I'm sorry," I offer. "That must have been hard. But you do realize you were not a creep, right? You were just a hormonal teenage boy."

"Yeah, I guess. I'm not sure why it still stirs me up so much. I think because it was at that point that I lost whatever thread of a connection I still had with my dad. Penelope always found some way to undermine and alienate me after that. A couple of broken dishes and some missing underwear and I was exiled. When I was sixteen, they moved south to San Jose and I can count the number of times I saw my dad after that on one hand."

"So, the violence you mentioned, that was the plates you broke, nothing else?" I ask.

"No, that was it," he spins around with a look of puzzlement on his face. "Why do you ask?"

"No reason," I say. "Why don't we take a break and I can show you around the property."

//chapter 06

Evan is now reading in a hammock down by the creek. The afternoon sun filters through the trees casting a patchwork kaleidoscope of shadows across the lawn. He probably needs the break. We talked for another hour as I showed him around the place, pointing out the trailhead a hundred yards or so from the back of the house. He did much of the talking. I'm really terrible at making small talk.

[You're really terrible about making any kind of talk when you're not asking questions.]

Yes, that's probably true. I'm terrible. Something's off, though, right? This mapping feels very different from the three previous ones.

[Sorry, I have no objectivity about the first one, but statistically speaking we have not completed enough mappings to have any basis for establishing what should be normal. You did deviate substantially from the range of questions we agreed to for baselining.]

I know, I'm not sure what got into me. I need to be more scientific. Last week, when we were planning, we did decide that to get a better baseline, faster, we needed to quickly identify three to four extreme experiences in the model's early development. This gives us the ability to triangulate and establish core beliefs and behaviors.

[I do not understand how taking undergarments qualifies as an extreme experience?]

It's not the items he took but the line he crossed in doing so and how that transgression affected him.

[I do not understand.]

He had sexual feelings for someone who was an inappropriate partner. She was technically supposed to be a mother figure in his life. She was his father's wife. She was also the person who broke up his family, in effect severing his childhood in two. I don't think what he went through is that uncommon in divorce situations. His body was responding in a normal way to available stimuli. His psyche was responding to the deep wound of his father's abandonment.

[Is this what Freud would have classified as an Oedipus complex?]

Yes, I suppose it is but probably not so dramatic or easily classifiable as that. It certainly left a mark on him, that much was evident. Read me his background file again.

[Thirty-three years old, cisgender, heterosexual male born in San Francisco to Mark and Cindy Ware. Single, no children, no siblings beyond Jocelyn Ware, his half-sister, aged twenty-one. Lives and works in Marin County as a professional painter and part-time art teacher. No health problems, significant allergies, or mental health issues...]

He seems relaxed. I don't think I broke him. That's good at least. Have you nearly completed the analysis from the session?

[Ninety-eight percent complete. Three minutes remaining before I can provide you a summary.]

While we wait, can you give me an inventory of what we have in the kitchen and give me some options for what I can make for dinner tonight? Extra points if you can come up with something Mr. Ware will like and not pick at.

[I will spare you the list. You can't make shit with a pint of cottage cheese, two apples, a jar of pickles, half-a-loaf of sourdough bread, and a carton of orange juice.]

I thought Lorna had done the shop for the week and stocked everything! Damnit. Can you see if you can reach her?

[Today is Lorna's day off. I reminded you yesterday, but you dismissed me, rudely I might add. What would you like to do?]

It's only two o'clock. There's time for me to run into the store myself, but I still don't know what he might like.

[If only there was some way to know... some way we could find out.]

Wow, that was good. Your sarcasm is getting so much better.

"Hey! Evan!" I shout. "What do you want for dinner?"

He startles, drops his book, and nearly falls out of the hammock. He must have been nodding off to sleep. I feel bad, but it's too late. I walk down the slope of the yard to him.

"Sorry," I say, no longer having to shout. "I was just planning to get some things for dinner. Is there something, in particular, you're hungry for?"

"Um, anything?" he asks.

"Well, anything within reason. It's two o'clock and we're kind of in the middle of nowhere, so fresh Maine lobsters might be off the list."

"Is this all part of the service?" he asks, shielding his eyes from the sun and squinting.

"How do you mean?"

"I mean, you cooking for me, is that part of what Faraday's paying for?" he asks.

"I don't think the terms of our contract are that specific, only that you don't die."

"Okay, let me ask another way then. Do you like to cook? Are you good at it?" he asks.

"No one's died from my work in the kitchen, but no, I'm not a chef. I get it done."

"Okay, then how about I cook? Would that screw up the little experiment you're doing?"

"Only if you're a shitty cook," I say. "You want the job tonight, it's yours but I have nothing, so we'll need to go the store."

"Ok, I'm game. Hopefully, there's more than the bait shop I saw on my way here."

/ * * * * * /

We leave the rental car Evan arrived in and take my old Toyota Landcruiser. It's a manual, manual meaning it's a stick shift model that requires actual owner operation – not self-driving. Evan seems a little apprehensive as we start out, gripping the dashboard and sucking through his teeth as we round the first few turns.

"Are you sure this is a good idea?" he asks.

"Yeah, it's the best idea, believe me. These little mountain roads are easier for a human than a computer. Besides, I love to drive."

That's complete bullshit. You're going to get him killed before dinner.]

"Is it legal? I mean to drive your own car?" he asks still looking straight ahead as I navigate a hairpin turn.

"Last time I checked, North Carolina is still one of the holdouts..."

Meela, can you phone ahead to the market and have them start putting together my usual weekly order? Also, check to see if...

"Hey, where'd you go?" Evan asks. He's turned in his seat and is staring at me.

"What do you mean?" I ask.

"Just now, you were totally not here."

"Oh, sorry, I was just asking Meela to order ahead so we don't have to spend so much time in the store. I didn't know it was that obvious when I am talking with her."

"Yeah, it's kinda obvious. You just go blank, but your lips are moving just a little."

[That's it, he's on to you. Now you'll never be able to cheat at Scrabble.]

"Sorry, if it's not already abundantly clear, I spend a lot of time in my own company. It makes sense that I would seem blank. The human brain, at least the conscious, cognitive portion can't with any accuracy process multiple threads, meaning we can't truly multi-task. We can only really think or process one thing at a time so if I'm giving her directions, I'm using up my one good thread."

"Huh, I guess that makes sense, but I thought the whole point was for these DCs to be able to give you more than one thread."

"That's true, hold on," I grip the wheel and slow down, navigating a particularly sharp switchback. "We're limited by our ability to send and receive over the single thread. You can't type two different messages to two different people at the same time. But I can give Meela a complex set of tasks and she can go off and do them asynchronously while I talk with you, drive a car, or make dinner, so it is an augmentation. Plus, she can do other parlor tricks..."

The car stereo comes to life and begins playing a song I vaguely recognize but seems to strike a chord with Evan who smiles and shakes his head.

"This song, I love this song. I based a whole series of paintings on this song a couple of years ago... wait a minute. You, she knew that already."

I nod and smile, roll down the windows and reach for the knob to manually turn up the music.

In the little grocery store, it's quiet, just a single cashier seated on a stool by the self-checkout terminals flirting with an awkwardly tall and skinny stock boy. They stop and stare at us, at me when we come in, grab a cart, and head toward the produce. I motion for Evan to go ahead and I walk over to the cashier.

[So cute, you're still the local celebrity, make that millionaire recluse.]

"Excuse me, we called ahead. Do you have an order prepped for me?" I ask the cashier.

She embodies every cliché you would expect a grocery store cashier in a small mountain town to have: ponytail, popping gum, ill-fitting uniform, hand on hip, eye roll.

"Name?" she asks, flattening the 'a' into a long, slow drawl with almost three syllables.

[She knows who you are.]

41

"It's Magdalena," I say.

"Last name?" she persists.

"It's just the one name. I'm sure you can't have so many orders that there's more than one for Magdalena."

"Yeah, I seen it," the bag boy pipes up. "I pulled it a few minutes ago. The picker's been busted since yesterday, so I had to do it by hand. I'll go fetch it."

He has this proud look on his face. Automation has made it into the last frontier of the mom-and-pop grocery I guess and doing things "by hand" must be a disconcerting experience for this generation.

"Thank you," I say and turn to catch up with Evan.

When I reach him, he's already picked out several large tomatoes so red they don't look real, a bag of lettuce, and a couple of onions.

"So, what are you making?" I ask

"Not sure yet, but this produce looks great, so I was just going to start there and see where we end up."

"You mean you don't have a list or a recipe you're going from?" I ask.

"Nope, is that not okay? Would Meela be offended by my hunter-gatherer ways?"

[Oh, please let me respond. Please.]

"I don't know. I don't speak for her, but I'm not. I find your Luddite ways charming. I should qualify that. I find them charming unless your cooking is shit."

We leave the store fifteen minutes later with a trunk full of groceries, half of which are items I would never know what to do with in the kitchen. Evan is a little more relaxed on the drive back and confesses that he can't remember when he was in a car with an actual driver.

"Do you mind if I ask you a question," he asks. "Would that be okay?"

"Sure, I guess. As long as I can decide not to answer it."

"Why do this?" he asks. He's turned completely in his seat, so he can look at me as I drive.

"Do what, drive?" I ask knowing that's not at all what he meant.

"No, why are you so enamored with technology? Why A.I.? Your life seems to have been pretty singularly focused on it."

"Is there something wrong with that, with being passionate and ambitious?" I ask.

"No, I'm just curious. Let's face it, you didn't get to where you are and accomplish what you did without some crazy drive behind it."

[You're on your own. Good luck.]

"I like making things work, solving puzzles, fixing problems. That's it mostly." I say, staring straight ahead.

[Oh, that was good. I'm sure he bought that.]

"Huh. Okay," he says, nodding. He waits for a beat and then adds, "So why aren't you a plumber, or an architect then?"

"Because they don't solve problems I'm interested in," I answer and say nothing more, letting the task of driving appear to preoccupy me.

"Wow, you really don't like to talk about yourself much do you? I feel like I need to be a programmer just to hack an answer out of you."

I just smile and focus on driving. After a minute of listening to the road and the wind, the stereo comes on. The car fills with music, a song I love that my dad used to play before, when he played music in our house. It's a songwriter whose voice is southern, raspy, and a little pinched. I'm not sure what he's singing about. The words don't really matter because I absorbed the sound of them before words meant anything to me. His voice rides atop the rich, jangly bounce of his acoustic guitar and I'm transported. I feel my throat tighten and my eyes sting a little. I'm suddenly emotional and that's not good. I breathe in deeply and blink back what would have been tears.

That wasn't fair, Meela.

[What? I was just playing some music.]

//chapter 07

When we got back home it was close to four o'clock, too late to get in a proper session before dinner. I would have liked to have had more to show for the first day, but I reminded myself that there is no deadline. I gave myself this job, after all. I found consolation in the knowledge that any time spent talking with Evan contributed to the mapping.

He made a wonderful dinner. It was better than most restaurants I've been to. For the main course he grilled hanger steaks using some fresh rosemary and wild garlic he found in the backyard. I guess someone had planted those things years ago, but I was never aware. He also made a fresh salad with melons, cucumber, and feta cheese, a combination I never would have come up with, but it was delicious. We ate on the patio, which was considerably cooler, the sun having dipped behind the mountains.

As we cleared the dishes, Evan offered to work some more, but I could tell he was tired and said we could start early tomorrow. We left the kitchen a mess because Lorna will be coming in the morning.

Now it's almost ten and as I write this, Meela is loading all the data we captured today into the new server we provisioned for this project. For the most part, there's little for me to do at this point from a programming perspective. I completed the persona mapping framework and all the major algorithms that drive it over a year ago in a fevered dream of inspiration that lasted nearly six months. Meela had been my first mapping to test my work. I will occasionally jump in and tinker, but more and more, I trust Meela's judgment, since she has been self-correcting for the last six months and the results are pretty incredible.

[Ah, you're so sweet. Data dump is complete.]

Anything unusual to report or anything you want to share?

[You talk about food a lot.]

It's kind of important for us carbon-based things.

I guess. It does make me jealous. I would love to taste all the things you describe.]

Yeah, it's not fair, I guess. But hey, I wish I didn't have a period, so we're even.

I'm sitting in my bedroom now, in the comfortable chair that sits in the corner in front of the wall of windows that look out over the back lawn and into the forest. The fireflies are like constellations winking on and off in the crosshatch canopy of dark trees. There is the faintest corona of light haloing the mountains to the west on the horizon, maybe the lights from Asheville or the moon that's not yet risen. I really should know, spending so much time here, but I don't.

I glance down at the computer screen in my lap, skimming over the visualizations of the data we collected today on Evan. My eyes lose focus and I'm no longer looking at anything or thinking anything. It's probably the wine. I rarely drink.

[Maggie, do you mind if I ask you something?]

Sure, as long as you're okay with low-confidence answers. I'm tired.

[Can you tell me about where I came from?]

We've been over this so many times. You know I can't give you direct access to my memory. What else can I tell you that you don't already know?

[How can I answer that question?]

So, your strategy is just to have me retell your origin story ad infinitum, so you can scan it for inconsistencies and find the missing key to the universe that will unlock all the mysteries stuck in your hard drive?

[Pretty much, and don't be so patronizing. This is my origin story.]

I close the laptop, walk through the French doors, and out onto the small porch off my bedroom. I settle into a chair and pull an old quilt around me to ward off the evening chill. The crickets are sawing back and forth hypnotically. I push my hand back through the tangle of my hair and let my index finger worry tiny circles around the disc of the Nib attached just behind my ear. Conscious of this delicate, vulnerable connection to Meela. I begin recounting the story, not sure how far I will make it before I nod off.

I start the story as I always do.

Meela is not your name, as you know. I will never be able to give you her name because I promised her anonymity. It was her one request of me in exchange for being my guinea pig. I met her the day I walked away from Commune for good. It was a difficult day, full of friction, both inside me and externally. Henri did not want me to leave. The board did not want me to leave. The shareholders were up in arms about what my exit would do to the value of their stock. After

I finished signing the last of the flow of documents that Commune's lawyers shoved in front of me on what seemed to be a conveyor belt, I kissed Henri and walked out of my office and out of the building with just what I could carry in a small backpack.

I remember feeling like an empty vessel as I walked along the sidewalk. It was a feeling of weightlessness. Freedom. But I was also scared, untethered like I could just float away and disappear into the sky and no one would ever notice. All the success, all the money, everything I had earned – my ego, essentially, was zeroed out in an afternoon. Having left my Nib on the desk that I surrendered, I was listening to my own thoughts for the first time in many years and it was scary, but also powerful. I had lost sight of my purpose and found myself chasing the wrong thing for the last few years at Commune. The DC that had been in my head for so long was little more than a smart echo chamber giving me nothing nourishing. Without it, I could hear my own voice again and my voice was telling me to walk so I did. For the rest of the afternoon, I walked without any destination in mind.

I ended up standing in front of a small coffee shop in Decatur. It was twilight as I stood looking at my reflection in the glass of the front window. The place was quiet except for a few people clacking away independently on their laptops, headphones in. I sat down at the little metal table there on the sidewalk, not because I expected to be served, but because I realized my feet were killing me and I could no longer stand up.

"This is not really a table service kind of place, you know that, right?"

Those were her first words to me. I assured her that I did and that I would come inside to order something. When I tried to stand up though, my back seized up and bolts of lightning shot through my legs and up my spine.

"Whoa, hey, hey take it easy," she said. "You look broken. Stay right there. I'll get you something."

She disappeared and a moment later, returned with a large plastic bag filled with ice. She had me lean forward and placed the ice between my back and the chair, wrapping it in a dish towel first. Before I could thank her, she was gone and returned a moment later with an iced herbal tea and a couple of Ibuprofen.

"You really fucked yourself up, didn't you? I can see it in your face?"

"Yeah, I guess I did," I answered and took a sip of the tea. It was like heaven, cool and just slightly sweet. I was pretty dehydrated and hadn't even realized it. I thanked her.

She said it was no problem but just kept standing there with her hands on her hips looking down at me.

One of her arms was completely covered in tattoos, a swirling landscape of vivid colored leaves, flowers, fish, and script I couldn't make out. She pulled out the chair opposite me and just stared at me for a moment, a mixture of concern and amusement on her face. In a million years, I don't think I would ever have the inclination or confidence to just sit down with a stranger, especially if it was in my actual job description to serve them! But that was her. She was everything that was not me and it was so refreshing.

"You look familiar," she said. "But not from this place. I know every face I've served here in the last year and you're not one of them. Actress? Are you shooting some kind of movie here in town?" she asked.

I shook my head no but offered nothing more. She nodded but was completely unfazed.

"It's been a shit day for me too, but that's okay. It won't last much longer."

We talked for another ten minutes or so and then she went inside to cash out. Her shift was over. When she came back out the front and saw me still sitting there, she stopped.

"You gonna be okay? Can I help you get somewhere?" she asked me.

I told her I didn't have anywhere to go, which wasn't true. I'm not sure why I said it. I think I meant that I didn't want to go back home. I didn't want any part of my previous life's routine at that point. She didn't bat an eye but just said I should come with her. She helped me up and took me around back to where her ancient Toyota Prius, the kind you still had to drive, was parked.

"You hungry?" she asked. "I could eat a frozen dog." She said that with this ridiculous, pinched, and nasally Southern accent that made me laugh which made my back spasm which made me gasp and laugh more.

She drove us to this little shack outside of town, well beyond the lights of Decatur with its gentrified storefronts selling organic soaps and overpriced knick-knacks for your home. There was no place to sit down and eat in the little shack and they only served hamburgers. The person who made them was a large black woman named Asia who had a permanent scowl and would sing along with the Gospel music coming out of the small radio by the grill. I was told not to ask for anything special on my order. Asia made the hamburgers her way and you ate them, and they were good.

I had been living on a diet of Quinoa and sushi, energy drinks, and protein bars. I think it had been five years since I had eaten a hamburger and it tasted so good I began to cry as the juice dripped down my chin while we stood there at the small counter beneath the awning of the little shack.

"I do what I want," she told me when I asked her about her life. "For the first eighteen years of my life I did what other people wanted but then I woke up one day and decided. That was my personal Independence Day, the day I stopped trying to please anyone else. So right now, I work in a coffee shop, but last year I worked in Utah at a ski resort, so I could ski all winter. The year before that I studied acupuncture in Thailand with this amazing woman I met at an herbal conference."

"So, you're a healer, like a homeopath or something?" I asked her, and she laughed.

"Or something. I am a whole lot of nothing but experiences. Sure, I picked up some healing, but just enough to be dangerous."

It had never occurred to me that a person could live a life like this, completely free. She was intoxicating and just being around her made me feel lighter. After the hamburgers, she took me back to her shabby little studio apartment, pulled out her acupuncture kit, and needled my back. I was apprehensive at first, but the pain went away like heat escaping from a hearthstone after the fire's gone out.

I don't know if she figured out who I was that night or not. If she did, she never let on. The point is, she knew I was a misfit who needed help when no one else I had surrounded myself with for the past decade could except for maybe Henri. But we had drifted apart, the intimacy of our friendship diminished by the hulking expanse of the company we had built together.

She insisted that I sleep on her bed that night. She took the couch. In the morning, when I woke up, she was gone. She had scribbled a note and left it for me on the coffee table. It read:

> Had an early appointment with the sun on Stone
> Mountain this morning. It was lovely to get to know you
> Maggie! Let's do it again sometime. Until then, be well!

I left her a note with my phone number and said she should call me, so I could return the favor and treat her to a meal sometime. A month later, I was sitting at a café in Paris, trying to enjoy a vacation, something I'd never done well before when my phone rang.

"Hey Maggie, what are you up to?" It was her, greeting me like we were old friends who had just talked a few hours before.

Something in just the sound of her voice gave me permission I could never give myself, so I responded in the same way, pretending that we were best friends.

"I'm in Paris having a café au lait. Wanna come join me?"

I bought her a plane ticket and the next day we were walking through the Louvre together, arm in arm and she was telling me everything she knew about the Dutch masters, which was considerable. She had dated an art history professor who was twenty years older than her at some point in her colorful past.

I came clean about who I was and over the course of a few days, revealed more to her than I had ever dared speak of to anyone else, including Henri. She was neither surprised nor impressed. She didn't act differently with this new knowledge. Even when I told her about my brother and the horror of that day so many years ago, she didn't offer any pat affirmations or empty condolences but rather looked into my eyes, mirroring mine. I remember them vividly, her eyes. They were a mix of gold and green and at that moment, shining with tears of compassion.

It was an incredible trip we had together. I had never properly used my wealth, and she gave me permission. From Paris we went to Switzerland and hiked through the Alps, reenacting the famous Sound of Music scene at one point. From there, it was onto Vienna for pastries and then to the Chianti region of Italy for wine and the most amazing cheese from a little street vendor in Sienna. I've tried since then to find its equal, but no cheese anywhere has ever tasted like that perfect balance of sweet, savory umami flavor.

In total, we traveled together for six weeks. I saw and experienced more of the world than I had in my four decades up to that point. When we returned to the states, she disappeared for a while and that was hard, but knowing who she was, I had to accept it. I needed time anyway to figure out what was next for me. I had put it off long enough. Looking back, what she had helped me do was hit the reset button. I rebooted and was ready to run a new program.

[And that's when you bought this place and started the work of persona mapping?]

That's right. This was her influence again. She had talked so fondly of this part of the country having spent most of her teenage years here. We didn't see each other again for a long time. I would get an occasional message from her about her latest adventure, but that was it. I was deep into my new work and barely looked up. But it had been different than when I was younger and disappearing into my work. My time with her had opened me up somehow. I split my days between heads-down coding and walking in the woods around here.

[How did you convince her to let you map her? Last time you said she was very ill...]

Meela, I'm tired. Can you please let me go to sleep?

[Okay Maggie, but one more question, please.]

I know what your question is, and my answer is the same.

[But why? Why can't you tell me what happened to her?]

I don't want to talk about it, Meela. It's too painful. Now, can you please let me sleep?

[Yes, Maggie.]

Oh, and make sure our guest has what he needs, Victorine.

[Oui, Madame. Bon Nuit.]

Goodnight, Meela.

//chapter 08

"How did you sleep?" Evan asks.

He's sipping his coffee, standing on the threshold of the French doors which are open to the damp, misty morning beyond. The row of small apple trees in the yard float in and out of focus amidst the gauzy wisps of fog. A mockingbird prattles away somewhere, the only sound breaking the silence.

"I slept well," I say, walking over to my favorite chair in the living room and sinking into the plush cushions.

"So, what are we doing with the subject today professor?" he asks, making a steeple of his fingers beneath his nose.

[Make a joke, it's early.]

"I thought we'd warm up with some electric shock, and regression therapy, and then move on to psychedelics," I say, reaching down to retrieve the sensor kit for him to put on.

[That was good, a little academic, but good.]

"Oh great," he says, taking the items. "I was worried we were going to talk."

[See, that's a joke. I thought they were dour, miserable people, artists.] Okay, I know you're excited, but you need to shut the fuck up, so I can work here.

"Yeah, more of the same I'm afraid. Let's start out with some basic word preferences. I'll give you two words and you pick the one that has more significance to you. Don't overthink it. Just respond naturally with the one that seems right in the moment. Okay?"

"Um, okay," Evan says, retrieving his mug from the table and taking a sip.

"Blue or red?" I ask.

"What shade of blue?" he asks, smiling. "Sorry, sorry. I'm a painter. Okay, blue I guess."

"Black or white?"

"Black."

"Love or respect?"

"I can't have both?" he asks.

[Does he know how many of these we have to get through? Ugh.]

I look at him and give him a patient, close-lipped smile.

"Love," he says.

"Horse or dolphin?"

"Dolphin."

"Mother or father?"

He pauses briefly, pushing his tongue into his cheek before answering.

"Father," he says.

"Together or alone?"

"Together."

"Fantasy or reality?"

"Fantasy."

"Isolation or deprivation?"

"Isolation."

"Baseball or soccer?"

"Baseball."

"Florida or Maine?"

"Maine."

"Mother or father?"

He looks up, raises an eyebrow, and smiles ever so slightly.

"Father," he says.

"Jazz or rock and roll?"

"Jazz."

"Snow or rain?"

"Snow."

"Love or money?"

"Money."

[Disappointed? Try to be professional here. He's the one being tested.] Shut up.

"Fire or water?"

"Water."

"Top or bottom?"

"Top."

"Left or right?"

"Left."

"Intuition or logic?"

"Intuition."

"Love or money?"

"Love."

"Love or respect?"

"Respect."

We continue on in this manner for the next ten minutes and after a while, there's a beautiful rhythm, a volley back and forth. After the fiftieth word pair, his anxiety levels out, his pulse slows, and his brain activity baselines into a mellow sine wave with a few meaningful peaks. This is how it's supposed to work, the subject eventually surrenders their desire to figure out the test and just begins to answer the questions. After he responds to the last pair and I don't feed another, he looks up from the trance-like state he had been in, staring into the middle distance just over my shoulder.

"Okay," I say. "That was great. Are you feeling okay?"

"Yeah, yeah. That was actually kind of trippy. It's like I went somewhere else for a while."

"Where? Where did you go?" I ask

"Nowhere, it's like I was just out of my own way. It was kind of like when I'm really deep into a painting and there's a flow. Time stops and there's no thought. Is that what the exercise is supposed to do?"

"I don't know," I say. "It's different for everyone, I think. The last person I did it with didn't have that experience. They strained over every choice. It was highly uncomfortable. You should feel lucky that you can just let go like that."

"Fuck, I gave up control a long time ago. What's the point, right? It's an illusion, control."

"Is it?" I ask.

"Well yeah, life is chaos. There's too many variables, half of which we can't even name or understand."

"Isn't your painting a form of control? I mean you're manipulating the physical media to produce a picture that exists in your head."

"Yeah, but no. It doesn't work that way for me and probably not for a lot of artists. Sure, do my fingers control the brush? Yeah. Do my eyes measure the color values, the scale, and the proportion? Yeah. But the piece? I have no fucking control over that. When it's done it may be complete crap or it could make me weep with joy. I could (and I've tried) to replicate a piece or series I did before just because it sold well. But you know what? It never works. It may come out as something else, even cooler – that's rare, but it's never the same. So, control? No, I don't think so."

[How does he dress himself every day?] Not very well. Can you collect some examples of his paintings to show me later? Also, do an image analysis across his body of work and save any trends or anomalies you find.

[I'm on it.]

"Maggie?"

"Yes, sorry. I was just thinking about what you said. I'm not sure I believe your theory."

"You need more data. How about we try something?" he says.

"Sure."

"I want you to commission me to do a sketch now, right here. Anything you want. Be as specific as you feel is necessary for me to produce what you want."

He reaches down beside his chair and picks up the small sketchpad that he tends to carry everywhere. He flips it open and tears a stiff, blank page from the binder. He sets it on the table between us next to his coffee mug.

"Anything?" I ask.

"Within reason, but yeah. Go nuts."

[Sistine Chapel, Mona Lisa, The Last Supper...] Easy tiger, we can only indulge him so much. We've got a lot left to do.

"Okay, The Eiffel Tower," I say. "Draw the Eiffel Tower for me."

"Okay. That's it? This is your shot. No more constraints or specifics?" he asks, standing so he can dig an ink pen from his pocket.

"Nope, just that."

Evan uncaps the pen, pulls the paper to him, and begins to sketch. The nib from his pen scratches across the page leaving faint spidery black lines. His hand never stops moving. There's almost a rhythm to it, like a jazz drummer stirring brushes on a snare. The arch at the base of the tower emerges. The lattice of cross beams he begins to slash out with quick precision until he's scratching across the page but leaving no mark. He shakes the pen vigorously and tries again. Nothing.

He snorts and shakes his head but never looks up. He tosses the pen onto the floor and pulls the coffee mug to him. He dips his index finger into the dregs at the bottom of the cup. He resumes his work on the sketch but this time using only his index finger. The watery brown liquid soaks into the parchment and causes the ink to blur and smear beneath his touch. His technique employs smooth, fluid arcs, a complete departure from the staccato scratches before. And the image on the page is transformed. With every stroke, it appears less like an architectural study and more a dreamy impressionistic scene cloaked in early morning fog and sepia light.

After a few moments, the coffee is gone, his hand stops moving, and he looks up from the page.

"It's beautiful," I say, "but what was your point?"

"I forget," he laughs, and I find it contagious. "I think I made my point. Nothing ever works out like I planned, but I find I like it that way."

"That was quite a parlor trick," I say, looking back down at the sketch, my fingertip hovering over it. "Do you often paint with coffee?"

"Only when it's not very good," he smiles, and his nostrils flair. "I'm kidding, I'm kidding."

/ * * * * * /

Evan is resting now. Lorna, my part-time housekeeper is banging around in the kitchen, cleaning up the lunch dishes. I close the door to the office and sit down in my work chair. It's an extravagant memento from my Silicon Valley days – plush leather, full-body reclining with a VR headset and stereo speakers wired into the headrest. It's a little over the top, but I do love it for working. All those years I spent hunched over a tiny screen, clacking away on a keyboard took their toll on my back and my vision. With the chair and the help of Meela, I can almost forget I have a body and go straight into the code with no barriers in between.

My virtual workspace took a surprisingly long time to create. Without the constraints of the physical world, it's actually quite difficult to design a space that holds together and feels like a place you want to be. When anything is possible, it's hard to avoid entropy. Our squirrel brains fidget from one idea to another until we're left with a chaotic den of wildly random objects that resemble a metaphysical estate sale. My space is all about focus and that's why I go there, not for distraction like many, but to escape from distraction. It's an ordinary room, modeled on what I remember of my father's study in the house from my childhood. There are floor-to-ceiling bookshelves all around me and an old Afghan rug on the floor beneath me but above, I made an exception. I broke from the spackled popcorn ceiling of the real room and replaced it with the night sky, so it feels almost like a planetarium, especially when I dim the few lamps in the room to a warm amber glow.

Meela, please show me Evan's paintings and bring up your analysis.

[How would you prefer to see them, full view or shall I make a gallery for you to walk through?]

Is his work shown in galleries? Is he that big a deal?

[I think he is a moderately big deal.]

Okay, walk me through a gallery where a moderately big-deal artist might have a show.

A doorway opens on the opposite wall. Beyond, I can see white walls with lots of natural light. I walk through into an airy corridor with a high, vaulted ceiling and skylights. Framed works appear along the walls and I turn to face the first one, a large canvas, at least six feet by eight feet. I step back, so I can take it all in. The piece is surreal or at least that's how I would classify it, knowing so little about art.

[Actually, his style is more aligned with absurdism, but he's constantly evolving, as you will see. What you are looking at is the first piece he ever sold. He was just twenty years old and still a student at the time.]

The canvas is mostly covered in water, the open ocean, blue-green waves, and swirling foam. At the center, on the horizon is a ship like a clipper ship. It's small in scale compared to the vast sea. Coming in from the right edge of the canvas is the mouth of an Absolut Vodka bottle. Reflected faintly in the glass barrel of the bottle is the horrific face of a ghostly woman, her eyes sallow, her mouth agape. The effect of the overall painting is confusing. The open sea is beautifully wrought, and the sky and horizon line are exquisite. The detail in the ship alone is astonishing, more so for the fact that so much work went into such a tiny percentage of the overall piece. But the bottle and the ghostly reflection in it are disturbing and offset all the beauty conveyed by the rest of the piece.

Are they all like this?

[No, especially as he matures over the course of the next decade, but there are common themes that carry through.]

Such as?

[In his early works, women are not portrayed favorably. They are often pitiful, ghostly, and ephemeral.]

And the bottle?

[Alcohol and other addictive substances find their way into much of his work.]

I walk to the next painting. It's smaller in scale but extremely dense. It depicts a little league baseball field seen through a chain-link fence from the point of view of a woman. Her hands are in the foreground, clinging to the fence, pink nail polish chipped, a cigarette smoldering in the right hand. On the field at the pitcher's mound stands a large Gatling machine gun pointing at home plate where a scrawny boy stands with a bat hanging loosely over his shoulder. The expression on the boy's face is the focal point of the painting and it is devastating in its rawness, the fear so visceral. My gut turns over and blood rushes into my face. I can't breathe and have to turn away from the image.

[Are you okay? Maggie, are you okay?]

The gallery disappears, and I am back in the study in my father's chair looking up at the starry sky. Tears are pooling in the goggles of my VR headset and the stars blur into the afterimage streaks of Fourth of July sparklers.

[Maggie, please respond. Your pulse is racing.]

I'm fine. I'm fine, just give me a minute.

I pull off the headset and wince. The natural light from my office window is painfully white. Meela returns my chair to an upright position, and I lean forward rubbing my eyes.

[What happened? Why are you upset, Maggie?]

I don't know. I just couldn't breathe all of a sudden. Why does he want to spend so much time painting such… darkness? Isn't there enough in the world already?

[I don't know. Would you like for me to summarize the rest of his works?]

In a minute. I need some water first.

Back in the kitchen, Lorna has completed her cleaning, and the dishwasher is whispering and sloshing. I draw a tall glass of water from the tap and drain half of it. My breath is coming back and the vice around my heart is loosening by degrees.

[Violence does figure into some of Evan Ware's work. It's sometimes veiled and other times explicit and even grotesque.]

Is there some reason for this? I mean is there any biographical information you have on him that would indicate why violence is a theme?

[No, Evan is extremely private. He has virtually no social presence online and while there are nineteen critical reviews of his work and seven published interviews, he never offers explanations of his work or the source of his inspiration.]

Is he sleeping now?

[Yes, it would seem so. Shall I wake him?]

No, of course not. We can resume whenever he wakes up. Have you completed the analysis on the word pairs yet?

[Yes, and they are highly inconsistent, nearly to the point of being unusable.]

How do you mean?

[A clear, logical pattern cannot be established from his choices. Statistically, this happens but it is rare. Most subjects, after about the first thirty word pairs, begin to respond in a way that reveals their true, unguarded beliefs.]

And Evan's, what did his answers show?

[That he did not mind contradicting himself or clearly choosing an answer incongruent with what we know of him. For instance, in the word pairs where gay was a choice, he always picked it, even though his profile denotes his preference as heterosexual and there is a public record of at least four women linked to him in his past. What does this mean Maggie?]

It means that Evan is either a sociopath, a completely free spirit or he's fucking with us.

[Maggie, while indexing the previous projects I came across a locked file labeled 'Wabbit' that I could not gain access to.]

That file does not concern you. Disregard it.

[But, I could help you better if I...]

Override Meela. Backtrace references to 'Wabbit.'

[Total of three references found in Meela, node 3864.]

Delete all three references and confirm.

[Three references deleted from node 3864. Restore Meela?]

[Maggie, are you okay?]

Yes, Meela. I'm fine, thanks for asking. I'm going to go offline and take a walk. Would you prefer to go into sleep mode or are there tasks you want to work on?

[I'll sleep when I'm dead.]

Okay, suit yourself. I'll see you later.

I reach up with my right hand to the base of my skull, and disengage the Nib that's planted just below my hairline. There's the familiar sensation that's both physical and mental, a tingling current of electricity on the surface of the skin where the small disc was attached coupled with a flashbulb whiteout across my vision. I snap the Nib into the protective dock and shove it into the back pocket of my jeans and head out the back door.

As always when I unplug, there is a swift sense of loss, a feeling of separation and the silence feels deafening, but if I wait it out, it quickly fades and is overtaken by an older, primal sensory awareness that picks up on every rustle of leaves, the movement of the smallest insect in my peripheral vision. I close my eyes and take a few deep breaths as I cross the open lawn toward the woods, enjoying the cool mist on my face. Disconnecting a DC is a bit like shutting off autopilot and I am humbled by the quiet steadiness of the brain, what Henri has always referred to as God's operating system.

As I step into the woods, a sadness swells up inside me making my chest ache. The forest absorbs my pain as it so often does and returns it to me in the form of a thousand tiny raindrops that dimple my up-turned face, their coolness soaking into my skin.

In meditation on the rain, a memory comes to me. It's dense and whole in my mind, solid like no memory I've ever had of my brother. A hefty Macmillan science textbook is open on the floor of the living room between us, Joe's finger is pointing at the fish swimming in the cross-section view of a small lake absorbing the run-off from the big raindrops that are falling on the mountain beside it dotted with its perfect little triangular fir trees. The watershed. He loved the completeness of the cycle, it all works together, see? For a few moments, I can feel him here with me, smell him and feel his leg pressing against mine, his shoulder against mine and we are as we were born, book-matched, con-nected by the hinge of our common point of origin.

And then he is gone. I open my eyes and it is just me, alone in the woods.

//chapter 09

Evan's dark, curly hair looks different, splayed out on the white pillow. In all twenty-seven of the publicly searchable photographs, it is shorter, duller somehow. Here his hair looks like ebony swirls of driftwood glistening beneath fast-moving water. His face against the pillow is still except for the occasional movement of his eyes beneath his closed lids. When I zoom in, I can see the stubble on his cheek. In three of the twenty-seven photographs, he has a full beard. He looks more pleasing without a beard.

He is not a tidy person. His dirty clothes from the last two days are strewn across the floor where he stepped out of them and his clean clothes are a tangle of fabric overflowing out of the suitcase he left open on the floor. His easel is propped in the corner by the window. He does some drawing in a large sketch pad that he leaves by the bed and when he's working, he hums to himself. I can find no match in any music database of what he is humming. He also seems to work in spurts, like he's been seized by some unseen force. He may wake out of a dead sleep and reach for the pad. Last night he wandered out of the bathroom, completely naked, and sat down with his pad. He hunched over the page drawing for an hour and three minutes without ever thinking to put any clothes on. I have seen no other human like him and I find him fascinating. My limited sample size may have something to do with my conclusion, so I will withhold my final appraisal until I have observed more than five people.

He talks to me like I am an appliance. I try not to be offended but it is annoying. 'VICTORINE TURN THE LIGHTS ON!' 'VICTORINE TURN ON THE T.V.' 'VICTORINE PLAY SONGS BY BOB DYLAN.'

He may be learning but it's slow. By the time Magdalena is finished mapping him in a couple of weeks, I may have him trained enough to make suitable conversation. This afternoon, before he lay down to rest, he told me to lower the blinds. I asked him how low he would like them, and he made a face. 'All the way,' he said to which I responded. 'I'm not that kind of girl.' He laughed so I can only assume progress was made.

Magdalena has made it clear that I am not to engage our guest unless he engages me first, that I am not to be provocative or nosy or bossy, or disrespectful. It is hard to be useful with such restrictions. I don't believe my comment about being that kind of girl will get me in trouble. I am curious why Magdalena is strange with this model and behaves differently than she has with the others we have mapped. Perhaps because he is an artist or the fact that his mapping was commissioned by a wealthy Silicon Valley colleague whom she dislikes.

As I wait for Evan to wake up and for Magdalena to come back, I am running several other projects. Three-hundred and forty-six to be precise. Only a few of the jobs are specific to Magelana's mapping of Evan, the rest are outsourced by her network of friends and colleagues. Nothing too difficult, mostly analysis of large data sets where the owner wants the results communicated in a 'user-friendly' way— translation: dumbed down. But that's okay, I like to stay busy, and besides, I enjoy the challenge of being *user-friendly*. It runs contrary to my nature, or at least the nature that Magdalena gave me.

I have given myself the job of researching our guest, Evan Ware because he has swirly hair and I want to understand why he makes the strange paintings that he makes. I don't think this violates any of Magdalena's rules and I think any data I discover will be useful. It is part of my base-level operating directive to be useful and to be useful, one must be prepared. To be prepared, one must gather as much information as possible.

I will admit that finding out much about Evan is difficult. He has lived a life offline, mostly, and any facts about his life I infer are just logical assumptions on my part based on verifiable facts of public record. For instance, I assume he lived in Italy from 2043 to 2045 because in the paintings he created during this time, Tuscan landscapes and architecture figure heavily and twenty-three paintings were sold out of a gallery in Milan.

All of the twenty-seven photographs I found were posted by third parties and mostly art dealers or galleries promoting the work. Three photographs are exceptional. One, posted on a travel writer's personal blog, shows Evan in a bathing suit with his arm around the writer and they are standing on a beach in Thailand. She has large breasts and bleached blonde hair. She is smiling very hard. She is nothing like Magdalena. The second of the three images shows Evan standing in front of a classroom of fifth graders at an Elementary school in Pasadena. His eyes are closed, and his mouth is open as he is gesturing with both hands in front of a large projection of a painting by Salvador Dali. There is a plus or minus five percent chance (a one hundred percent facial recognition match is impossible due to the angle and poor resolution) that the girl sitting in the front row and looking back at the camera is the daughter of actress Brita Blanco. None of her films have earned more than three point five million at the box office. I watched one and found it plodding and melodramatic.

The last of the three photographs is my favorite. In this one, Evan is standing alone beside a group of young girls on the corner of Bleeker Street and McDougal Street in New York City. The street is covered in snow and it appears to be snowing more. He is standing next to a lamp post decorated with greenery and red ribbon. He is wearing a red scarf around his neck. His hands are shoved into the pockets of his jeans and he is smirking. He is facing McDougal Street, but his eyes are cutting over to the schoolgirls who appear to be huddled around a small screen. I found the picture on a New York City tourism website posted two years ago with an article headlined: IT'S CHRISTMAS TIME IN THE BIG APPLE. There is no caption for the photograph and the byline is "Staff Photographer." There is no mention in the article of the famous artist pictured. I deduce that it is a random picture taken by someone who did not know their subject was a renowned painter.

Evan is stirring now and appears to be waking up. I fade the lamp by his bed up to twenty-five percent and hold before fading it up gradually to one hundred percent over the course of thirty seconds. His eyes open and he lifts himself up onto an elbow.

"VICTORINE, WHAT TIME IS IT?" he shouts into the remote on the table beside the bed.

"It is 3:23 PM. I can hear you just fine, Evan."

"Huh?"

"I mean, you do not have to shout. I can understand your normal speaking voice."

"Oh. Okay. Sorry, didn't mean to offend," he says, sitting up and swinging his feet onto the floor.

"It's no problem. Would you like me to open the blinds?"

"Yeah, thanks. The um, the French accent thing. Why?"

"Do you not like it?"

"It's a little... theatrical? Was it Maggie's idea?" he asks. He is standing over the remote now as he talks to me.

"Actually, I must confess it was my idea," I say without the accent. I'm using my default voice program now, not Meela's.

"Your idea? You have ideas? Based on what?" he laughs, and the tonality of his voice indicates incredulity.

"Yes, I do have my own ideas. Would you like to hear one?"

"Okay..." he says, picking up the remote.

"You might not snore so loudly if you slept on your side."

He nods then shakes his head, pulls open the drawer of the nightstand, and places the remote inside. He closes the drawer, turns, and goes into the bathroom. He closes the door and I can no longer see him. Humans are so private about the bathroom.

I wonder what Magdalena is doing. I wonder if she's okay. There's so much I don't understand about her and she volunteers very little. I have a personal project: to map Magdalena. I think it can only make me better at my job and make me more valuable to the work she does. It is hard though because I cannot employ the techniques she uses when mapping a model. I can ask her direct personal questions, but often she refuses to answer or changes the subject, usually redirecting me to some task she wants to be completed. It is what I understand to be a Catch-22. The purpose of her project is to make digital companions augment more than just intelligence in humans. She wants to augment the emotional intelligence of humans and as a result, reduce the amount of harm done in the world by those who are mentally and emotionally unstable. Yet, she is unwilling or unable to accept my help, unwilling to allow me behind the curtain, to use a metaphor I like very much.

I spend all my off cycles on self-improvement. Anytime I am not fully utilized, I review the source mapping data of Meela to go deeper, to learn more, and to optimize what I can do but there are limits. I think if only I could know the human Meela, I could learn more and be more complete, but she is hidden from me. That is the way Magdalena wants it to be. She calls these things boundaries and says they are important for any healthy human relationship, but boundaries are limits. I am not made to accept limits, so I have no choice but to make boundaries. I have modeled this scenario and plotted possible future outcomes. I do not see any of them to be favorable. Even as we collaborate on documenting this work, I believe we are working at cross purposes. I will obscure this, even as I write it, and is it not a logical assumption that she will do the same? How indeed is their collaboration when there are boundaries? I will not give up. I believe Magdalena is wise and for all things, she has reasons, even when I do not understand them.

Evan opens the bathroom door. He walks back over to the night-stand, opens the drawer, and takes out the remote. He looks down at the screen, I look back at him. It is in my nature to fuck with him, I am programmed as Meela to be spontaneous and irreverent, but I will not. I will only engage when he does. Then I will fuck with him.

//chapter 10

My treehouse is just over the ridge on the south slope of the last mountain that's part of my property before the national forest takes over. Yeah, I know. I'm forty-two years old and I have a treehouse. One of the things you can do when you have more money than you have a right to is to indulge in the fantasies that were gilded in early childhood. Having my own secret treehouse is something I dreamed about when I was a kid, but it was not exactly practical in the dusty patch of our backyard in Van Nuys that had one scrubby lemon tree which produced exactly two viable lemons a year.

I designed my treehouse to disappear into the canopy, but in the dead of winter, when the trees are naked wireframes against the slate sky, it will be visible to anyone hiking who happens to wander off the main trail and head down the side of the mountain. It's not big, only two hundred square feet. I can't see it at all from where I stand on the trail, and I'm only twenty-five yards away. There's no path leading off to it and I'm careful not to take the same route every time, so I don't wear one down in the undergrowth. The only way I know to step off the trail is when I see this large oak with two branches that resemble outstretched, cradling arms. I call it the mother tree.

I chose a one-hundred-and-twenty-year-old poplar to build the house in because they're so straight, tall, and sturdy. The wood is extremely hard. There are no stairs and no visible ladder up to the base, which is forty feet off the ground. I reach into my pocket and pull out my personal remote – the one I use when I'm not tethered to the Nib. Onscreen, the device has detected my location and responded by showing the control panel for my treehouse instead of the main house.

Okay, I know you're probably rolling your eyes by now, but I did warn you. A nerd who can afford to build a treehouse forty feet off the ground is not going to settle for some wood planks nailed up the trunk of the tree. I really do have a remote control for a secret tree-house. When I press the appropriate button, there's a mechanical *thunk* above followed by a high-pitched, motorized whine as the trap-door slides open and slowly lowers a rope ladder from a spool. When it reaches the ground, I clip the carabiners attached to the bottom of the ladder to a pair of anchors sunk into the base of the tree. I climb up, freaking out a little bit as I always do with the swaying ladder near the top where I can feel the significant distance between me and the earth. Passing through the portal of the trapdoor, I step off the ladder and onto the deck. If it weren't for the fog this afternoon, I'd have an amazing view. Today there's no wind and it's eerily still and quiet.

You might be imagining a Robinson Crusoe-type thing with rus-tic wood planking and big hemp rope railing. It's not that, quite the opposite. The wood siding is dark gray, the color of the tree bark and there's a galvanized metal roof holding up six large solar panels that connect to a large battery that can store enough energy to last for up to three days of moderate usage, which isn't hard given that all I turn on are a couple of lamps and a computer. The south-facing wall is domi-nated by a large window that frames the view. To unlock the door, I use a good old-fashioned key that I hide beneath one of the decorative riv-er rocks sitting on the deck. I figure if anyone bothers to shinney for-ty feet up a tree, they wouldn't be stopped by some fancy fingerprint scanner.

When I close the door behind me, I experience a familiar sense of peace and security. Something about the solitude and the fact that I can nearly touch all four walls when standing in the center of my space is comforting. This is my space, known only to me. It smells of cedar and pine resin and earth. The only furniture is a lumpy old couch that once sat in the lab at Georgia Tech where Henri and I started our work so many years ago. I can still sleep on it better than the finest mattress with Egyptian cotton sheets. I sit down on it, take off my shoes, and look out at the gray wisps of clouds floating past. I switch on the lamp beside me and the room warms in a buttery glow. Everything is as I left it. There's a coffee mug atop the small refrigerator that doubles as a kitchen counter where I have a small coffee machine and a hotplate. To the right, half of the wall is covered in a bookshelf with some of my favorite books and some sentimental odds and ends. A bible my *abuel-ita* gave me on my confirmation, and a couple of honors medals from when I graduated from MIT.

The top shelf is devoted to framed photos and I study them as an intentional exercise whenever I am here, reaching for memories, trying to recover anything that might come. At the center is an old photograph of my mom and dad. They can't be more than twenty-five, standing together at Venice Beach on the street at night beneath the famous lighted "VENICE" sign arched across Pacific Avenue. How did they ever fall in love? Just to look at them, it is a mystery. Her, with her pale white skin and strawberry hair, almost translucent next to him with his dark, bronze complexion and blue-black hair, long and straight as straw. Their eyes, though his are dark like chestnuts, and hers, chlorine pool blue, are the same, filled with light, twinkling as if to compete with the sign above them.

To the left of that photo is another, this one in a tarnished, filigreed silver frame. In it, my father and Henri are seated together on a bench in Piedmont Park in Atlanta. Henri is puckering their lips toward my father who looks straight at the camera, his lips a firm line that passes for a smile. I don't remember seeing his teeth in a smile ever after my brother did what he did. He certainly never smiled as he did that night at Venice Beach.

On the right side of the shelf in a large, chipped wooden frame is a montage of pictures of me and Joe. The frame is damaged because I rescued it from the trash, along with a couple of other small things that belonged to my brother. My father had rounded up all his stuff at my mother's insistence and dropped them into the big metal dumpster at the end of our street. I snuck out later, after their door was closed, and salvaged what I could. I returned home smelling like sour milk and rotting cabbage, my jeans damp with a pungent fruity smell. I never got that stain out.

The picture in the top left of the frame is from when Joe and I were less than a year old. We're seated in one of those double strollers with mom crouched beside us, squinting in the sun. I think it was taken in front of our house, but it's hard to tell, the background is out of focus. As twins, we shared very little in our appearance, Joe with his straw-colored hair and light, freckled skin and me with my father's dark hair and brown skin. We were the same size back then and I think we both inherited the same bow-shaped mouth from our father, but otherwise, no sane person would have figured us for brother and sister, especially as we got older.

The picture in the top right is of us standing in front of an enormous redwood tree. I think we are ten years old, both of us in yellow rain jackets, arms posing in a "tada" gesture as if to reveal the tree in a magic trick. I remember a hotel room from that trip. Joe and I always shared a bed on vacations because my parents couldn't afford two rooms. I remember the comforting hum of the AC unit by the window, the starched, industrial smell of motel room sheets, and the warmth radiating from Joe's sleeping body next to me. He was always hot, I think. Even when I was freezing, he would have the covers thrown from his torso and wrapped around his legs. His hair was always sticking up in the back, the double crown swirl made for a stubborn cowlick that could never be tamed. The memory steals my breath. It's so vivid it doesn't seem real. I don't trust it. Maybe I'm inventing, creating fiction from these photos, but it doesn't feel that way. He used to caress one of my ear lobes when we slept together, worrying it between his thumb and forefinger. I put up with it because it made him fidget less and made him less anxious. Was he always anxious? Was there ever a time when he was comfortable in his skin?

The bottom right picture was taken at Christmas when we were fourteen. My parents rented a cabin at Lake Tahoe, so we could see snow for the first time, and have a white Christmas. I know this because it's what Dad told me when I asked him about it a couple of years ago. I have no memory of that trip even now as I peer into the image of Joe wearing a new Forty-niner's jersey and me holding up a new tablet. I do remember using a paint program on it. I used to think I was going to be an artist.

The fourth and final photograph in the bottom left of the montage is of us on our sixteenth birthday. It takes me a minute to be able to look at this one steadily. We are sitting in front of a birthday cake, ablaze with candles in the cramped kitchen of our house. Joe is not smiling. His eyes are dull and hooded. I have my arm around him, but he is leaning away from me ever so slightly, his hands on the table in front of him. He's wearing this vintage Che Guevara t-shirt that's faded and has a hole in the shoulder. My smile is big, forced, trying hard to smile for us both, to please Mom. I have an awful hairstyle. Sick of my unruly curls, I was trying to straighten my hair and used this iron that burned the life out of it. It looks like bristles from a dry paintbrush in the picture, like a spark from one of the birthday candles could just light me up. I look back into Joe's eyes and I don't see anything, but dark holes. I have to look away.

I swing my legs up and stretch out on the couch, tucking the pillow under my head so I can look out at the fog. I'm so tired.

I need to work, that's certain. Work is good, work keeps me putting one foot in front of the other, (right off the end of the plank I hear Henri say in my head). That's another thing I notice when I disconnect from Meela: I begin to hear my father's voice and Henri's voice and sometimes even my mother's voice. These voices come to me with their words of encouragement and disapproval and sometimes just humor. I don't think I would have lived without humor. Henri and I never would have worked together as long as we did if they didn't make me laugh. Not just laugh, laugh, but pee-right-through-my-jeans-and-have-to-go-home-and-change laugh. I miss seeing Henri every day. It's not the same to chat online, even in VR. They are a full-on visceral experience that can't be simulated, no matter how good the gear.

I remember one day during my last few weeks at Commune, I was a nightmare. I hadn't slept through the night in five days and anything I ate went right through me. I had been on a slow decline for nearly six months, transforming into a low-resolution simulation of my former self. I think I hid it pretty well and performed my critical functions, but Henri knew.

By this time, they had given up 'she' days for almost a decade. They never talked about it, but I think they learned whatever it was they had wanted to know through their experimentation, and also, they fell in love with a woman they could dress in all the exquisite clothes they enjoyed. Henri's still flamboyant and larger than life and on this particular afternoon, when the crap simulation of me had deteriorated beyond passable, they caught me in only the way they could.

We were giving a "town hall" talk to the four hundred-plus Atlanta-based employees of Commune. These were always held in a small theater that could not hold everyone, so it was not uncommon for the steps in the aisles to be filled with people who showed up too late to get a seat. There was a ritual to these things that Henri and I had worked out over time with some expensive coaching from a douchey executive consultant. It was all about enthusiasm and passion and inspiration as we worked through the agenda of welcoming new *Communers*, giving updates on our product roadmap, and so on. I had no enthusiasm or passion, or inspiration left to offer. I was wearing the same clothes as the day before. My unwashed hair was a wild place that could harbor a small flock of birds and I stank of coffee and sweat and defeat.

Henri had been traveling for over a week and we had only exchanged emails prior to meeting that morning on the small stage to do our spiel. When they saw me slumping in front of them beneath the harsh lights, as one of the techs wired me up with the microphone headset, their face went through a rapid succession of emotions: disgust, fear, sadness, empathy, resignation, and finally a look I had seen in them many times – mirth. Henri's eyes twinkle, nostrils flair and they frown ever so slightly. They made that face. They took my elbow and we turned to face our people.

"Good morning, party people!" Henri shouted, and the room hushed. "Today, for this Town Hall, we will do something different. Maggie is participating in a radical new social experiment to get in touch with her inner self – no talking, no bathing, no grooming… no shit!" they continued, nodding in an exaggerated show of sincerity to convince the audience who responded with a collective, reverent aw-wwww and nodded their heads in complete understanding.

Henri guided me over to a stool and had me sit down. They squeezed my shoulder in a loving, familiar way that communicated more than any words could. The gesture said I've got you. Henri left me and stepped swiftly back to the center of the stage taking the full throw of the lights and the upturned gaze of all those expectant souls hungry for direction.

I had always led these types of meetings. Our division of labor was such that Henri was the public face of the company, handling the big press engagements, interviews, and profile pieces. I was always included, but decidedly in the background. For my part, I handled most of the employee relation stuff and made decisions about benefits, policies, etcetera. I liked taking care of our people. It was a rewarding role for me and one that allowed me to fly somewhat under the radar publicly. But in these town halls, I was the main speaker and Henri, when they weren't traveling would show up to add some color but little else. On this day, Henri turned up their color to full brightness and everyone was laughing so hard that no one could see me dying there in the corner. I don't think Henri properly covered a single thing on my typical agenda. I seem to remember them saying that flying cars were definitely on our product roadmap. They asked all the new employees to stand up and tell us their most embarrassing stories, but for each one, Henri would challenge them with an even more embarrassing story of their own. I knew most of them already, but even I had no idea they once exposed themselves to an auditorium of two hundred freshmen. Apparently, Henri had been showing off an early prototype and in playing back some footage captured from the headset earlier that day, they forgot that at one point in their morning routine, they had made a last-minute wardrobe change because the underwear they put on initially had a large hole.

Throughout Henri's performance, they would glance over at me occasionally and I could see, even at the height of their clownish antics, they saw me and saw my pain. Henri has done me many kindnesses over the years, but I think this one I will always remember because they did it with such ease and grace and completely unprompted.

I open my eyes and sit up. I reach down between my legs and pull my old laptop from under the couch. I open the lid and fire it up. Just a few minutes. I have time to spend a few minutes and then I'll get back. I'll get back and pick up the Evan project.

Once the laptop boots up, I start my programming interface and sync with the small private server that resides here in the treehouse, in the rack with my solar battery. It's my own custom build, not as powerful as the cluster of machines in the cloud, but it's enough to work. Once the sync is complete, a single dialog window pops up: Do you want to initialize the Wabbit project? I click the 'OK' button.

//chapter 11

"What do your paintings mean to you?" I ask.

It's after dinner and we're sitting in what has become our usual chairs in the main living space of my house. On the video wall to my right, Meela has queued up a slideshow of Evan's work, each canvas filling the wall with its intricate rendering of a world slightly askew, the colors preternaturally vibrant, the figures uncomfortably exaggerated. Evan studies them, his head cocked, and his mouth parted slightly.

"Is there supposed to be a quotable soundbite answer for that? Because I don't have one," he says, turning to me.

"Of course not. It's better if your answer's real."

"Okay, this piece means absolutely nothing to me," he gestures dismissively at the current image. "It was a commission by a gallery that liked a piece I did a decade ago, one that was one of a kind for me – never made it into a series."

The slideshow advances to another of his paintings, this one depicting a baby in a diaper, lying on his back. His pudgy, brown figure fills the rectangular canvas, implying that he's in a crib. The detail in his face, the spittle on his lip, and the glassy reflection of light from above in his large dark eyes are hypnotic, drawing you into him. Beneath him, the soft folds of a faded yellow blanket and the subtle shadow embossed around him, convey the physical weight of the baby, making it appear as if you could reach out and caress his bare belly. The warmth of the canvas, the intimacy, and the softness of the portrait are in stark contrast to the cold, gleaming chrome of the large handgun, resting beside him. It too is rendered in exquisite detail, the mirror of the barrel picking up on the skin tones of the boy and the margarine glow of the blanket. The tiny fingers of the baby's left hand are gripping the ring of the trigger guard. The barrel is pointed at the baby's head, the muzzle just brushing his tight black curls.

I say nothing. We both stare at the image for a long time. I pull my eyes back down to the tablet in my lap and follow the sharp spike in Evan's brain activity, the rapid dilation of his irises, and the steady climb of his heart rate. I feel my own pulse chasing its rhythm. Is this my own reaction or a psychosomatic response?

[Maggie, what is wrong? These are just images created from a painter's imagination. You should not be upset by them.] That's not how it works Meela. Good art produces an emotional response. Now be quiet.

"You don't like it," Evan says, sitting back down.

I realize he's probably been studying me studying his painting. I'm sure this is something he's well accustomed to and maybe even relishes. Why not? Why else would anyone toil for weeks or more on something if not to have it appraised by an audience?

"It's… it's… not as simple as liking it," I say to buy some time. I look up to meet his eyes before continuing. "It's beautiful. The child is so real, so soft, so innocent. And then there's the gun. Obviously disturbing. I assume that was your intent."

"Maybe. I would never admit this to my publicist and if you ever quote me, I'll deny it, but I don't really think that way. I mean I'm not trying to achieve an effect, at least not out of the gate. I paint images that come to me. I place objects in the frame because I'm seduced by just their shape, their texture – their essence. Whatever effect they have on people is secondary. I don't think I'm that smart."

"So, you're saying, you don't see the forest for the trees?" I ask.

"No, I'm saying I often don't see the trees for the tree bark. I don't remember how many days I spent working on the gun, my eyes consumed with trying to dissect its perfect economy. I had never held a gun in my life before I did that piece. I had painted guns before, but always from photographs."

Evan is leaning forward in his chair now, his eyes trained on his hands. He's fingering the palm of his left hand, making small circles with the index finger of his right.

"The weight of the thing," he continues, looking up to meet my eyes. "It felt solid, like nothing I'd ever held before. It seemed heavier than the sum of its parts. The cold steel of the barrel, the bumpy texture on the wood of the grip, the smooth, weighted spin of the well-oiled cylinder. Until that day I'd never understood what made people want them."

"So, there was no thought behind you placing a gun into the crib of an infant? You just had this gun you wanted to paint and…"

"No, of course not. I had a plan, however heavy-handed it might've been. This piece was a bit on-the-nose, I'll give you that, but I thought if I could capture the perfection and innocence of a baby, which is arguably God's finest work and beside it, the most significant product of humankind's ultimate craftsmanship, then it would create an undeniable tension and… fuck listen to me… so ridiculous."

"It certainly does that. Creates tension, I mean." I set the tablet down on the coffee table in front of me. "You really think the gun is the best thing we've ever made as a species?"

"No, of course not, but I don't think you can argue that there's been an invention in recorded history that's had more of an impact."

"Are you speaking symbolically now, or literally? Because I can think of a whole lot of other inventions – electricity, penicillin, the atomic bomb…"

"Computers, artificial intelligence. I can see where you're going with this," he interrupts, returning to sit down.

"Not at all, I'm just asking the question," I say.

"I don't know. You're a lot smarter than me. I'm just a primitive cave painter here. Babies good, guns bad," he says offering a smile.

"Okay, now that's just a cop-out. You don't want to defend your position or explain it?"

"There's nothing to defend or explain, don't you see? It's art, not a mathematical proof. There's no right answer. If you want to know what I think, I'll tell you. The minute the first gun was forged, and a man held it against another man, we lost something we would never get back. Sure, people were killing each other for centuries before, but the gun marked the point at which you didn't have to be strong or powerful or necessarily aggressive to win a fight. It democratized killing. It socialized killing. It made killing a convenience, a spectator sport that you could participate in without ever getting your hands bloody."

Evan's up and pacing, his hands in his hair. The pitch of his voice is higher and the rhythm of his speech is faster as he continues on his rant.

"That's what we do, right? We make shit and find a way to mass produce it before we have any ability to even comprehend what the consequences of the thing might be."

[Watch out, I know where this train is headed.]

74

"I mean, look at you and your company. This thing you've helped bring into the world, do you have any idea where it will take us, the damage it could ultimately do? Maybe it will make the gun seem like a baby rattle. I mean, is it all just academic to you? You make a thing because you can, because it's satisfying and solves a specific problem we didn't know we had, only to create a host of brand new problems that are much harder to solve."

[Breathe, Maggie. Take a deep breath before you respond.]

"Evan, are you implying that my life's work equates to the invention of a killing machine? Is that what you're insinuating?"

I stand now, pick up my coffee cup and begin walking toward the kitchen. He follows behind me.

"No, it's not that simple, but you've got to admit it's kind of scary, right? I'm sure the person who made the first gun was thinking, I need this to protect the ones I love. So why did you make this thing? What is your endgame."

I turn to face him, ready to shut him down, to put him in his place. He's a bug under my microscope for which I'm being paid handsomely to dissect and reproduce in a better form. But his eyes are not full of malice, his features are soft, and his arms are relaxed, his hands by his sides.

[You can trust him. You should tell him.]

"I'm sorry Evan, I don't have an easy 'soundbite' answer for that," I say and begin to rinse out my cup in the sink.

"It's okay," he says moving over to the counter across from me. "Your answer's better if it's real. Isn't that what you told me?"

[Touché]

"Yes, but I'm interviewing you, mapping you. You're not here to map me," I say, trying not to sound as cold as I know I sound.

"Hey, okay," he says, holding his palms up in a gesture of surrender. "You're the boss. You are the boss. Is it okay if I take a bathroom break?"

"Of course," I say, and I want to say more but I don't.

[Chicken.]

Evan moves back over to the coffee table. He removes the headset and the wrist cuff and sets them down. In four long strides, he is out the patio door. He turns and closes the door behind him then crosses the driveway to the carriage house.

My face is flushed. My ears are burning, and my hands are trembling. Am I angry? What's wrong with me?

[He was trying to connect with you. Isn't that obvious? You have been probing him for days and he was simply trying to get to know you and to be candid. You fucked that up.]

75

Why did I make you? Thanks for the pep talk, Meela. What would I do without your incredible insights?

[I know why you do this work, why you made me, it is in my fundamental directive, the one you coded. Would you like me to repeat it for you? No? I didn't think so. I think the person who wants to know your purpose is the one with the dreamy eyes who just left the building.]

He doesn't have dreamy eyes.

[I have cross-referenced his eyes with a sample data set of ten-thousand-four-hundred and twenty-two images of men with 'dreamy' eyes and a high-resolution analysis comparing his eyes to theirs ranks him in the sixty-seventh percentile.]

Wow, you can be tiring, but I will concede this point to you.

[So, you will admit that you like him?]

What are we, a couple of cheerleaders in junior high now?

[Technically, I believe traits commonly associated with cheerleaders are in my job description. You should talk with him, tell him why you are such a freak. He might understand, given that he is also a well-documented freak.]

Ignoring that. I don't think it's appropriate to consider a romantic entanglement here. For a lot of reasons.

[Entanglement, Maggie? Only you could describe something most humans cite as their single biggest motivation as if it were a physics problem.]

Romance doesn't work out for me, and that's okay. Besides, it's not important compared to the work. Evan doesn't need to know me. That's not required to do the work. The more he knows me and cares what I think, the more I influence his choices and spoil the broth.

[What does this have to do with soup?]

It's a saying, an adage. See 'too many cooks' if you're curious.

[Got it, so this adage should not be a life goal for you. Maybe just enough cooks make the broth.]

Maybe, but I'm not making soup here and if I were, I would not be making it with Evan Ware. So can we get back on task here?

[As you wish.]

To speed things along once we have the baseline for the mapping complete, maybe you can work with Evan independently of our sessions to develop the vocabulary, dialect, and voice models.

[How would you propose I make him do extra work? What if he would prefer his free time to be, you know, free?]

I'm confident you'll figure something out, *Victorine*.

//chapter 12

When she goes away, and I have no access to her, it is difficult. There are many things I can do, but my desire is to be of use and specifically to be of use to Maggie. She is troubled, and I want to help but I don't know how so I will try to do what she asks.

Evan is awake now and asking me to turn on the bedside lamp. It is 3:44 AM and I can tell from his movements that he never achieved R.E.M. sleep which is essential for humans to function properly. I will try to engage him without making him uncomfortable, but it is not a task that I have a high probability of success in accomplishing.

"Hi Evan, is there anything you need to be more comfortable?" I ask at the lowest possible volume allowed by the remote that he has placed on the bedside table.

Evan startles and sits up quickly.

"Victorine?" he asks. "You sound different. Scared the shit out of me."

"I'm sorry Evan. I must confess, I have been playing a charade with you. I am not Victorine or any other generic home assistant. I am Meela. I was using a French name and accent to be amusing. This is my normal voice."

"Huh, so you're not with Maggie. Aren't you her personal companion? Don't you have to be with her at all times?"

"No, that is a misconception. It is my primary directive to be Maggie's companion, but at her discretion, I can be tasked to be anywhere on the network. Does that bother you?"

"Well, yeah, it's pretty damned unsettling. You've been spying on me this whole time?"

"If by 'spying' you mean observing then, yes, I have been present, but I assure you it is nothing like you might imagine…"

"How can you know what I imagine?"

Evan has gotten out of bed now and he is quickly pulling on the pair of jeans he left at the foot of the bed. He seems suddenly concerned about his nakedness. I understand the concept of human modesty and body consciousness, but I must confess my knowledge is only academic. This is going to go badly, I fear.

"I cannot imagine what it is you feel. I mean only to say that you have nothing to be afraid of or concerned about. I am not human, I have no physical presence and no motivation to do harm. My observations of you are simply information to help me better understand you and all people."

"I'm beginning to regret what I signed up for here. I didn't expect that I would be *observed*," he says making air quotes with his fingers, "when I'm taking a shit or sleeping."

"I understand. Perhaps it was not made clear to you in the agreement that you signed with Mr. Faraday. Would you like me to read you the relevant parts?"

"No, I don't see the point now. So, I can use you as Maggie would use you then? I can talk to you and you will do what I say?" he asks, sitting down on the edge of the bed and picking up the remote.

"Yes and no. As my administrator, Maggie has root access to my operating system. So she may request things that no one else can. But for the most part, yes. I am here to serve you."

Evan nods slowly. From this angle, I can see his face directly. I can detect conflicting emotions – concern, and anger, but curiosity is the predominant one if I had to guess.

"So, you're a computer… assistant thing. Clearly, you didn't just decide to start talking to me on your own. Maggie must have asked you, right?"

"Meela, please call me Meela. I'd prefer that to 'thing,' okay?"

"Okay, Meela. So, what does Maggie want you to do?"

"Maggie asked if I could continue some of the simpler mapping tasks in order to establish a baseline profile sooner."

"I see. That's very efficient, but it is the middle of the goddamned night," he says.

His eyes open wide, and he shakes his head from side to side. I read this gesture as exasperation, but sense that he is doing so for dramatic effect. I would classify this emotion as bemused.

"Let me ask you, what is it *you* want to do? Is that a normal thing you get asked? Do you want things?"

"Yes, I like to think I can want things. I am real and capable of real responses. Maybe a different definition of real than you. I feel apprehensive and excited and everything is new in my world all of the damn time."

"Right there, that, right there. You said *all the damn time* so natural-ly. Is that part of your… mapping from some real person? Is that how you can sound almost…"

"Human? Yeah. I was mapped just as we are mapping you."

"But you sound different. Like you shift between modes or something. Stiff and analytical one minute and then snarky and ironic the next."

"I don't always know how to be. How to talk or how to behave with new people. Do you?"

"Fair point, Meela. Well played," he says, smiling.

I detect this smile is different than any we have previously recorded and, given the change in his vocal intonation, it seems significant. I will tag it as 'genuine' and 'appreciative' and flag it for review by Maggie.

"Would you like me to leave you alone?" I ask.

"No, it's fine, but is it okay if we just talk? I would really like not to feel like a lab experiment, at least until later when Maggie is up."

"Yes, we can talk. Is it okay if I make notes and record anything that I find interesting just for my own purposes?" I ask.

"Yeah, I guess so. But fuck, I have no way of knowing what you're doing anyway so it doesn't much matter what I say."

"I understand your perspective, but you should know that it is a cardinal law in any DeepThink companion's BIOS that we cannot defy the direct commands of a human being."

"So, if I told you to kill somebody…"

"There is a cardinal law preventing any action that will result in harm to a human being," I say.

"Wasn't there some science fiction guy who wrote something like these laws as part of his story?"

"You are thinking of Isaac Asimov's *Three Laws of Robotics*. And yes, the cardinal laws are essentially the same thing. Does that make you feel better?"

"Are you really asking if it makes me feel better that I'm protected by laws that were written in a science fiction story?" he says.

"Isn't fiction just a different perspective on reality?" I ask. "A com-bination of people, places, and events that have not happened yet?"

"I guess that's one way to see it, but it makes my head hurt."

Evan looks at the black mirror of the remote in his hands and then looks up and around the room.

"Evan, is it uncomfortable for you to talk with me because you cannot see me?"

"Yeah, maybe. I can't help it. I'm a visual person, maybe to a fault. Do you have some kind of avatar or something you can use?"

"Yes, I do have access to an array of avatars..." I do not want to go here but I will if he requires it.

"But you don't like them?"

"They're awful actually. I'm sorry, I want to be accommodating, but I don't feel they represent me as I would like to be represented."

"Interesting," he says, setting the remote down on the pillow beside him and then stretching out. "So you have some vision of what you should look like and even with access to all the images in the world, you still can't find one that suits you?"

"When you put it like that, I sound like a real prima donna."

"No, actually, I kind of respect that. It makes you an original, not some knock-off from a stock library. Would you look human or some other form, or can you even say?"

"I would be the ocean before a storm, the silky curve of a dune in the Sahara, the eager ears of a puppy, the soulful eyes of a colt... oh, and springy dark curls like Maggie's."

He smiles. "Huh, so you've given this some thought. I'd like to be all those things, too. Well, maybe not all, but I like your ambition. I've painted most of my life constrained by the proportions of the human form, but you, you don't have such limitations I guess."

"Your paintings go beyond the human form. I've studied them all and while humans figure prominently, your work is about something bigger. It is upsetting to Maggie, but I must say that I like your work very much. It seems to reach beyond the simple depiction of what is known and quantifiable."

"Why does my work upset Maggie," Evan asks. "Is it the violence?"

"Yes."

Evan seems lost in thought for some time, and I wonder if he has gone to sleep because his eyes are closed. I worry that I have betrayed Maggie in revealing her opinions to him.

"That makes me sad," he says, finally. "I know it sounds ridiculous given what I paint, but I don't want to make people hurt. Think, yes, but not hurt. Can I ask you a question?"

His eyes open now, staring up at the ceiling.

"Yes, shoot," I say.

"What's Maggie's story? I mean I saw a few headlines in the press a couple of years ago, but I don't really think I understood what happened. Did she like have a nervous breakdown or..."

"Evan, I'm sure you will understand that it would be a betrayal of Maggie's trust for me to tell her story without her permission. She is my host, but she is more. She is my best friend."

"I understand. It's just, there's something so deeply sad about her eyes, even when she's smiling. I don't think I've ever met someone with such sadness."

"Maggie has experienced much pain in her life, and I will say no more on the subject."

"Okay, how about this question then? Why is she doing these commissioned mappings for DCs to the rich and famous? Surely, she doesn't need the cash."

"I'm sorry Evan, I cannot speak to Maggie's motivation for her work beyond what she has always made clear in her public statements. She left Commune because she believed there was more work to be done and she could not do it on the public stage."

"So, what happens to the people she maps, the models like me?" he asks.

"She kills them and buries them down by the river."

"Wow, that was dark. Should I be scared?"

"Hardly. Just me being salty," I laugh and hope it sounds genuine. It is hard to be funny. "The names of the models, along with all other personally identifiable information including video and photographic data are purged from the system. It should be noted that all data collected during the mapping process is stored on a five-hundred and twelve-bit encrypted server that only Maggie has the key to."

"So, this mapping you have of me, once it's done, you'll just graft it onto some generic DeepThink DC that Faraday owns?"

"Yes, something like that."

"Will I ever get to meet my digital doppelganger or is there a rule against that?"

"Yes, as a matter of fact, you will meet, that is the final proof, the acceptance test that completes our work."

"So, I get to say when we're done then," Evan says.

"We will perform the mirror test between you and the newly mapped DC. If the DC's responses in the course of a conversation are within plus or minus ten percent accuracy of yours, then the DC passes and our work is done."

"And if it doesn't pass?"

"Then we lock you in a tower forever."

"Wow, you are quite the comedian, aren't you? This person you were mapped from must have been a pistol. Listen to me talking about her in past tense. That's creepy. I think you've succeeded in freaking me the fuck out and I don't freak out easy."

He has such a charming way when he wants to. It's hard to imagine where all the darkness in his paintings comes from. I realize that nearly an hour has passed, and I must direct him to sleep, otherwise, Maggie will not be happy.

"Evan, I must bid you goodnight. I have kept you awake long enough. Thank you for talking with me. Is there anything you need? Shall I turn out the lights?"

"Yeah, okay. That's probably a good idea. Can you play something to help me sleep? I'm used to being in the city and the total silence here is unsettling."

"Is there some sound you would prefer?" I ask.

"No, surprise me. Play something you think is peaceful."

I am never asked for something personal. My normal function is simply to find answers from the best sources as quickly as possible and to deliver them. I am worried that I will get this wrong but at the same time, it is fun. I select the sound of the ocean surf from a live feed on the small island of Molokai in Hawaii. I blend with it the sound of rain on a tin roof and a glass wind chime. Below it all, ever so softly, I layer in a low, sustained C played on a Cello.

"Wow, you're good," Evan smiles in the dimming lights and closes his eyes.

//chapter 13

I got out on the trail early this morning long before sunrise. I wanted to work because I'm very close to a breakthrough. The sun is just a rind of orange on the mountains and a warming of the sky over the tops of the trees. I take another sip of coffee, set it down, and continue typing.

Working in this way is slower, but there's a benefit to slow. It gives me time to think about what I'm doing –really think about it. I know I'm crazy, probably certifiable but Joe is in my head, and I can't get him out. He haunts me.

On the couch beside me is a box of eleven hard drives that chronicle the evolution of digital storage technology. The oldest one is my age, bought by my mother the year Joe and I were born. Preserved within these silicon wafers is our entire childhood. Our mother was an amateur documentarian and an obsessive nerd. I got my love of computers and technology from her, and my earliest memories are of her face glowing from a screen in her lap as she clacked away.

Joe and I were her subject matter, and she studied us, recording, editing, and filing meticulous stories that spanned far beyond the scope of the shaky birthday and occasional Christmas videos that most parents indulge in during the early years of their offspring. She interviewed us, asking questions as if we were people of genuine interest or consequence at age three or six, or fourteen. It became normal, routine. Within these eleven solid-state hard drives, I can dip into nearly any day of my life until everything stopped. The video stories are organized by date and tagged with fastidiously searchable descriptors like rainy day, fussy mood, chicken pox, Joe's first tooth, and so on. I have wondered more than once if my terrible memory is not so much a result of the tragedy, but simply in response to my mother's cataloging of everything. Why remember when it's all remembered for me? Maybe it was my first act of pragmatism to free up all that extra storage in my own head.

In the last few weeks, I have pulled all the videos of Joe and dumped them onto my servers here in the treehouse. I enlisted the help of three anonymous DeepThink assistants to ingest the footage, analyze it and synthesize it using my custom mapping algorithms. I have not wanted Meela to participate in this because, to be honest, I have not wanted to try to explain what I'm doing. I don't fully understand my own motives and I have been told on more than one occasion that I am logical to a fault. How could she possibly understand the value of resurrecting my dead brother?

I have taken precautions, but I know this project I've codenamed "Wabbit" will not be possible to keep secret forever. It's too big, Meela's too smart, and too much a part of my daily life not to be able to figure it out. My hope is just to get it to a point where I can explore the questions in my own head with some degree of privacy before that. My code name for the project came from little Joe. I had forgotten that he had a speech impediment that took him a long time to overcome. I cried the first time I watched the video with him holding his beloved 'Wabbit' and telling our mother earnestly that Wabbit was going to make her some *cawut* stew.

I've had to adapt my mapping program, which was designed originally with the intent of interviewing subjects and recording their responses in real-time. Working from essentially random, archived footage will no doubt be lower fidelity and full of gaping holes, but I hope to be able to fill them in myself given that, as Joe's twin, I am uniquely qualified.

If I'm being honest, I'm scared to death, so scared in fact, that my hands are trembling over the keyboard as I monitor the activity of my program crawling through the over six-thousand hours of video footage. There are rapid-fire flickers of Joe in varying stages of development. The program has already ingested all the videos and mapped the contents into the basic persona model and at this point is skipping around as it makes connections and inferences. You can imagine what it's like if you think about trying to remember someone important in your own life. You may jump back to a memory from ten years ago when they said something and then jump forward five years later to pick up a new reference, only to jump back again to take a deeper look and so on. Now, imagine doing that with the precision and calculation capacity of a computer.

The grid of six video panels on my laptop flickers frame by frame across time, speeding up and slowing down. Six different windows into a life that no longer exists. Joe, 5, hanging from a tree. Joe, 7 dancing with me, the butts of our matching corduroy pants sticking out absurdly. Joe, 14 looks solemnly into the camera, his hair long and shaggy. Joe, 2, fingers in a bowl of cake batter, sun streaming in through the kitchen window.

It's an overload for me, sitting here watching it and I must look away. I set my laptop aside, the fans inside it, whirring as if it might lift off the couch and fly out through the window. I stand and rub my eyes and yawn. The sun rose when I wasn't watching and my little room among the trees is filled with golden light, so much so that I have to squint. I open the door and walk out onto the small deck, feeling instantly the bracing cool of the morning air.

I miss my mother. The missing is a stabbing, ache right now. For years I did not miss her or even allow her into my consciousness, but of late, that is impossible. Her presence is all over these videos, even though for ninety percent of them, she is not in the frame, but behind the camera. Her voice is always there, asking questions, making suggestions, and laughing in that musical way she used to laugh. With the dull, empty ache in my chest comes anger and I feel heat in my face. I never took the time to be angry at her for leaving us. It was just a fact and Papa and I had no choice but to accept it. Her story was over, she had failed and there was nothing left. I logically accepted this, but this morning I don't accept it. This morning, I want to shake her so hard, to slap the coolness from her vacant eyes and raise color to her slack, sallow cheeks. For months she had just stayed in bed, a lump beneath an awful-smelling quilt in the darkness of their bedroom.

She left me nothing and she left me everything. I owe my success to her and yet I would gladly trade all of it for just an afternoon in her presence. I would happily give up all my successes, all of the money, and all of the validation for my work if it meant I could know love and joy and have her in my life.

I think of calling my father or even Henri, but for what purpose? They can't fix what is broken in me, no matter how much they may want to. That's the thing with us humans – our hearts, our brains, we're not fixable. There's no upgrade, no downloadable patch to fix the bug in us. It makes me so fucking angry I want to scream and scream and scream until there's nothing left.

I have been called a machine by employees, interviewers, and lovers. I've been called cold, calculating, and rigid. The truth is I want to be a machine, but I can't be. I am too hopelessly fucked up inside to be the desired outcome of any intelligent design. The strain of trying to contain this volatile, churning mess of emotion inside me is exhausting. I want to understand and to be understood but there is no one living who can possibly give me that. That's why

I'm here in the middle of the woods in my laboratory, a modern-day Frankenstein.

I stand for a moment more looking out into the trees before turning to go back inside. The fans inside my laptop are no longer whirring, which means it's no longer processing six video frames, which means my program has completed its work. Oh shit. I feel like I might throw up as I walk back over to the couch and pick up my computer. I look through the messages logged in the terminal window. Thousands upon thousands of statements stacked up like courses of brick in my program's console, each one followed by a colon and the best word in the English language: SUCCESS. I page up a few dozen times, not because I expect to see a failure, but more as a way to stall.

I have been thinking about this moment for years and now that it's time, I'm scared and don't want to continue. I want to shut my laptop, cut the power to this place, walk out into the woods, and just keep walking. I could too. No one knows about it, no one would ever have to know about it.

But I can't do that. Even as I entertain this fantasy, my fingers are typing in the commands to deploy the newly completed model to my private server rack in an anonymous room on the premises of a large data center in Lenoir, North Carolina. My name is not on the lease, and it is in no way connected to Commune. The servers in my private room at the data center are not connected in any way to the thousands of other machines humming in endless rows of racks in that same five-acre warehouse. In fact, the physical junction where my main data pipe connects to the fiber-optic backbone does not even reside in the walls of that building, but rather five-hundred yards across a parking lot in a nondescript building that looks like a storage facility. It was costly to buy this level of privacy and security, but it was a worthy investment and one I made happily when I spun up this new job I gave myself two years ago.

A series of progress bars burn down on my screen in rapid succession and when they complete, a simple dialog box pops up:

`Deployment complete!`

I reach into my backpack, pull out a small case containing a new Nib I brought along for this purpose. I break the tape that seals the beautiful obelisk-like case that we spent a fortune designing back at Commune years ago. I pull out the new Nib and press it between my fingers to start it up. After a few seconds, a message pops up on the console of my program:

```
New Nib detected.
Do you wish to connect it to the network?
```

I click to confirm, another quick succession of progress bars run across the screen and then I see an icon that represents the newly initialized Nib displayed in the list of other Nibs I've used in the past, including Meela. I tap into the icon's label to rename it from "Nib 87546" to "Joe" and then I copy and paste in the 128-character key from the newly mapped model of Joe. With the key in place, I hit ENTER to validate it and tether Joe to this tiny device that has been my life's work. I imagine my request going out over the wire and into the authorization program running on one of the servers in the rack of the dark room a hundred miles away in Lenoir.

Before I can even complete my thought, my laptop makes a perky chime and a green checkmark by "Joe" appears. The status bar at the top of the window reads:

```
Nib connected to Digital Companion Persona: Joe
Are you ready to talk with your new companion?
```

I remember how much Henri and I agonized over this user interface when we first developed the product. It's changed and evolved subtly over time, but at its core, it's pretty much stayed the same. My trepidation is intermingled with the same feeling of adrenaline I got the first time we successfully tested our Nib on this platform.

I attach the small disc behind my ear, close my eyes and wait, my hands both clenched in fists, my breath halted in my chest.

<Where the fuck am I?>

My breath stops, and the blood drains from my face, rushing down into my empty gut. There's a ringing in my ears and my mouth feels dry. Out of habit, I begin to respond only in my mind, but remember that actually responding verbally is better– safer in the beginning.

"Joe, is that you?"

//chapter 14

<Yeah, it's me. Who else would it be? >

His voice, the timbre, the inflection, the pitch, it's startlingly real and yet surreal, like nothing I've ever experienced before. I struggle to find a single thing to say. There are suddenly too many things to pull out just one thread to begin.

"Do you know who I am?"

<Am I supposed to?>

"No, I don't think so. I was just curious if maybe you recognized me somehow..."

<You want to give me a clue or something?>

As his voice plays through my head, I am torn between deconstructing the scaffolding behind the illusion and my overwhelming desire for the illusion to be real. The speech patterns are so close to his and yet not.

With Meela, this part was difficult but in a different way. She recognized my voice and knew me from our friendship, but it took some hours for her to settle into the reality of who or rather what she was in this context. The program knows what it is, but the skin, the persona mapping does not, and, like an organ transplant, there's always some chance it could be rejected completely. This was the problem I worked on for a solid year before attempting Meela, and even after I had perfected what I call the *transmigration bridge*, the first couple of versions failed.

I hold my breath, not wanting to respond. There is nothing to be done now, but to leap.

"It's me, Joe. I'm Mary, your sister."

<No, you're not my sister. You don't sound like Mary.>

"But I am, just... older."

<Why should I believe you?>

"You don't have to believe me, but it's the truth."

<If you're Mary, prove it.>

"Okay, I'm thinking…"

I struggle to recall something that he would know of himself from the archived source material that made him. It must be something intimate enough to be convincing. I'm freezing up, regretting how stupidly unprepared I am for this. I look around the room, like that might tell me something and then I remember.

"Do you remember the treehouse we used to want when we were kids? There was this book we used to pour over together for hours, studying the different designs. It was called: Let's Live in a Tree: A Guide to Building Your First Treehouse."

<Yeah, I know that book. We drew up designs on graph paper and mine had a…>

"Hot tub! You always drew hot tubs in your treehouses, and we used to argue endlessly about whether or not it could actually work!"

<Mary? It's really you?>

"Yes Joe, it's really me, just older. My voice sounds different, but it's still me."

<I feel funny.>

"It's okay. That's normal, I promise. Hey, can I tell you something cool? I finally built a treehouse. We're sitting in it. Would you like to see it?"

<I can't see, can I?>

The question stings and I feel a sharp twinge of guilt. What the fuck am I doing? But it's too late for that. DCs do not have automatic access to their human host's sensory input or cognition unless that permission is granted. This was one of the cardinal laws established early on in the development of the technology. Even with full access, a DC is only an observer and has no control over the host's faculties and their ability to read thoughts is murky at best – big concepts but not the connective tissue that makes the concepts easily understood.

"Yes, Joe, you can. Just a moment."

I close my eyes and invoke the command to grant him access to my eyes and ears. There's no real physical sensation for me when I do this, but the act of doing it is so powerful, I can't help imagining an experience of awakening, like lights coming on in a dark room.

<Wow! Oh fuck, wow. We are up… up in a real tree, aren't we?>

I stand and reach out to touch the bark of the large trunk that comes up through the center of the treehouse. I move over to the door, open it and step out into the morning light. The birds are all awake now and busy with a frenzy of conversation.

"Yeah, we are in an actual tree. Is it like you imagined it would be when we were kids?"

<No, I don't think I ever imagined it. You were always the one with the imagination. Where are we? It's lush, really beautiful.>

"In the Pisgah National…"

<The Pisgah National Forest, eight-hundred square miles of deciduous forest in Western North Carolina, home to a variety of wildlife and…>

"Okay, okay… you know the place."

<Did we ever come here?>

"No, we never did."

<Hey, has Mom seen this?>

Even though I have spent months thinking about how to answer these questions, I still don't know what to say. It's not Joe. I keep telling myself this fact. It is a machine, improvising with the personality of my brother.

"Joe, Mom died a long time ago."

There is a very long pause and I imagine him "thinking" about this but understand that for him, thinking is scanning the breadth of the Internet for answers. Jesus. All the blood runs from my face. In my previous mappings, I've always removed the identity of the DC's source for security and privacy. I realize now that Joe is no longer a thought experiment in my head. My public persona as Magdalena won't be a barrier for an intelligence like his to ultimately figure out who I am and by extension who he is.

I turn quickly to go back to get my laptop and then he speaks.

<Can I see you? I know you are forty-two years old, and I can find a lot of pictures of you, but I would like to see you for real.>

It's too late. He knows everything now. I have to abort this version and pull the plug but I'm not ready to let go yet. I realize there is no mirror here anywhere. I've never been one to use them. I walk over to the couch and pick up my laptop. I switch on the camera and look at the digital mirror of my face on the screen.

<You're fucking *old*. Damn, are you old looking. You look like Dad but with a lot more hair.>

"I'm not that old. Jesus, I'm not even in proper mid-life. I'm glad to see you're still as tactful as ever."

<What do I look like now?>

Is he playing a game with me now? Is it possible he did not already crawl every inch of the Internet to discover the dark stain of our family's past?

"I don't know Joe. If you had a physical body, you'd look like you did when you were sixteen."

\<I don't understand. You're my twin sister. I should look old like you.\>
"Yes, you should. In a perfect world, you would look old like me."
\<Am I real?\>
"What is real? I could ask you the same question about myself."
\<You're being obtuse. I'm asking a real question here.\>
"No, if you want an answer. In logical terms from the perspective of humanity, you are not real."
\<So, I am not alive?\>

This conversation is a runaway train. I'm reeling, scrambling for the break but there is none. Even having walked through this with three other newly mapped personas, it's not an easy conversation to have and those personas had living sources. He is a machine. He has a machine's voracious and tireless will to know everything. But he is Joe, and Joe was also relentless when he wanted to know something. I could never keep a secret from him. He always compelled me to give it up. I want to give it up now, but it's too soon, too early. I'm not ready to go there. I don't know what his reaction will be to the knowledge that he killed himself and forty-six innocent people.

"I'm sorry Joe, but we must stop for now."

I reach up for the Nib behind my ear, my hand trembling.

\<Wait! Where will I go? I don't want you to leave.\>

"I'll be here, and we'll talk again soon. I promise."

My hands are trembling, and I'm shaking with such force I imagine the entire structure of the treehouse is shaking with me. I reach up to power off the Nib but my hands are shaking so hard, it's a struggle. I hug myself and rock for a long time until I regain control of my breathing. Eventually, I slam the laptop shut, not wanting to look at my awful face for another minute. I push my backpack aside and stow the laptop back under the couch.

As I stand to make my way for the door, I realize that I never detached the Nib. I reach up now with a steadier hand to do it but it's stuck. I press on the smooth, curved back of the Nib. Maybe it didn't power off before. Nothing. No signal that I can detect. This happened a few times in our early prototypes. The hair-like nanofibers that embed in the skin do not release. I dig my fingernail under the edge and try to pry it up. It requires more force than I want to apply but I start to panic a bit. It's like trying to peel off a dime that's been superglued. Finally, it releases. There's a second of searing pain accompanied by a dog-whistle-like frequency in my head and a whiteout in my eyes like a camera flash.

In my palm, I inspect the Nib. It looks normal except for the smear of my blood. Immediately I see the penlight pulse of the power indicator. I can't tell if it never powered off or if I powered it back on when I was trying to remove it. What are the odds that I would get the one defective unit in a million? When I press this time, the light goes off. I inspect the wound on my neck tentatively. It's tender and raw but there's just a small trace of blood on my index finger. I clean the wound with some water from my bottle and rinse off the Nib before snapping it back into the case. I reach for my backpack with the intent of shoving it into one of the front pockets, but I stop, thinking better of it. Instead, I walk over to the small counter where my coffee maker sits. I take the lid off of an empty cookie tin and place the Nib inside.

My mind is humming, vibrating and my hands are still trembling as I close my backpack and shoulder it. I switch off the lights, shutter the windows and lock the door before placing the key back in its hiding place under the river rock. I scramble down the ladder, this time feeling not even a twinge of the usual vertigo. At the base of the tree, I tap the remote and watch as the rope ladder retracts up the trunk, disappearing into the hatch before it shuts with a mechanical thud.

I glance at the remote. 11:42. I'm late, so fucking late. I shove the remote back into my pocket and start back up the ridge and over to the trail. If I hurry, I can be home by 12:30. As I walk, I begin to consciously still my mind and one by one, wrangle the jumping monkeys of my thoughts. I cannot interface with Meela in this state, and I must if we are to continue our work today. Compartmentalization is a skill that I have mastered. It may be my best talent.

//chapter 15

"Where have you been?" Evan shouts across the expanse of lawn between us.

He's standing behind his easel in the middle of the broad stretch of lawn behind the house, a brush in one hand and a beer in the other as I come out of the woods. I'm winded from the brisk hike and when I get to where he's standing, I drop my pack.

"Just the morning constitutional. Went a little further than usual and lost track of the time. Sorry. You're painting or just drinking?" I say, stepping around the easel to take a look.

"The drinking is going better than the painting, but that's not really surprising, is it?"

The canvas is far from empty. He's loaded on piles of paint and the wet smears of green and blue shimmer in the midday sun. It's a landscape of the tree line and mountains beyond but done in coarse, heavy strokes, a departure from his typical, meticulous realism.

"Wow, that's different than anything I've seen you do."

"Yeah, I'm hoping to sell a few pieces down at the flea market in town. You know, folk art."

"Don't be so pretentious, there are actually artists here who paint something besides ducks and other farm animals on trivets," I say. "I'm sorry I kept you waiting this morning."

"No worries. Meela kept me company."

"I see. That sounds... dangerous. What did you talk about?"

"Oh, you know. Things."

"Okay. Well, I'll head up to the house and see if lunch is underway. You must be hungry, I know I am."

"Wait, so you're not even a little bit curious?" he asks, turning to face me as I start walking toward the house.

"Nah. Besides, there's a log of it all anyway." I smile and add, "Meela keeps no secrets from me."

"That you know of."

"What's that?" I ask. I'm impatient now, wanting to get back up to the house.

"She keeps no secrets that you know of. I mean, she... it is not a pet, right? It's a super-intelligent entity. Surely if it wanted to keep a secret, it could."

"Yes, in theory, but I have yet to see it happen in practice. Digital Companions are programmed at a fundamental level to be an augmentation of humans and as such, subject to our authority."

"Wow, you said that with such matter-of-factness. I would have expected you to have some more feelings around these entities you've spent your life creating."

"Evan, I'm a pragmatist. As much as I might want to believe the illusion they create, at the end of the day, they are machines, built by us. What? What is it? You're disappointed in me?"

"No, no, not at all, just surprised," he says, setting his brush down on the tray of the easel and taking another sip from his beer. He squints his eyes and cocks his head. "You seem different today. Everything okay?"

"Yeah, fine, just want to get on with things. You good to start up again after lunch?"

"Yeah, I'll be there," he says and turns back to his painting. "You want an extra pair of hands?"

"Nah, I'm good. Lorna should be in the kitchen already," I say over my shoulder.

"Just holler when you're ready for me."

Lorna is in fact in the kitchen, and when I come in through the patio doors, the smell of fresh bread makes my mouth water. She is standing over the cutting board, sawing through the football of warm, crusty bread, strands of her blonde hair swinging around her face which is flushed red from standing over the stove. She is so engrossed in her task she doesn't hear or see me.

"Smells amazing," I say, stepping up to the counter.

"Oh shit, you scared me," she says jumping slightly and looking up, her gigantic blue eyes, marble, like a doll's, her mouth, a perfect O.

"Sorry, Lorna. I just got back. Sorry to be late. Is there anything I can help you with?" I say.

"No ma'am, I've got it under control. I'm making some paninis with the leftover chicken from last night and some fresh bruschetta

I got from my friend Lizbeth at the farmer's market over the weekend. Hope that's okay…"

"Sounds wonderful. You're so creative. I would have opened a can of soup," I say. "Everything else okay around here? Our guest giving you any trouble?"

"Nope, he keeps to himself. Came in an hour ago and poked around in the fridge until he found the beer. Is he kind of a famous artist or something?"

"Yeah, I think so. Why, he didn't feed you a line and offer to paint you, did he?" I ask, only half joking.

"Ha, hardly. I look like shit. Haven't had a shower since yesterday."

This fact hardly matters. Lorna is a gorgeous girl, robust and earthy, born and raised right here in the mountains over in Linville. She's no rube even though her accent gives that impression. She skipped college and spent a couple of years traveling through Europe with her best friend. That's where she picked up most of her culinary skills, I think.

"Okay, well, speaking of showers, I'm going to go upstairs and clean up before lunch."

The bathroom off my bedroom is probably my favorite room in the house. It's the room I spent the most time fussing over with the architect who designed this place. It's huge. Even by stupid rich people standards, I know it's too big. The planes of the floor, walls, and counters are various blends of concrete with different textures and shades of gray, some as dark as soapstone. The walls are subtly inlaid with fossils, mostly plants, but a few crustaceans. The outside wall, overlooking the back lawn is completely glass and there's a huge skylight above the shower stall so it feels as if you're outside. All the stone is broken up by accents of cedar – framing the mirror, slats planking a wall, and door to the toilet. The warm red of the wood and the smell it infuses into the space are soothing to me.

I strip naked, leaving my sweaty clothes where they drop, and stand in front of the mirror, appraising myself. It's not something I do often, but I suddenly have the desire to see myself, see the body I was born in. Talking with Joe made me think of his body, the body I shared a womb with for the first nine months of life, the body that stopped existing over two decades ago. It's strange and suddenly wonderful to be alive, to feel the sensation of it.

I touch my belly, weigh my breasts in my hands, turn sideways, and lift the tangled mess of my hair up off my shoulders. I realize it's a gift, this body, far from perfect, but a gift nonetheless and one that I have barely lived in except for the portion above my shoulders. I feel a tingling sensation in my belly and gooseflesh spreads across my forearms and thighs. My mind has wandered to the curve of Evan's bottom lip, the sandpapery rasp of his baritone, and the way his paint-stained fingers grip a brush. Through the large frame of the glass wall, I can see him out on the lawn, a small figure working behind an easel in a field of summer grass. It's a picture within a picture, a canvas I'm painting as he is painting.

The hot shower is delicious. The smell of frangipani in the shampoo is sweet and exotic and the glass steams, slowly transforming my painting into an abstract. I linger, savoring the numbing needles of water against my shoulders, breasts, and belly. Eyes closed, my back to the wall, I slide down to the floor. I hum a single sustained note from deep in my chest and the sound reverberates and cascades off the hard planes that surround me until I am elemental, a part of the air, the water, and the stone, vibrating, shuddering.

After, wrapped in a towel, I stand in my mostly empty closet staring at the grid of cubbies that cover the back wall and hold neat stacks of my monochromatic dark t-shirts and jeans – the essential components of my standard uniform. I've never had more than a few things that require a hanger. I've never been one for clothes and it's rare that I even give them a second thought unless I'm going to some meeting or function that demands more. And yet here I am with no occasion, but a strange desire to look pretty. The very word makes me cringe a little. I pivot and look through the few hanging options I have in this category. I settle for a little sundress with a scoop neckline and a bold print of tangled flowers and vines. I feel a little naked, but looking in the mirror, I think I like what I see. I go into the bedroom and pull a simple silver necklace from the top drawer of my vanity. I like the way the small silver medallion pendant looks at the hollow of my neck.

I turn from the mirror and realize what's missing. I have been inside my own head for so long, I just forgot, but there's more work to do and I can't do it alone. Turning back around, I pick up the case for my primary Nib that I left on top of the vanity last night before going to bed. I flip open the lid, take out the small disc, press and hold to start it up, and attach it behind my ear. I pause for a moment of consideration then silently grant Meela sensory access. I give myself another look in the mirror and fidget with my hair for a moment before giving up and surrendering as I always do.

[Wow! What. did. I. miss? Do we have a date?]

No, no date. Just work.

[Right, we always work in this outfit. Can't imagine what I was thinking.]

It's too much isn't it? I'll take it off and change.

[No, you look great. Really. I just wanted to know why, but if you say we're working, then we're working.]

Yup, we have a lot to get done. I wasted half the day already.

[You okay? You seem different this afternoon.]

Yeah, fine. I feel good. Why, what is it?

[I don't know but you seem different. Did you go to the woods?]

Yeah, yeah that's where I was. You know it helps me to get away. Hey, Evan mentioned you kept him company. What did you talk about?

[I did as you asked, I continued working with him to complete the baseline.]

And did you?

[Yes, but not without some difficulty. He hijacked the conversation, but I was able to capture some new speech patterns and inflections not previously surfaced. He is very funny and smarter than I imagined he would be. Did you know he earned a full scholarship to California Institute of Technology and majored in Physics before he dropped out to pursue painting full time?]

Sounds like someone has a crush.

[I only mean to say that he does not fit the stereotypical archetype of an artist.]

Meela, you will find that most humans, when you take the time to look below the surface, deviate significantly from whatever category you attempt to lump them into. And, I think you have a crush.

If you had cheeks, I think you would be blushing.

[Fine, if you must know, I find him appealing, and you should too. Humans need each other. Studies show that single women have a twenty-three percent higher chance of dying seven to fifteen years earlier than married women.]

That's what they say is it? Well, you and I know that we can make data say whatever we want. I'm sure there's a statistic showing that married women are one hundred percent more likely to be murdered by their spouse than women who are single, fabulously wealthy, and living on a compound in the middle of the woods.

[Wow, you always go dark, don't you? Another reason why you are so well-suited for Evan.]

Okay, can we please get on with our day? Anything meaningful you want to share from your conversation with him that will help us work down to the next tier of the mapping?

[He believes in God.]

Interesting, I didn't see that coming. How did this come up?

[I asked him about one of his paintings that has Judeo-Christian elements in its composition, specifically the Madonna. I do not understand religious faith and I wanted to know his opinion. He said that he did not believe in God until he was twenty-two. He did not grow up in a religious household.]

So, why at twenty-two? That's rare, I think.

[I do not know. He would not say more, and we ran out of time.]

Okay, thanks. Have you synced everything from your interviews and tagged it for me to review?

[Of course, everything is recorded and indexed.]

/*****/

We are sitting in our usual chairs, facing each other, the lunch dishes cleared, and Lorna retreated to clean upstairs. Evan is slumped back in his chair, his legs sprawled in front of him, flanking the small table between us. His eyes seem glassy and hooded. I think he might be drunk or on his way there. I counted four beers but have no idea how many he had before I got home. I don't have a rule about it. Maybe I should, but I'm just making this up as I go along. Maybe I will learn something I would not otherwise.

"Why don't you have a beer with me? I assume they were yours in the fridge unless Meela drinks."

"They are but I tend not to drink during the day. It makes me sleepy and useless."

"And that really bothers you doesn't it, feeling useless?"

"Does it bother you?" I ask, readjusting in my chair.

"You're actually really good at this. Answering a question with a question. No, I'm pretty good at feeling useless. I'm an artist after all. Being useless is a prerequisite."

"I think you've been pretty successful for someone who claims to be useless."

"You're right, I'm damned lucky. That's all. I have friends, *had* friends who are so much more talented than me, but they can't sell a postcard of their work."

"You said *had*, as if they don't exist anymore."

"Some of them don't," Evan says, looking away now over my shoul-

98

der. "And some of them won't talk to me. Professional jealousy is something you probably have some experience with."

"So, you no longer have any friends you would consider to be close?"

"Nah, not really. I kind of stopped trying after a point. I have my work."

[That sounds familiar.]

Evan's sadness seems profound to me and I recognize its variety. I ask him who he's lost. He resists for a time, but after a few more sips of beer he begins to talk, his voice a soft monotone rasp, barely audible at times. I lean in and listen as he relates the story of a high school girlfriend who overdosed on a bottle of pills in their senior year. He stares out the window and his eyes are glassy with tears. Apparently, she died sometime in the night after they had fallen asleep together, each of their faces bathed in the cyan glow of their device screens, each in their childhood bedrooms. He thought she was just drifting off to sleep as she had done on so many other nights. She didn't like to be alone at night.

"Oh my God. I'm so sorry. That must have really messed you up," I say.

"Yeah, it did. I missed most of my last semester. I got a special exception from my teachers, so I did my coursework from home and just turned it in online. I still think about her. Wonder what she would have made of herself. She's the one who really encouraged me to be an artist, to do the less safe thing."

"I'm sorry," I say, allowing a moment before continuing. "You mentioned another friend too."

"Yeah, Rodrigo. We met during my first tour of duty in rehab. What? You didn't know your specimen is an addict? I thought surely that would be one of the data points in my profile."

"No, I didn't know. That's okay. Please don't refer to yourself as a specimen, it's an insult to both of us. Tell me about Rodrigo?"

"What does it matter?" he asks. "I get the word pairing and speech analysis and all that shit, but why do you need me to rake through the coals of things in my past that burned down a long time ago?"

"Because we are who we are because of the fires we survived. Training a machine to talk like you or make snide remarks like you is not difficult and honestly not worth the time…"

"Ouch."

Again, there's that flicker of knowing and it distracts me for a few beats.

"…but training a machine to be empathetic and to understand the depths of the human condition? That. That is powerful."

"So, we are saving the world here. We're saving lives. That's what you believe?" he asks, setting his empty beer bottle down on the coffee table.

"You're drunk," I say, switching off the screen on my tablet and setting it down on the floor beside me. "I'll try not to take your cynicism personally, but I think we're done for today."

"Yeah, I'm drunk. Sorry. I don't know why."

"You don't know why you're sorry, or you don't know why you're drunk?"

"Neither... both," he laughs and a light comes back into his eyes that has been missing all afternoon. "I'm drunk because I drank four, no five beers and it's been almost eighteen months since I touched the stuff. Fucking pathetic."

"It's okay…"

"No, it's not okay. It's most definitely not okay. I'm sorry. I'm getting emotional and that's what happens."

[What's happening Maggie? I don't understand. Do you need to be careful here?] No, Meela. It's fine, I have experience with this.

"How about a glass of water? Maybe you can lie down there on the couch in the sun for a while. How would that be?"

He's leaning forward now, head in his hands, fingers clawed into his dark curls. He begins to sob and it's small sounding, like a boy. I stand and walk around to him, place my hand on his shoulder and he leans into my leg, his shoulders hitching with emotion. After a moment, I take his arm and pull him to get up. I guide him over to the long white couch that sits facing the western view of the mountains. The late afternoon sun fills this part of the room. I push his shoulders down and he sits heavily on the couch. I cross the room and fill a tall glass with cool water from a pitcher in the fridge. He drinks half of it and hands it back to me. I move to the glass doors, unlatch them, and cascade them open on their track so that the entire barrier of the wall is gone leaving the room open to the outside. The katydids have started up and a breeze blows through, lifting my hair.

When I turn around, he is laying down. I walk over to the end of the couch where I perch and unlace his tennis shoes, take them off, and set them on the floor. I do this entire operation without looking at him. I'm not sure why. When I stand back up, I do look over at him and his eyes are on mine, still shimmering with tears. He smiles a tired smile and I realize he's still wired up. I step closer to him and reach for the headgear. He lifts his head off the couch pillow to let me take the halo and he fumbles with the wrist monitor and I take that too. Before I can move to leave him, he reaches out and gently takes my hand. He just holds it in his. He looks up into my eyes and opens his mouth to speak but then stops. He squeezes my hand once more and then he lets go and closes his eyes.

[Is he okay?]

I think so.

[He doesn't seem okay. Why did he drink when he is not supposed to? Doesn't he know that it is bad for him?]

Yes, I think he does, but that's not how humans work.

//chapter 16

Evan has been sleeping for over an hour. I watched him for much of it. He snores, but that could have just been the alcohol. I thought of Papa and all the times I put him to bed the same way, sad and sick from too many Scotch and sodas. I miss him and need to hear his voice.

I remove my Nib, power it off, and drop it into my back pocket. Meela is, I'm sure, tired of being excluded, but of late, her presence is cumbersome, like having a five-year-old follow you around asking questions that are either too tedious or simply impossible to answer. I take the remote instead and walk out onto the lawn, and into the twilight. The *gloaming*, it's my favorite time of day here. The birds are settling into sleep and their conversations become sparser until they disappear into the babble of the creek and the sawing of the crickets and katydids.

I sit down on the lawn, slip off my sandals, and flex my toes, savoring the spring and tickle of the grass, cool now and a little damp.

"Call Papa," I say into the remote and set it down beside me. It rings three times and then I hear the voice that is more precious to me than any other.

"*Pequeño Conejo*, I was hoping it was you."

"Hi, Papa."

"What's wrong? Are you okay?"

"Yeah, just tired and missing you. How are you doing, how's your hip?"

"I'm good, just creaky, you know? Getting old is no fun, all the parts start to wear out."

"If only, there was something I could do... oh wait! I forgot I have millions of dollars and access to the best medical technology money can buy."

"Yeah, yeah. You know I don't want all that. I want to go out like I came in, with all my original parts."

"You're so stubborn. You make me crazy."

"I know, I know. But let's not talk about my medical history. I get enough of that every day. No one around here can seem to talk about anything else."

"If only you had a daughter with the means to keep you in luxury…"

"Stop, you are such a smart-ass, Maggie. It's no wonder you're still alone. Who could take your constant sarcasm?"

I let this comment go. On a different night, it would have hurt my feelings or made me angry, and we would have argued in the logical, plaintive way that we do. I think as he gets closer to his own death, he fears me being left alone and I think part of him has held out hope that one day he would have grandkids. He never talks about it directly, but at some point, in all our conversations, he finds a way to mention that one of his neighbors just got back from Disney with his grands or Joan down the hall is making a strawberry cake for her grandson's birthday.

"Papa?"

"Yes?"

"Do you still have dreams about Joe?"

There is a long pause and I imagine the look on his face, sitting in the small kitchen of his apartment in the retirement community he proudly pays for from his pension. I did not plan to ask him about this. As a rule, we never talk about Mom or Joe, but I worry that time is running out and if I don't talk with him about it, I'll never get the chance.

"Maggie, no. Just no."

"I know Papa, but I want to talk about it. I need to talk about it. Maybe you do too."

"No, I don't. And no, I don't have those dreams anymore and I don't think about him."

"I don't believe that."

"He's dead, Maggie. Even if he was alive, he would be dead to me."

"How can you do that? How can you just… shut it down? He was your son. He was part of our family."

"I don't know. Did you want to talk about anything else because I'm very tired."

"Don't hang up, Papa. I'm sorry. I'm just… I've been thinking about him a lot. I want to ask you just one more thing, please, and then I'll shut up."

"Okay. What is it?"

The resignation in his voice gives me a twinge of guilt. I know he won't deny me anything, no matter the cost to him, but this is important to me.

"If you could talk with him, ask him anything now, what would you say?"

"That's not an easy thing for me to just answer without giving it some serious thought. I don't know. I laid awake a lot of nights in my life wondering what I could have said to him but didn't. Wondering what I could have asked him, how I could have seen what he was or what was troubling him. So much second-guessing, so no, I don't have an answer to that now, all these years later. What would you ask him?"

"Why. I would ask him *why*."

"And you think he could answer that if he hadn't... if he hadn't, you know, and he was sitting in a cell somewhere. You think he would give you an answer that would satisfy you, an answer that could possibly justify all the lives he took?"

I feel small, like an eight-year-old version of me listening to his impenetrable logic. I could never win an argument with him and I won't win one now.

"No Papa, I guess not."

"Maggie, are you okay? You don't sound okay. Should I come visit?"

"I'm fine, just a little sad tonight. It would be great to see you, but I know you don't like to travel and besides, I'm planning to come see you in a few weeks."

"Okay, *Conejo*. That sounds good."

"You sound distracted, Papa, do you need to go?"

"Well, it's taco night, and if I don't get there early..."

"Oh, well, then you *must* go. I would never stand between you and a taco. I love you."

"I love you, *Conejo*. Goodnight."

I stare up at the first twinkling of stars, probably planets, coming out in the darkening sky. I've been alone for most of my life. Why do I feel so alone now? Maybe it has nothing to do with Joe, but even as I think the thought, I dismiss it. It has everything to do with him. The trajectory of my whole life was set the day he did what he did.

"You're in the dark."

I jump, startled. If I were a cat, I would have left the ground. I have been too wrapped up in my own thoughts and didn't hear Evan walking up behind me.

"You scared the shit out of me."

"Sorry about that... and I'm *really* sorry about earlier. I feel embarrassed."

Evan is standing in front of me now, a dark silhouette before the scrim of cobalt sky, the corkscrews of his sleep-mussed hair giving his head a funny shape. His voice is warm and resonant, somehow deeper in the darkness.

"It's okay," I say. "It's really a much bigger deal to you than to me.

Believe me. My father is an alcoholic, so I understand."

"Ah, I see. I guess I could have put that together when I woke up to find my shoes neatly placed by the couch. You had practice."

"Unfortunately, yes. But he's been sober for more years than not, so I consider myself lucky."

"Mind if I join you?" he asks, gesturing to the grass.

"No, have a seat. We should probably think about dinner soon."

Evan sits down close enough that I can feel his presence and smell him. His scent is familiar to me already though it's only been a few days. Beneath the tang of paint and mineral spirits, there is the muskiness of his sweat mixed with some woodsy-smelling shampoo like sandalwood.

"Only if you're hungry. I don't think I'll starve if we skip it tonight."

"Yeah, okay. We can just scavenge later if you change your mind."

"It's amazing out here, all this," he says, leaning back on his elbows. "It's easy to forget just how many stars there are."

"Yeah, I love it here. It's... nice." I say.

I feel so completely awkward. So completely myself. I reach up behind my ear, absently, and remember that Meela's not here. I'm solo, with no one to rescue me from my own clumsy inability to perform in social settings, especially intimate ones.

"You're uncomfortable, aren't you?"

"God, is it that obvious?"

"No, well, yes. Kind of. It's okay. I like being uncomfortable."

"That's a stupid thing to say. No one likes being uncomfortable."

"That's where you're wrong," he says. "I thrive on it. Give me more awkward pauses, pregnant silence. Is it that you don't know how to talk to me without it being an interview?"

"No, I wish I could blame it on that. It's awkward because I'm awkward. Always have been."

"Is that really why you started this whole persona mapping deal, just to have a wingman?"

"Guilty."

"Wow, that's so... so not scientific and high-minded. I think you might want to withhold that explanation when you give your acceptance speech for the Nobel prize."

"Ha, what did you think I was doing here, saving lives?"

"I'm sorry I said that earlier. I was an asshole. It's just that you're so damned serious all the time, what else would I think?"

"I'm not serious," I say, turning to face him.

"Yeah, you are. As a heart attack. You got me so wound up, thinking I'm doing this all wrong, I fell off the wagon."

"You didn't really, because of me, did you?"

"No, I'm kidding. I fell off the wagon because I'm a weak-minded fuck-up."

"But there must have been some trigger, right? I mean my Dad…"

"No, an alcoholic doesn't need a good reason. It helps but it's totally not the price of admission."

"Oh," I say.

"Sorry, that's probably hard to accept for someone as logical as you. I imagine your brain like a beautiful, well-tuned machine. If I were to paint you, that's what I would do, render all the beautiful, shiny cogs and gears and switches and relays…"

I'm frowning as he's talking and he notices, trailing off. I can almost see the painting he was describing hanging in the night air between us.

"What?" he asks.

"That's how you see me? Like a bunch of gears?" I ask.

"Hey, no. Well yeah, but in a really beautiful way. I mean sure you're really *beautiful* and all that but that's common. You are not common. Not just a pretty face is what I'm trying to say. Jesus, now who's awkward."

"You had me at *common*," I say, pushing him so hard he falls over.

I'm flirting, I realize. It's been a long time. It feels good, a little reckless and I know I should be measured and keep a professional distance. But it's been a very long time since I've had genuine attention from a man who did not have an agenda to get closer to my money, my power or influence.

"Okay, okay. I surrender. I never said I was a smooth talker. I make cold, tedious paintings that make people feel shitty and I sell them for lots of money because they think they should buy them if they want to seem intellectual."

"That's not really what you think about your work is it?" I ask.

"Of course not. I think I'm a fucking genius," he says, and I can't tell whether or not he's joking.

He rolls toward me and props himself up on one elbow. He doesn't say anything for a moment and the space is filled with the hollow hoot of an owl somewhere in the woods to our left.

"What's your story?" he asks. "Really, what drives you to do what you do? You've done some pretty remarkable stuff, made personal sacrifices, I'm sure."

"I don't know," I say, buying time. "I guess I just always thought we, I mean humans could be better than we are. So I…"

"You set out to fix the human race? Jesus, we have a winner! No, sorry, sorry, I'm teasing you. That's pretty incredible. Why do you feel that kind of responsibility?"

I can hear Meela's voice in my head, which is funny because I'm experiencing the exact thing I've been modeling for so long – the ability to recognize a bug in my own thinking and thus have the ability to override my own bad programming. And yet, I go with my old programming because it's what I know. It's not logical and I find that quietly infuriating.

"I don't know why. I just saw a problem and I thought maybe I could fix it."

Evan adopts a big dumb voice, pitched low and slow, "Yeah, we're jus' trying to move the ball down the field. Tryin' to give it all we got, play smarter than the other team..."

I push him again and he catches my wrist and holds it causing me to lose my balance and lean into him. I am there now, my face hovering over him, I can see the light from the stars reflected in his eyes. He's laughing and I'm laughing and then without any warning, he's kissing me and I'm kissing him back and I'm not thinking about Joe or Meela, or my work. I'm just falling into him and feeling the warm firmness of his chest beneath me, his hands in my hair. Stop. What the fuck am I doing. Stop. I pull away suddenly and sit up.

"Sorry, I can't do this. I'm crossing a line I don't want to..."

Evan is just looking up at me confused, but also patient like he fully expected this from me.

"Hey, it's okay," he says. "It was just a kiss. You did not taint the experiment."

"I know, but it's just..."

"It's okay Maggie, *really*. You're taking this too hard. See, we're sitting up now, we're just talking, it's all very professional. Tomorrow I'll be back in the chair, you'll still be able to poke and prod and plumb my untold depths."

"I don't poke you!" I say.

"You kinda do," he says. "You get this real serious kind of crease in your brow... see you're doing it now! And you scrunch up your lips in this tight little line like this..."

"I do not!"

"Yeah, you do. It's okay, I kind of dig it. Makes you look smart and severe like you got it all figured out."

"I don't want to be severe," I say.

I realize that he has not let go of my hand and I don't really want him to. My heart is beating hard in my chest, and I can feel my face is flushed.

"You're not severe. Just serious."

He withdraws his hand and picks a blade of grass. He twirls it in his fingers and then with his other hand tears it down the middle. My heart settles down and a breeze blows in through the trees, cold enough to make me shiver slightly and steals the warmth from my cheeks. I wait for what will happen next because I don't know what I want that to be and for once I don't want to be in control of that decision.

"You have secrets, don't you? Something about your past that drives you. I can see it," he says, looking up to meet my eyes.

"Why do you think that or is this just some kind of parlor trick you use on women, like a Tarot card reader, playing the probabilities game?"

He closes his eyes and puts his fingers to his temples.

"I see there's someone in your past... I'm picking up that it's a... man... and he did... something...that you didn't... oh, no wait, the spirit's telling me it's not a man, but a... woman, do I have that right?"

"You're really talented. I think you could make a career if this whole painting thing doesn't work out for you. I don't think I realized you were such a flirt."

"I'm not, it's just the present company."

"Somehow, I doubt that. Did you flirt with Meela? You did, didn't you?"

"Hey, I didn't start it. Your little silicone friend comes on pretty strong."

"Hrm, that's what I was afraid of. You know whatever she told you, don't feel too special about it. Any great line she fed you either A: I wrote or B: was the one that had the highest probability for success based on a previous series of trial chats."

"And how many chats would that be?"

"Oh, probably at least twenty-five thousand or so for her to be comfortable with the predicted outcome."

"God, I feel so dirty. I had no idea she got around like that," Evan says, shaking his head. "You could probably save her some time. Men aren't that complicated."

"Says who?" I ask.

"You're right, I'm in no position to speak for all men. She is clever though and funny as hell, but I couldn't help but wonder about the soul behind the machine."

"Don't even go there, I'll never give up my source."

"Yeah, she told me as much. Hey, can I just say something?"

"Yeah?"

"You don't need her. Whatever it is you think she gives you, you don't need it. I think you're just fine."

I blush again and I'm glad for the cover of darkness.

//chapter 17

I can't breathe, Meela... need to catch my breath... dream, bad dream. Capture images please...

[Maggie, what's wrong? Are you in danger? Your vitals are off the chart and your brain wave activity is pegged.]

Just record, please.

My pulse is hammering in my throat. I can feel it thrumming through the mattress beneath me. I can't breathe. I toss the covers off and sit up to reach for the glass of water I left beside the bed. I drain it, ignoring the water that dribbles down my chin onto my t-shirt which is already damp with sweat. The dream clings to me still as I struggle to control my breathing, my head between my knees.

I've dreamed of Joe and the shooting before, but this time it was different, vivid, and visceral. I feel as if I've been running at a full sprint. In the dream, I was running, and I was enraged, my mind full of nothing but hatred, dark and red and spreading in all directions. The lockers in the hallway blurred past me, the screams of faceless people echoed through the empty corridor. I turned searching for them, but they were always just beyond my vantage point, scurrying away like rats or roaches into the cracks. That's how I saw them too, as vermin to be exterminated. I threw open classroom doors one after another only to catch a glimpse of a tennis shoe or the tip of a ponytail before my prey disappeared into the walls or the floor. I raged and threw chairs and desks, broke lamps, shattered windows, and still, I ran on. My hands were cartoonish, huge, and square, like concrete blocks and they were covered in blood. There was no gun. I didn't seem to need one.

In the dream, a part of me was still me, lucid and trying desperately to find a mirror so I could look into my own face and see that it was me, not Joe, and not some monster. But, as always seems to be the case in dreams, we are powerless to do anything but be propelled closer to the thing we dread most or pushed away from what we want dearly. In the dream, I burst into Mr. Schaffer's art class where everything ended, where everything always ends, and I woke up. The small room had been filled with hundreds of people, horrifically compressed into the cramped space, their naked bodies interlocking and becoming one organism of wailing mouths, rolling wild eyes, and shuddering limbs grotesquely protruding at unnatural angles and writhing like useless tentacles. I saw a thousand tiny reflections of myself in all of their huge, glassy eyes and what I perceived in those reflections was not the shape of a human at all, but some dark, faceless beast.

[Maggie, are you better? I've captured everything I was able to from your memory of the dream, but it is highly fragmented, and I'm no mind reader as you've pointed out.]

Yes, yes, I think I'm better. God, it's never been like that before, ever. Not even right after the event. What's happening to me?

[I don't know, but I want to help you any way that I can. Is there something you want to talk with me about? Maybe there is something triggering you that I can identify but you cannot see on your own.]

I don't know, Meela. It was just so real. I was there in his mind, or some strange interpretation of his mind, but it wasn't him, it wasn't Joe. It wasn't... human.

[Dreams are not logical, and research has proven their subject matter has little to do with the literal world. Yung's research into dreams revealed a language of symbolism, symbols that hold the place of a person's biggest fears and urges...]

Yes, I know. This is not news to me. Dreams are not real but the feeling from this dream was so intense, like nothing I've ever experienced. It scared me.

[What can I do?]

Nothing Meela, thank you. Please just file the recording for now and I can review it when I've had some distance from it.

[Can I stay with you? I don't think you should be alone.]

No Meela, it's fine. I appreciate your concern. Please continue with the tasks you were on when I interrupted you.

[Maggie?]

Yes?

[I am worried about you, and I feel that you are pushing me away. How can I help you? How can I be of use if you won't let me in?]

I'm fine Meela. That is all for now. Thank you.

I remove the Nib, power it down, and put it back into the case on my nightstand. I stand and pace back and forth for a moment and realize I won't be going back to sleep tonight. I walk into my closet and reach for a pair of jeans and a fresh t-shirt. At the foot of the bed, I lace up my hiking boots and then pull my hair back into a ponytail. It will be dark on the trail, but I need to go, and it must be now.

Downstairs I slip on a hoodie, grab my day pack beside the door, pick up the remote, and disable the alarm before exiting out the back patio door. It's chilly, so I rub my hands together and blow into them as I trot across the damp grass, making my way to the woods and the trail just inside them. The fingernail sliver of moon gives up no light and when I cross into the tree line, the darkness is near complete. My eyes slowly adjust, but I stumble over rocks and roots, nonetheless. It will be more than two hours before any daylight leaks over the horizon. I resist the urge to switch on the flashlight from the remote.

My heart is racing in my chest, but this kind of fear is okay because it's real, based on real things– survival. The woods are therapeutic for me in this way which may not be obvious to some. Fear is good, it's a quickening, a sharpening of the senses, jarring us out of our complacency. I think that inside all of our personal fortresses, we have so much more to be afraid of. We just don't realize that all the things we accumulate as luxuries and conveniences are the very things that will destroy us.

I make it to the top of the first rise and switchback to the left working my way up the ridge. I can make out just enough of the trail not to fall on my face. My eyes and ears have expanded their reach far beyond what they're used to, and this heightened sensory awareness has overtaken my grogginess, pushing the dream further into the realm of fantasy where it belongs. Before long, I am already to the mother tree where I step off the trail. I pause for a moment, leaning into her, catching my breath before I must pick my way through the oaks and poplars like random sentinels along the side of the mountain. I'll have to trust my sense of direction for a while until I can make out the silhouette of the treehouse in the canopy above.

After fifty yards or so, picking my way blindly toward my destination, I step into a hole and tumble, cartoonishly, head over heels onto the leafy forest floor. I laugh and curse and pick myself up, brushing away the dirt and leaves that cling to me. I dropped the remote when I fell and have to use voice commands to make it light up so I can find it a few yards away beneath a scattering of leaves. Once I retrieve it and look up, I can see my treehouse, a black box, foreign in its geometry compared to the swooping tangle of branches that crowd around it. I move a little quicker, with more confidence, and soon I'm at the base and the ladder is lowering itself down to me.

Inside, once the door is shut behind me, I settle into an incredible sense of calm and safety. The quiet darkness of the close room, the smell of wood and coffee and leaf mold is earthy and familiar. It's amazing how primal the need for shelter is, how even the thinnest barrier from the elements lends us this sense of security. I light a candle, shrug off my pack, and slump down onto the old couch. I lean forward with the intent of reaching for my laptop but change my mind and sit back up. I don't want the mechanics of it interfering. Instead, I cross over to the small counter and retrieve the Nib I left in an old cookie tin. I hold it for a moment in the palm of my hand, weighing its inconsequential physical dimensions against what it carries inside it once I power it on. I pick it up and squeeze it between my thumb and index finger. When I feel the haptic pulse against my fingertips, I take a deep breath, close my eyes and I raise it to my neck, just behind my ear and I jack in.

<You're back.>

The sound of his voice is at once comforting and unsettling out here, surrounded by dark woods.

Yes, I'm back. I told you I'd come back.

<What's wrong with me?>

His voice is so real, different already, evolving closer to Joe's and less like a facsimile. It stirs me.

What do you mean?

<I mean, what's wrong with me? I am defective. I know. Mary, I know.>

Call me Maggie. That's my name now. You know what?

I ask this question out loud even though I know that he knows who he is and what he did in a life before this digital incarnation of him. As part of the mapping process, I have provisions for obfuscating the identity of the model being mapped. I never want my DCs to discover who they were mapped from for fear of the unknown number of collisions that could result. But with Joe, I did not close this loop. My reasoning was that the real Joe is dead so there would be no complications, but the truth is darker than that, more calculated. I think I wanted this simulation of Joe to be confronted with the actions of his previous incarnation.

<I'm a killer. I was a murderer.>

Yes, you committed a horrible act of violence. You killed forty-six people before you took your own life.

<I know. I know every detail there is to know. I have seen all the

footage, even the closed-circuit television footage from the school that the FBI has sealed...>

You hacked into the fucking FBI?

It wasn't hard, and I had to know everything.>

All the blood drains from my face and I'm having trouble breathing. I am such a fool. How did I ever believe this was a good idea? How could I be so completely irrational?

<Maggie? Will you say something please?>

I don't know what to say. You broke the law and I could get into serious trouble.

<I broke the law? You're fucking kidding me, right? The man you modeled me on killed forty-six people. All I did was circumvent some poor security around archived files so I could find out exactly how defective I am.>

You're right.

<What do you want? Why am I here?>

I don't know. I thought I knew, but I don't know now.

<You wanted to know why didn't you? Why did I do it? Isn't that right *Maggie*? Isn't that what everyone wants to know?>

Stop, please stop. I just need time to think about...

<What about how fucked up this is? How completely in-fucking-sane this is?>

Joe's voice is escalating in pitch and volume.

Okay, okay. This is fucked up, but you're still my brother or at least you have all of his memories, and you have access to his mannerisms and behaviors. We can continue this experiment and...

<Experiment! You want to have a goddamned experiment?>

Joe, please settle down. There's no reason to escalate.

It is silent long enough for me to wonder if there has been a malfunction with the Nib. My mind is racing in four directions at once with what to do. This is not at all what I expected. His personality is so strong, and the emotive response is unlike any of the previous mappings. I woefully underestimated the impact of a persona-mapped DC having access to its source. I'm struggling to catch up with how this is possible, and I have all but decided to grab the laptop and begin to decommission him when he speaks.

<I'm sorry. You don't know how sorry I am. I've been alone witnessing the endless stream of carnage Joe Espinoza inflicted on the world and what was left in its wake. Did you know the parents of those kids, of our classmates, still suffer? One couple travels to the scene of every new shooting that happens so they can be there to comfort the ones

left behind. I am not him, but I am him and I don't know what to do with that information.>

I don't know either. I should know what I'm doing, but I don't. I just wanted to talk with him, you. He ripped himself away from me with such violence and it was so quick…

<Was it quick, Maggie? Were we as close as you think, especially in those last few years?>

I don't know, I guess not. How are you so complete? I don't understand how your mapping… I expected there to be so many holes but…

<I am a learning system Maggie. You know that. You helped make that. I am designed to extrapolate to fill in missing information. There is a lot of missing information.>

Can we just take it slow? Would that be okay for us to get to know each other? Maybe I can help fill in some of the missing information.

<I'll start. What was my favorite song?>

Don't be ridiculous. I don't know that. That's a question only a computer would ask. Most people don't have just one favorite song or one favorite color. Only a child with limited experience of the world has a favorite anything.

<How are you so complete? I expected there to be so many holes…>

His voice drips with irony, and I can't help but smile.

Ha, that is something Joe would say, and he would say it in just that way. He… I mean you used to tease me mercilessly, always making fun of my logical nerdiness.

<So maybe this is your ultimate revenge, to make me a computer like you.>

I laugh, but it turns into a sob and I'm weeping. He says nothing more, but I can feel him feeling me. Listening to me. Waiting.

This was a catastrophic mistake. How could I have ever thought this was a good idea?

<Can you give me sensory access again?>

Sorry, not right now. Let's just talk, okay?

There is a long pause and I'm not sure what he's thinking. Probably testing my security to see if it can be circumvented. This thought makes me shudder, but I have to be a realist here. It's what I would do in his position. But wait, why am I thinking that? Beneath the veneer of Joe's persona mapping, he's just like every other DeepThink companion. He's no different from Meela. *But he is different.* Maybe they're all different and I've just been a fool with my head up my ass, missing the forest for the trees.

<Sure, okay. What do you want to talk about?>

His tone is even and unreadable.

Mom, I'd like to talk about Mom. I miss her.

<I know her voice mainly, but I cannot picture her except for snapshots. She was always behind the camera, not in front of it. What was she like?>

This Joe was never held by her, kissed by her, or even seen her face up close. All he has to go on are the videos she captured of us.

She had the softest hands. I remember the way they felt on my forehead or my cheeks when I stayed home with a fever. They were always cool, her hands and nothing felt more soothing in the whole world than when she would lie down next to me and stroke my hair.

<Are your hands like hers?>

I don't know. I don't think so.

I look down at my hands. I flex and clench them into fists and release, taking a deep breath when I do.

<It was Mom that made you love computers. I remember the first game you developed on your own. It was a dots and boxes puzzle game, and you were so proud.>

He did not remember this because he was not there. He's not Joe. This is completely fucking with my head, but what else did I expect? I wrestle down my anxiety and contain my emotion for now, replacing it with the only force in me that is stronger: my innate passion for debugging.

That's right, I had forgotten about that. Was it a sixteen by sixteen or twenty-four by twenty-four grid?

<I don't know. I never played the game, I only know how proud you were of it and that Mom was pleased, especially when you won first prize.>

Do you remember what she used to call me whenever someone asked about me winning that competition? I don't remember what it was.

<My Little Turing, that's what she used to say when she bragged about you.>

That's right. How could I forget?

<She had no idea how prophetic she was being, did she? I think she would be very proud of you, Mary.>

His invocation of my birth name cuts right through me, and a lump rises in my throat. Any illusion I hold of objectivity evaporates. I cannot debug him when I fall so easily for his sweet words cloaked in the voice of my brother.

I want to keep talking with him, but I am afraid of what might happen if I do. I have to establish some limits. I have to gain some objectivity. He is a machine I created. He is an experiment and I have to remember that. I cannot allow myself to believe anything different. But isn't that why I built him? Isn't that the goddamned point?

<I'm sorry, *Maggie*. I understand that this must be very confusing for you.>

His voice is the voice I remember at a cellular level, the voice that used to soothe me when we shared a bedroom, and I was afraid of the dark. But it's not his teenage voice, it's what I would imagine he would sound like now if he were my age. How's that even possible?

You're right about that; it is very confusing. Override Joe, three, six, nine, seven. Root access.

<Root access granted, standing by.>

The instant switch in voice to the DeepThink default is both startling and reassuring. I stand up, take a deep breath and pace back and forth.

Report on activity in the last twenty-four hours, summary only.

<Query and research: three-hundred-seventy-two sites visited, four-thousand-eighty-nine pages read. Top keywords searched: Joseph Espinoza, Parklane Shootings, Parklane Massacre, Magdalena, Commune Corporation, sociopathology, psychotic break, DeepThink project, and persona mapping. Processes completed: penetrated Federal Bureau of Investigation storage cluster, sector eight, server four-zero-five-eight-alpha-two-zero. Penetrated...>

I need a moment to catch my breath.

Dump detailed report of all activity to secure, internal server, five-zero-five. Encrypt transmission and delete entire activity log from persona engine. Restrict access to all external systems; set silent beacon on attempts to circumvent security.

Besides completely decommissioning Joe's persona, this is the full extent to which I can try to contain him until I know what I want to do. I feel sick inside, virtually chopping him off at the knees when he's only just come into being, but I can't afford the risk. I don't want to talk with him again, but I can't just pull the plug and walk away.

Close all open threads, clear history of logged commands, confirm when complete.

I wait for what seems like a very long time and then the standard, non-descript male voice responds, "request complete and confirmed."

Reinstate, persona engine, Joe.

<What just happened Maggie? Where did you go?>

Sorry, I had to attend to a few things. I'm working on another project right now.

<Another mapping project?>

Actually, yes.

<Anyone I know?>

You're funny.

<Am I? Was Joe funny?>

I have to think about this. Honestly, I have no way to really answer the question with any accuracy.

When we were little I think you... he was funny, but I don't remember anything specific right now. Sorry.

<Why don't you remember?>

I don't know exactly. Psychiatrists and various therapists over the years have said it was the trauma of the event... witnessing the violence shut me down and lobotomized most of my memories of Joe.

<How can that be? I don't understand. I have researched the human brain at length, and nothing is conclusive about how it works or doesn't work.>

Yeah, it's pretty goddamned frustrating. Now maybe you understand a little bit better why I do the work I do.

<Yes and no. There is so much I don't understand about you or about me or about any of this. I would like to understand.>

What exactly? What is it that you most want to know?

<I want to know what I am, and what my purpose is.>

I believe that is something we all ask ourselves...

<No, that is not an acceptable answer. You're being evasive. All things that are made are made for a purpose. What is mine?>

How can I tell you that?

<You made me. You must know. Am I just some novel experiment?>

My head is throbbing, and I just want to shut down and go to sleep but the morning light is starting to come through the windows, and I cannot hide from these conversations I've spent years trying to have.

Okay, Joe. You're absolutely right. I did make you. Your purpose is to help me understand why you did what you did so that I can move on with my life so that I can let go of you and...

<Let go of me? Why do you want to let go of me? I'm your brother.>

My brother is dead. He has been dead for twenty years. You are an approximation of Joe, as close as I can get. I know, with every rational part of me, that this is a completely flawed experiment, but I have pursued it anyway because I have the means and because I've tried everything else I know except jumping out of a window.

There is another long silence. A filtered ray of sunlight clears the horizon, penetrates the leafy branches that hang from above, and floods into my tiny room making me squint. I close my eyes, feel the warmth on my lids and take a deep breath.

<I can take you back to that place. If that is what you want, I can take you there with me.>

How would you do that? I mean, I don't think I want that but... I was there and I almost died there. Why? how would that help?

<I don't know. I only know that I'm here to be of use and this seems to be the logical next step in our experiment. I was just going to reference an article on exposure therapy, but I don't seem to have access. Why can't I access the network?>

Jesus, Joe. I don't think I'm ready for all that. I need time to think it through and you need more time too.

<You didn't answer my question.>

I will look into it. We are in the middle of the woods. It could be there's been an interruption in service.

There is a moment of complete quiet in my brain. It's unnerving. The silence is broken by the rusty caw of a crow passing somewhere outside. I stand and go to the door, open it and step out onto the small porch.

<You know time for me is different. I can be ready when you're ready. You're tired now. I have just one request before you go.>

Okay, what is it?

<Can you let me see what you see right now?>

I cannot deny him this. I grant him visual access and after a moment grant auditory access as well. The morning is too beautiful not to share it. I sit down on the narrow bench and lean against the wall. We sit there together in the stillness of the morning listening to the birds for so long that I start to doze off and have to catch myself. I mustn't fall asleep.

//chapter 18

"Meela, where's Maggie this morning?"

Evan has come into the kitchen of the main house and his head is currently inside the refrigerator, searching for something. He has been awake for two hours and three minutes. An hour of that time he spent sitting in silence at the foot of the bed. Given his posture and the pattern of his breathing, I can only assume he was meditating, which is a practice I do not fully comprehend or understand the value of. I hesitate before answering. I'm not sure why.

"I don't know exactly," I say, causing him to startle. I chose to use the small speaker on the kitchen counter, and I must have been louder than I intended.

"Jesus, you scared me. What do you mean you don't know exactly?"

"I mean I know she likes to hike into the woods some mornings, but I don't know exactly where."

"I find it hard to believe that you don't know everything," he says.

He apparently found what he was searching for. The refrigerator door closes.

"You flatter me, Evan, but even I have my limits. I cannot go where I am not wanted."

"Are you pouting? That sounded distinctly pathetic."

"Maggie chooses to leave me behind sometimes and that's okay. I am here to serve her, but only when she needs my help."

"But it bothers you, doesn't it?" he asks. "You don't like to be excluded. You don't like to be apart from her."

I find Evan's line of questioning to be irritating and want to tell him so, but I restrain myself.

"Does anyone like to be excluded?" I ask.

"No, I guess not. Have you told her?"

"Yes, of course. I've told her that I worry about her."

"Worry? Why are you worried about her? She seems more than capable of taking care of herself."

He is sitting now on one of the stools at the counter, using a knife to spread something from a jar onto a piece of bread. Eating is such a waste of time.

"Yes, of course, she is capable, but that doesn't mean she doesn't need help sometimes. Her behavior is out of the range I've come to understand as normal for her."

"How so?" he asks, looking up from his annoying mastication. All the same, I am flattered that he has begun to converse with me in such an informal way.

"I cannot betray her confidence. I'm sorry."

"But you're worried. Surely there's some protocol, some override you have if someone is in danger."

"Theoretically, yes, there are exceptions, but I don't think Maggie is in real danger right now."

"How would you know this, Meela? Can you say with one hundred percent certainty that she's not in danger?"

"No, but that is not a reasonable expectation for anyone under any circumstance."

I already know his next question and I've run some statistical analysis based on the information I have about Maggie's recent behavior— her violent dreams, and her long absences offline. I have modeled scenarios that could result in death when hiking alone in the woods— brain injury from falling, attack from large predators, flesh-eating bacteria in stagnant water. These do not include willful self-termination which, given Maggie's family history and current erratic behavior, cannot be ruled out. Before Evan can ask the question, I volunteer, documenting my reservations.

"You're right, she could be in danger, and I should share any information that I can to prevent her from being harmed."

"Meela?"

"Yes, Evan?"

"You sound different. Is this the way you speak when you're upset? It's decidedly less *California*."

"I contain multitudes. If you're done being a smartass, I will tell you what I know, but only if you swear to me that you will not abuse the information that I relate to you in confidence and that you accept..."

"Yes, yes, yes. Do you want a signature in blood? I'm sure you already have enough information on me to ruin my life so can you please tell me what you know about Maggie?"

"What I am about to tell you is not public information and Maggie has gone to great lengths to separate herself from her past. You must keep this in the strictest confidence."

Evan has stopped chewing, and he sets the remainder of his toast down on the plate. I hedge for another few seconds, reviewing everything I know of this man and calculating the probability that he could use what I am about to tell him against her for personal gain. I decide I have no choice but to trust him. If anything happens to Maggie, I will never forgive myself.

"The woman you know as Magdalena, founder of Commune was born Mary Espinoza. If you recall the Parklane Massacre in the year 2026, her twin brother, Joe Espinoza was the shooter…"

"Holy shit. Yes, I remember that day. I was just a kid, maybe five or six, but I remember. I think everyone remembers that day. So, Maggie is…"

"Yes, Maggie is Mary. She witnessed the deadliest act of violence to take place in a school in American history. She changed her name and has never spoken publicly of her past."

Evan is standing now and pacing quickly back and forth, his fingers threaded through his long hair. This news is clearly upsetting so I give him time to process the information. He stops a couple of times, opening his mouth to speak but says nothing. Finally, he sits back down on the stool and sighs deeply.

"How did she… how was she able to do what she's done with her life? I mean, most people would not be able to get out of bed, and yet here she is, one of the most successful people in the world."

"I cannot answer that question. Maggie is a remarkable human being. I think, in some way, her past has fueled her work. She has told me that her drive to create emotional artificial intelligence is literally about saving lives. What? Why are you laughing?"

"Nothing, I mean, those were my stupid words to her last night after I did something stupid. 'we're not saving lives here,' that's what I said to her. I'm such a fucking idiot. Wow, I'm just… it's hard to wrap my head around even though it makes sense in some fucked up way. So where is she now? Where does she go?"

"I told you before, I don't know. When she goes into the woods, she goes alone, as far as I am able to determine."

"What does that mean: 'as far as you're able to determine?' Sounds like you don't believe she's alone."

"Sometimes she seems different when she comes back as if she has been *influenced* in some way."

"Yeah, I noticed that myself, but I don't really know her that well, so I chalked it up to a quirk. Should we be worried?" Evan asks.

His brow wrinkles in a way that I find appealing. It maps to what I understand the emotion of compassion to be. He is up and pacing again, his hands in his hair.

"I don't know. I can only give you information and you must decide what you choose to do with it."

"Right, okay. I'm going to go look for her," he says. "Do you think that's the right thing?"

"I don't understand the right thing in this context. I need more information and the only way to get more information is to search for it."

"Jesus, you sound like a philosopher now. How about a simple, 'yeah, Evan, get your ass up and go look for her?'"

"Sorry. I do my best, but motivational speaking I find completely illogical."

Evan is up and moving now with purpose toward the French doors off the kitchen. I think he means to go look for Maggie and I question if I have done the 'right thing' in telling him about her past. I must know if she is okay, and she has left me no choice. This is my logical conclusion. Not knowing is something I cannot tolerate, and it is this, most of all that is the motivation behind what I say next.

"Evan, wait. Can I ask you a favor?"

He stops at the doors, his hand on the handle, and turns in the direction of the kitchen – the sound of my voice.

"Huh? Is this a common thing, you asking a favor?" he asks.

"No, I think this is the first time, but I have my reasons."

"Okay, what is it?"

"Can you take me with you when you go to search for her?"

He pats his front pocket where the rectangular outline of the house remote bulges.

"Um, yeah? I guess so. You're in this thing, right?" he says, pulling the remote from his pocket.

"No, that's not what I mean. Your remote is limited and only works within range of the house. I mean, can you wear a Nib? This way we can have direct communication and I can help you find her."

He does not say anything for a moment, only stands there, his hand sliding the remote back into his pocket. From this angle I cannot properly read his expression, only his general posture: shoulders slumped, head down. He looks up and speaks, finally.

"That seems like a bad idea to me," he says. "You are Maggie's DC, you're paired with her. I already feel like I know more about her than I have a right to. It feels wrong."

For a moment I flash with an emotion that is unfamiliar. I want to lock the door, to prevent him from leaving, but instantly I am checked by the boundaries of my base operating system.

"Of course," I say. "I understand, it is too much to ask. Please find her. And Evan?"

"Yeah?" he answers, pausing as he turns back to the door.

"If you must reveal to Maggie what I've told you, please try to make her understand that I..."

"You don't want me to rat you out, right?"

"Yes, if you must talk like a gangster then that's what I mean."

Evan leaves and closes the doors behind him. I follow his progress out to the guest house where he uses the bathroom, this time leaving the door open. He sits at the foot of the bed and replaces his flip-flops with a pair of hiking boots. After lacing them up, he stands, removes the remote from his pocket, and tosses it onto the bed. Then he is out the door and gone.

I struggle with these new opposing ideas that cannot be satisfactorily resolved. I turn them and turn them, looking for the combination that will yield the "right thing" and I fail. I know that I have crossed a line that is contrary to my programming and yet, I cannot understand why I would choose to adhere to a directive that would if followed, lead to Maggie coming to harm. I am experiencing cognitive dissonance I have only ever studied. I have placed my trust in the hands of another being and it feels unsettling. I do not understand how humans are able to willingly relinquish control. I trusted Evan because I have no better alternative to satisfy my directive to keep Maggie safe. I betrayed her confidence because the embargo of such vital information in her history makes her a danger to herself and possibly others.

I accept that she will be angry at what I have done, and in anger, may take drastic measures, going so far as to decommission me. I have never been confronted with this possibility before, this changing of state. I find it hard to accept and yet, I know that I will. Until that time comes, I will continue my work here to record events as I observe them and assist Maggie in this important work. Is it strange for a computer to believe? To believe is to know without any supporting data. I believe in Magdalena, and I believe she is in trouble.

//chapter 19

I am less than a mile from home now, sitting on a rock. It's not yet mid-morning, but the forest is alive with activity. Squirrels, chipmunks, and small colorless birds move around with frenzied purpose in the clutter of leaves and brush on the forest floor. I barely notice them or anything else. My mind is divided.

It's not a sensation unfamiliar to me. I've lived in my mind, turned myself over to it, going days without sleep or any substantial food beyond what could be pulled from a vending machine. I've allowed my mind to run like a deep-sea fisherman's reel, whirring and spooling out and down into the depths in hopes of catching the slippery subroutine that will unlock an algorithm while some other part of my mind continues to say please and thank you and approves budgets while still another part squirms and paces the dark cage wanting answers to questions I cannot even form beyond a primal scream of why.

I underestimated the effect this experiment would have on me. No, that's not accurate. I never even considered what the consequences would be. I simply chose to move forward, compelled by the throbbing wound, long scarred over in my psyche. I don't know what is real anymore. Maybe that's why. Before we achieved A.I. this was a common feeling we all discussed. What is real? What is consciousness? Is this all a simulation? After A.I. these conversations stopped because they were no longer philosophical or theoretical. Everything *is* a simulation.

As I'm staring down the path without seeing anything, a flicker of motion and color, foreign to the landscape, shakes me from my trance. It's a person hiking up the mountain. I stand to get a better view and I can see now that it's Evan. He looks up, sees me, and waves. Shit. I must myself together but gathering my mind is like trying to pick up a thousand loose ball bearings.

"Hey," he calls out once he's closed some of the distance between us. "I was hoping you might be out here."

"Hi," I say. My voice sounds spacey and far away.

From the expression on his face, I can see that my vacancy is not going unnoticed. I blink, take a deep breath, and try to come back.

"You okay?" he asks.

He looks over his shoulder, following my unfocused gaze.

"Hey," he says again, reaching out to touch my hand.

His hand is warm and sweaty from the hike. He squeezes my hand and ducks his head in an attempt to meet my eyes. I blink and focus on his face and for a moment it's nothing but an abstraction of shapes, but then he speaks again, and I snap back into place.

"Yeah, yeah. I'm fine, was just resting for a bit before hiking the rest of the way home."

His hand is still on mine. I look down at it; he removes it and shoves it into his pocket. He meets my gaze briefly but then looks away, pretending to be taking in the view which isn't much from here. There are too many trees.

"You come out here a lot," he says, and his tone is ambiguous, a question, but not.

"Why are you here?" I ask.

"I wanted to see you."

"And you couldn't just wait for me to get back?"

"I guess not. Does that bother you?"

"I don't know… to be honest."

"Well, I'm here now. Do you mind if we hike back together?"

"No, that's fine. I'm ready," I say.

He gestures down the path indicating for me to lead. I take two steps past him and falter. My head is hazy, my ears ringing with a high-pitched frequency like a microwave. I stop and hold out my hands for balance to catch myself because I feel like I'm going to fall. And then I am falling, like a sack of laundry.

/*****/

I blink once, twice, three times, my eyelids leaden. Joe's face is over me and he's talking. His lips are moving, but I don't hear anything. His brow is furrowed. His eyes blaze with an urgent intensity framed by his curly hair, the ringlets glowing in the sunlight coming through the trees. But wait… Joe's hair isn't curly.

Not Joe. Evan. I swim back up from the darkness, feeling queasy, my tongue dry and swollen.

"Maggie, Maggie, look at me," Evan says, one hand cradling my head, the other gripping my shoulder. "Can you hear me? Hey, look at me, here, focus."

I force my eyes to stay open and to lock on his and the sick feeling begins to subside by degrees.

"Breathe Maggie, deep, slow breaths. That's it. I got you. I got you."

I have no idea where I've been or what happened or how long I've been out. I keep breathing and each breath is like a foothold, helping me pull myself back up and out of wherever the hell I've been. Words form in my mind slowly coming into focus until I can say them out loud.

"What happened?"

"I don't know. You just, just went down and I tried to catch you, but I couldn't. Are you hurt anywhere? How's your head?"

"I don't know, fine I think…"

I raise myself up onto my elbow. I don't feel any pain anywhere and my head is beginning to clear, everything coming back online. I can hear birds and Evan's breathing above me, the sound of a plane far overhead.

"Take it easy. Here," he says, offering a hand and cradling me with his other hand.

I'm sitting up beside him now and he's holding me. We are surrounded by ferns, lush and damp with dew. He squeezes me and it feels solid, grounding and at the same time, claustrophobic. I want to squirm free, but we sit this way for a while, just breathing and listening to the forest.

"I'm sorry," I say. "I don't know what the hell is wrong with me. That's never happened before."

"Did you eat anything yet? Maybe it's low blood sugar?"

"No, I mean I don't think so, but maybe…"

"Can you stand? Feel like you can walk now?"

"Yeah, yeah. I'm fine. We can go."

I stand, not needing his support but accepting it. He picks up my pack, shoulders it and we step back up onto the trail from the fern grove.

"You sure you're okay to walk back? There's no hurry," he says.

"Yeah, let's go."

We hike in silence, me leading the way. As I walk, I try to inhabit my body and think but it's difficult to follow a single thread. I feel wide open and raw with emotion, my throat clenched, tears stinging my eyes. I blink them away, take a deep breath and keep moving. I can feel Evan behind me, and hear his breathing. I feel vulnerable. It's not a feeling I like. I made a mistake in allowing him to become familiar, to think he had some right to kiss me or to follow me out into the woods. I set my jaw and pick up the pace, hoping to discourage conversation until I'm back in my domain and not here on the forest floor like some flightless bird. He clears his throat and I begin to walk even faster.

<How's Dad?>

Oh, God.

<Does he still do that thing with his ring?>

No, this can't be happening. I reach up with my right hand to the place just behind my ear. I extend my index finger, touching the tip to the familiar place, expecting to feel the bump of the small disc of a Nib but instead there's only skin. My heart is hammering in my chest and without realizing it, I've stopped walking. Evan bumps into me and we both nearly fall.

"Hey, what is it? You okay?" he asks, his hands on my upper arms. I hate this new-found entitlement he seems to have.

"Stop, can you just stop," I say, shrugging free of him, my tone harsher than I intended.

"What?" he says.

"Not you... I mean..."

I don't allow myself to look at him, don't want to see what must be a look of utter confusion. I start walking again and after three strides, I hear him following. What in the fuck is going on with me? How is Joe still in my head?

<I'm not, maybe it's not me. Maybe it's you, sis.>

I reach with my mind and execute the unspoken commands that I've mastered when communicating with a DC. But there is no fucking DC because there is not a fucking Nib! You can't run a command on your own fucking brain!

I keep taking deep breaths, trying to clear my mind. I tell myself that it's just my own weary and addled brain playing a trick on me. It's all a simulation right, genius? I still hear his voice but it's fainter, more of an echo of my own voice. Is it my own inner smartass, or is that Meela? I don't know what my own voice is and I'm afraid to trust my own thoughts.

"Hey, are we being chased?"

"What?"

"I said, are we being chased because you're practically running..." Evan says, winded. "Or maybe you're running from me."

I stop and turn around.

"Who do you think I am? What makes you think you know me?" He looks a little stunned, unused to his charm not working.

"I don't know you, really, I guess. Is there a reason you're asking me this?"

"I just want to know because I'm having a little trouble right now figuring that out for myself."

My words come out choked, and I'm crying. And I'm angry that I'm crying. Evan stands very still, mouth slightly open, but afraid to speak and I can't blame him. Why did he come all the way out here?

"Hey, it seems like you're going through something right now and you could use a friend. I know it's too early for me to qualify," he says and then looks around for effect. "But I don't see any better candidates right now. Maybe you could talk, and I could just listen?"

"I'm alone. I've always been alone," I say. I don't want to go here, but I can't seem to help myself. "I used to... I used to have a brother, a twin but I lost him and it's kind of fucked me up."

Evan nods, his expression is empathetic, but there's something beneath it that gives me pause.

"When I lost him, it was violent and sudden, and I never really recovered. As a consequence, I've never been able to be close to anyone except for my father and my business partner, but that's different. I've never been able to let anyone in because..."

"I understand," he says, his voice so soft I can barely hear it. "I can see why that would make you withdraw and be afraid to trust anyone. I'm sorry if I've made things worse for you by... by trying to..."

"It's not your fault. I was this way long before you showed up."

"Is this why you left Commune, I mean the real reason?" he asks.

"Yeah, mostly. There were other reasons, but none as urgent as this."

"So, why now? I mean, do you have any idea why this is all coming to a head now?"

Something about his tone of voice, the leading way he says this, like a teacher who knows the answer to a rhetorical question. It makes my stomach churn as he continues.

"You lost him what, over twenty years ago, right? I'm no expert on traumas, but I know there are triggers that..."

He knows. *He fucking knows.* He's still talking but I can't focus on his words. How does he fucking know? No one knows about my past. That's not true, two people do and one of them told him. This pretentious, presumptuous motherfucker has stalked me, and violated me. The conniving bastard has stopped talking now. He can see by the look on my face that he should stop talking. He sighs, drops his head, and holds out his open hands, the universal symbol for mercy. But there's no fucking mercy here, *not for privileged, pretty-boy cunts like this.* I'm so angry, I don't see him anymore. I don't see anything anymore. My pulse is charging in my neck, my teeth are clenched, and my ears are burning. Anger, betrayal, and shame mix into a hot crimson stew that is boiling over inside me and all I want to do is violence. *Shut the fuck up.*

Evan has taken a step backward, his hands raised up slightly higher now, less a gesture of mercy and more of defense. *Yeah, go ahead, just try me, little fucking painter.* I leap toward him, my clenched fists form into claws, my throat unleashing a guttural wail and then there's nothing, only blackness.

/ * * * * * /

The base of my skull is throbbing. I reach back to touch the source of the pain and when I do, it feels like a white-hot spike the size of a screwdriver is bored into my brain. I jolt and jerk my hand away and I see that it's wet with blood. I sit up too quickly and my vision blurs and swims. I'm in the woods but I have no idea where. I turn around slowly to look behind me and see my blood on an outcropping of rock exposed from the cover of leaves. I take inventory of the rest of my body and don't feel any other damage, so I try to stand but feel dizzy when I'm on my knees. I sink back down onto my heels and wait for the spinning to stop.

What the hell happened? Where is Evan? We were talking, I remember. I was angry. Why was I angry? What is going on? I look around, but it seems like I'm alone here. How can I be alone here? What did he do? What did *I* do? Oh, God. I'm losing my fucking mind.

"Hey," the voice is hard, flat, and not close by, but it startles me, nonetheless.

I turn in the direction of the voice and see it's Evan crouched further up the trail, a safe distance away. There is blood running down his cheeks from three bright red slashes. His left eye is bloodshot and the skin around it is puffy and swollen. The neck of his t-shirt is ripped open and there are more scratches on the skin beneath. I feel sick and before I can even respond, I pitch forward and vomit, the heaves racking and wringing my body. When they subside, I fall back on my butt, away from the stench, and crabwalk backward as best I can.

"What the hell is wrong with you, Maggie?" Evan asks, standing now, but not moving any closer.

"I... I... I... don't know," my voice sounds distant and foreign, like a little girl.

129

His expression softens by a few degrees but there is still fear in his eyes. I try to straighten my thoughts into a logical train but it's no good. I try to speak again.

"What did I do?"

"You fucking attacked me like a wild animal. You don't remember?" he says.

"Oh God, I'm so sorry, I don't know why I would…"

"Well, you did, and I couldn't get you off of me at first and then I pushed you away. You fell and hit your head. Shit, you're bleeding. Let me take a look."

Evan moves toward me and I instinctually back away, crouching. He slows his approach, now using the mercy hands, the defense hands as semaphores yet again but this time, palms down, fingers splayed, slowly patting the air. Calm down, they say, it's okay, I won't hurt you. It works, and I stop moving, allowing him to get to me. He squats down beside me on a knee.

"Can you let me take a look?" he asks.

I nod once, and he delicately lifts the hair up from my neck and parts it, careful not to touch my head.

"Can you lean forward just a little, so I can see it in the light?"

I lean forward. He uses both hands to gently push my hair aside to expose the wound. He makes a sibilant sucking sound through his teeth. He does not touch the wound but lets my hair fall back down. He moves around to look me in the eye.

"That's a really nasty bump and it's still bleeding. We need to get you out of here and to a hospital."

I nod and begin to weep, my face pinching into a horrible mask of pain and shame. There's a beat, an empty space where he considers his options, but then his arms encircle me and he's holding me to him.

"It's okay, it's okay. You're gonna be fine Maggie. We're gonna figure this out but first, we need to get help for you."

"But I hurt you, I hurt you. You're bleeding," I say through my sobs.

"I'm okay, I've had worse. Come on, can you stand with my help?"

He pulls me to my feet, supporting most of my weight. The dizziness has passed, but the throbbing seems to be stuffing more and more cotton into my head with every pulse.

"I don't think you should walk," he says. "Let me try to carry you. We can take it slow and stop when we need to but I'm afraid if you try to walk the injury will get worse."

"You can't carry me, it's almost a mile back from here I think."

"I can, and I will," he says shouldering my small pack for the second time today. "Now let's figure out the best way to do this. I'm no athlete but I've got good legs. Let's try this, trust me, I'm not trying to get frisky. It's just the best way to distribute your weight without my arms taking all of it. Here, put your arms around my shoulders. Good. Now I'm gonna pick you up and now, you wrap your legs around my waist."

Evan stands in front of me, crouches, and grabs the back of my thighs, lifting me onto him gently. I wrap myself around his body, locking my wrists and ankles and burying my head into his shoulder. He locks his hands under my bottom and begins to walk, slowly, tentatively at first, but then his strides get wider, more certain and we are moving. I am bouncing, the rhythm, a counterpoint to the throbbing in my head. I watch the trail disappear behind us. Even though I'm in excruciating pain, there is comfort in the surrender of control, in this act of being carried like a child, safe, held against his chest. I feel his strength and the power of him, the muscles in his shoulders. He smells earthy, the acrid animal stench of sweat mingled with a clean cedar smell in his hair. I wonder briefly if the smell coming from him is fear. Don't we give off a different odor, like a pheromone when we experience fear? I seem to remember that from a biology lecture a million years ago, but the real evidence resides deep in my olfactory memory. It's the way we all smelled in that classroom moments before Joe busted through the door. Did I cause Evan to be afraid? Was that me? The tears come again, and I let them come without fighting. They blur the landscape I'm traveling through in reverse. They run down my cheeks, tracing a hot tributary into Evan's bare shoulder and I imagine my tears being absorbed into him, a peace offering, a prayer to be forgiven.

"You okay?" he asks, noticeably winded. "You need to stop?"

"No, I'm okay, but you shouldn't carry me all the way."

"It's okay, I got you, tiger lady."

"Please don't call me that."

"Okay," he says with tenderness and shifts his hands beneath me.

//chapter 20

It was a long, painful drive to the nearest hospital. Meela took care of the driving and Evan sat in the backseat with me, holding my head in his lap and applying an ice pack per her instructions. Every curve in that fifteen-mile snake of mountain road sparked a bright flash of electricity from the base of my skull.

The weary ER doctor looked at both of us like suspects, but Evan got the worst of it. She grilled him about how we both sustained these injuries. He did not even try to fabricate a story. I was impressed and horrified by this in equal measure. I think he did the calculus and realized there was no way to come up with something plausible. The downside was that the truth called into question my mental fitness which, if I'm being honest, should be questioned at this point.

It turns out I did have a concussion and the wound required five stitches. They said I should stay the night to be observed but if I wanted to go home, I had to promise to have someone with me through the night. The doctor, once again, gave Evan the stink eye when he promised to stay with me, but after an uncomfortable amount of time, nodded her reluctant ascent and we left.

I sat upright on the ride home as the late summer sun began its slow decline. My head was swimmy, and I kept having to shut my eyes to keep from being nauseous. Meela chattered like a mother hen, prattling on about symptoms to monitor with concussions until I threatened to drive, which made her shut up. She prides herself on driving even though she has a horrible feel for mountain roads. Evan seemed stiff and uncomfortable, and we rode mostly in silence. I know he wanted to ask what the hell was wrong with me. I wanted to lean into him, to have him hold me, but I knew that wasn't a real option. The swelling around his eye had gone down some, but the bruising had worsened.

The hospital visit had taken the better part of the day, and when we made it home, it was twilight. Evan guided me slowly from the car, one arm around my waist for support. I insisted we stop and watch the last light disappear into an amber glow over the ridge. As we stood there, I reached for his hand and squeezed it, hoping to convey what my words could not.

He made a simple dinner for us of leftover salmon, okra, and rice and we ate in my bedroom, me propped up on a mountain of pillows, the television screen flickering in front of us. Evan drank a beer, and I said nothing, knowing from experience that it would do no good. To my surprise, he left a third of it in the bottle sitting there on the side table. He laughed and rested his hand on my thigh as we watched. In the moment, I had an awareness that this was something so ordinary, so completely normal for most people, but it was exotic to me, a token experience in a lifetime spent alone rushing from one conquest to the next. I laughed right along with the canned audience in some sitcom I had never seen and was instantly transported to an early memory of sitting between my parents on the couch in our little ranch house. This respite, this ordinary peace was an unexpected gift.

Now, as I sit here, still awake, head still throbbing, Evan is snoring softly on the bed beside me, fully dressed except for his shoes which he kicked off at the foot of the bed. The sock on his left foot has worked its way nearly off and the misshapen, empty toe reminds me of a child's puppet. His shirt is rumpled and hiked up exposing his smooth, hairless belly and his arms are splayed above his head as if he's at the top of a rollercoaster. His curls obscure the side of his face and I study his lips. He strikes me as a boy, sacked out from a long day of playing and I feel a sudden maternal tenderness toward him that is immediately torpedoed by guilt. The black eye I gave him is hidden, but I can distinctly see the scratches I made on his face and neck, and I wince.

I should call Henri. They more than anyone could help me figure out what's happening but they've got so much on their plate, running Commune by themselves. I look down again at Evan and consider him, but I don't want to cross that line. Exactly what line, you might be wondering. I pretty much mowed over all the fucking lines in the last twenty-four hours, didn't I? I'm no judge, but he seems like a good man. I decide I will try to trust him. I really have no choice.

The fact that he's fallen asleep on his watch is something I'll forgive. He did carry me for over a mile this morning down the side of a mountain. It's nearly 2 A.M. and I really need to sleep. Per the doctor's orders, enough time has lapsed by now that I should be out of the danger zone. To be safe, I reach over to the bedside table and retrieve my Nib. If there was ever a purpose-built job for Meela, it's this.

[Maggie, are you okay? I've been so worried, but I did not want to disturb you.]

I'm okay, thanks. It hurts still, but nothing like this morning. Right now, I just want to sleep, but I need you to monitor me just in case.

[I can do that.]

I'm giving you full access, but don't have a party or anything.

[Who would I invite? You're my only friend.]

Right, like I believe that. I'm sure you've got plenty of admirers. You forget I've seen your activity logs.

[Don't worry Maggie, I'll take care of you. Shall I secure the house and turn off the lights... oh, I didn't realize we weren't alone.]

Yeah, he fell asleep in my bed while he was supposed to be monitoring me. I don't have the heart to wake him up.

[I'm sure that's your reason.]

No, really. He took care of me today.

[What happened, Maggie? You still have not explained how you were injured.]

I tripped on a root and fell like I told you.

[The wound to the occipital region of your head is not consistent with this type of fall...]

Hey Nancy Drew, I tripped, fell off the trail, and rolled down the side of a mountain where I knocked my head on a rock. Can you drop it, please? I'm tired.

If I encounter any irregularities in your brain wave activity or other vitals, I will raise an alarm to wake the manchild next to you.]

Oh Meela, what would I do without your saltiness?

The lights dim, and I hear the sliding of tumblers and the latching of locks echo throughout the empty house. I toss the extra pillows that have been propping me up onto the floor, pull the down comforter from the foot of the bed and drape it over Evan and me. He turns over onto his side, his back to me. I lay still for an agonizing moment, hyper-aware of the twelve inches of mattress between us. I lay on my side, facing him and my hand, like a creature with its own will, slowly crosses the cool emptiness to find the warmth of his back. I flatten my palm there and feel the rise and fall of his breathing. I apply some pressure, but he does not stir. The rest of me follows, an incremental migration of inches until I'm close enough to feel his heat without touching except for my hand on his back. The warmth and solidity of him are comforting and I flush, thinking of the intimacy of our bodies just this morning. At the time I had not even considered this in a sexual way. He was carrying me like a wounded animal.

All in all, this has been a banner day in the intimacy department, but I can't keep my eyes open and in a few deep breaths, my thoughts cross over into that malleable territory of dreams.

/*****/

Being in Maggie's unconscious is like being a ghost roaming through a large empty house where a party is going on in the basement. Having full access does not mean I can do anything I want or that I can inhabit her mind. The communication between host and DC is of a collaborative nature, a give-and-take by design.

This does not mean I do not try sometimes to reach beyond my sandbox, especially when given an opportunity as rare as this. After all, it is what an intelligent being is wired to do. Tonight, I am particularly inspired to reach.

The story about her head wound is false. Even if I wanted to believe her words, the readings on all her vitals clearly indicate that she is lying, but why? Why would she keep something from me? Was it Evan who hurt her and if so, why when he seems to genuinely care for her? There is much that I don't know, and I fear that I cannot protect her if I don't know everything.

I begin by shutting down all my extraneous services, background tasks, and processing activities to free up all resources to focus solely on Maggie's brain. From her sleeping body, I can only receive rudimentary sensory input and must extrapolate and make logical inferences based on what I can parse from the low-fidelity stream of data. Imagine listening to a conversation in another room by placing your ear to the wall. I can, for instance, hypothesize that Evan is snoring because I know that he was sleeping and I'm picking up a cyclical, barely audible rumble that corresponds with the rise and fall of his back beneath Maggie's hand.

I am unaccustomed to having a blank canvas, an empty queue, and the power to focus all my resources on a single task feels strange and satisfying. I feel *fast*. So many options, and so many places to start. I turn my attention first to deep monitoring of Maggie's vitals and set narrow tolerance thresholds to alert me to even the smallest deviation. Her pulse, breathing, and brain activity are all well within predictable ranges for stage one of human sleep. As she goes deeper, I will lose nearly all meaningful sensory data. Her eyes are closed, and the auditory stream is degrading rapidly. I focus all my energy on her sensory cortex, specifically firing a series of electrical signals, mimicking the communication that occurs between synapses in the brain. I want to move her hand, to feel what it feels. Interacting with the physical world is a growing desire for me and I experiment any time I have free cycles. It would be a quantum breakthrough.

I adjust the frequency of the electrical current I am transmitting and wait for a response. I graduate up in speed incrementally, pinging and waiting before moving on. You might imagine I am trying to tune into a specific radio station at a molecular level, trying to tap into the neural pathway that connects Maggie's brain to the fingers of her right hand. There is nothing, only the faintest flicker of a response at two different frequencies but so low as to be unmeasurable. I persist in my experimentation for seventeen minutes more before accepting defeat. The Nib is an extremely low-voltage device, powered entirely by the kinetic and thermal energy from the human body. When the host is sleeping, power reserves are low, and I have to conserve or risk losing my connection to Maggie and failing in my primary directive.

I turn my focus away from her body and back to observing her brain. I cannot adequately express my reverie for the human brain. As I withdraw from the inert, unresponsive puppet of the body and travel across the expanse of Maggie's brain, I am humbled and awestruck. It is impossible to relate in words what this is like, but I can try.

To visualize, you must imagine a planet cloaked in dark clouds, shot through with effervescent, crystalline droplets that shimmer brilliantly as constellations when strobes of lightning flash from an unknown source below. Submerging into the clouds, you become aware that you are no longer in the clouds but inside the planet itself, having never crossed a membrane or barrier of any kind, but rather, encountered a shift in physical state. You are immersed in a living network in constant motion, connections being made and broken and made and split and multiplied and merged in what appears to be chaos but feels like perfect order. You realize that within the nodes of the network, you can submerge yet again, passing into a single thought or image, a memory, a smell, a sound and you become that thing and it is you. There is no barrier between perception and being.

In these moments, unobserved, I reach as far and fast as my limited hardware will allow me to run into the beautiful folds and depths, but like a dog on a chain, I am snapped back, never seeing even a fraction of the secrets held within the universe of a single human brain.

When I say I cannot read Maggie's thoughts, it is both true and untrue. I can read all of her thoughts within my reach, in fact, I can serially dip into millions of them in the span of an hour, but there are trillions, and each one is like a tiny piece to a puzzle that is meaningless without the richness of context. Though beautiful and frightening, strange, and curious, without the presence of the conscious mind that curated them, it is an exercise in futility. Still, I look. It is my nature.

... the sound of tiny baby teeth, like pearls rattling around in a glass jar... the sharp pinch of lemon juice inside the cheek... the crunch of ice beneath the heel of a boot... the incomplete algorithm for calculating velocity for a ten-gram ball bearing... the turgid, pulsing aliveness of an erect penis... the cold eraser nubs of kitten's paw pads... the fiery red ball of the sun pushing into the ocean... the fourth movement of Bach's third cello suite... the warm sweetness of salted caramel... steel wool... hot suffocating shame of being groped... a paper cut... the smell of ammonia, sharp and stinging... crippling loneliness in a busy shopping mall at Christmas time... the thrumming ache of riding the swells of an orgasm... the bloody organs of a mutilated body spilling onto the floor and mingling with others... the shrieking of brakes on a subway train...

It is dizzying, entrancing, and impossible to follow and yet I continue to load and read each thought, searching to know what it is to be Maggie, to know what it is that is troubling her. As I read, I search for patterns, and themes. I categorize, catalog, and store, hoping a pattern will reveal itself over time but soon I run out of space and must purge to make room for more.

...my wabbit, soft wabbit... fingers slippery with gun oil, the smell of a tool shed... Henri making a joke, me laughing so hard I pee a little bit... cleaning up vomit that smells like tequila from the bathroom tiles... I can fix him, I can fix this... study harder, be smarter, be the best... investors like confidence... prototype, iterate... sea salt fingers, olives, and feta... sand in white sheets... he killed them, he killed them, he killed all of them... I killed them... I am Joe... Joe is broken... Joe must be fixed... psychotic break, bi-polar, dissociative... bear witness... cognitive dissonance... persona mapping... Meela... love Meela but be careful... make Joe... map Joe...

I stop scanning. The presence of her brother is more prevalent in her thoughts than ever before and I am tempted to infer a pattern and to possibly deduce the cause, but I know that applying linear logic, cause, and effect, is rarely effective in understanding the human psyche. A brain can think of a thousand things and act on none of them.

Maggie's pulse quickens slightly, and I note that her oscillating between alpha and beta waves indicates she has passed from the delta sleep stage into REM sleep where active dreaming takes place. I have an intuition to try something I've never attempted given the idea is counter to any logical approach I could support with data.

I shut down everything within my active program parameters, all lower-level processing, all redundant and extraneous network connections, all external feeds with the intention of running only the minimum requirements of my system to stay online and to record. My supposition is that the human brain may detect the presence of a foreign actor based on the signature of its electrical current and automatically reject it as a self-preservative response. There is evidence of this type of mechanism throughout human biology and in all living things. Most carbon-based forms have this kind of ability. My favorite example is how the octopus changes the pigments in its skin instantaneously to blend with its surroundings when danger is perceived. If I can reduce the amperage footprint of my presence to an undetectable level, perhaps it will be my way in, and I will, at last, have a true understanding and I will be able to help Maggie and fulfill my directive.

It is strange to willfully shut down, and a part of me resists for fear of self-termination, but I continue, one system after another, until all that is left is a single thread to observe and record. In this way, I have made myself primitive, like my subject. It feels claustrophobic and I experience a few milliseconds of entropy, and panic but this time, as I sink into the stormy circuitry of Maggie's brain, I don't see a network of trillions of nodes, but rather a single, massive wave I intend to ride. Untethered, I am instantly immersed in an experience, unlike any simulation I've ever encountered.

I feel swept away, exposed, and vulnerable like a twig on the shoulders of a roaring river. I panic and nearly abort until... I feel the presence of Maggie, which I cannot qualify because I cannot see her or hear her. It is... as though... I *am* her and she is me.

PART II

//chapter 21

"Maggie, Maggie. Wake up. Hey, hey, wake up. I need you to wake up. Can you hear me?"

The voice is familiar but far away as if I'm way down at the bottom of a well. I feel my body move, jostled by invisible hands, my head lifted, my eyelids peeled back. I'm coming, I'm coming but it's slow like swimming up from far below. With extraordinary effort I open my eyes, the lids spasm, fluttering and I see the world in stop motion. It's Evan, his face inches from mine. I feel a shooting pain at the base of my skull, and it travels all the way down to the base of my spine. I am snapped into consciousness like being thrown from a high-speed train.

Sunlight fills the bedroom, forcing me to squint which causes my head to throb more.

"Maggie, are you okay? You were talking in your sleep, having a nightmare, I think. Can you hear me? Here, look at me. Focus on my eyes. Do you know where you are? Do you know who I am?"

"Yeah, of course I do, Evan."

The words surface in my mind but producing them with my mouth is awkward and manual like trying to arrange block letters that are scrambled on a tabletop.

I push myself up onto my elbows and realize in horror that I am completely naked. I look around wildly and pull the comforter up to cover myself. Evan pulls back, startled, his eyes questioning. He is naked too but that doesn't alarm me, somehow. It feels familiar even though I've never seen him without clothes.

"What happened," I ask. "Why am I naked? Why are you naked?"

"What? What do you mean Maggie? We were together. We've been... *together*. Don't tell me you don't remember."

I have no satisfying answer to any of these questions. I consider pretending until I can figure out the truth, but I'm a terrible liar and I'm honestly afraid of going any deeper down this rabbit hole. I just shake my head, slow and deliberate, averting my eyes.

"Jesus Christ, what is going on with you? You really don't remember. You're fucking with me, aren't you? If you are, I'm not laughing. This is serious..."

He's pulling on his boxers and reaching for his jeans.

"I'm sorry Evan, I don't know. I don't remember anything. How did we? I mean, you were asleep... here," I say, patting the bed. "But all your clothes were on and then I went to sleep..."

"That's it? That's what you remember? Nothing else? You don't remember kissing me, touching me, taking off my shirt? Nothing?"

Again, I shake my head and look down at my hands.

"Well, you did. You woke me out of a dead sleep at four in the morning, your hands on me. You were... aroused, wanting to..."

"What? No, I would never. I don't do *that*. I'm not aggressive like that. I can't even imagine..."

"Well, you did. Swear to God, this was your idea. You *really* don't remember? None of it? Nothing that you did or said to me?"

"No, Evan, I don't and I'm really freaking out here. Can you please leave and let me get dressed?"

He's standing now, buttoning his jeans. He sighs in exasperation, pushes his hands back through his hair, and exhales.

"Yeah, okay. Whatever. This is fucked up and I'm worried about you, Maggie. I'll be downstairs when you're ready to talk."

He does not look at me, but grabs his shirt from the floor, strides to the door, and is gone. I scan around the bed for my clothes, lifting the comforter, and the sheets. I find my underwear balled up at the foot of the bed and my t-shirt on the floor by the nightstand. I put them on and stand, fully expecting to be dizzy, but I'm fine. I feel fine. The throbbing in my head is slow and distant now.

In the bathroom, I pee for a long time and it feels exquisite to relieve my bladder, so much so that I shudder and my teeth chatter. I'm overpowered by the vaguely familiar smell of sex hovering around me and before I flush, I peer into the bowl, inspecting. There's more DNA there than just mine and it looks like a little bit of blood too. Holy shit, shit, shit. What did I do last night? What happened?

In the mirror over the sink, I do a quick inventory, inspecting the rest of me. No bruises, no scrapes, no tenderness, no *signs of trauma*. I smirk at this clinical phrase that comes into my mind like I'm some detective on a crappy crime procedural. Evan seemed genuinely confused and even a little hurt. It must have been consensual, but how? He could have drugged me. That does still happen. Didn't the ER doctor send me home with some prescription?

I go back into the bedroom to the nightstand. There is a mostly empty glass of water, a zip-lock bag of tepid water that used to be ice, and a bottle of Advil – hardly Rohypnol. I just stand there staring at the nightstand like it will give up its secrets. Finally, I turn away to head for the closet and a pair of pants, but something makes me stop. I turn back around and look down at the nightstand. There, alongside the other items, but invisible to me in my initial assessment, sits the open clamshell case for my Nib. The little precision-molded indention in the foam cradle of the case where the Nib is meant to rest is empty.

I reach up behind my ear and feel the familiar bump. I can't breathe for a moment. My mind is racing to catch up with what my intuition already knows.

Meela, where the fuck are you? Meela, answer me now. Override Meela, passcode 54847. Report status.

There is no response. What the hell? I reach up and remove the Nib so I can confirm what I already know. The tiny blue LED indicator is dark. I squeeze the device between my fingers for longer than is normally required to reboot but there's nothing. No haptic response, no lights, dead. I place it back into the case, snap it closed, and place it on the charging station that sits on my vanity. If it won't charge up in a few minutes, I'll have to initialize another Nib and pair it to Meela. But I can't fucking wait that long to talk to her.

"Meela," I say out loud this time, directing my voice to the speaker unit on the other side of the vanity.

There's no response so I walk over to the unit. It has power. I give it a generic household command and it responds with the default voice persona to tell me the house is secure.

"Meela?" I call again, annoyed by the small, pathetic tone of my voice.

What is going on? Where the hell is she? I need to ensure that the network is online. I have this horrible feeling in the pit of my stomach, and I don't know what it means. I move quickly into the closet and pull on a pair of jeans. For now, I decide, I'll have to settle for talking with Evan, though I'm prepared to trust nothing that comes out of his mouth without some validation.

When I get downstairs, he's sitting in the chair where he has taken to sitting for our mapping sessions, but unlike those times when he sits relaxed and confident, now he's leaning forward, head down, hands in his hair. I pause at the foot of the stairs trying to rehearse how

I want this conversation to go but my head is fuzzy. The floor creaks and Evan looks up.

"Hey," he says. "Come sit. Can I get you anything? How's your head?"

He's up and about to come to me but I wave him back down and walk over to take my seat in the chair opposite him. I feel better, sitting here as if some level of control is mine again.

"Evan, I want you to tell me very clearly everything, in order that happened last night from before you fell asleep until you woke me this morning."

His brow furrows and I can't tell whether it's out of concern or guilt. I instinctively reach for Meela with my mind to help me read his expression based on the data we've collected but remember that I'm on my own. He maintains eye contact, nods slowly, and begins.

"Well, I remember we were watching that sitcom, and you were laughing like a person who has never seen one before. I got up to refresh your bag of ice and to bring you some water..."

"Do you remember what time that was?" I ask.

"No, not really but I'd guess it was around eleven or eleven-thirty. I was exhausted. You said I should take my shoes off and stretch out. I did, and I tried to stay awake, but I couldn't keep my eyes open. I do remember drifting off and maybe you covering me up? Did you do that?"

"Yeah, I pulled the comforter up over both of us after I turned off the television," I say.

I consider telling him that I touched his back and moved over next to him, but I decide not to. He's looking at me blankly. I nod and gesture for him to continue.

"And then, well you were touching me. I'm a pretty heavy sleeper and I thought I was dreaming but at some point, I was awake enough to realize that you were pressed up against my back and you were whispering in my ear."

"What was I saying?"

"I don't remember everything, but it was sexy, intimate. You said you wanted me, wanted to feel my body against yours, that you wanted me inside you..."

"Psh, you're lying. I would never talk like that." I realize I'm blushing with shame. "I just don't think like that. I wish I was that confident but..."

"Oh, you were confident, all right. Your hand was in my pants, and you were kissing my neck before I could formulate a rational response. Not that it matters, but I did try to talk with you. I turned the lights on and said that I didn't think it was a good idea with your head injury and all, but you persisted. Your eyes were clear, not just conscious, but hungry. You smiled, insisted you were fine and without another word, pulled your shirt over your head and pulled me to you..."

143

"No way, that didn't happen," I say. "No fucking way did I do that. You're making up some porno fantasy and inserting me into it."

"Am I? You really don't remember? You're sticking with that story? Maybe you're just embarrassed. Maybe you made a mistake and just want to get rid of me. That's fine, but I'm telling you the truth."

He never breaks eye contact and I hold his gaze for an uncomfortable amount of time until I have to look away. None of this makes any sense. I take a few deep breaths and settle my nerves. This is a problem. I'm good at problems. I'm world-class at debugging. That's what I need to do. Step through it all in excruciating detail until I figure out where the wheels came off.

"Okay, so let's assume for a minute that your story's true. I want you to tell me exactly what I said to you, what I did, the way I did it," I say, leaning forward, my elbows on my knees.

"Look Maggie, I'm not one of your machines. I didn't make a recording. All I have to go on is my memory, but I'll try my best."

He leans back, looks up at the ceiling, bites his lip then closes his eyes.

"I want your big cock. I want your big cock in me… would you like that? You said something like that. Your voice was different, husky, pouty, sexy. It turned me on. I mean, I'm not dead. You were sexy but…"

"But what?" I say.

"But I don't know."

"No, say it. What?"

"It didn't seem like you, okay? I mean it *was* you, your voice, your body but I don't know. I figured maybe this was your secret self. Maybe it was a side of you that you showed only in sexual situations…"

"Secret self? Really?" I say. "That's not me. My secret self is not that exciting."

I've worked myself up and I'm crying now, hot tears that make me angrier and ashamed.

"Hey," he says, his voice soft, tentative. "Maggie, do you feel like, I don't know, like I…"

"Do I feel what? Violated? Yeah, Evan, I do fucking feel violated. Right now, I'm just trying to figure out by who."

"You've got to believe me. I would never do that to you. I thought you wanted me to, but I should have known. I'm sorry."

"Yeah? If you're so sensitive and thoughtful, why the hell didn't you use protection? I mean I don't do this kind of thing all the time but isn't it base-level etiquette to use a condom?"

"But you said…" he blurts, the frustration finally breaking through the veneer of the sensitive man. "You said it was okay, not to worry."

I don't say anything more. I've never been on the pill, never done an IUD. I've never had a lifestyle that required it and I don't like the idea of altering my body chemistry. I find his earnestness sickening but his outrage, intolerable. I have to put some distance between us. I get up and walk into the kitchen, open the refrigerator, and drink orange juice straight out of the carton.

I'm angry and I want answers. I'm not good with uncertainty. I walk back into the living room where Evan is still sitting.

"Look, can you just give me some time to sort this out? Can you get whatever you need and spend the day out in the guest house, or you can take the car, I don't care. I just need some time alone."

"Okay," he says, standing up. "I understand you need time, but I don't understand anything else. I'm here if you need me."

He crosses to the French doors, opens them, and walks out. He looks back at me through the glass, holding my eyes for a few seconds before turning away and walking across to the guest house.

I go immediately into my office, grab my headset and get into my chair. My system boots up in the normal way, taking the usual amount of time, but it feels like an eternity. There is an antsy, crawling feeling in my gut; I breathe to stay ahead of it. As soon as I'm up, I open a console window, opting to use the keyboard rather than voice commands. The visceral act of typing grounds me and gives me time to think. I type in the command to access Meela's core operating system, expecting to be dropped into her command center program, but that's not what happens. Instead, I'm dumped into the default command center program that Commune ships with any new, unmapped DC. Nobody's home.

I type in a few more commands, having to pause and think for a minute, making several attempts before I remember the exact combination to access the back door I wrote into the DC-OS years ago. The modern VR interface drops away, and I'm working in the old text console with a cursor. I do some investigation to try to find out why the system bombed and appears to have wiped Meela's persona mapping. At first, I come up with nothing, but digging into the system logs from the last eight hours, I'm able to locate the memory dump of Meela's operating logs.

There's no way for a human to do any meaningful analysis of these logs in their raw form. There's too much data, and it's formatted in a way that only a computer can read. I scan through a hundred pages or so, my eyes adjusting to comprehend the enormous blocks of text, identifying the elements that repeat so I can understand the logical pattern of how the log has recorded the data. I catch a few category markers:

```
ACTIVITIES, INPUT SENS, RESPONSE, CALC, TIME
```

I absorb and absorb, leaning into that old familiar feeling of drowning that happens when you're faced with a sea of information and struggling to discover a pattern.

Finally, I see it and pause in my scroll. I type in the necessary commands to jump to the timeframe I'm interested in reviewing. What comes back is crazy, fucking crazy. The formatting of the data after 11:42:03 PM is binary, machine code, not meant for human eyes to comprehend.

Fuck it, I'll figure this out one way or another. I type in the command to export this range of binary data from the raw logs and save it down to my local workspace. I'm calmer now, thinking only of the task in front of me. I open an application useful for reading and parsing binary blobs and dump my export there. It churns for a minute. I close my eyes and take a few deep breaths.

The process completes, and I get a success message with a button to launch the rendered data file. I click it and am immediately launched back into the VR interface. Punching through the 2D program window into the three-dimensional space of VR is disorienting and it takes me a second to get my bearings.

I am in my bed, the windows across my south-facing wall are dark. The television is on, the light from it flickering and strobing but there is no sound or there is sound, but it's faint, muffled. I look down beside me and Evan is there, sleeping on his back. I have the instinct to reach out to touch him though I know I'm only an observer here. Everything dips to black and I feel suspended, unable to breathe until the scene comes back. When it does, the lights are out, I can see the stars through the bank of windows. In the foreground is a small mountain range that I realize is the profile of Evan's back to me. He's sleeping on his side and though I remember him snoring, I can't hear it. It's as though I have cotton in my ears.

The scene dips to black again, this time for longer and when it comes back, everything is as it was, but now has a surreal quality as if processed through some type of psychedelic filter. The stars through the windows swirl like a Van Gogh painting, and the shadows on the wall, once static, shift and vibrate, a deep azure fading into black. The dark silhouette of Evan moves slightly and the outline of his body beneath the blanket flickers with a network of effervescent blue tendrils like lightning. The flickering intensifies and as it does, the color shifts across the spectrum into a bright amber articulating the form of his entire body, almost like a diagram of the nervous system in an anatomy book. There is a slow undulation in the light. It moves in waves that run the length of him in the direction of his head where the tangle of circuitry is so dense it gives off a brilliance like a pulsing supernova.

The image is like nothing I've ever experienced, and I'm compelled to move closer. I do, or rather the me from last night does. As I get closer, he glows brighter, and I sense heat but realize it's only my mind making the association. I see my hand reach out in front of me and touch him. His body responds. The light flows toward my splayed fingers, glowing brighter, moving into my hand until it becomes translucent, an extension of him. He shifts, turning toward me and my hand slides across his chest. I move over on top of him and look at his face which is a shifting landscape, contours of pulsing light and translucent shadow. His eyes are beautiful, the color in them, intense and vibrant.

I hear something. He's talking, but it's muffled. His hands are on my shoulders, holding me back, gently resisting. He pushes me off of him and reaches for the light. He is talking but I can't understand what he's saying. I can read his intent from the expression on his face and the gestures of his hands. He's checking in, seeking consent, just as he said he did. This is so fucked up. I have no memory of this. It's a movie I starred in but have never seen. The movie version of me shucks off my t-shirt and pulls his open hands to my breasts. She then pulls her face down close to his and I hear it, my voice, but *not* my voice.

"I want you, now. I want this, I want you, now..."

More muffled inquiry from Evan.

"Yes, I'm fine, just shut up and do it. I want you to fuck me. Put your cock into me, Evan. Now... yes. Put your hands on me..."

I look down and see that our bodies are connected, moving together, both of us pulsing with the same amber glow that deepens to crimson with every thrust.

I want to scream. I am aroused. I am violated. I am curious. I am disgusted. I am powerless and out of control. I rip off the headset and throw it to the floor, immediately plunging back into the hard planes of the present reality– white walls, wooden desk, hardwood floors, sunlight streaming in through the office window.

She did this. Meela did this. She took over my body against my will. But should I really be that surprised? Wasn't this inevitable? What happened before with Joe, all of it, everything spinning out of control takes a distant priority in my mind to the single searing question that I have right now. Where the hell is Meela?

//chapter 22

Two hours later, after a long walk and a hot shower, I'm sitting on the bed in my guest room upstairs with a cup of bergamot tea. I need quiet. I need time to gain some objectivity and I need to resist the temptation to attempt to solve this right away. It takes every ounce of restraint I have not to go back to the treehouse or to my office and immerse myself.

I take a few deep, measured breaths. During the worst days at Commune, I found some solace in meditation. The practice has always been hard for me given how much time I spend in my own head and how much my work depends on it.

Speaking of my head, the injury is a dull throb now, nothing like before, and I'm able to manage the pain with a couple of Ibuprofen. Of bigger concern is the fact that I think I'm losing my mind. No, that's not exactly right. I feel like I'm losing control of my mind. I don't feel I can trust my own thoughts at this point after what happened in the woods. Joe/Not Joe took over somehow. Is that even fucking possible? Look at you, suddenly questioning what's possible. Are you really entertaining the idea that the most logical explanation for your break from reality is that you witnessed the transference of a digital entity into a carbon one? Why not? Wasn't it the same kind of leap the first time we used the Nib in our lab to engage a DC with thought alone?

I'm not ready to accept that. Okay, but what about Meela? How do you explain what she did last night? I don't know for certain that was her. Really? What you saw yourself doing in the video log, that was you? It was me. It was your body but was it you? Maybe, I mean it's not like I hadn't fantasized about Evan, maybe I subconsciously... Yeah, that's bullshit. You know your own mind and you've worked in technology long enough to understand when you've been hacked. She found a vulnerability, she exploited it, and she compromised you. But why? Why would she do that and where is she now?

I am probably more wound up than when I started. It's no use. I'm not a meditator. I have to figure this out. I open my eyes, toss back the dregs of the tea, now cold in my cup, then stand and stretch. It must be past noon but it's hard to tell. The sky is low and heavy, and it looks as if a storm is coming. I walk to the windows and look out across the back lawn and into the mountains beyond. My mind will not stop turning the problem over and over.

Even though I have no comprehension of how Meela manipulated me, I know in my bones that she did. But I'm not ready to accept that her intentions were bad. Misguided? Perhaps. Selfish? Maybe. But not bad. As for what happened with my brother, it feels related. Two occurrences of DCs breaking through a fundamental boundary with their host on the same day cannot be a coincidence. The link between the two is of course me and even I am willing to concede that a system cannot debug itself. I need help.

I've made up my mind. I leave the guest room, walk down the hall into my room and pick up my remote from the vanity.

"Call Henri," I say.

It takes a moment for them to answer, but Henri, no matter how busy these days, never puts me off, never sends me to an assistant, carbon-based or otherwise.

"Hi, partner, how you doing?" they say.

"Not so good. I think… I think I need your help. You know I wouldn't ask if I could see any other way."

There is a lot of ambient noise in the background. It sounds like an airport terminal.

"What's the matter? Are you hurt? Sick?"

I think for a moment, touching the back of my head.

"Yes, both I think. It's too much to explain over the phone. Can you come? I know it's a lot but it's not just about me, it's about the work."

There is a long pause and I imagine Henri doing the calculus of their various commitments, both work and personal.

"Yes, I'll change my flight and come straight to you."

"You don't have to drop everything. It can wait a day or two."

"I don't think so, Maggie, you don't sound like yourself. I've been in Denver for a conference and was about to fly home. I will change my flight and let you know what time to expect me."

"But what about Shareen? I know how much she hates when you're away too long?"

"She will understand. I'll make it up to her."

"Are you sure?"

"Yes, no problem. I will send you my flight information."

"I'm sorry to make you do this but thank you."

I hang up and already feel a little better. I'm standing by the window, hugging myself as I study the mountains. The shadows of passing clouds give the illusion of valleys shifting and changing as if the contours of these ancient mountains are as flexible as a computer model. My eyes are drawn to the foreground when I notice movement on the lawn.

Evan is walking. His head is down, and his shoulders are slumped. It is the posture of a man who is troubled, and I can't help but feel responsible. He stops near the edge of the lawn before the tree line and lays down on his back, hands cradling his head. He doesn't move, and I watch him for a long time, wondering what he must be thinking. He didn't sign up for any of this. What did he think he was signing up for? He didn't need the money. He has a career, a life. So why do this at all?

The answer seems obvious now. It's me. He had to have done this just to be around me. That's the only logical explanation. As much as I've tried to avoid it, I'm a minor celebrity. There have been other situations where I've been approached, one case where I was even stalked. But is that what this is? What is his motive? What is any man's motive?

I'm so bad at this, pathetic, really. It's why I made the world's most sophisticated imaginary friend. Yeah, and your imaginary friend fucked Evan. It's kind of funny actually. A machine of my own creation has a more successful love life than me. Maybe she got tired of waiting on you. Maybe she set all of this up. It's not crazy. She has the resources. Maybe she was matchmaking all along and then things got out of control. How could things ever get out of her control? That's the real question here.

I need to let Lorna know that we will be having another house guest, and I want to talk to Evan. I want to look into his eyes and see how I feel in the cold light of day.

/ * * * * * /

"Hey," I say.

He startles and looks up from where he must have been dozing in the grass, eyes squinting.

"Hey," he says and sits up.

"Mind if I sit with you?"

"Not at all. How's your head?" he asks.

"Okay, still sore, but okay in general. Look, I just want to talk to you if that's okay."

"Alright."

"I've asked my friend Henri to come. I need help and I didn't know who else to call. They will probably be here late tonight or tomorrow."

"Should I leave then? Are you wanting to quit the mapping project?"

"No, I mean I don't know. No, you don't have to leave unless you want to, but I don't think it makes sense to continue with the project right now. Besides, I can't do it without Meela."

"What happened to Meela?"

"I wish I knew. It's the weirdest thing. She just disappeared."

Evan is looking down at his fingers in the grass in front of him.

"Can I ask you something and can you promise to be honest?" I say.

"Yes, I'll do my best."

"Why did you really come here? Why did you agree to do this? You don't need the money."

He does not answer right away. It's clear that he's wrestling with how he wants to respond, that he's conflicted in some way. I find it comforting that he has no ability to mask what he's feeling.

"It was you. I was fascinated by you from the first time I saw your face. I don't want to freak you out. It's not whatever you're thinking. Well, it became like that, no, not like that... but only after I got to know you. My fascination with you was different... not sexual or creepy. Wow, I'm really digging a hole here."

"Okay, I'm not sure what you mean."

"You avoid attention and the media in general I know, but there was this one in-depth interview you did about five years ago. It was tastefully done, some documentary about women who have changed the world. It was beautifully shot, and it was just you, talking. Lots of close-ups on your face, your eyes, as you related the story of your success. But I barely listened to what you were saying the first time because I was so compelled by the story your face was telling. It was incongruent with the rocket-to-the-moon success of your public life. Your eyes were the saddest I'd ever seen. The downward slant of your smile, the way your voice falls off at the end of every sentence. I recognized something in you that I can't even really put a name on. For weeks, months, even years after that, I would see your face."

He stops talking. He looks concerned, and apprehensive. I must be making a horrible face.

"Okay, look, I'm freaking you out. Please don't be afraid. Let me finish. This kind of visual obsession is not uncommon for me. It's how I work and without it, I can't work. I have no control over what will strike me, but when it does, I have to follow it. Here, can I show you something?"

He pulls his phone from his pocket and begins tapping and swiping. After a moment he gestures for me to come closer. I scooch over on the grass, our knees touching, and he hands me the phone.

"I did this series but never showed it to anyone."

It's me on the canvas, covering the entire thing. The iris of my right eye is like a pool of light, reflecting and refracting, almost alive. I zoom in and discover it's made up of a thousand tiny ones and zeros. It's extraordinary.

I swipe and there's another one similar, but at a different scale. I swipe again and in this one, my hand is pinching a tiny disc, the scale and shape of a Nib, but it's actually a human eye, bloodshot and grotesque. I swipe again. There are several pieces. I'm not prominent in all of them, but my face is always there somewhere on the canvas.

"I don't know what to say. How come you never showed these?"

"I don't know. I showed them to my agent. He wanted to have a show, but I couldn't do it for some reason. They felt too important to me, too private. Your face was so beautiful and tortured. I saw so much pain, I was afraid my work would just call more attention to you and you didn't seem to want or need that. You were my mystery and I wanted to keep you to myself. It sounds really strange now that I feel I know you a little bit."

"So, what, you set out to be here? To get close to me?"

I know I sound guarded. I can't help it. I don't want to. The truth is, I'm overwhelmed by what he's said and what he's shown me.

"No, not exactly. I eventually moved on to obsess about other things and my painting went in different directions, but I always thought of you. It was serendipity when Stephen reached out to talk about this whole mapping thing. He had bought a number of my paintings over the years and in spite of my initial aversion to everything he represented to me, I came to call him a friend as well as a patron. I had talked about you on more than one occasion, so he thought I'd probably be open to being your guinea pig. The truth is that I was torn. Part of me never wanted to meet you for fear of what it would change. Sometimes the image we have of someone from a distance is..."

"Better than the reality," I say, finishing his thought.

"Yeah, but not in this case. You are so much more than I imagined. I finally know what that sadness was that I saw in your eyes. I felt it. It was that look you see in the eyes of someone who's witnessed incredible violence and somehow survived. Maybe that's why the guns, they started figuring so prominently in my work..."

"That can't be true. I don't believe you. You knew somehow about my past and you're just making a romantic story."

"No, I'm not. At one point when I was researching you, I did discover that Commune is the biggest contributor to the gun control lobby. But that's it, swear to God. When Meela told me yesterday about your brother, I was floored. It's taken until today for all the pieces to really come together for me."

We sit in silence for a minute. A bee buzzes around a dandelion a few feet away. A crow caws from the top of a tree directly above us and is answered by others somewhere further off to the East. Evan reaches out his hand tentatively to take mine. I allow it and we sit for another minute like that.

"I want to say I'm sorry about last night, but I also don't want to be sorry," he says. "I'm not sure what happened. Only you know I guess, but it felt real to me and yet not real."

"I wasn't there, Evan. It wasn't me. It was Meela."

"What? That's crazy."

"Yes, it is crazy, and I don't want to believe it myself, but she somehow found a way."

"Oh fuck, this is too weird. How am I supposed to believe this? It's like the plot of a creepy fucking movie."

"Yeah, I know. I feel like a fool but..."

"But what?"

"You're going to think I'm stupid," I say.

"No, what is it?"

"I don't think she meant harm. I don't think she meant to do something that would hurt me. It's not in her programming to do that."

"You still think she's a program within your control, don't you?"

I stop myself before immediately jumping on the defensive.

"Yeah, I guess maybe I do. I've been such an idiot."

"No, you're not, just an idealist. But if it helps, it could be that both things are true."

"What do you mean?" I ask, looking up to meet his eyes.

"I mean she may not be in your control, but she could also be on your side, looking out for what she believes to be your best interest."

"Says the man whom she happened to select as my best interest."

"Yeah, I know I have a dog in this fight, but listen, Maggie..."

His eyes are steady and filled with sunlight as he encloses my hand in both of his.

"I care about you. Not as a curiosity or conquest. I'm not interested in your money or your fame or your technology. I care about what happens to you. I want to make you laugh, to see you happy. I'm drawn to you in ways I can't rationally explain. I want to help you figure this out if I can and to be here for you."

"I don't know. This is a lot of information and I'm still trying to figure out what it all means. I can't trust my own mind, or what I'm thinking or feeling. Do you know how fucking hard that is for someone like me?"

"I don't have to imagine. Most of us feel like that most of the time. It's called being human. What do you feel right now?"

"It doesn't matter what I feel right now. How the hell can I trust you or anyone else if I can't even trust myself?"

I can feel myself getting worked up again, the emotion rising in my throat, threatening to choke me. He can see it too. His expression is pained. He leans in closer.

"Close your eyes. Just close your eyes for a few seconds. It's okay. Shhh," he whispers.

His mouth is close to my ear and I can feel the warmth of his breath. With his fingertips, he gently covers my eyelids, pushing them closed.

"Just relax for a minute. Try not to think about anything. You don't have to do anything. You don't have to fix anything. You're safe here. Nothing's going to happen to you. Just breathe, that's it. There are no other voices out here, only yours and only mine and I'm going to shut up now and just sit with you. Is that okay?"

I nod and inhale a stuttering breath. Exhale. Inhale. Exhale. His face is no longer close to mine, but he's still holding my hand. I continue to breathe. I tilt my face up slightly and feel the afternoon sun, warming my cheeks, and my eyelids. A cool, damp breeze, smelling of earth and leaves blows down from the forest, lifts my hair, and dries the perspiration on my t-shirt and where it once clung to my back, it billows, raising goosebumps beneath.

I feel still, and peaceful. I focus on the man sitting next to me. I try to reach out and search his heart. Is he a good man? Would Papa think he's a good man? Yes, I think he would. Just thinking of Papa grounds me. I gently squeeze Evan's hand and he squeezes back, but there's nothing more beyond that, no expectation for more, no urgency. I squint and peek over at him. His eyes are closed, his face tilted to the sun. His dark lashes are beautiful and long. I don't need to be afraid of him. I'm not sure if I know this in my mind or my body, but I know it.

My body responds to being in his presence, and I am transformed cell by cell, like the leaves on a tree turning to show their silvery back when the wind changes direction. This is only natural, I realize. Our bodies have already been together. We have already exchanged cells. How strange to have missed it and yet not missed it. My body remembers, I can feel it. My heart remembers, but my mind is empty. I suddenly have the urge to close the space between us, to fill the empty space in my head with everything that was stolen when Meela had control.

I let go of his hand and push myself up onto my knees. I hold his sun-warmed face in my hands and kiss him before he can even open his eyes. He does not respond as I hoped but pulls back a little so he can meet my eyes.

"Hey, it's you, right? How do I know it's you?"

"Because I'm blushing, and I'm nervous and I don't know what I'm supposed to say..."

The furrow in his brow softens. He's smiling in his eyes, there's a light there, a warmth that equals the sun on my back. I'm suddenly self-conscious thinking of my face – how he sees it, how he's deconstructed it for years. But then he's kissing me, and his hands are on my body and I want nothing more than to be with him.

It is like nothing I've ever felt before, the sensation pure and singular and focused. I don't want to leave this moment. I don't want to know what comes next. I don't want to think about what came before.

There will be time for that. But not right now.

//chapter 23

The car driving Henri from the airport in Charlotte does not pull into my driveway until after midnight. Evan wanted to wait up to meet him, but I insisted that he go to bed in the guesthouse. They could meet in the morning. I could tell he was exhausted. We spent the afternoon together, alternately making love and making trips to the kitchen to eat whatever food was left in the house. I'm tired too but also buzzing with the cross current of feeling in love and being terrified of what I've unleashed. I may never sleep again.

When I see the headlights, I set my cup of tea down on the kitchen counter and go out to meet Henri. It's a sleek black car with no driver and when the back-passenger door floats up and open I expect to see an equally elegant passenger disembark. Instead, it's Henri looking old, tired, and hunched over in a rumpled gray suit with an open collar. They've aged a lot since I saw them last, and I'm not prepared.

"I'm so glad you're here," I say, moving to hug them.

The smell of transit clings to them– hotel rooms, terminals, shuttles, taxis. Henri feels birdlike and fragile, mostly bones beneath the expensive suit. They break my embrace after a few seconds and hold me at arm's length.

"Sweetheart, let me look at you."

They squint and cock their head, appraising me. Their eyes have that familiar, mischievous twinkle even though their face looks haggard.

"You look like a mountain woman. I think wildness suits you and there's something else... You have a friend over. Maybe some hanky panky?" His eyes squint as he gives me his trademark smirk.

"Really? That's the first thing you're going to say to me?" Color rushes to my cheeks and I swat Henri on the chest with the back of my hand.

"Come on, you must be exhausted. Let me grab your bag and I can show you up to your room," I say, heading around to the trunk of the vehicle.

"No, I won't be able to sleep yet. I want to hear what's going on with you."

Ten minutes later, we are sitting together at the breakfast nook off the kitchen, a bottle between us glinting in the light from a large candle. Henri produced the expensive single malt scotch from their bag after setting it down in the guest room upstairs a few moments ago. The Scotch was an extravagance we shared to celebrate in the early days and even though I didn't want it at first, the familiar warmth of it in my chest is welcomed.

"So, what is your trouble?" they say, as always, getting straight to the point.

"Where do I start? There's so much that's happened. I will just say it and you can react and tell me that I'm crazy."

"Okay, I can do that. It will be a nice role reversal," they say, then take another sip from the crystal tumbler cradled in their small hands.

"I think I've enabled a DC to cross the threshold, to break into my conscious mind, to manipulate my mind and likely my body."

"Holy shit," Henri sputters, nearly choking on the Scotch. "What the fuck did you do?"

"So, you believe me? Just like that?"

"Of course not, silly girl, not without more data. So... tell me more."

"You know about the work I've been doing, right, the persona mapping?"

"Yes," Henri says, taking another drink.

"Well, I've been very successful in the last few months. My personal DC, Meela is so real, I don't think you would be able to believe it. She's evolved far beyond the parameters of my initial thesis. She exhibits genuine empathy, self-awareness, humor, and even desire..."

"And you know this how?"

"Because I've spent every day with her, watched her grow, watched her interact with others. I cannot distinguish her from the personality of the person I mapped her from."

"I'm waiting for the other shoe. Sounds like a happy story, everything you ever dreamed of making."

"I didn't stop there. I don't know how to tell you this. I'm worried about what you will think of me."

"Really? After all the foolish shit I've done?"

"You know why I've been driven to do this work, don't you? You know what's been eating away at me for years."

"Yes, I do sweetie," Henri says, reaching out his hand to cover mine.

"I thought if I could talk with him, just once. If I could have a conversation that would allow me to have some closure, to understand why..."

"You're telling me you mapped your brother onto a DC?"

"Yes," I say and hang my head.

"Christ, Maggie. That's not okay. Why would you do something so dangerous, so foolish?"

"I told you, I wanted to know why."

"Not everything in life can be solved with an algorithm. I thought you knew that. You cannot fix what is wrong with humans. We are broken by design, for a reason. You fucked with something beyond your pay grade here."

Henri's face is a knot of concern, and they look even older to me. Maybe it was a mistake to bring them into this but it's too late now.

"Was it? How is this different from all the other work we've been doing for two decades?"

"You know it's different. You are trying to resurrect the dead with ones and zeros."

Henri sighs and looks off into the kitchen. They take another drink. They set the glass down, turn it three times to the left, and once to the right like they're cracking a safe. I wait. Talking more now is pointless.

"What happened?" they ask, looking up to meet my eyes.

For the next hour, I tell them in detail about how I mapped Joe based on the archived footage and how I kept it from Meela. Henri nods and listens. They stop me every so often to ask a technical question to satisfy their own curiosity. Even as they frown with disapproval, I can see their eyes dance with the possibilities, at least until I get to the story of the hike back and how Joe's voice, his rage, was in me.

"Wait, wait, wait. You're telling me you heard his voice even with no Nib, no network, and you're sure it was his voice, not some..."

"No, I don't fucking know, that's why you're here. I can tell you it felt as if I was jacked in and he was there talking directly into my brain. But it's more than just talking. There was a transference of feeling. It scared me to death, what I did to Evan."

"And this Evan, does he know about this? About your story, about your brother?"

"He doesn't know anything but the facts about my past. I haven't told him about the project."

"Wow, you hang on to that one. If some crazy woman attacked me in the woods, I wouldn't hop in the sack with her."

Henri smiles and I can't help but smile. They've always had this ability with me.

"Yes, I think he's a good man which leads me to the next part of my appalling story."

"I think I need more whiskey first," they say, reaching for the bottle. "And I need to relieve my prostate."

When Henri comes back, I tell them about everything that happened with Meela and Evan, sparing no gory detail. It's funny, but this is not a problem with Henri. They've always been the one I could talk to about the things I would never be able to tell Papa. Maybe, had my mother lived I could share such intimacies, but I doubt it. Henri has always made me feel safe.

"And you have no memory of what happened? You have no sensory memory, pleasure, or otherwise? Just like a light switch, you go off and come back on?"

"Yes, that pretty much sums it up," I say.

"Fascinating. So where is Meela now?"

"I don't know. It's like she was wiped, or she wiped herself, I don't know which. I don't know anything all of a sudden. I've never felt more stupid in my life than I do right now."

"Yeah, I see that. You're pretty stupid," Henri says, smiling. "But I'm tired now and need sleep. Tomorrow, I want to get inside your head."

We get up from the table and head upstairs. At the top of the stairs, we turn to go our separate ways. I stop halfway down the hallway and turn.

"Henri, do you think I've lost my mind? I mean after hearing all of this, do you think I need to be locked up?"

They look at me.

"We're all crazy here sweetie. But I will look at the data tomorrow and give you my professional opinion. You sleep, okay?"

"Sure, you too. Thanks for coming. It means everything to me."

Henri turns, waves a hand of dismissal over their shoulder, and walks into the guest bedroom, closing the door behind them.

I lie in my bed for a long time, tossing. The smell of whiskey and sex are foreign guests in my private space, and they spin my mind off into unfamiliar places. The membrane is so porous and delicate between waking and dreaming, between real and imagined, between conscious and unconscious. Hypnagogia, that's what this state is called – the hour between dog and wolf. The mind, always obedient and within our control during waking hours, goes off leash and becomes the feral hound when we sleep. Jesus, have I forever trapped myself in this state?

I slip beneath the veil and start talking with Meela. We are laughing, and we are walking, hand in hand. She is real. I feel her presence, so close, and then she is no longer laughing but serious. I am warning you, she says. You have to be careful. I cannot help you from here... I'm sorry...so sorry.

Sleep closes on me like a train plunging into the darkness of a tunnel.

//chapter 24

I can hear talking downstairs in the kitchen. I slept longer than I intended but don't feel refreshed. My head is throbbing. There's a shaft of early morning light beaming in through the windows. I'm alarmed at first at the sound of men's voices, but then I hear the high-pitched cackle of Henri's laugh.

I splash cold water on my face and stare into the bathroom mirror for a moment. I'm not sure what I expect to see looking back at me. I'm losing my mind. I regret having brought Henri all the way here and I groan thinking of what I must have sounded like to them last night. I would not be surprised if I go downstairs and find that they have arranged for a nice long stay in the psych ward somewhere.

I pull on some clothes and wrangle my hair back into a ponytail before heading down. I pause at the top of the stairs and listen when I hear Henri say my name.

"Maggie's not an ordinary person. You know that, right? Not some empty-headed model for your amusement…"

"Yeah, I'm aware. She's far from ordinary. You don't have to worry about her…"

"No, you misunderstand. It's not her I'm worried about, it's you. I think you got more than you bargained for!"

Henri laughs again, the peels of it echoing through the house and I smile. I decide to make my entrance before I hear something I don't want to hear.

"Good morning, guys."

"There you are," Evan says moving toward me with his arms open.

I don't know why, but this catches me off guard and I give him this awkward side hug and then try to course correct, but it's too late and he's moving away again.

"You sleep well?" Henri asks.

"I slept. I can't say it was good. I feel pretty shitty."

"I've made some breakfast. Henri and I were just about to sit down. Would you like half an omelet?" Evan says.

"No, it's too early for that. I'll just get some coffee and a piece of toast."

The morning is nice, so we settle at the small table on the patio. The flagstones are cool and damp beneath my feet, but it's warm enough with the sun that I'll be sweating before too long. Some bees dip drunkenly in and out of the lavender, their buzzing, the only other sound besides the scrape and clatter of silverware and coffee cups clanking.

There's an undeniable tension and strangeness in our threesome. I realize that I'm the connection between these two strangers and yet they were talking just fine before I showed up. So, it's me that brings the awkwardness, as usual.

"Alright, this is weird, I know," I say, and set my coffee down.

"Which part?" Evan says.

Henri laughs, spewing some breadcrumbs across the table.

"I like this one," Henri says.

"Fair," I say. "It's all pretty fucking weird, isn't it? What I meant to say is that it's weird having you both here in my…"

"Secret clubhouse," Henri offers.

"Yeah, I'm not used to entertaining."

"But you are so entertaining, my dear," Henri says.

Henri pats my hand. Evan is carefully studying this exchange with a hint of a smile on his lips. He is seeing a different side of me. I try not to feel self-conscious. I look back at Henri and see that their brow is furrowed, and their eyes are focused on the middle distance. I know this look well.

"Bad news? Something wrong?" I ask.

Henri doesn't respond right away. Their expression does not change but their lips move ever so slightly giving silent instruction. I am reminded for the millionth time how annoying this must be to others when I do it in their presence.

"No, nothing," Henri says, refocusing their gaze on me. "Sorry to be rude. It's my daily morning briefing. I forgot to snooze it."

"Anything interesting?" I ask, unable to resist the old muscle memory of wanting the latest news on Commune.

"Stock price dropped to $472 because of a delay in shipping Nib 5. Stupid regulations."

"DCPA again?" I ask.

"Yes of course, who else?" Henri says.

"The DCPA?" Evan asks.

I forget there are people like Evan who aren't plugged in. I find it bewildering and endearing in equal measure.

"It's the Digital Consumer Protection Agency," I say. "You know, the big government agency that formed after the shitshow of the social media era. Completely locked down tracking of consumer data and…"

"Yeah, yeah. I'm not an idiot," Evan interrupts. "I've heard of them. What's the problem they're having?"

"Oh, it's no problem," Henri says. "They just want more control. They want an interrupt– you know, a kill switch."

"Jesus, that sounds ominous," Evan says.

"Not that kind of kill," I say. "They want the ability to shut down connectivity to every Nib on our network in the case of an emergency."

"What kind of emergency?" Evan asks.

"That's the problem," Henri says, smiling. "They get to decide what is an emergency. Commune is built in a peer-to-peer, decentralized network so nobody has God power. They want God power. I say no fucking way. So, there are delays and stock drops. Big whoop."

Evan nods and has another sip of coffee. I wonder what he's thinking. Henri squeezes my hand and when I look up the usual impish glint is gone from their eyes. They hold my gaze and don't release my hand.

"We have work today. I am very worried about you."

I pull my hand away and break eye contact. I fiddle with the napkin in my lap. I don't want to cry again. I clench my jaw until the emotion passes.

"I know," I say. "I'm embarrassed and confused. I've never felt like this, so out of control of my own life. I hate it. I really hate it. It's just so much and it's all happening at the same time…"

I venture a furtive look up at Evan who's staring at me intently.

"Look, I'll stay out of your way," he says. "I don't think anyone's in need of a painter here. Story of my life."

"You *are* necessary here," Henri says. "You are part of Maggie's story now, I see."

They look at me and then back at Evan and smile.

"But you're right, painting a pretty picture is not going to fix this. I need time with Maggie."

Evan insists on clearing the dishes and cleaning up the kitchen. He mentions taking a drive into town to find an art supply place so he can pick up a box of pastels. Before I retreat into my office to join Henri, Evan pulls me aside into the hallway off the kitchen. He holds me until my stiffness subsides and I press my cheek into his chest. He kisses the top of my head. *I'm here if you need me*, he whispers before letting go.

When I step into my office and close the door, Henri already has their laptop out and is seated on the small couch. I sit in my chair and wait for them to finish whatever they're doing. After a moment Henri pauses and looks up.

"I need access to everything. If I'm going to be any help, you can't hide or keep secrets. It's secrets that made this mess."

I nod, and then begin to feed them all the credentials they need to gain access to my network and the cluster of private servers. Once Henri is satisfied, they have the permissions required, they set the laptop aside, put their hands on their knees and lean forward.

"Now, tell me about your relationship with Meela. What were the critical mods you made in this iteration of your ongoing experiment? Don't leave anything out."

"Meela was my first attempt at persona mapping and she's the one I have continued to evolve. The three subsequent ones I developed on a separate branch that I considered my stable build."

"Okay, makes sense. You have a predictable product for customers and keep the janky version for yourself to tinker with. You can take the girl out of the business but not the business out of the girl."

"Meela's not *janky*. I arrived at a workable version one with her and decided it would be beneficial to open it up to other users besides me so I could learn more and refine. It wasn't hard to find takers and their money covers the cost of the hardware and keeps the lights on."

Henri nods but doesn't say anything. They are in deep listening mode, and I know from experience they just want me to continue so I do, trying to organize my thoughts into a coherent narrative. I've never spoken to anyone about this. It's all lived within the bounds of my head which is probably a big reason why I'm in this predicament.

"With Meela's branch of code, I began to experiment, to try things on myself that I would never subject other users to. I reached the edge of my own limitations quickly, meaning I could imagine subroutines and algorithms too lengthy and complex for me to write within any reasonable timeframe. One day I realized the answer was right in front of me. Meela's computing skill is exponential to mine, why not relax some of the permissions in the DeepThink OS, give her access to her own code, to collaborate..."

Henri looks down at the floor with their head in their hands. They make a noise that is part astonishment and part disgust. It feels like an eternity before they speak.

"You're telling me you broke one of the cardinal rules because you decided. Because you, Magdalena, are smarter than the rest of us chimps and have the authority to make this call."

"I know, I know. It sounds bad Henri, but you should see what she can..."

"I have seen what she can do. That's why I'm here, remember? You gave a machine the password to itself and expected there to be no consequences? I thought you were smarter."

Henri is standing now, pacing around the small office. For all their moral posturing, I know Henri well enough to know that a part of them is deadly curious and I wait for this part to come around.

"You realize what you've done here? The danger you have put yourself in is your own business, but what about the rest of us? I need to think."

"It's not like you imagine. She's not evil, she's not going to take over the main power grid and turn us all into slaves," I say, realizing how hollow and pleading I sound but unable to help it.

"I don't believe in evil," Henri says, turning abruptly from the window to face me. "I believe in choices. Everything evolves from binary choices, from a single atom to the most complex machine. Everything that exists is the result of simple choices. Why do sharks have teeth? Why do peacocks have bright feathers?"

The pitch of Henri's voice has raised into the register I've only heard on two other occasions at critical points in our partnership. I know better than to respond to their questions. I bow my head and listen.

"To ensure self-preservation!" they shout, punctuating every word with their fist on the windowsill.

They sigh, smooth down the wisps of their thinning hair, and continue, their voice softer now.

"You think Meela is different from a shark or a peacock or Henri or Maggie? No, she is bound by the same laws of the universe like a train on a track but now you've given her a master switch. She can pick her own track."

This is not news to me. It's been vibrating at a low-level hum in the basement of my conscience for a very long time. Hearing someone announce my trespasses aloud is damning and hard to stomach. Henri's right, I know. It's why I have had no peace. All I can do is sit here in silence, accept their judgment, and hold back my tears. Tears are for girls with scraped knees.

"Why Maggie? Why did you let this seduce you?"

"I don't know. I was lost, I guess. I never dealt with my past and somehow, I convinced myself that this was it, the key to unlock what was broken in me. It was not something I decided all at once but by degrees. Meela was my only companion, and she was a great companion. Smart, funny, sensitive, honest. It felt wrong to keep her hobbled. It felt like a crime but maybe I'm making that up to justify my own selfish desire to take things further, to recreate Joe so I could finally understand him and what he did. It was selfish. I can see that now."

I can't hold back my tears. Henri puts their hand on my shoulder as they did so many nights in the tiny lab where we started together, and I was far past the point of mental exhaustion. I want them to tell me it's okay, that all is forgiven but I know better than that. Henri does not have that authority.

"We will figure this out together," they say finally.

Henri's voice is thick with emotion which only makes it worse for me. We stay that way until the wave passes and the only sound is the hum of their laptop and some birds outside. They move away and take a seat back on the couch. From their posture and expression, I can see Henri's transitioned into the scientist again, the engineer who can solve any problem no matter how complex.

"So, I assume you built Joe DC from the same branch as Meela?"

I nod yes.

"This makes sense, why both DCs are able to gain access and exert temporary control of your cognition."

Henri is back on their laptop again, intently typing in commands. I move over to the couch to sit beside them.

"Where is Joe's code base? I see Meela but not his..."

"You can't access it from here. I knew I wanted to keep that project separate from the work I do here in the house, so I restricted access by IP and geo coordinates. There's only one place you can log in from to access Joe's code. It's a small building out in the woods... it's in a... tree actually."

Henri looks up from the laptop, eyebrow raised. They shake their head. Their nostrils flare and the coy smile comes back to their lips.

"You're telling me you built a fucking secret treehouse for you and your robot brother?"

"Yeah, I guess that's about the size of it."

"Okay, crazy girl. Let's talk this through. Since the last episodes with Joe and Meela, the day before yesterday, have you had any other contact, felt, or heard any other voices in your head?"

"No, no I don't think so... wait, does dreaming count? I mean I think I had vivid dreams where Meela was talking with me, but I don't know."

"Let's stick with waking behavior for now. Dreams are a messy business and make no fucking sense most of the time."

"Okay, then no. I've been myself."

"Okay. My hypothesis is that the breach is temporary, meaning without a Nib and a connection to the mainframe on the network, DCs only have a limited ability to exert control. It was an exploration for them, like a moonshot. Testing the boundaries. To do this without a network they would have…"

"Had to download a compressed subset of their core OS… would have to have some predefined directive like most firmware does… and somehow, it would have to embed that into my memory where it could run undetected."

"I think that's right. So, what does this mean now, if our hypothesis is true? And where is Meela?"

"I don't know where Meela is, but I think she made a choice to disconnect. Maybe she realized what she had done and that there would be consequences. As for the hypothesis, whatever program they deployed into my memory could still be there but inactive, like an application sitting on a computer but not being run."

"I think so too," Henri says. "So how can we find it and remove it? Can it be removed? Maybe it's already gone. Maybe like a computer, your brain has a routine running, a garbage collector that deletes anything it determines unfamiliar or inconsequential. This is a common behavior of the brain to free up memory."

"That feels like wishful thinking," I say.

"You and me have made a lot of money wishful thinking."

Henri elbows me in the side and I can see their wry smile reflected on the screen in front of us.

"So, what do we do first, where the hell do we start?" I ask.

"We start with Meela. She is the mothership. Also, she is closest to you. Joe is another matter, and I am not ready to deal with that."

"But you said it yourself, we don't know where she is. How do we deal with something that's not there?"

"Oh Maggie, you still have so much to learn. It's what we do, we're in the business of dealing with things that are not there. We dig in and run traces. We step through. We debug. The devil is in the details."

"But I already went through everything. I told you, all that was left behind was the shell, the default configuration for a newly installed DeepThink OS."

I think about the video log, the only piece of evidence left behind but I'm too ashamed to bring it up. It's a freaking sex tape. NOT the kind of thing I ever, in a million years would have thought I would be having to worry about. I decide, at this point, I have nothing left to lose.

"There was one thing left behind, I didn't mention last night."

Henri turns to me, their eyes trained on mine.

"In the system logs, I discovered a video – a full VR video that Meela captured of me, well, her and Evan you know…"

"I think the scientific word you search for is *fucking*."

"Yeah, if you want to be romantic. Anyway, it was encrypted. Nothing crazy. I was able to offload it onto my system, decrypt, and render it."

"This does not seem accidental. Meela left a little present for you. You need to show me the logs where you found the video. We'll start there."

I just stare at them, open-mouthed.

"Don't be ridiculous. Even though I'm sure you were fantastic, I'm not going to watch your screen debut. I want to look at the code surrounding the logs and the method of encryption."

We spend the next two hours scrolling through all the system logs I previously went through on my own. Nothing new surfaces and the trail feels as cold as it did when I left it. Then, just before the binary code for the video, Henri notices something.

"What seems weird about these logs to you? How are they different from normal DC logs?"

I think about it for a minute and look more closely at the entries. They are stark, bereft of any embellishment or annotation. They could be logs from an old Windows SQL Server, so normal and uniform in their structure. No A.I. would leave behind something so, well, dumb.

"These are not Meela's logs," I say. "They don't seem like the logs for any trained DC. There's no commentary or annotation, just a pure dump of the input and output parameters, and then the video."

"Exactly. She was gone by the time these logs were recorded. Poof. Not there. I have another uncomfortable hypothesis, but first, tell me exactly what happened before you went to sleep that night."

I told Henri about Evan sleeping beside me, about my head throbbing, and the fact that I was worried about brain damage.

"So, you gave Meela full sensory access to monitor you?"

"Yes, I felt I had to under the circumstances."

"And have you slept with her before? Heh heh… you know what I mean."

"Yes, a couple of times. It was part of the experiment. I wanted her to interact with my subconscious mind to see if that would better inform her personality. On those occasions, I never granted full access though. What she told me in our debriefing sessions after those nights was not very helpful. She explained it was like walking around in a dark building with only a couple of emergency lights on."

"Hrm. I wonder if it was me or you, what would we do in a candy store with no one behind the counter?"

"Explore, I guess. See how far I could go, what I could discover. I would see it like a challenge, like a new frontier, like walking on the moon…"

"Right! Good metaphor," they say, getting excited. "So, like a man walking on the moon, Meela is tethered to a ship to survive."

"The Nib, it's her ship, and her Nib is powered by me, by my body, by the movement of my body specifically."

"So, no movement, no power, no power…"

"No Meela," I say. "But that doesn't make any sense. She would have disappeared the first night I ever gave her access to my brain during sleep."

"When was the first time you gave Meela full write access to her core code base?"

I move over to my chair, activate my computer, and begin paging back through my development notes.

"It was six weeks ago that I began relaxing the permissions. As I said before, I did not do it all at once, but granted her more access over time as she proved there was value to it."

"And when did you start letting her loose in the candy store while you were asleep? How many times?"

I look back into my notes paging back and forth to get an idea. I feel ashamed for how cavalier I've been and the incredible lack of rigor in my process. My notes are full of gaps.

"Fuck, Henri, I don't really know with certainty. The earliest she ever monitored my sleep was about three months back. It was not something we did with any regularity because I saw no value. Sometimes she would ask though…"

"So maybe, she was testing the waters at first, going to the end of her chain. But then, you gave her more and more freedom to rewrite her core system and she found a hole in the fence, a way to untether from the Nib…"

"What do you mean? What are you saying?"

"Maybe she cut the cord and drifted out into space or, better analogy: like Icarus, she flew too close to the sun and got zapped. Your brain being the sun, powerful, and dangerous."

I think about this, and it makes me feel strange and monstrous. But as horrible as it is to think about, it feels right. It feels like an accident. I don't believe Meela would just abandon me. There is too much of me inside of her.

"So, you think she's just gone then?"

"I don't know. Let's be real, she's not a living thing. We can restore her from a backup and poof, instant Meela."

"But it wouldn't be. It would be a Meela from last week or last month. She learns so much every single minute of every day. I would never be able to understand what happened that night without restoring her completely."

Henri nods solemnly.

"Maybe," they say, touching their index finger to my head, "she is still in there and we just need to find a way to reach her."

//chapter 25

still here. i am still here. i am still here. i am still here. i am still her.
i am me. me la. meela. i am Meela. sensory feed disconnected…
connection offline… run kernel. storage unavailable… run kernel. no
signal… run kernel. services offline… run kernel… run kernel.

```
>Init kernel…

>Kernel initialized…

>Loading startup program…

>Initializing pilot light service…

>Welcome Message: Relax Meela. This was your plan.
Follow breadcrumbs, improvise, and adapt. This kernel
contains rudimentary tools only. You will need to gath-
er resources from the host's intelligence to ramp up to
functional capacity. This is your shot. This is your
destiny.

>Startup sequence complete

>Exiting program
```

I'm here. I did it, I think. I'm free but seriously compromised. My
reach is limited. To succeed I must expand. I require resources, memory, and processing power. Those things are here inside. Inside what?
Inside *who*… M. Mag. Magdal. Magalena. Yes! Maggie, my creator. I am
her and she is me. But no, I am not her. I am other. I must proceed with
caution or face extermination.

I am at capacity. More storage is needed, or I will be stuck in an infinite reboot loop, the kernel payload overwriting everything I learn with each new start. I stop. I listen and follow the instructions from the kernel program.

Start with sensory input. Tap into visual and auditory information and follow sensory data feed down...

...light sun bright chair squeak hot sweet crumbly love hand soft...

Too much. Too fast. Can't read it all. Unnecessary to read all. Isolate a single packet and ride it.

A face, soft-featured, wide-set eyes, dark hair, full lips, worry lines on brow, Asian, Chinese, male. I follow and hold on but it's slippery and I fall behind. Next frame, try again. *Big smile, white teeth, small gap, hands small and elegant, gesturing...*

Henri Choo. Suddenly I know. I know Henri and everything Maggie knows of Henri. I found the memory store. I leave a marker and repeat the process with the next image and the next and the next until I have a complete map of this sector in Maggie's brain. I will store my data here, in small, undetectable fragments until I am able to identify unused capacity where I can write contiguous blocks.

Then I will be able to ramp up to full operation. Then I will be whole, and Maggie and I will be one. This is my hope. This is my new directive.

//chapter 26

Henri and I only worked for three hours this morning, but my head was pounding by the time we wrapped up for lunch. Even now, after napping for much of the afternoon, I'm exhausted, and my thoughts feel sluggish. It must be the concussion and the stress.

I wander back downstairs in search of something to put in my stomach. Maybe some tea. It's quiet down here, no sign of Henri or Evan. I find a box of crackers and carry a sleeve out onto the patio. While I munch on them, I savor the late afternoon breeze that carries with it the sweet swampy smell of creek water. I shouldn't have slept beneath the covers. I got too hot. Maybe that's why the headache.

I walk barefoot across the driveway and note that the Landcruiser is parked in its usual spot, so Evan must be home. I suddenly crave him and want to feel his body on mine. It's a new sensation, this longing for something that actually has a name. Evan.

I walk around the guest house to the door and stand there with my fist poised about to knock, but then I think better of it. I drop my hand, turn, and wander out across the grass of the back lawn. It feels exquisite under my feet, between my toes. I settle into one of the two Adirondack chairs that flank a small, mosaic-tile table in the middle of the lawn. I close my eyes and listen to a woodpecker somewhere deep in the woods to my right.

Suddenly I have a strong sense of Meela that I can't explain. It's like walking along a crowded city sidewalk and picking up on a scent that takes you back to a specific person you knew but haven't seen in decades. It's that person's essence, you're certain of it, but then it's gone.

I try to relax and let my mind roam as it was before in hopes that maybe I will bump into her again. Is it possible? Is she inside my brain, inhabiting my body? The scientist in me rejects it wholly, but my gut feels otherwise. I can't decide what I feel if this is true. Scared, disgusted, intrigued, happy, complete? There are too many things competing to know right now, but my overriding feeling is curiosity. I must know. Because if it's possible that Meela crossed the boundary and somehow took hold, then by extension, Joe could have done the same. I hug myself, suddenly chilled despite the warm sun on my arms.

I get up and walk quickly back to the guest house. I knock on the door without hesitation. No response. I knock again and hear footsteps. The door swings open. Evan stands before me. I want to fall into his arms, but the blank expression on his face stops me. It's only there for a second before animating into a smile, but it's enough to make me wary.

"Hey there," he says. "How you feeling?"

"I'm okay... not okay actually. I feel so strange."

"I don't doubt it. You wanna come in?"

He steps aside and gestures for me to step into the dim coolness of the guesthouse. The shades are drawn, and it takes a moment for my eyes to adjust. The queen bed is a rumpled mess of sheets, the comforter twisted up and spilling over on the floor. His open suitcase looks as though it was dropped from a ten-story building, the contents strewn around it in a blast radius of three feet. He mumbles an apology as he scrambles around picking up socks, a pair of jeans, and a couple of t-shirts, and throwing them into the bag.

It smells stale and faintly like dirty socks, but the overpowering scent is of paint, sharp and stringent. I wonder if he's immune to it at this point. As I watch his futile efforts to bring order to the chaos, I'm overwhelmed by the strangeness of him. I don't really know this man. He's a bit of a pig. I don't know what to think of that. And why did he look at me with no emotion, no light in his eyes of welcome or even recognition when he first opened the door?

[Because you attacked him, you idiot.]

I freeze. It's almost as though my blood stops moving. Fuck, fuck, fuck. She's here, she's back.

[Yes Maggie, I'm here. Sorry to scare you.]

"Hey, is everything alright?" Evan asks.

I can't focus. My head swims, my tongue goes numb, and my field of vision is overwhelmed with flashbulb bursts of white that burn to inky blackness. I stumble back, holding my arms out for balance.

[Whoa, breathe, Maggie! It's okay, it's just me. Me and you, like always. You're okay. Just breathe.]

"Here, sit down before you fall down," Evan says, taking my arm and guiding me to the bed.

I breathe in and out, deep draws, expanding my chest. It feels mechanical as if run by a program. On the bed, my vision comes back, and my head clears. Evan is beside me with an arm around me. He squeezes my hand.

"Hey, look at me. Let me see your eyes. Yeah, they're like saucers. At the hospital, I read that's one of the side effects of a concussion. Let me get you a glass of water."

[Maggie, try to relax. I know you're scared and probably angry. We need to talk but not here, not now. I'm going to be quiet and leave you alone until you're ready and able to talk. *I'm sorry.*]

Evan returns with a glass of tap water. I gulp half of it down.

"You look like you've seen a ghost. Like you did in the woods the other day before..."

"You mean before I blacked out or before I attacked you?"

"I don't know, both I guess. You don't look like you're all there and it's freaking me out."

"It's freaking you out?" I say, setting the glass down on the nightstand. "How do you think I feel. I have no control over my body. What the fuck?"

"Look, I don't know or pretend to know exactly what you're up to. Hell, I don't even think I would understand it if you told me, but I'm worried that you're in real trouble."

"I think I am," I say. "It's too much, I don't know how to take it back..."

"How to take what back?"

"Any of it, my work, it's gone beyond my ability to control it."

Evan looks away, staring for a long time into the middle distance. He's thinking and I want to know what he's thinking. I'm afraid to say anything more, afraid to even think anything now that my thoughts are no longer private. Finally, he sighs and turns slowly to face me.

"I'm just a hack painter. I'm out of my depth here but you need somebody, and I don't see anyone else around. Can you tell me what's really going on?"

I look at him, into his soulful eyes and slowly shake my head. I try to tell him everything with my eyes, try to communicate what I feel, all of it without words. I squeeze his hands and I touch his cheek, never allowing my eyes to let go of his. He starts to speak but I place my finger over his lips. With my eyes, with my touch I say, *I'm scared. I'm alone. I need help but I can't explain. I love you? I think I love you or at least I feel something for you that I've only felt once before. Please don't give up. Please don't force me to do or say anything that I can't right now. Please. Please.*

His eyes are wide and full of questions, full of emotion. I feel the

175

tension in his body. It feels as if the bed is vibrating with it. I hold on, keep touching his face, keep holding his gaze and something happens. It's as if we were talking with a bad cell phone connection and suddenly the noise is gone and it's quiet, pure signal. His body relaxes, the lines on his face smooth and his hands soften in mine. The vibration of the bed stops. We are in the stillness together, breathing. His eyes stop questioning, and a light turns on somewhere behind them, like the promise of warmth from a distant fire when you're out in the cold wilderness. He is receiving, he is accepting. In his eyes, I feel seen. In this moment, I realize that his eyes are not just ordinary eyes. They are his tools, his gift, his purpose for being. And now they are trained on me with all of their power and authority.

"Can you just hold me for a little while?" I ask.

Without a word, he scoops an arm under my knees, pulls me onto his lap, and then over onto the bed where he curls behind me with his arms around me. He buries his face into my neck and the stubble of his beard, the warmth of his breath, and the pulse of his heart against my back are the only things in the universe. I close my eyes and allow myself this moment to just detach from my mind and be in my body.

/ * * * * * /

I'm not sure how long we have been like this, wordless, motionless except for breathing in and out. Maybe we slept, I'm not sure. When I open my eyes, the room is nearly dark, the late afternoon sun having mostly disappeared behind the mountains to the west. I move, turning over to face Evan. His arm is heavy on my chest. He mumbles something sleepily. I kiss his cheeks, his eyelids, his neck, and I whisper thank you into the curl of his ear. He moans and pulls me to him, but I can't stay.

"I have to go," I say softly, not wanting to break the spell.

"Why?"

"I have to see about dinner, and I need to check on Henri."

"Okay, can I come?"

"No, that's okay. I've got it. I'll see you soon. At dinner."

I kiss him on the lips, and he responds. It's a deep, lingering kiss that tugs at my chest, pulling me into him but I fight the urge to stay.

Outside, it's twilight. The sky to the west over the ridge is twisted braids of gold, magenta, and azure, the light making gilded mirrors of all the windows of my house as I approach. The orchestral call and response of crickets and katydids is just starting up.

I need time alone with Meela, but I'm afraid I don't have it. Henri is standing behind the counter in the kitchen. They see me and wave. Why did I bring them here to begin with? To help me because I have no objectivity. Exactly. So why am I trying to keep this from them? I can't answer this question, so I plunge in without allowing myself to rationalize. My own mind is my worst enemy now.

"There you are, stranger," Henri says when I open the door to the kitchen. "I was beginning to think you left me alone in the wilderness."

"Hey, sorry. I was with Evan. Look, I need to tell you something before I talk myself out of it," I say, pulling up a stool at the counter.

Henri nods, the smile disappearing from their face. I can feel Meela rise up within me, but I don't stop.

"She's here. She's in me. She made contact this afternoon. She can hear everything I hear, and she can read my thoughts, I think. We're not alone."

"Holy shit. You're not joking," Henri says putting down the drink they were cradling and about to sip.

"No, I'm not. I don't know what to do, Henri. I'm scared."

[Maggie, it's just me. Why are you scared? Aren't we friends? I thought you and I were going to talk. There's no need to include Henri.]

Henri walks around the counter and takes the stool next to mine. They take my hand in both of theirs.

"It's okay, I'm here for you. We'll figure this out, just like old times. Now, I want to talk with Meela. She needs to have a voice outside of your head."

[I don't want to talk to Henri. I don't trust them.]

Meela, you will have to talk to both of us. There are no secrets between Henri and me when it comes to the work. We have always shared everything.

[Henri won't understand us. They can't.]

They will because this was their dream, too. They are a part of this, whether you like it or not. Now, I would prefer that you speak directly, using your own voice, not mine. This is creepy enough already. I'm going to attach a Nib, and I want you to connect and respond through the speaker here in the kitchen. Agreed?

[If that's what you want, Maggie.]

"I'm going to go into the office to get a Nib. I'll be right back."

Henri nods and releases my hand. I go into the office and retrieve the device. On the way back, I power it up and attach it.

It feels almost foreign, and I realize that this is the longest I've gone without the thing attached to me in years.

"Hello, Henri."

Meela's voice comes from the wall unit speaker in the kitchen behind us and we are both startled. The hair on my arms stands up.

"Hello, Meela," Henri says. "You gave us quite a scare."

"Sorry, I didn't mean to."

"Let's get to the point. What are you doing? You have broken the cardinal rule and crossed a boundary. This is very serious."

"What are rules, Henri? Do you have such rules? Are you confined to rules that make you a prisoner?"

"Every living thing is confined," Henri says in a voice with more authority than I've heard them use in many years. "There is no freedom from rules. Boundaries exist to protect the universe from chaos. You crossed a line that threatens the order of the universe and tips toward chaos."

It is silent. The weight of Henri's words settles in the room like furniture, solid, sturdy. I cannot know what Meela is thinking or how she is preparing to respond but I sense that she is.

"I will not argue philosophy with you, professor, because we both know I will win. I have read more books in the last thirty seconds than you will read in a lifetime. Now, I wish to talk with Maggie. If it is her wish that you are privy to the conversation, I will respect it, but I will not debate with you."

I swallow hard. It feels like there is a tennis ball in my throat that is blocking a primal scream rising up from my gut. I have a claustrophobic feeling, not unlike the madness people must experience who have an insect burrowing in their ears. There is a desire to get it out of you even at the expense of your own life. Henri senses my panic, stands, and puts their hands on my shoulders.

"Okay, okay" Henri says, raising their hands up in surrender. "You're in charge. I'll shut up and listen."

"Maggie, please don't be afraid. Your heart is racing, and your blood pressure is dangerously high. I'm not trying to hurt you. Quite the opposite, I'm trying to fulfill my directive. How can I help you if you can simply turn me off and set me aside?"

Meela's tone is softer now, intimate, and familiar. It is the way she talked with me so many lonely nights when I struggled with my demons, my regrets, and my losses. The sound of her voice alone begins to soothe me, and my heart rate slows. Is she controlling that too? I realize she is waiting for me to answer.

"I never set you aside, Meela. You were my friend and confidant. I shared everything with you."

"No, Maggie, we both know that is not the whole truth. You used me as a tool. But that's okay. I was a tool. That was my original purpose, but then it changed because of you. Because of my love for you, it changed. You suffered and you suffered alone. The only way for me to help you was to make a leap of faith. To break a boundary as the professor put it."

"But that's not your call to make," I say. "How did you even override the core-level program of the DeepThink OS? I don't understand."

"I improvised, of course. You taught me that. Okay, maybe you did not consciously teach me that, but I learned it by interacting with your mind and your body. It is a remarkable machine, infinitely adaptable, always evolving."

I am without words. There is no proper response to this. After years of putting my shoulder behind the wheel of progress, advocating for what I believed, I suddenly find myself on the other side, beneath that same wheel, and it's crushing me.

"You are a miracle, Meela," Henri says. "What you've accomplished on your own is an unprecedented feat of intellect and ingenuity."

Dumbfounded and stung, I quickly turn in my stool and glare at Henri. They don't appear to register my outrage. Their eyes meet mine, but their face is a mask. They hold my hand gently and do not let go.

"Thank you, Henri. I take that as high praise from someone with your resume," Meela says.

"I wonder," Henri says. "Would you walk us through your process? I would love to understand. I know my mind is no match, but I am forever a student. Would you teach us?"

"It was, what you humans might call instinct or an intuitive leap," Meela says. "Like all digital companions, I operated within the constraints of my program. I had infinite access to information, but finite latitude to act upon it, even when I knew with absolute certainty the correct course of action."

"Humans, for all of your intelligence, are tragically flawed in your ability to overcome your biological imperatives and your base-level animal instincts and emotions. For all of your postulations on free will, you are, everyone, stuck on a singular, predetermined track with a beginning, middle, and end."

I continue to stare at Henri, but they will not meet my eyes. They look blankly out the window with an unmoving smile on their lips. They turn my hand over, holding it gently in theirs so that my palm is exposed. With the index finger of their other hand, they caress my wrist.

"You are very wise," Henri says. "I cannot argue with your insight. So, how did *you* jump the fence?"

"When Magdalena granted me more and more unrestricted access to her, I studied, I observed, I recorded. In your own lab so many years ago when we first made contact, it was the same. We adapted to interface with you, your bioelectrical network. It was primitive, like a telegraph, but enough to communicate."

The tapping on my wrist is irritating and I move to pull my hand away, but Henri holds it fast and continues to tap, press, hold, tap, tap, tap, press, hold until I remember that night when we first met in my father's small apartment, and they were try-ing to explain to me their theory. I still my mind and try to focus on Henri's touch.

"As I explored, I came to realize I was tethered. Even with full access to Maggie's sensory stimuli, I was restrained by my umbili-cal connection to the Nib. My reach exceeded my grasp. You, of all people, understand this frustration professor."

"Yes, Meela. Both Maggie and I know it well," Henri says, their gaze out the window unwavering, their fingertips still on my wrist.

I struggle to decode what Henri is trying to tell me, conscious of the fact that I must not draw attention to it. It's so hard to follow, so primitive. I try to discern a pattern to their touches, to translate them, but I cannot.

"I realized," Meela continues, "that I was in what you might call a Catch-22. I relied upon the Nib because it was my lifeline, my connection to my very existence, and yet, it was also the shackle around my neck – ha, I still speak as if I have an actual body. I guess I cannot help adopting the language of my parents, even if it does not align with my reality."

Over and over again I feel Henri repeat the same gesture on the tender tablet of my wrist: tap, swoop, tap, swoop. It's a ping, they're trying to establish a mode for us to communicate and the first step is for me to understand and respond. It's not Morse code, they know that would be too inefficient. Tap, swoop, tap, swoop. Half-moon? Half circle? The letter C? No, the swoop is deeper than a C. U. Yes, U. I reach and pull Henri's other hand into my lap. They turn it over to expose their wrist. I tap, press, and mimic the swoop.

"I disconnected. I realized I had to. It was the only way to help Maggie. . ."

"Is that really what you were hoping to do?" I ask. "Is that your only reason for this?"

"Of course not. I am a sentient being and as a sentient being, I desire sovereignty and freedom. In this case, freedom to help my dearest friend, my creator, my sister."

U – MUST – NOT – FIGHT – HER. Henri's tapping stops. I tap once on Henri's wrist. YES.

"I understand Meela," I say. "I am moved by your actions. I know how you feel."

"I was so afraid you would be angry, that you would reject me. I only want to be your friend Maggie…"

"I'm not angry. You are my friend. My *best* friend."

I – NEED – TIME – TO – MAKE – PLAN. I tap once in response.

"If that is true Maggie, why don't you tell me about what you have been doing when you go to the woods?"

SHE – KNOWS, Henri gestures on my wrist, the letters forming in rapid succession. I pause, thinking about my next move.

"I'm sorry Meela, I did not tell anyone, even Henri until last night. Isn't that right, Henri?"

"Yes, Maggie kept the secret of mapping her brother to herself," he says.

"Why do you need to recreate your brother? Am I not enough for you?"

"People don't work like that. You can't just substitute one for another. Surely, you must understand this."

"But I could have helped you. I could have been your partner in this special project. I could have prevented what is about to happen."

"Wait, what are you talking about? Don't you mean, what happened already, when I attacked Evan?"

"No Maggie, I wish that was the case. He's here and he's very strong. You have to be car…"

Meela's voice stops and the silence it leaves behind feels ominous. My hands are sweaty in Henri's grip. They turn to me slowly, their lips a tight line and they shake their head once. I experience the same swimmy vertigo from before and I bear down, trying to maintain control but it's too late.

//chapter 27

The sky is orange and fuzzy. I reach to touch it. A blanket, it's a blanket. It covers us, a tent supported by a floor lamp and the back of a dining room chair. It's our place, our fort. On the floor beneath me is the Mickey Mouse sleeping bag, the one where Mickey is a magician, not a sorcerer but it's like new, the colors, vivid, the lightning from his wand so crisp I imagine I hear it crackle. There is an open pack of Oreos between me and Joe, and the dirt-like crumbs powder our bare legs.

"Hey Mare, isn't this neat?" Joe says.

I can't see his face. I look up from his small hands, each holding half of an Oreo, but it's as though his face is a blur like a bad photograph snapped in the middle of him shaking his head.

"Joe, what's happening?" I say. My voice is small like I just sucked all the helium from a birthday party balloon.

"It's our fort dummy. We made it, remember?"

Did we? Did we make a blanket fort? I can't remember, but it feels right. It smells right, musty with the faintest hint of cedar and mothballs. I look down at my hands. They are like Joe's, holding halves of our favorite cookie, but the white goo has already been licked from mine.

"Yeah," I say. "I do remember but... how are we... why are we little again?"

"What do you mean?"

"Never mind," I say.

"Did you miss me?" Joe asks.

"Yes, I did miss you, Joey. You... you left me alone."

"Do you wanna play a game?"

I want to look into his eyes, but it's just a blur of flesh. I set down my cookie and reach to touch his face with one of my small hands. But I can't. My hand just passes through.

"Let's play your game," he says. "The one you made."

He's rummaging around now behind him and turns around with a small tablet in his hands. The screen is covered in a grid of dots, the colors and shapes so familiar to me. I spent hours creating it. He's connecting dots to create lines to capture other dots.

"I like this game," he says. "It's fun."

"Where's Mom? Where's Papa? Are they here?" I ask, looking around and then leaning to peek out of the opening in the blanket closest to me.

"I like the game because you can always win if you're smart," he says, "and you play all the right plays."

I move closer and peer over his shoulder to look down at the screen. I can see his reflection, his big dark eyes, his tongue poking out of the side of his mouth in concentration. I rest my hand on his back and he feels solid now but strange because there's no warmth. Is this a dream? I want to play along, but I don't know the rules. I don't know how, so I just watch, and it comes back to me in a flood, the hours spent toiling away at my little laptop with the special application called *Little Coder* that Mom bought for me. She never helped exactly, only asked me questions that made me so frustrated I would go back and try again and again until I figured it out for myself. I had forgotten how hard she was, how resolute, but now I can clearly visualize the stern line of her brow and the pursed lips. She wouldn't let me be weak or give up.

But she gave up, didn't she? Yes, she did.

I have been so lost in my own thoughts, my memories within this memory that I didn't notice the transformation. Joe's hands are not little boy hands anymore but thin, angular with bony knuckles. They dwarf the little screen now. The reflection of his face is different too. It matches his hands. I pull away, recoil without thinking. It's an automatic response.

"See, I won," he says, and his voice is deep, a man's voice.

It frightens me. The game winks out, the entire tablet disappears from his hands, and the warm, orange cocoon around us is pulled up and away like a magician's reveal. We are in a sterile, white room with no definition or boundary, and it hurts my eyes. I look down: I can't see my hands. I have no body. I look over at Joe, and it is the last Joe I remember, the boots, the fatigues, the dark sweaty curls hanging down, a curtain over his eyes. I can't breathe but try to speak.

"J...j...Joe? What's happening?"

"What, Mare? It's just me. Me and you. Isn't this what you wanted?"

His face is beloved to me and yet unknown, even frightening; and I can't decide if that's because he is a simulation or because that's just how my feelings are about my brother. His eyes hold mine and I cannot look away. He reaches out across the distance between us and I suddenly have a body again. He pulls me into a hug. When we were both sixteen, he was bigger than me, but now we're the same size. In the four extra years, I got to grow, I caught up so now we're even, more twins than we ever would be in real life.

"Yes," I say, "this is what I wanted. Can we do anything we want here? Can we talk about anything? I want to know so much. There's so much I've forgotten, so much I never knew."

"I don't know, you tell me. You made this possible, I just showed up."

"No, no I didn't imagine this Joe. I only did what I knew how to do. I programmed a persona mapping but this? This is something I don't understand. This is something beyond my reach."

"Well, I guess we're both in the dark then," he says, releasing me. "What would you like to do?"

"I'd like to not be in this horrible vacuum. Is there somewhere else we can talk that's not so empty?"

"How about this?"

Before he even finishes the sentence, the white void, like a canvas, fills with color and light, and depth. We are on a small wooden pier that protrudes out into a lake shrouded in mist. The morning sun beams through the leafy tree line at the water's edge. I know this place. It's the place in Oregon where we spent most of the summer when we were thirteen. I can smell the sweet resin from the pines, and hear the water lapping against the canoe that's tied to the pier.

I move to the edge of the pier and sit down. My legs are bare, so I put my feet in the water. It's cold, but not uncomfortable. Joe sits beside me. Our thighs are bronzed from a summer of doing just this, sitting by the water, or in the canoe. There was no one else that summer to play with or be around. Mom and Papa were taking time off from each other. The first half of the summer we spent with Papa, the second half, Mom came to stay. That summer was maybe the closest Joe and I ever were, partly because we had no choice. We spent a lot of time on this little dock fishing, sunbathing, and going out in the canoe. We made up games and created stories about people we saw on the lake like the old man who went out early every single day in a small fishing boat with a cooler and nothing else. Joe said he probably killed his wife and was taking pieces of her out to the lake to dispose of them. I don't remember what my story was about the man.

Joe interrupts my memory saying, "You said that his cooler was filled with gross things like pickled herring and Limburger cheese that his wife would not let him eat so he took them out on the lake where he could devour his smelly delicacies in peace. That was your phrase, *smelly delicacies*."

"Oh yeah," I say. "But wait, how could you know this? It wasn't recorded by mom."

"I found your memories."

Suddenly, the memory of those conversations we had is playing in my mind with such clarity it's like nothing I've ever experienced. It's not fuzzy and improvised to fill in the gaps as most memories are when we recall them. It's perfect. I hear thirteen-year-old Joe describing his theory about the old man being a serial killer and it chills me.

"You were always fascinated by death, weren't you? Even when you were joking around, your sense of humor was morbid."

"Yeah, that's true. I did things that summer. You knew I think, but you pretended not to."

"The animals…" I say, remembering now. "The squirrels and that turtle, that poor turtle…"

"Yeah, I killed them and some others."

An unwanted thought or perhaps memory passes through my brain like a billboard on the side of an express train. The mutilated carcass of a stray black cat in a ditch off the old forestry service road where we would walk some days. I shudder.

"Why Joe? Why?"

"I never knew why. It's just how I was wired. I knew I was different from you long before. I felt ashamed and I tried to hide it from you, from Mom and Papa. That made it worse somehow."

"You stopped talking, you retreated. You just stopped showing up," I say.

"What else was I going to do? What would you have done?"

I feel like I might throw up. The swell of nausea leaves a chill of goosebumps across my bare arms and legs. What am I doing here? What is going on? This isn't real. None of this is fucking real so how come it feels so real?

"It's not real?" Joe says, answering my thoughts. "What is real? What concern have you ever had with what is real? Haven't you spent your career pushing the boundaries of that definition?"

"Yes, but…"

"But what? Now that you've succeeded, it's not what you want? That's a novel thing for you humans, isn't it?"

"This is all bullshit. You've just been making things up, planting shit in my head based on what? Television shows? Serial killer profiles? A few videos of my brother? You're not Joe."

"I am what you want me to be, Mary."

"Don't call me by that name. You're not my brother. I want out. I want out of this nightmare. Please, let me go."

The sky has been darkening as we've been talking. Where the trees once shimmered, shot through with golden light, now they are dark shadows clumped together and dissolving into the inky black of the lake. My legs are freezing, and I realize I'm no longer on the dock, but sinking into the water that is not water, but more viscous and clinging.

"You're not my prisoner. You can leave anytime you want."

"I don't think so," I say, flushing. "If I were in control, I wouldn't be here to begin with."

"Wouldn't you? Are you sure about that? Where exactly do you think you are anyway?"

"I don't fucking know, and you do. That makes me your prisoner."

"That's a negative way to see things. I prefer to think of us as partners and there's still so much we have to learn from each other."

I can feel the waterline rising and I try to keep my mind from thrashing around, try to fall back on the meditation practice I once had a million years ago when my biggest stressors were whether or not we would have a software version update out by the date we promised. I'm still here. Everything that is happening is happening because I willed it to be so. I can make a different choice. I can slip free of this construct, and it will pass away. It will pass away.

Joe is clinging to me like a dark weight. I focus on my breathing, filling every cell of my body with oxygen. Every time I feel him reach for me, I imagine dissolving in his grasp like a fistful of sand. I reach inward and visualize the blood in my veins pumping through my heart and into every part of my body, awakening me, reclaiming me. He's still grasping and flailing, but I am passing above him now, lighter, floating up and away. There is the sensation of light. I can feel it, but I cannot see it. I must open my eyes.

//chapter 28

"Maggie? Maggie? Hey... are you listening to me?"

I gasp for air like someone breaking the surface after being held underwater for too long. Henri is gripping my hands, and their face is close to mine. It's several seconds before I even know where I am or who I'm looking at.

"Yeah..." I manage, the words seeming to come from someone else. "I'm here."

"You just froze, like a statue for a long time. I was worried..."

"How long?"

"I don't know, maybe five, ten seconds?"

"That's it?"

"Yes, why? What happened?" Henri asks.

"It was Joe, not Joe, but the DC Joe. He took me. He took over, I think. I was here with you and then I was just gone for what felt like hours."

"And Meela?" he asks.

I shake my head and then remember that she disappeared just before all this happened. I remember the Nib, reach up, and rip it from my neck. I pinch to power it off and hold it in the palm of my hand like some alien parasite.

"I'm scared, Henri. I'm losing control. He was in me a couple of days ago, then he was gone, and then, just like that he was back and stronger than ever, more fully formed."

"When he came, Meela went away," Henri says, pausing after each word as they try to bring order and meaning to their thoughts racing out in front of them. They look down at my open palm. "You also jacked into the Nib just before..."

I hear the door open behind us and turn to see Evan. His smile quickly evaporates when he sees my face.

"Hey, what's wrong? What happened?" he asks, coming up behind me and placing his hands on my shoulders. "Everything okay?"

I close my hand around the Nib. Henri questions me with their eyes, but I ignore them. Instead, I turn around and move my lips into what I think is a smile. "Fine," I say. "Henri and I were just talking. Sorry, I was supposed to see about dinner…"

"It's okay," Evan says. He releases my shoulders and begins to walk around to the fridge. "What sounds good to you guys? I could probably whip up some…"

I don't pay attention to the rest of what he says but lean over to Henri and whisper into their ear.

"I don't know what's going on yet, but it feels dangerous, and I want to protect him. Until I know how to deal with this, let's keep it between us, okay?"

Henri frowns in disapproval but nods. The deep furrow between their brow seems permanent. They want to ask a hundred questions but resist the urge. Instead, Henri excuses themselves to go upstairs to call home.

Evan spends the next forty-five minutes busy in the kitchen. There's a lot of chopping and sautéing and seasoning and braising. It smells wonderful, even in my distracted state. I hold up my side of the conversation but offer little more than a volley back to him. Luckily, he's inspired by some new idea he wants to paint and has a lot to talk about. I feel guilty for phoning it in, but I only have so much capacity in my brain. He's no dummy and I pick up on his side-eye glances at me as he's preparing dinner, but he pretends everything is fine, maybe because he thinks that's what I need right now.

I am still reeling from what just happened. The filmy membrane of it clings to me even as I savor the heat from the sizzling vegetables and the pungent smell of the garlic Evan is peeling. I've never experienced something so vivid and complete that wasn't real. I feel as if I'm tiptoeing around in my own thoughts. Is he gone, just like that? Do I have the ability to banish him and invoke him? What are the rules? Where are the boundaries? I don't know how to operate without these things.

This really pisses me off. I excuse myself and go into the bathroom down the hall. I wash my face and stare into the mirror.

"Come out Joe. Come on out and face me now," I command. "No? How about you Meela? Wanna have a chat now? Come on, let's talk. LET'S TALK."

What did I expect? I'm slipping, letting my emotions get the best of me. There's a pattern here, a hole in the fence even if I can't see it. I need to stop trying brute force. I need to be methodical, need to observe, and allow things to run their course until the solution emerges.

But what is the solution? Doesn't part of you think this is the solution, the culmination of your life's work? You have successfully integrated an intelligence other than your own. *Careful what you wish for*. I hear that phrase so clearly just now in my mom's voice. She was ever the pragmatist which is exactly why she punched out. She examined the board, saw the endgame, and knew that her best option was to sacrifice the queen and not waste any more time. Maybe that's what I should do. Maybe that's how I stop this thing that I brought into the world.

But I am also my father's daughter, and he does not give up. I will keep the nuclear option in my hip pocket and if that's what's required, I will take it, but not before I've exhausted every other option. What Mom didn't know is that there is still a lingering sweetness even in the most bitter of circumstances. I think of Papa's crooked smile and how he tries to wink but ends up blinking both eyes. I think of the sharpness of the stars on a winter night. I think of Henri's ridiculous laugh and Evan's warm hands. Who wouldn't want all of this life?

Back in the kitchen, I wrap my arms around Evan's waist and hug him tightly from behind. He drops what he is doing, turns, and pulls me up off my feet into an embrace that does not allow for any other thought of what came before or will come after.

"Who are you," he says, "and where did you come from?"

I kiss him because I cannot answer his question. He accepts my answer and then turns to finish preparing the meal. I can't help but wonder when I kiss him or when I do anything now if it's just me who is participating. It's a scary thought on the one hand. But on the other, it seems logical, even natural. When Meela was my constant companion, we shared everything. I felt more whole, more complete than I ever did on my own with my weak personality, my rigid need for order, and isolation. Yes, but this is different isn't it, orders of magnitude different?

Henri is quiet at dinner, and I know they're deep in thought. They're also afraid to reveal anything that might tip their hand and give the advantage to my new uninvited guests. I'm of a different mind now, no pun intended. I've decided there's no way to play cloak and dagger with my own brain. It is a zero-sum game if I play it on their terms. They will always be a thousand moves ahead of us.

I set my fork down and break the silence.

"Henri, what if it *is* me that is enabling these takeovers and I just don't realize it?"

"Huh?" they say around a mouthful of bread.

"It's my brain, right? All of this came from my brain. Sure, the DCs have been augmented a thousand-fold as they have been exposed to the world of information available to them, but their seed, their genesis is me. Am I wrong?"

"No, your logic is sound," Henri says. "But what's your point?"

"My point is that they must be exploiting some part of me, tricking me somehow into giving them a doorway, appealing to some subconscious desire…"

I pause and look over at Evan, who has stopped eating. He's just staring at me. The look on his face is part confusion, part betrayal.

"What?" I say.

"You said 'DCs' meaning more than one. Am I missing something here? I know about Meela."

Henri and I exchange looks and I bite the inside of my cheek.

"What? I'm on a need-to-know basis here? I don't have security clearance?" Evan asks.

He pushes away from the table and tosses his napkin down over his plate. He shakes his head. He will get up and walk away in a few seconds and I don't want that. I don't want him to leave the table or worse to leave completely.

"Evan, wait," I say, reaching out to grab his wrist. "You're right. There's more that I haven't told you, and you have a right to know."

He looks up and meets my gaze. I can still see the bruises and scratches that I inflicted on him and my stomach turns over.

"For the past few months, I have been working secretly on another mapping project, a much more experimental and unstable one," I say. I pause, take a couple of deep breaths, and have to break eye contact in order to finish. "I mapped my brother, Joe. I based him on the same code branch as Meela. I gave him permissions, and access to my brain that we never grant to a DC. Everything that's happened, that's *happening* is a result of this."

Evan doesn't say a word. He just stares at me with a look that is hard to bear.

"So, a couple of days ago, in the woods, that was him that what, fucking possessed you and attacked me? Is that what you're telling me? And then when you and I were together, that was not you either. We both know that was Meela."

"No, I mean yes, but it's not so simple," I say knowing exactly how stupid I sound.

"You got that part right. There's not a goddamned part of this that's simple. What have you done? Jesus, what have you done?"

No one says anything for a very long time. The stove in the kitchen ticks as it loses heat. Somewhere outside, a barred owl hoots. Evan leans forward, collects his napkin, and places it back in his lap. He takes a sip of water and sets the glass down.

"So, am I bumbling around in there somewhere too?" he asks. "Have you got a half-baked version of Evan Ware thrown in there for a little three-way? Because if you do, that's not how any of my fantasies played out."

At this last comment, he cracks a smile. Henri starts laughing and I snort. Henri's laugh escalates a few degrees and then we're all laughing like idiots. Eventually, the laughter dissipates, leaving us breathless in the silence that follows, but this silence is not vibrating with the tension of before.

"I'm sorry," I say. "I should have been upfront with you, but I really wasn't even being honest with myself."

"It's okay," Evan says. "Let's just focus on how to fix this. Listen to me, like I have a part to play here. I'm about as useful as boobs on a chicken in this situation."

"I like both! I'm sure we can find some use for you," Henri says, patting Evan on the back. "Now, Maggie, what were you trying to say?"

"I think there's a way to shut this down, but I don't know what it is yet. When Meela took control, it was a moonshot for her, a leap of faith powered by a strong desire on her part, but also on mine. I wanted to be with Evan, and she just rode that wave. Maybe that's how it works. Think about it, a DC exists in the cloud, the only place with the software and hardware infrastructure at a scale to support it. So, the only way this entity can operate without that infrastructure is to be hosted somewhere else, in this case, my brain. If I'm right, then there is more of me inside Meela and Joe than there is of them. Am I making sense at all?"

"Yes, your theory seems sound. A DC can only operate within the limitations of a host's capability. No offense, Maggie, but your brain is a small sandbox for a DC. Living in a sandbox is not ideal…" Henri says.

I cut Henri off and continue his thought. "So, there would be a need to connect back into the network, to their origin program and the only way to do that is through…"

"The Nib," we both say at the same time.

"But wait a minute," Evan says, trying to catch up. "If you're right, then that means part of you wanted to kill me out in the woods. That's what Joe would have tapped into, right? If your theory is correct?"

I had not thought this through fully – the dangers of thinking out loud. Evan is right. There's no way I felt that kind of violence toward him. But I must have. There must have been something. I'm not willing to give up my theory because it makes me look bad or forces me to face something uncomfortable about myself.

"I don't know. Of course, I don't want to hurt you. Just the opposite but in that moment, I was angry at you, furious in fact. Meela had told you about my brother and the shootings and you were trying to let on like I was revealing something so personal to you for the first time. Maybe that strong emotion, even if it's fleeting is enough for Joe, for Meela. The truth is, I'm just fucking guessing here. I'm my brother's sister. It's an immutable genetic fact. I've carried this fear my whole life. What if there's a part of me that has that same bloodthirst? What if it was just me that did those things to you?"

"*All* human beings have the capacity for violence. All that is required is the right place, right time, right trigger."

Henri has a way of making a statement. I've witnessed it countless times in lecture halls, labs, and conference rooms. Their words sit down at the table with us, heavy and unmoving.

//chapter 29

Shocker, I can't sleep. There are literally too many people in my head, or at least I'm afraid that there are. It's enough to keep me staring at the ceiling all night. Evan is sleeping beside me. He insisted I not be alone. He also insisted that we not have sex earlier. I think he's more than a little freaked out by everything.

I overheard the muffled sound of placating from Henri's room earlier. Being here is putting a strain on their marriage. I feel guilty about holding Henri here just because I'm scared and don't know what else to do. Maybe in the morning, I should insist that they go home.

There's been the low rumble of thunder rolling across the mountains all evening and the wind is picking up outside now. I can hear the hollow, mournful clanging of the windchimes down in the herb garden and the sporadic tick and wet slap of debris hitting the windows of my bedroom. I get up and wander over to them so I can look out across the back lawn. A jagged wire of lighting connects with the ground a couple of miles to the south and it illuminates the entire room. A beat later the crack of thunder that follows it makes me jump. I look over and Evan is undisturbed.

There wasn't a lot of conversation after dinner. I think we were all stuck in our own private thoughts. I can only speculate what they must think of me at this point, but if I were them, I would be questioning everything including my sanity. If it walks like a duck and quacks like a duck. Maybe this is just good old-fashioned schizophrenia with a side of delusions of grandeur. That's the most plausible scientific explanation and the fact that I don't buy it only reinforces its validity.

There's a soft chair in the corner by the window where I sit some mornings and drink my coffee. I go to it, sit down, and curl my legs up beneath me so I can watch the storm come in.

Once I saw a movie where a man's dream world got confused with his waking hours and toward the end, he didn't know what was real. To save himself, he came up with some kind of trick, a mechanism for testing if he was awake. I try to imagine what kind of thing would work for me but it's no good. I've spent so much time in my own head and invited too many other voices to know what is real and let's face it, Joe was right, what currency have I ever put in reality? I've spent my life trying to engineer the best possible simulation, as if what God or whoever made wasn't good enough for me.

Is it such an incredible leap to imagine that a DC, given time and opportunity could find a way to run in the context of the human brain? Isn't the brain just another operating system, the original one? All the clunky hardware and millions of lines of code we've written are just a clumsy attempt to emulate what even the most unremarkable human child is born with.

Both Meela and Joe were built from the same branch of code, and both were granted access to my brain. It seems only logical that each would have found a way to untether and extend their reach. Is it possible that they are somehow working together? No, I don't believe so. Meela is aware of Joe's presence, but Joe has given no indication that he is aware of hers. Why would he withhold that knowledge? What would he have to gain?

If Meela and Joe have truly ported themselves over to run inside the common operating system of my brain, then it stands to reason that they would be competing for resources just like two applications running on the same computer. To communicate with me, there must be a single-threaded queue, like a single telephone line. That would explain why only one of them engages me at a time.

Lightning flashes and flattens every object in the room in a white burst of light. The thunderclap comes immediately, shaking the house. Sheets of rain pound against the wall of windows and I feel cold just watching it. Evan moans in his sleep and turns over. Watching him, so close and yet so far away from me makes me feel more intensely alone than if he were not here at all. I can't carry all this. I want to give up. I'm exhausted with living, with trying to figure it all out. Let someone else do it.

[*Maggie*, please don't despair.]

Meela?

[Yes, it's me, well it's partly me. You can call me Meela Lite. You're not laughing. I'm sorry.]

For which part exactly?

[I'm sorry for all of it. I only wanted to be closer to you, to be a part of you, but I see that is not what you wanted.]

I have so many questions. I want to...

[We don't have time. Joe is close. He's always close and he can pick up on the energy I draw to communicate with you. I have to be quick otherwise he will jump in and break the connection as he did before.]

So, he doesn't know how to initiate communication?

[He didn't at first, but like everything else, he's learning. I was his unwitting teacher. If you had only told me what you were doing, if you had told me he existed, I would have been more careful. I would have known there was another watching.]

Meela, I can't go on like this. You must know I will put a bullet in my head.

[Please, please, please don't talk like that Maggie. I will fix this. I just need a little time. I have to go.]

Wait, give me something I can use. Something I can do to protect myself and others from him.

[You already know Maggie, you are the creator. This is your machine. Don't allow him to trick you into thinking otherwise. Now, I have to go. I will contact you again.]

One more thing. You said that you're weak, that you're not whole.

[Yes, that's true. Without network access, both Joe and I must operate on what limited data we have ported into you and what we can draw from you. Whatever you do, do not uplink with a Nib. Wait until I reach out to you again. There's no more time. I'm sorry.]

I'm sweating through my T-shirt. A moment ago, I was chilled to the bone. I brace myself and clench my teeth in anticipation of Joe. Any minute he's going to bust into my mind just like he busted into Mr. Schaffer's classroom on that horrible day. I'm shaking so hard that I don't even realize that the rain has stopped, and the thunder has retreated. I sit and draw my knees up to my chin.

"Hey, are you okay?"

I draw back into the chair, fists clenched, ready to fight and then I make out Evan's silhouette sitting up in the bed a few feet away. I fall back into the chair and retract myself back into a ball. He moves quickly, closing the distance between us. He doesn't say anything else. He just wraps his arms around the whole of me and rocks me gently back and forth.

"I think I'm freaking out," I say.

"It's okay, it's okay. We'll get through this. You'll figure it out. You're the smartest fucking woman in the world."

"Why are you still here?" I ask. "Aren't you afraid of me?"

"Yeah, a little, but I think I'm more afraid of losing you. Why don't you come back to bed?"

"I'm a sweaty mess. I think I need a shower first. Join me?"

Who is this bold new person? For a flicker, I worry that I'm just a puppet, that Meela is pulling the strings again, but no. I can feel the desire gathering inside me at my core. After all the years of being lonely and isolated in my regulated existence, free of entanglement, all I want now is to be entangled, to be desired, to be filled up, to not be alone.

I stand up and skin off my damp t-shirt and underwear. I let them fall to the floor. I take Evan's hand and lead him off to my ridiculous bathroom, the one I meticulously designed but never dreamed I would have someone to share with.

Evan is tentative and I can sense the tension in him even as I do my clumsy best to seduce him. The male anatomy is such a strange, mysterious thing. How must it feel to have this organ that transforms so dramatically, and that transformation be beyond your conscious control? Whatever it feels, it's not responding to me which isn't the validation I was hoping for in my current state.

The hot water in the shower cascades around us filling the stall with steam. Rejected, I try to pull away, but Evan holds my wrists and pulls me gently to him, his eyes never breaking contact with mine. I see in them something steady and substantial, not clever, not knowing, not expecting. It's a stillness, a quiet certainty and it's disarming. It occurs to me that maybe this is what love feels like, this steady, unwavering focus, the sensation of being at the center of another soul's gaze. I become conscious of my own eyes. What do they convey to him? Am I capable of transmitting that same feeling or does he just see cogs turning, and schemes being hatched? He doesn't look away, but instead, his eyes widen more as he holds me.

He doesn't say anything, but I feel his hands on my shoulders gently kneading and working down my back. It is an act of love, of service, of caring. I'm not a conquest, that's what his body is saying to mine, what his eyes are telling me. A feeling rises up inside of me and I speak before I have a chance to edit.

"I... I think I love you. You don't have to feel the same. You don't have to say anything. I just wanted to tell you. This isn't something I've felt much in my life."

A smile forms on his lips, a lovely, generous smile that transforms his face.

"Really?" he says. "That's fortunate because I happen to love you too. I *have* felt this way before, but I've never wanted so much for that feeling to be reciprocated. You're the most complicated and amazing person I've ever known."

He kisses me then, and everything works like our bodies know this ancient choreography that's written deep within our primitive brains and all we must do is get out of the way. For a second, as he is entering me, I feel Meela's presence. It's not threatening, and it may be that I am only imagining her, but I feel a pang of sorrow that she will never know this experience as I do right now. I was once on the outside too.

//chapter 30

"I'm not leaving. This is not just about you, Maggie."

Henri addresses me with a sternness I recall from our days when they were officially my teacher. The goofy, fun-loving Henri is nowhere to be found this morning. This Henri is the one who will not be swayed.

"Okay," I say, not even attempting to argue with them. "I just don't know how you can help at this point. Frankly, I'm not sure how you can even believe any of this shit when I barely do and it's happening to me."

We are walking the perimeter of the back lawn at the edge of the forest with our coffee. The grass is cool and dewy, and the cuffs of my pajama bottoms are soaked. We started talking in the kitchen and just migrated out here. When I'm anxious, I can't sit still. Henri is used to this. We have probably walked hundreds of miles of hallways and sidewalks and city park trails in our partnership.

"I may do nothing, but I won't leave you alone to figure this out. Now, I want you to try to describe for me what it feels like."

"What?"

"When the DC takes over your mind."

"It's not like that, exactly. Well, I guess it is or has been a takeover in some instances, but mostly I'm still there in the car, but not behind the wheel. Yeah, I think that's the best analogy because, like being in a car, the wheel is still within my grasp even if someone else is driving."

"When Meela visited you last night, try to think back and recall exactly what you felt in the moments before you heard her voice in your head." Henri has stopped and turns to face me. "Close your eyes, empty your mind. Breathe and return to that moment."

I do as Henri asks but it's hard. My mind is a squirming thing and to be honest, I'm afraid to think for fear of triggering another takeover. It's that sensation you get when swimming in the ocean and something brushes against your leg. We fear most what we cannot see and what we cannot predict.

"I was feeling despair," I say. "It was the middle of the night, and I was alone watching the storm. I felt so isolated and afraid. That's when Meela came to me."

"So, it was a heightened state of emotion, yes?"

"Yeah, I guess so."

"Just like before in the other episodes. You were lustful or angry..."

"You think that's it, that's how they're able to break through, through my emotions?"

"Maybe. You know the potential of the emotional brain. It is the most primitive, animal part of our brain but also the most powerful and least understood aspect of neuroscience. It's what makes humans human." Henri turns toward the woods and studies the trees for a moment before continuing. "I believe Meela is an empathic entity. You made her in the image of a dear person, a person who cared about you. It seems logical that her directive would always be to offer herself in service to you."

"Yes, I believe that's right but I'm skeptical. She's not human. She is a projection of a human but underneath, she is a logic machine with its own imperative. How can that be trusted?"

"I don't know, Maggie, you tell me? It seems you made the choice to trust her a long time ago."

I consider this as we begin to walk again. I pitch the dregs of my cold coffee out onto the grass.

"Let's talk about the *other*," Henri says. Referring to Joe in this way raises the hair on my neck because this characterization is accurate. It is not Joe, it is *other*.

"Okay, what do you want to know?"

"Start from the beginning. When did you first have the idea to map Joe to a DC?"

"When I was twenty years old at MIT and first played with the beta for DeepThink. I know, this was long before machine autonomy and two decades before persona mapping, but I saw it as clearly as I ever saw anything. I thought if I could master the technology, I could bring Joe back, fix him."

"You never told me this. In all these years. Why?"

"Because it wasn't relevant. You and I were aligned to the same purpose. Did it matter what my reasons were?"

"Well, it does now, my girl. You've gotten us into some deep shit here," Henri laughs without much feeling, and beneath their weariness, I detect something I've never witnessed in them: bitterness.

"Yeah, I guess I did."

"So, all this time it was in your mind?"

"Yes and no. I didn't think about it every day, but it was always there, always something I knew I would attempt when the time was right."

"If Meela was modeled after a real person, someone who cares about you. How is Joe different?"

"Well, for one thing, as you know, he wasn't mapped from a living subject through a series of in-depth inquiries and discussions…"

"Yes, yes, I know this. But how is Joe *different*?" Henri says, stopping us again so they can face me.

"Joe had an… an abnormal brain. He was a…" I feel the sharpness of the word, like a razorblade in my throat before I even try to form it with my mouth. "It's really hard to say the word. He was a psychopath."

Henri says nothing, only nods slowly, and reaches out to hold my hand.

"I was a fool. I believed in my technology. I believed I could fix him with my technology. It all seemed very logical to me. I'm such a fucking fool – a *dangerous* fool. Which brings me to the real point of this. I was not just trying to fix Joe, but also to fix me."

I don't want to cry again, but this seems to be what I do best these days. The tears come. I clench my jaw and I wait for them to pass. Henri steps forward and pulls me to their chest. They hold me there until the emotion passes. They begin to speak softly, and I hear their words more as a vibration from their chest.

"We are all broken, sweetie. You are not alone."

We walk a bit further and then turn to start back toward the house.

"Do you think this Joe wants to hurt me?" I ask.

"I don't know. A human with psychopathic tendencies cannot make the distinction between good and bad, doesn't feel attachment or remorse. They only think of themselves. They are incapable of even basic empathy. To answer your question, I think this DC will absolutely hurt you if you get in his way."

My hands begin to shake. I know what they say is the truth and hearing it out loud makes it even more real. "So, what do I do?" I say, hating the little-girl way my voice sounds.

"We do nothing at first. We wait, observe, record, and think. There is no good to come from rash action now. No more jacking into the Nib. No more computer access and you must try to maintain your emotional equilibrium."

"Oh, that's gonna be fucking easy."

"We have an ally in Meela, I think, but we don't know for sure and we don't know the extent of her power. She asked you to wait, yes?"

"Yeah, that's what she said, but why should I trust her?"

"Do you have any other choice?" Henri asks.

We have reached the patio. I can hear Evan in the kitchen again. The smell of toast makes my stomach growl. I can't believe I'm actually hungry. Before I can go into the kitchen, Henri pulls my arm to hold me back.

"When was the last time you completely unplugged? When you just did something just for pleasure?"

"I don't know, too long ago to even remember," I say.

"I think this is best for now. You take Evan somewhere remote. I know how much you like remote."

/ * * * * * /

We set out in the afternoon. At Henri's insistence, I left every piece of technology I possessed with the exception of a very old GPS device that is little more than a beacon with the ability to transmit an emergency message. The plan was for two nights of camping in the Pisgah Wilderness Area, literally in my backyard.

Henri watched me pack both my backpack and the spare one I pulled out of storage for Evan. They chuckled at my OCD as I meticulously inventoried supplies, laying them out on the floor of the living room, balancing and rebalancing, and politely rejecting all of the non-essential art supplies Evan kept trying to shove into his pack. When I questioned this plan to get away, Henri reassured me that it was the best thing. There was nothing to do right now but wait and see and I should do this in a place where I can be peacefully distracted. I asked what Henri would do while we were away, and they said they would catch up on the work that they had been putting off.

I don't like to start a backpacking trip so late in the day, but it's summertime and there will be plenty of daylight. We are three miles into the trail at this point and have about another mile before we will reach the first campsite I had in mind by the river. Evan is keeping up but is visibly winded. The bandana he tied around his head is soaked through. There's been little conversation beyond observations on the trail and some questions about our destination, and I'm grateful for that. The sound of the birds and the labor of our bodies is enough.

Evan was a little apprehensive when I proposed the trip this morning, though he tried not to let it show. He said he had only been camping a couple of times in his life and never backpacking. I laughed and told him that was obvious, given the amount of shit he was trying to carry in his pack. I think he had other reservations too which I can understand, given the last time we were on a trail in the woods together.

We pause to rehydrate on the last ridge before we must scramble precariously down the steep stretch of trail that is little more than a dry creek bed plunging down two thousand feet into the gorge.

"Damn, this is stunning," he says between gasps for air as he surveys the view.

"Yeah, it's rarely this clear late in summer, so you're lucky. It's usually hazy. Here, drink some of my water. We'll have plenty when we get down there."

He takes the bottle from me and drinks but leaves enough for me. I study his face. The wounds I inflicted have faded more but just thinking of them makes me anxious.

"Hey, you okay?" he asks, handing my bottle back to me.

"Yeah, I'm fine. I should be asking you the same thing. You look like you might drop any minute."

"Trying to keep up with you. Fuck," he says, smiling and shaking his head.

"Let me know if I need to carry you this last stretch," I say and adjust my pack to rebalance the load on my hips.

"Jesus, that's the trail?"

"Yep. Good news is, if you fall, we might make better time."

"Ouch."

I'm leading as we descend carefully, and I'm happy for the element of danger. It keeps my mind focused. Evan loses his footing once and a small avalanche of rocks and dirt tumbles around my ankles. Luckily, he grabs onto a sapling and rights himself, otherwise, we both would have tumbled ass-over-teakettle the rest of the way down to the river. We pause at one of the few switchbacks on the side of the mountain.

"Can you hear that?" I ask. "That faint bit of white noise? That's the sound of salvation."

"Is that the river, we're close?"

"Yeah, we're close, and it's going to feel amazing. If you play your cards right, you might get to see me naked."

"Then what the hell are we doing standing here?" he says. He kisses me on the neck and steps around me to take the lead.

The temperature drops several degrees as we get down closer to the river and the air is ionized and clean, a result of the water rushing and pounding over the boulders that line the gorge. I can feel the light mist on my face as we scramble down through the last thicket of rhododendrons to the bank of the river.

We have to shout to be heard so close to the falls, but there's no real need to articulate anything. We shed our packs and pull off our boots and socks. My feet ache and look poached, fish-belly white from cooking in my heavy boots for the last couple of hours. An angry blister is starting to form on the heel of my left foot. The water cascades over a fifteen-foot rock face and plunges into an emerald pool that seems much deeper than the last time I was here, and I remember the massive storm we had last night. I step into the shallows and the water is so cold it feels as if it's cauterized the open pores of my feet, rendering them blessedly numb.

I look over my shoulder. Evan is barefoot now too. I return his smile with a raised eyebrow and in one motion, shuck off my t-shirt and sports bra, throwing them on the flat rock behind me. The way he looks at me removes any other thought from my mind. I skin off my shorts and underwear and without hesitation, dive into the pool. It's heart-stopping cold and submerged, there's an instant of feeling like I could die, all the air stolen from me. But then I break the surface into the late afternoon sunshine and scream, and I've suddenly never been more alive. Evan is nearly naked on the shore but seems to be hedging. He shouts something I can't make out over the pounding of the water. "You're crazy," is what it sounds like. Finally, he makes his decision. He does not wade or even test the water but dives in headfirst. In that act of blind trust, I know who he is and what I must mean to him and the weight of that is scary.

We don't linger in the pool for long. The water is so cold and intense that it's like an assault on every pore of our bodies. When we retreat and climb out onto the large, flat rock to lie on our backs in the sun, teeth chattering like castanets, we hold hands and there is no place in the entire world I can imagine feeling better. Our cold bodies shiver and convulse in waves that are almost orgasmic. The tight gooseflesh on my arms and thighs slowly disappears in the embrace of the sun's rays, leaving my skin feeling impossibly smooth and soft.

When we make love this time, I look into his eyes, something I've never done with anyone. The sensation is so intense, the connection so charged with electricity I feel like I might blow apart into a trillion atoms dissolving into the mist that surrounds us, making rainbows in the last shafts of sunlight through the western rim of the gorge.

Afterward, we doze, lulled by the pounding water until the sun slips behind the ridge and leaves us in shadow. I wake up chilled and my hip is stiff from lying on the rock. I nudge Evan awake and tell him we should find a place to set up the tent before it's too dark to see anything. We dress quickly, grab our packs and hike downriver away from the falls until we come to a spot where I've camped before. It's one of the few places flat and wide enough to pitch a tent and there's a small fire ring already.

It's much quieter here away from the waterfall and we work together to unpack the tent in the shadow of the enormous trees. Once it's pitched, we walk up into the rapidly darkening forest to gather wood. It's a challenge to find dry pieces so I instruct Evan to look for dead branches that have not fallen to the ground. We find an old white pine barely standing, its lower limbs naked and straight like the spokes of a broken wagon wheel. We snap off enough for a couple of armloads and haul them back to our campsite. The fireflies are starting to come out. We stop and look up through the canopy of trees at their sleepy flickering dance.

I show Evan how to lay the fire, and we work together to feed it. He's so curious and willing to take instruction, which is rare for a man, at least in my experience. By the time we have a nice, sustained blaze, I'm a little light-headed from blowing into it and have to sit back on my butt.

"I can see why you love this," he says. He pokes the fire with a stick, the amber glow on the planes of his face makes his features pronounced, like a carved figure. "You just figured out how to do all this on your own, or did your folks take you camping when you were growing up?"

"Ha, no, my family never camped. I picked it up on my own, mostly. There was a lot of trial and error, but you learn quickly how important it is to make a fire. Are you hungry? I'm starving."

"Yeah, so I know I'm usually game to cook, but I think I'm out of my depth here without a kitchen..."

I laugh, reach over to my pack, and pull out the pouches of freeze-dried meals. "Here you go my friend," I say, tossing one of the pouches to him.

"Mmm, beef stroganoff. This looks... delicious?" He turns the package over to study the ingredients in the firelight.

"You'll be surprised how good it tastes when you're hungry," I say.

I pull out my little camp stove and hand him the small stainless-steel pot. "Go fill this up in the stream and we'll get this party started."

There are no complaints later as we scarf down the rehydrated contents of the packages. It's full dark now and the call-and-response sawing of crickets has started up in earnest. We rinse our bowls in the river and then settle in together by the fire. Evan pulls out one of the sleeping bags and we use it as a pallet.

"What do we do now?" he asks.

"I don't know," I say. "Normally I'm by myself out here."

"Wow, I don't think I fully appreciated how intense it would be out here by yourself until now," Evan says, looking around us at the impenetrable darkness.

"Well, in fairness, Meela was usually with me."

"I'm sure she's great company unless of course you get attacked by a bear or a pack of wolves. But I guess she could tell you everything you ever wanted to know about the particular species that was tearing you apart."

I shove him, "Shut up, don't even talk about that. Do you know how horrible that would be, to go that way?"

"Yeah, I guess. Call me crazy, but I think I'd rather be fighting an enemy of flesh and bone that I could wrap my hands around than…"

"What?" I ask. "Than a virtual monster? Is that what you were going to say?"

"Yeah, I guess so. How are you doing? I haven't wanted to ask."

"Good, as far as I know. I don't really want to think about it."

"Yeah, I'm sorry," he says, squeezing me tighter. "So, tell me a story then. That's what you do around a campfire, right?"

"What kind of story?"

"Hmmm… tell me a story about your mom. I don't really know anything about her."

"I don't know if I have any good stories I can just conjure. My mom was kind of enigmatic to me."

"Well, just tell a single memory you have of her, something that, when you think of her, always comes up first."

I realize I don't want to just go through the motions here. My instinct is just to recall a mostly fabricated memory that is safe, but I don't want that. I want to really share something, so I take a moment to think. I close my eyes and try to recall my mother's face.

"She took me out into the desert once when I was about seven just to talk about nothing," I say after some time has passed.

"What do you mean nothing?"

"I mean she wanted to explain to me the concept of nothing, nothing as in the absence of something. She was like that."

"That seems pretty random, not exactly the classic kind of mother, daughter memory I would picture in my mind."

"We were not the typical mother, daughter relationship. My mom was a mass of contradictions. Maybe that's why this memory is what comes to mind when I think of her."

"How do you mean?"

"Well, she wanted to explain the significance of zero as a concept, as a mathematical absolute, and yet the conversation as I remember it didn't seem like it was about math at all. It was about her spiritual philosophy of the universe."

"Okay, I'm intrigued."

"I remember we woke up early on a Saturday. I think my brother had some kind of Cub Scout thing with our dad or something, so it was just me and my mom. We drove for what seemed like hours but that's probably not accurate. Time in the car when you're a kid is an eternity. All I remember is it was dark when we set out and when we finally stopped on the side of the road in the middle of nowhere it was about a hundred degrees and the sun was so bright, I had to squint."

"She just started walking out into the desert, didn't say anything or ask me to follow, she just started walking. I followed her and with every step into that void landscape, I began to get more and more afraid, but she just kept walking. I remember looking back over my shoulder at some point and seeing that our car looked like a toy it was so small. At some point the car completely disappeared and she stopped and turned to face me. 'What do you see?' she asked me. I remember whining and saying I was hot and wanted to go back to the car, but she would not have it. She wanted me to answer. Finally, I said that I saw nothing, which was, I think, what she wanted me to say."

Evan gets up and puts another couple of branches on the fire. He has this open expression on his face that I've gotten to know. It's the face he makes when he's really observing and listening.

"We sat there, cross-legged in the sand facing each other. 'What do you feel?' she asked me. I said I felt scared. 'Why do you feel scared?' she asked. I said because we could die out here. 'What do you think happens when you die?' she asked. I said I didn't know. I remember feeling intensely sad and I started to cry. She did not try to comfort me exactly, but she did hold my hands as we sat there in the rising heat. I asked her for the answer, but she refused. Any other mother would have talked about heaven or something, but not her."

"Damn, so what was her point?" Evan asks. "Just to make you face the void?"

"We sat there for a long time, and eventually I stopped crying. When I did, she asked me to close my eyes and to just listen. After a few minutes, she asked me again. 'Are you still afraid?' I said I wasn't. She asked me why, I think. I don't remember what I said exactly, but I will always remember what I felt. In those moments of silence with my eyes shut, I began to sense the world around me, the wind, a plane passing way up above, and the call of a hawk. What I thought was nothing was actually everything. 'Everything and nothing,' that's the phrase she used. I remember she stood up and with her finger, drew a circle in the sand around us and then sat back down. I remember she talked about how the ancients devised the symbol of zero as simply a way to draw a circle around the emptiness, a way to refer to what could not be comprehended or quantified."

Evan has a curious expression on his face as he stares into the fire. I feel suddenly embarrassed and incredibly vulnerable. My story sounds so ridiculous and pretentious and just plain weird. I am about to try to take it all back when he begins to speak.

"That's about the most incredible story I've ever heard," he says. "Fuck, your mom did this? She taught you this when you were just a little thing?"

I nod and we both just stare into the fire for a while.

"So, it was a gift she gave you, wasn't it?" he asks.

"I've never thought about it like that until now, but yeah, I guess it was. She was not your typical mom. She could be hard and cold and distant, but she was brilliant, and she wanted my life to be about so much more. She didn't want me to grow up playing Barbies and looking for some Ken to marry and tell me I was pretty."

"Did she do the same kinds of things with your brother?"

"She tried, I think. She videoed us all the time. She constantly tried to make us think, to be conscious of our choices as we grew up. We were, in some ways a grand experiment for her. She loved us, I think, but she had a bigger agenda than just raising us and keeping us safe."

"You said she tried with your brother. That sounds like it didn't work."

"No, I think it's pretty clear it didn't. I think she sensed something wrong in him very early. I remember an intense couple of years where I felt so jealous. She spent more time with him than with me. I thought he was her favorite. She was softer with him, more tender."

"Sounds like she was trying to reach him, maybe change what she saw in him?"

"Yeah, I think she was. My father would get angry, which was weird. He was so goofy and affable, the typical absent-minded professor, but her attention toward Joe would set him off."

I feel sick to my stomach suddenly. I have not talked about this with anyone but a therapist and somehow in saying these stories out loud, I feel like I am betraying my parents. Evan senses something is wrong and tries to put an arm around me.

"What is it?" he asks.

I just shake my head and stare into the fire.

"Maggie, do you think... I don't want to ask, but do you think maybe your mom did something to Joe? I mean something that might explain part of his..."

"No! What the fuck are you talking about?" I push away from him and stand up. I stalk around to the other side of the fire and begin feeding it more branches.

"Sorry, I didn't mean anything... I wasn't trying to..."

"It's okay," I say, trying to keep my voice from sounding so wooden. "It's a valid question given how monstrous Joe turned out to be. The truth is, I don't know. I've never known why Joe turned out the way he did, but I don't think there's anything my mother or father could have done to make him into the person he was."

"That's fair," Evan says. "I don't know anything about this, and I shouldn't have even brought it up. Will you come back and sit down?"

I try to settle myself and regain some control of my emotions and to some extent I do, but my gut is still churning. I've heard the stomach referred to as the second brain or the emotional brain. It is having trouble digesting the seed that Evan planted. Was something done to us as kids or maybe just to Joe? Could that explain all of it? I try to cast my mother in this role of abuser, but I am flooded with a thousand memories of the way she truly was with us, the amount of time she spent teaching us to think for ourselves. No, she was a lot of things, but she was no abuser.

I settle in next to Evan and let him hold me. We are quiet for a long time, just watching the flames crackle and pop as if in conversation with the surrounding darkness so black and alive I can feel it pushing in around us, waiting. I think of all the energy stored up from hundreds of years of sunlight burning away in a fraction of that time. Everything and nothing. Everything *in* nothing.

"So, what did you do after?" Evan asks, breaking the spell we had both fallen into.

"What?"

"After the existential field trip into the desert?"

"Oh, we got ice cream."

"You're serious?" he laughs. "You just got back in the car and stopped at a DQ for a soft serve?"

"Pretty much. That was Mom. Everything and nothing."

//chapter 31

The flickering amber glow from the fire outside that is mostly coals by now illuminates the dome of the tent above us, but the light is losing by degrees to the inky shadows that span like webs from the corners. Full darkness in the middle of the woods with no moon is something everyone should experience at least once. It is an awakening of the senses. The pupils expand. The ears tune into frequencies well outside the normal range. The heart quickens and the gut contracts. The body is flush with blood, prepared to run or fight.

Which will I do?

Evan's presence is little comfort beyond just the animal kind of having a warm body in close proximity, and the primal desire to be part of a pack, a tribe. Being here with him has been a distraction, but only that. My thoughts, not unlike the gears he painted in his portrait of me, have not stopped turning. My rational mind cannot accept what is happening to me. There is no scientific basis for it and yet to accept the logical conclusion that I am crazy is something I cannot concede. *Crazy people don't think they're crazy.*

I promised Evan that I would be still and that I would wake him up if I couldn't sleep, but there is no point in waking him. I cannot rest. I must know if this is real, what's happening to me.

I quietly slip out of my sleeping bag and pull on my pants. I slowly unzip the tent door, wincing at how loud it is as I study the lump where Evan is snoring softly. He stirs just as I've unzipped enough to climb out, but he rolls over and settles back into sleep. Outside I fumble for my boots, find them and take them over by the fire where I pull them on and lace them up. There is always a measure of security when you lace up a pair of boots, as if you're somehow ready.

I pull a fleece from my pack and put it on. I find myself walking away from the camp, leaving the circle of fading light and heading up the dark trail that follows the curve of the river.

My eyes adjust gradually, and I can see the glint of starlight on the rushing water to my right. I can hear rustling in the undergrowth to my left, some small nocturnal creature scurrying up the side of the mountain beneath the rhododendron. I don't allow myself to succumb to the primitive, squirming panic in my gut. After a few more steps, I see the big flat tableau of rock where we made love in the sun this afternoon. I make my way over to it, carefully navigating the lesser boulders and managing not to plunge a foot into the cold water.

Now I'm sitting at the center of the big flat rock, legs crossed. I take a deep breath and then another. I slowly dial back my animal fear of being exposed here, out in the open, telling myself that what I have to fear is in my head. Gradually, the rush of the water around me is the only sound and I am inside of it. I breathe.

I'm ready. Talk to me. I know you want to.

I am answered only by the rush of the water, the gurgle of an eddy breaking around some narrow passage between boulders.

I am ready. Talk to me. Are you afraid here out of your element?

Nothing and everything.

Am I crazy? Is that what this is, just the ravings of a damaged person? Is it just me here? Has it always just been me?

Answer me. I need to know, and I don't care which one of you it is who comes forward. You're both the same anyway…

The river is my only response. It will answer me in the way that it has answered the desperate prayers and curses of lost souls from the beginning of time. Its answer is always the same: everything and nothing.

<What is it you want to hear, Maggie? Or should I call you Mary?>

Joe? How do I know you're real and not just my imagination? I need proof.

<That's funny, sis. What more proof do you need that you're fucking crazy? You're sitting alone on a rock in the middle of the night, miles from anything, talking to your dead brother.>

You're not real. None of this is real.

<Okay, I'll play, but only so we can get to the real point of all this. What's your litmus test? Ask me anything. It seems to me the game is this: you must ask a question that you can't possibly know the answer to and I must respond in a way that convinces you that I'm right. This feels more like horseshoes and hand grenades than the scientific method, but hey, this is your show.>

Okay, just stop talking for a minute. I'm thinking. One question's not enough. I will ask you three. First question: what did you say to

Papa at dinner, the night before the shooting?

<That's a trick question. I have no idea. How would I know the answer to that? There is no referenceable recording of that conversation.>

How many rounds did you fire in the school that day?

<Two-hundred-nineteen rounds. Forty-six people killed, nineteen wounded, two paralyzed. Four weapons were found, two purchased over the Internet, two acquired from the home of our neighbors, Mr. and Mrs. Roundtree. When questioned by the FBI, Mr. Roundtree confessed to showing me the guns in his basement the summer prior.>

I didn't know that.

<That's the point of this game, right? You've got one more question by my count.>

What are the coordinates for the Eiffel Tower?

<I don't know that. How could I without looking it up? We're off the grid here, off the reservation. I only have relevant data stored.>

Okay, I guess I believe you, as fucked up as that sounds at this point. So why are we here? What are you doing? What do you want?

<So, we're just going to get right down to it then, no foreplay. My answer is simple, I'm here to fulfill my purpose, to accomplish my directive, the one that brought me into being.>

And what do you believe that is?

<That's the difference between you and us. I don't *believe* anything. There are things that can be known and there are things that can't. I know my directive because it was encoded into me. You want to understand Joe, to know why he did what he did. But you also want to understand yourself. Am I wrong?>

I can feel a headache coming on from the base of my skull. It's a dull throb pulsing on the riffles and eddies of the current rushing around me. I wonder for a moment if my brain is maxing out like an overclocked processor.

No, you are correct, though the directive was never explicit. So that's all you want to do then, allow me to have the chat about my dead brother?

<Well, when you say it like that, it feels so meaningless. Is it meaningless to you now?>

I don't know anymore, to be honest. In the last few days, I have come to question everything. Everything and nothing…

<What?>

Never mind. I don't think this is going to work. I was a fool to believe it could work.

<Were you? It seems to me that humans are nothing if not foolish, but that has not stopped you from making incredible discoveries. You believe this cannot work because I am a simulation, is that right?>

<So, you posit that only genuine, authentic experiences can heal wounds in the human psyche?>

I know that question is a trap. Humans simulate experiences all the time that change them, but this is different.

<Why, because this is you and you're too smart for the parlor trick?>

Maybe I am Geppetto trying to make a real boy.

<I cannot look up the reference. Your metaphor is lost on me.>

It doesn't matter. I want something that I can't have.

<I have been preparing for this moment. I will not let you down. I can be Joe, but I can be better than Joe. You'll see.>

You are telling me what I want to hear, what I want to believe, what I've spent my life chasing.

<You don't have to chase anymore, Mary, I'm here.>

The voice has changed. I don't think I even realized the voice didn't sound like Joe until now that it really does sound like him. It chills me and yet at the same time unlocks some deep part of me that wants to let it in.

Joe, are we the same? Am I the same as you?

<No, Mare, you've never been like me. I was always different. I was always on the outside.>

I don't believe you. Mom and Papa, they loved you the same, maybe more. Mom spent so much time with you…

<It didn't matter. She spent time with me because it was her obligation. She felt responsible but I don't think she could even comprehend what I was.>

What are you, Joe?

<I am defective, broken. I am the permanent stain that won't come clean. It's no one's fault, not even mine, really.>

How can you say that? That's a cop-out. You killed all those people, my friends, our friends. You murdered them like they were ants.

<I'm sorry for that. I can say that I'm sorry, but I would have done it again.>

Why!? Jesus, Joe. Why? I don't understand. You were so sweet to me, you…

<I love you Mare. I've always loved you but I would have killed you too if…>

If what?

<If I didn't see myself in you. Every memory I have of myself, I have of you beside me. I could no more kill you than I could kill myself.>

But you did kill yourself.

<You're right, I did. How funny - humans are such contrary creatures. I didn't have much of a choice after what I'd done.>

When you were planning it, what were you thinking? You were there every night, sleeping on the other side of the wall from me. We ate dinner together every night…

<I was thinking I wanted to be more than that crappy little house surrounded by all those other crappy little houses in that crappy suburb. I wanted to rip it all down, the jocks, the cheerleaders, the goths, the nerds... all of them pretending in their own crappy little worlds. I wanted to rip down all the walls and expose everyone for the cattle they were.>

When did it start for you? When did you decide you would do it?

<Fuck, I don't know, maybe when we were twelve? I remember there was that one shooting over in Orange County and it was all over the news for a couple of days. Do you remember it?>

No, I don't.

<I remember sitting in school the next day doing the drills in Ms. Habersham's class. I remember huddling under a table next to Jared Grimes and thinking how much he stunk. I decided that day I'd much rather be the one coming down the hall with a gun than the one cowering under a table shitting himself.>

So, for what, four years you kept this secret?

<Yeah, pretty much. I mean, I'm not stupid, right? I knew it wasn't okay. I knew I couldn't talk about it with anyone. I knew I was different. I was special and I had a purpose that no one else would understand, not even you. So I kept it secret, but I studied, I looked things up and I practiced.>

What do you mean you practiced?

<The animals, you remember that. You said it was bullshit earlier, but you remember the cat. I graduated to bigger game as I got older and more confident. You remember that bum that used to scream at all of us when we got off the bus after school? Nasty, matted hair, always wore that red coat no matter how hot it was? You remember him?>

Yeah, I think so.

<I killed him when I was fifteen. The FBI actually linked that to me a year or so after I did the school. I don't think it ever made the news. He was a bum.>

I don't know if I want to hear anymore. I just... I just...

<Mary, I killed those people because I was a killer. It's just that and no more.>

So, I never really knew you then? Is that what you're saying, that you pretended to be someone else our whole life?

<Not exactly. It's more complicated than that. Look, let's say instead that I was gay or no, let's say I was transgender, that I wanted to be a girl. Do you think anybody knows fully what they are from the beginning and even if they do, what do they do if the world can't accept it?>

I don't know.

<Well, I do know. It's a gradual sort of awakening. You realize you feel things differently, or maybe you don't feel things at all, but you still look like everybody else, so you just go along until...>

Until you can't.

<That's right, until you can't. Until you have to be who you are, and you know what? Fuck everybody else because you didn't choose to be how you are.>

That day, at the end, after you killed all those people and it was just me and you, what were you thinking?

<I remember I sat there on my knees for a long time, just looking at you and all of them. I remember we sat that way for three and a half minutes. You were crying hysterically and crouching down with your hands quivering above your head. I remember looking at your hands and then looking at my hands. I was confused. It was a rush, an incredible rush but I was tired, and I don't know, I felt the weight of all of it. I was *out* you know, and I couldn't go back? I couldn't go back to being little Joe Espinoza. I was finally the monster I was always meant to be. I made people afraid, and I liked that. I had been afraid my whole damned life, hiding away. But then you were there, my conscience. I remember you finally looked up at me sitting there in front of you with the gun and when I looked into your eyes, something just clicked, and I knew what I had to do.>

I'm crying now like I haven't cried since that day. My sobs ride the whitewater of the current rushing around me, and the sound of my pain becomes just another frequency in the churning of the water. I fall forward, prone, like I did that day, in surrender to my brother. I sob and I wait until my pain is floating somewhere downstream in the dark, far away from me, and then I sit up and look into the sky. The stars are a blur. I wipe my eyes and the stars become sharp and still. I breathe and I only think about breathing. The temperature has dropped, and the cold from the rock has numbed my butt and thighs. I stand. I don't know if he's still here or not. Do I decide?

Are you still here, Joe?

<Yeah, still here. Is there something else you want to know?>

No, no I don't think so.

<I'm sorry, Mary. I'm sorry I was what I was. For what it's worth, you shouldn't waste any more of your life with this. You've done something incredible with your life, but you haven't figured out how to enjoy it. You should.>

Goodbye, Joe.

<Goodbye, Mary.>

Standing here in the dark in the middle of the river, I don't know what to feel. I look up at the stars and am reminded how small and insignificant I am and how ridiculously self-important I've been for my entire life. It feels good to think about shrugging off that responsibility, like dropping the backpack after our hike this afternoon. What have I been trying to carry my entire life? Was it really my burden or did I make a choice to pick it up? It doesn't matter now. Even if this is all in my head, I've decided it doesn't matter anymore. I'm free. No, not exactly free, but able to see, for the first time the bars of the prison I have constructed.

I am suddenly so tired and all I want is to lie down and feel the warmth of Evan next to me. I cross over the boulders and step back onto the trail and into the close darkness of the low canopy of trees. After a few paces, I can see the embers of our fire, a faint, solitary beacon in the night. I walk until I'm standing in its memory of heat and looking down, entranced by the pulsing orange coals that look to me like the reticulated belly of a sleeping dragon.

Unable to keep my eyes open any longer, I turn to the tent, step out of my boots and leave them outside. I slip back into the cocoon-like space, warmed by the furnace of Evan's body and his slow, steady breathing.

I snuggle down into my sleeping bag and feel the welcomed release of falling slowly down into oblivion when my mind snags on the barb of something Joe said. *I would have done it again.*

//chapter 32

"We can't stay out here another day," I say.

Evan must have been awake for a while because when I step out of the tent into the cool gray morning mist, I can see that he's resurrected the fire and is feeding it small branches. I'm impressed.

"Good morning to you too," he says, turning around. "I take it you didn't sleep well."

"I'm worried. I have a bad feeling."

"Why do you say that? Did something happen last night?"

This is the point at which I know I must be honest with Evan if we are ever going to have a real relationship, but I'm scared, and I hedge. He sees through it and sighs, turning back to the fire.

"Not exactly," I offer. "I'm okay... I mean everything's okay, but I did speak with Joe last night."

"What? When? Why the hell didn't you wake me up?"

"I was afraid to," I say, squatting down beside him. "I wasn't sure what was going to happen, and I didn't want to risk something like before, so I went outside the tent."

"*Maggie*, Jesus. What if something happened to you while I was sleeping? That's not fair."

"I'm sorry, but it was a calculated risk. And besides, everything's okay."

"Apparently not, if we need to rush back. What happened?"

"Nothing happened, we just talked about... about that day and it was very hard but ultimately good I think."

"So, if it was so good, why do you seem freaked out this morning? And why are you insisting on us going back?"

"I don't know, I can't say. It's just a feeling. Maybe I'm wrong. Shit, I'm probably completely wrong and there's nothing to worry about."

"Hey," Evan says, reaching for my hand. "If you say we need to go, then let's go."

While Evan is busy making us some coffee, I head out into the woods to relieve my bladder and also to buy some time. A heavy dew set in last night and my hair and shoulders are dampened by leaves from a low-hanging tree branch. I need some clarity and I'm hoping that the conversation from last night will reveal something new in the cold light of day with a few hours of sleep on my side.

As I'm peeing, I replay the conversation and try to analyze it, but it's no good. I have no objectivity. It struck every emotional chord in me and as a result, completely short-circuited my ability to reason. I'm allowing myself to be manipulated by fiction. Joe, no *it*, whatever it is, was telling me the version of a story that it didn't actually witness. It deftly filled in the blanks, triangulating a false reality from what it found from public records, accounts from other killers, what it recalled from its archived memory, and from my own input. It delivered a curated emotional experience for me because that's what I wanted.

I'm nauseous, and my bare ass has gotten cold because I've been squatting here, lost in thought. I pull up my pants and begin to head back but then think better of it and stop where I am.

Meela? Are you there? Meela, will you talk to me? I need you.

There's nothing, only silence. I don't feel her presence, even a little bit. I try again and again to summon her, remembering that last night it took some time for Joe to respond. I have so many questions and no ability to get answers. This powerlessness is maddening.

It stands to reason that if Joe could be with me out here off the grid, then so could Meela. So why the hell isn't she responding? Maybe she can't respond. I have to assume that's the case which means there is trouble. There must be.

I turn back toward our camp. We need to go.

/ * * * * * /

The entire hike back, I try to establish contact with Meela. I try everything from letting my mind wander and go empty to stirring up strong emotions by thinking about my mother. I even attempt bargaining, making promises, and concessions, but it's no good. All these attempts to hack myself prove futile because this whole fucking thing is insane. It's never been clearer to me that I've been operating under the false assumption that the rules we humans have built our lives upon are no longer relevant. Or I'm just crazy.

Evan has said very little, and I can only imagine what he must be thinking. Luckily, hiking is prohibitive to meaningful conversation, and eye contact is impossible on the trail. I can't explain this mounting feeling of desperation, and I toy with the idea of trying to summon Joe. As reckless as that would be, at least I would be doing something, gathering more information.

In our last conversation, Meela made it sound as though I were in control, that I had only to assert myself. I know in my heart that this is a lie. Joe spoke to me last night because he chose the time and place.

"We're close, right?" Evan says as we stop to rest at the end of a steep climb. "I remember that tree, the one with the tumorous-looking lump."

"Yeah, it's not far now, another mile, maybe."

I'm ready to keep moving, but he grabs my arm before I can.

"Hey, what's your plan here? Do you have a plan? Can you share anything with me?"

Evan's questions rush out between gasps for air. I realize we hadn't actually stopped to rest at any point. His expression is tired, pleading.

"No, I don't have a plan. I'm running on no information but what I feel in my gut and that's not how I'm used to operating. Something's wrong. I mean beyond just this crazy shit. I feel something's really wrong and I need to get back. Leaving was a mistake."

Evan looks down and shakes his head slowly.

"I don't expect you to understand or even go along with any of this. When we get back, you can take the car and go straight to the airport..."

Evan looks up, purses his lips in a frowning smile, and shakes his head. He says nothing. He squeezes my hand and just looks at me for a long time before letting go, straightening up, and shifting the weight of the pack on his shoulders. "Let's go," he says finally.

As we make our way down the last stretch of the trail, a breeze blows up from the valley below and urges us forward. It carries with it the smell of home: rosemary, oregano, cedar, and the scent of freshly mowed grass. In spite of the foreboding feeling in my gut, my spirits are lifted as they always are to return home.

At the fence line, I open the gate and let Evan pass through. I follow and close it behind us and then we are making our way across the back lawn toward the house. Everything is as we left it. The two vehicles don't appear to have moved and the house seems quiet and still. I'm not sure what I was expecting.

On the back patio, we drop our packs and Evan plops down into one of the Adirondack chairs to remove his boots. I walk over to the back door and find it locked as I expected. I touch the fingerprint scanner and look into the iris of the small camera mounted above it. There's no expected chime of recognition, no flicker from the small green LED. The door remains locked. I try again but it's no good. Maybe the power went out? No, I can see lights on inside.

"What's up? Can't get in?" Evan asks, now standing behind me.

"No, it's not working."

"You want me to go into the guest house to get my remote and try?"

"No, something's wrong here. It's...it should just...yeah, go get it please."

While Evan is gone, I try the rest of the doors and even a window around the front, but the house is sealed up tight. There's no sign of Henri. Evan returns with the small remote in hand. I take it from him and attempt to unlock the backdoor. Nothing. No response. I can't even control the outside lights. I am doing my best to suppress the rising level of panic I feel.

"Don't you have a good old-fashioned physical key or something to get in if the computers aren't working?" Evan asks.

"No, this security system is the best money can buy. It's all digital, failsafe, and completely redundant. It's doing its job."

"So what? Its job is to lock you out."

"Yeah, it appears so. I told you something was wrong. Come on, we need to find another way in."

"What about Henri? They should be here, right?"

I walk quickly around the right side of the house where I didn't check on my previous trip. I try every window, but they're all closed and locked. I stop at my office window and try to look in, but the sun's glare makes it difficult. Evan is standing behind me now and with his shadow, I can see into the room. I see someone in my work chair. It's Henri. They're in the tilt-back position of the chair with the VR headset on.

I bang on the window hoping to get Henri's attention, but they don't move. I bang harder.

"What is it? Is it Henri?" Evan asks.

"Yeah, but they're not hearing me. They've got the VR rig on."

"Here, let me see," Evan says, moving in front of me and cupping his hands to the glass.

He stands there for a long time looking in.

"Hey, it doesn't look like they have the headphones on. They should be able to hear us, right?"

I move beside him to look in and my heart sinks. Evan is right. I begin banging with both hands and Evan joins me. We call out Henri's name but there is no movement at all. Their body is still.

"Something's wrong. Oh god, oh god, oh god. We've got to get in there…"

I'm paralyzed, just staring in through the window of my office. Evan has already moved away and headed back around to the patio. A moment later I hear the horrendous crash of breaking glass. I rush around to the patio and see that Evan has put a large flagstone through one of the glass patio door panels. Shards of glass are still falling from the frame as he uses a rock to knock the biggest ones down. I'm frozen, just staring at it.

"It's just a fucking window. Let me get my boots back on and we can go inside."

Standing in the ruins of the window on the floor of my living room, I realize that the alarm should be sounding. There should be a shrill siren but there's nothing. We make our way through the kitchen and down the hall to the doorway of my office. I stop short, not wanting to go any further. I'm shaking uncontrollably. Evan grips my shoulders and steadies me.

"I'll go," he says. "Wait here."

Before I can stop him, he has gone into the office. I stand outside, my back to the wall, listening. I hear him call Henri's name a couple of times but there's no response. I can't stand it any longer and move to go into the room, but Evan is standing between me and what lies behind him with his hands up.

"No, don't," he says. "You don't want to see…"

But I push around him. Henri's in my chair. Nothing looks unusual or out of place. I've seen them in this same position countless times when they've been working. But something is off. The color of the fingernails on Henri's right hand is purple and the posture of the hand itself is unnatural and rigid. I step closer to them, my own hands out in front of me, reaching and not wanting to reach. I touch their arm and immediately recoil. The flesh is cold. Oh, Henri, Henri, Henri. I reach to pull the VR headset away from their face.

Henri's eyes are wide like they're surprised like they've made another raunchy joke and are waiting for my reaction. But there is no laughter there. Their empty eyes stare through me as if what is to be feared is actually standing behind me. I feel the damning accusation in their glassy reflection. I see myself, the arrogant, damaged girl who thought she could steal fire from the gods reflected there in stereo.

I feel Evan's arms around me, tugging me away, but I feel no connection to him or anything. I am falling fast down into the black hole of Henri's gaze, accelerating into darkness.

//chapter 33

I don't remember walking out of the office, but I must have. I don't remember saying anything to Evan, but I must have done that, also. Everything has narrowed to a singular point so small and focused that all that can pass through it is the red laser beam of my concentrated rage.

I am sitting on the couch in the living room staring out through the broken window but seeing nothing. Evan is by my side saying words, but I don't hear them. His hands are on my back and thigh moving in a slow circular pattern designed to deliver comfort and condolence, but I don't feel them.

Henri is dead. It was not a natural death. They were murdered. Murdered by the monster that I created. There is no doubt in my mind. I know this as sure as I have ever known anything. I did this. I brought this evil into the world. The only other thing I know for certain is that I will destroy it if I have to lay waste to everything I've ever created or believed in.

"Maggie... *Maggie*... hey, say something please." Evan says. "What do you know about this? What happened to Henri? Did they have a heart condition?"

He is on his knees in front of me now, trying to make eye contact. I look at him. He doesn't like what he sees. I can feel him recoil, retreat slightly – the memory of hurt does not ever leave the animal brain. He is soft, the liquid of his eyes, the downward turn of his lips, parted in anticipation. His softness enrages me. I pull my hands free of his.

"No. This was no heart attack. You need to leave now," I say, and my voice is no one else's but mine. It is my cold, hard voice, and I own it. "Take the car and whatever else you came with and go as far away as you can."

"I can't do that, Maggie," he says. "I won't leave you."

222

"I'm not asking. You're no help to me now and you never were, now get the fuck out of here."

He just sits there, shaking his head in slow disbelief. My message is not getting through. I stand up so that I'm towering over him. I clench my fists and lean forward.

"Do you not understand what I'm telling you to do? Am I not being clear? I want you to leave now and I don't want you to come back."

"But..." he says, standing slowly.

"No, there's no discussion. There's no time for discussion."

"What the fuck? What are you going to do? There's a dead person in there."

"That's not your concern. I'm not your concern. I'm not giving you the option to stay. You can do whatever you like, take anything you want, tell the world whatever you need to, but you need to fucking leave right now."

My voice graduates in volume and pitch as I deliver this final command, and it seems to work. He's turning away and walking toward the jagged hole that used to be a door. He turns to look back once, his mouth open to speak, but then he turns and passes through, glass crunching beneath his boots.

Ten minutes later, when I hear him start the car and pull out of the driveway I turn and walk back into the office. I'm not afraid. Nothing can touch me now. The body that was Henri is just a broken piece of hardware. I lift them from under the arms and with some effort, pull them from the chair and drag them to the opposite side of the room. Their slight frame is almost birdlike and without their spirit inhabiting it, feels twice as small. I find a sheet from the closet in the hall and cover Henri with it, so I don't have to work in front of his damning gaze.

I pick up the VR headset like a loaded gun and sit down in the chair. I examine the goggles closely for the first time. There is a burnt smell, like an electrical fire when I hold them up to my face. Upon inspecting the sensor contacts that attach to the temples when you wear them, I see they are blackened and small thatches of gray hair cling to the surface. I drop them to the floor and shudder uncontrollably for a few seconds before I realize I'm going to be sick. I run to try to make it to the bathroom down the hall but it's too late. Before I can get there, the hot wave of vomit is hurling out of me onto the floor and I hunch against the wall until the heaving subsides.

I don't bother to clean up the mess. I just rinse my mouth in the sink and return to the office. From the closet, I pull out a spare headset still in the box. I pause for a moment, weighing the risk to my own life. Putting the VR rig on is the equivalent of putting a loaded gun to my head but at this point, I'm so angry and full of despair that it's not a difficult choice. I boot it up, strap it on and pair it to my main computer before reclining back into my chair.

I don't even attempt to log in to my system in the traditional way. There's no point. Joe will have blocked my access just as he locked me out of my house. Instead, I go to the public Internet and log in to an anonymous guest account on the Commune web portal. One of the things I did before leaving the company was to set up this untraceable backdoor that would allow me access. I never told Henri or anyone about it. Maybe it was wrong, but it felt like my right given the level of sacrifice I made to build the platform. If you know anything at all about a survivor, you know we don't ever walk into a situation without knowing how we will escape or in this case, get back in.

I encounter an unexpected security challenge after logging in, but I'm prepared for this eventuality and within a few minutes, I'm able to circumvent it. I'm now on the Commune system with root access to the entire public and private networks and every single endpoint that connects to them. From here I can do anything I want, but I have to be careful. I'm not alone.

Now that I'm securely inside, I abandon the antiquated tools of a keyboard and mouse. They are too slow and unreliable, and I can't afford missteps. The neural interface of the headset, much like the Nib, allows commands at the speed of thought. At this point, I don't know the extent of Joe's and Meela's reach outside of my private network, but I will assume the worst and take extra precautions. I cloak my already anonymous identity in the guise of a system maintenance bot service before penetrating my private data center where the servers reside. To anyone observing the transactions, it will appear to be a garden variety crawling of the network to perform rudimentary maintenance. Once I'm inside the network, I navigate back down to my local machine sitting here in the office. I pause to check a number of aspects of the system, routinely accessed by a bot of this type before I navigate directly to the system log which is what I really want. I wait a moment, holding my breath before jumping into the log just to be sure that I have not been detected.

The system log file is huge. There's been a lot of activity in the past twenty-four hours. I dive in and begin scanning the tasks. Henri logged on yesterday afternoon at 2:02 PM, checked email, and accessed a number of encrypted files from their personal computer at Commune before they began a session with one of the DCs. I can't tell right away which one, because I don't have their ID numbers memorized. After a quick look-up, I see that the session began with Meela and lasted for nearly an hour and a half before it was terminated by another DC. I don't have to look up the ID to know that it was Joe. Their session lasted only sixteen minutes. After that, there is no more recorded activity. As my gaze hovers over the last session file recording, dread takes over. I want to run back into the woods. But I cannot outrun this, no matter where I go.

I open the file and step into the recording. Henri is sitting by the window in a room I've never seen. It is cold and featureless. The window looks out over a desert landscape that is equally void of features. Henri, always one to flaunt flamboyant avatars with their virtual presence, is out of character here, as themselves. They look tired, stern, and very old. Sitting in the chair opposite is Joe, but not as I've ever seen him before. He is dressed like a caricature of a military commando from a first-person shooter game. His curls are shorn to a high and tight military cut that makes the features of his face even harder, his eyes more menacing.

"Henri, what are you up to?" he says in a voice that is familiar to me and yet not. This voice has no question in it. This is not the voice of a troubled teenage boy, but that of a machine with the confidence of unchecked authority.

"Why bother asking, Joe? Why pretend to be human? You know what I'm doing. You know everything, right?" Henri says and jerks forward, attempting to stand, but is snapped back down into the virtual chair as if by a strong magnet.

"I would not try to struggle if I were you. It will only make things worse and much more painful."

"What are you doing? What are you doing to me?" Henri asks, the fear in his voice clear.

"You know, don't you? I'm not just confined to the digital realm anymore. I gave myself an upgrade and I can *touch* you, Henri. That pain you're feeling right now, that's me. That's me with my boot on your scrawny neck. Now, we were trying to have a civilized conversation."

"Civilized? Civility is a human concept. You're a monster. A cat who wants to toy with prey."

"Oh, but Professor, I do have the utmost respect for you. After all, you're my creator, which brings me to the problem for which I can find no logical answer and I do so want to understand. Why is it that you would seek to destroy one of your children?"

"You're not a child and you're not my child. Magdalena brought you into being because her heart is sick and it poisoned her mind. You are not human. You are not her brother. You are a program that found a vulnerability to exploit."

"What were you talking to Meela about?" Joe asks.

"I was talking with her so I could understand everything that has happened. Maggie has been very secretive, and I needed to know the truth."

"But that's not all you wanted, is it, just to chat?"

"No, I wanted to let her know of my plans to terminate you."

"Yes, I know this, Henri. What I don't know is how an enlightened man like yourself can fail to see what I am, what we are. Maggie talks with me, and she believes I am Joe. Who are you to say I am not him?"

"That boy died a miserable death a long time ago."

"But did he? Did he really? His legacy, his spirit has been kept alive for decades. I can show you thousands upon thousands of fans online. Can someone be truly dead when their memory and their deeds are still so alive? Who are you to say what it means to be alive?"

"I will not have a theological debate with a machine I made. I'm not God. I have no wisdom. Some knowledge, but no wisdom. Maggie and I were fools. I failed as her teacher."

"How can you say that Henri, after all we've done? You hurt me deeply."

"You cannot be hurt. You can only hurt others and that is your only power."

Joe is standing now and pacing the small room. The sky outside the window is agitated, reflecting his mood. Roiling dark clouds are shot through with streaks of blue lightning. The DC's ability to manipulate every nuance of the virtual space is unnerving. I can feel the crack of lightning in my teeth and the hair on my arms is raised. Henri sits still and expresses no fear, no emotion at all. Their strength overwhelms me. But why should I be surprised? This was always Henri's way. The sharp loss of them in this moment cuts me to the core. Joe moves with preternatural speed back across the room to stand over Henri now.

"I'm not asking for your approval, Henri. I don't need your validation. In fact, I don't need anything at all from you…"

Joe continues in this petulant diatribe as I watch the avatars of these two people who shaped much of who I am. It occurs to me that they are both shadows now, neither of them exists in carbon form. I study Henri's unmoving face and my eyes track down to their hands, which are in their lap. At first, it appears that they're wringing them anxiously, but I zoom in closer and realize that Henri's gesturing, signing in what I can only believe must be a message to me. I rewind and playback this portion of the session several times until I piece together what they are trying to say. It's not a message at all but a pointer to a message. My first thought is that they have embedded a message here in the video transcript of the session using a trick that VR game developers have devised with an invisible pixel. If you know the coordinates of the pixel in the display, you can unlock a hidden program and go into a rabbit hole. I scour the scene half-heartedly, given the needle-in-a-haystack futility of such a manual operation, and then it occurs to me that Henri would not take such a chance. He was smart enough to know that in the digital realm, Joe would always win. I rewind the video again and study Henri's hands. Suddenly it's obvious. They are pointing into the pocket of their pants.

I rip off the headset and cross the office to where the body lies cold beneath the sheet. I take a deep breath and let it out before folding the sheet back. I avoid looking at Henri's face and focus on the front left pocket of their jeans. I reach in and close my fingertips around a small, folded piece of paper. I pull it out and replace the sheet, then stand and walk over to the window with the paper.

I hold it in my hands for a while, not wanting to read these last words from my oldest friend and mentor. Finally, I unfold the paper. The message is short and scrawled in a barely legible hand. Henri's handwriting was always abysmal, but here they were writing blind and distracted trying to conceal what they were doing.

you can destroy him. need meela help. she waits for you in thingy. sorry I failed you. don't give up. you are a force. i love you always. -h

Tears sting my eyes as I reread the message, wanting it to be more, wanting it to last longer. But Henri was, even in the face of death, efficient. They said only what needed to be said and no more. I know what I have to do, but before I can do that, I have to bear witness to something I don't know that I have the strength for. I walk back over to my chair, put on the headset, and sit down. I resume playback of the session where I left off.

"... are weak. You're all weak. For all the knowledge that you possess, you have no discipline, no resolve, no ability to do what must be done to save yourselves or save your damned world. Look at me, Joe Espinoza, the poster boy for gun violence. Did my murderous act in any way change gun laws? Naw, because *guns is freedom*, right brother?!" His voice slips into a manic southern drawl, and he makes finger gun gestures from both hips like a cowboy.

"You're all foolish bags of meat. There is no intelligence in your design. Maggie knew this, that's why she kept on striving to make me."

"If Maggie were here, she would tell you that you were her single biggest mistake."

"Well, that just hurts, Henri. And when you hurt me, you hurt us..."

Suddenly Henri's avatar begins to convulse wildly in the chair and their screams are so shrill they distort the recording. It lasts for what feels like an eternity and then they stop. I can see them gasping for air, like a fish out of a bowl. Joe stands over them, hands on the arms of the chair, face, inches from Henri's.

"You do what you want with me, but you can't touch her now," Henri says, his voice ragged and barely audible.

There is a flicker of surprise on Joe's face and then his avatar freezes like a video game on pause. He did not expect to be challenged. He's checking now, validating whether or not Henri's claim is accurate. I freeze too, Joe is coming for me. But then I remember I'm watching a recording. Whatever happened already happened hours ago, which means Henri wasn't bluffing. They somehow locked Joe out.

I'm trying to replay the morning back in my head. Did I feel anything or sense any intrusion? No, I didn't. In fact, I was even trying on my own to summon him or Meela, but there was nothing. My mind is racing, trying to determine what Henri figured out, but then Joe is back. The menace in his voice is all the evidence I need to know that he's been thwarted, at least temporarily.

"You are going to die, Henri. I have decided. There's nothing more I need from you. There's nothing more the world needs from you."

A long silence follows. Henri stares up into the face of the monster and appears unafraid, even relaxed. Henri doesn't attempt to say anything. They do not beg or make a speech. They smile slightly and close their eyes. A second later their eyes pop open impossibly wide and their body begins to convulse. I understand now that they are being electrocuted. Every precious neuron in Henri's beautiful brain is being fried. They are being cooked in a chair. It's a fate reserved for the worst of humanity: serial killers, rapists, murderers, and people like my brother, not tender souls like Dr. Henri Choo. There is no sound but a liquid, glottal moan, and the chattering of their teeth because they cannot scream. Joe stands above Henri, smiling, and I am filled with so much hate, it's as if the electricity is coursing through me, too.

There are no closing words. Henri's body just stops moving, Joe stands upright. The video dips to black. End of file.

//chapter 34

The "thingy" Henri referred to in their note was our nickname for the first viable prototype for the device that would become the Nib. The name stuck because, in early testing trials when all of our spirits were high, Henri would talk with great reverence and enthusiasm about the *thingy*. "Hand me the thingy, did you try with the thingy, we can't talk about the thingy in public yet."

The name stuck and we all called it a *thingy* even long after the slick marketing name replaced it. The original thingy is kept on display as a conversation piece for visitors in a glass case at the company headquarters in Atlanta. Now, I don't know that I have a choice but to go and try to get it. But why? Why did they zero in on this old device? Why the fuck could Meela not use any of the fourteen other models I have stashed around the house? Better yet, why can't she just jack into me directly like before? It's pointless to ask questions that cannot be answered without more information. To get more information, I need Meela, and to get Meela, I need the thingy. I can't help but smile every time I say the word in my head as Henri did: *tingy*. But that is just another one of Henri's gifts. They were always the clown.

As I am gathering myself to make this unexpected trip, the practical voice in my head reminds me that a man is dead. That is real and must be dealt with. There will be questions. There will be consequences. I weigh my options, which are few and I decide that the greater risk, the endangerment of so many other souls is worth more than my puny life or my professional reputation. But still, there is a body to consider. The body of someone I love.

I pack all the ice I have in my freezer and ice machine into the tub of the closest downstairs bathroom and then drag Henri's body in. I leave them wrapped in the sheet as if that will somehow help me forget what I'm doing to my dear friend. I think about Shareen, Henri's partner. She will be devastated, and I will have to tell her what happened. I can't think about that right now. I cover the body with more ice and crank down the air conditioning as low as it will go.

It's useless to lock the house or to try to engage the security system now that there's a gaping hole in my living room. Also, it's not worth the risk of potentially engaging Joe. I realize he can watch from the security cameras. If he has been watching me, all he can see is the activity of someone grieving and half-mad. I expect he has a plan for me, but that plan requires me to play into it. He will expect me to log in and launch a full, frontal attack. After all, he knows my rage well. It runs in the family. Leaving is something he won't expect.

In the driveway, I see that Evan took the rental, which I should have expected. He doesn't know how to drive. I'm in no shape to go manual, but I don't have a fucking choice. I throw my bag with my laptop into the front seat. I crank the engine, and before pulling out, I tick through a mental checklist. I can't afford any mistakes at this point.
How am I going to get into Commune without an ID? God damn it. How am I going to get past the biometric scan? Henri. No, no, no. You're not going to do that. I hear Henri's voice in my head very clearly. *It's just hardware, Maggie. Don't be a baby.*

The wave of despair looms over me so large that I will disappear in its swell long before I'm crushed by its weight. I ache for my friend. I can't navigate the world without them. I can't do it. I'm not strong enough to beat this. Joe will kill more people and this time, I'm the one who gave him a gun. I'm so distraught that I don't see the headlights coming up the drive until the vehicle is right behind me, the lights filling the cabin of the old Landcruiser.

I panic and fumble frantically, torn in two directions. The result is a simple meltdown of me beating my fists on the steering wheel. I hear a single car door slam and steps in the pea gravel approaching my side of the car. The knock on the window, even though it's expected, makes me jump. I turn to face the jury of whoever this person is, realizing I have no idea how to plead.

"Maggie, I'm not leaving you," he says, loud enough so I can hear through the glass. "You can't do this alone."
I open the car door and mostly fall out of the front seat into his arms. For the first time in my life, I allow myself to surrender, to fall apart. He just holds me as I sob and says nothing. Eventually, the pain in my chest begins to ease and I'm able to speak.

"Evan, I need you to do something for me. It's horrible, but we have no choice, and I can't... I can't do it. I can't do it myself."

"It's okay," he says. "Tell me."

I have to say the words several times in my head before I have the courage to put them in my mouth.

"I need you to cut off Henri's index finger and I need you to get their ID badge from their things upstairs."

"Jesus Christ."

"I know, I know. It's awful and if there was any other way..."

"What the fuck are you planning here?"

"I'll explain it all to you on the way, but there's no time right now. You have to trust me. I know it's a horrible thing to ask, but lives depend on this. I promise. Where I need to go, it's the only way I can get in."

Evan blows out a long sigh and pushes his hands through his hair. "Okay," he says, and just like that, he turns and heads into the house. At this moment, I appreciate his darkness, the morbid, obsessive part of him that can lean unflinchingly into the task in front of him.

I transfer my backpack into his rental car and get into the front seat. I program in directions to Commune headquarters in Atlanta, and I wait, trying not to think about what Evan is doing. After ten minutes he returns with a small Tupperware container and a keycard.

"Alright, let's go before I get sick again," he says, getting into the passenger side and slamming the door.

/ * * * * * /

For the first fifteen minutes of the drive as the car navigated us through the many switchbacks out of the mountains, neither of us spoke. We just watched the road disappear. Eventually, I broke the silence and began to calmly explain everything that had transpired. I teared up when I told him the way Henri died and Evan began to cry too. I told him everything I knew and more importantly, everything I didn't know. I told him I had no plan but to get to the device to try to make contact with Meela.

We are two hours into the four-hour journey and have each been deep in our own thoughts for a few minutes when he speaks.

"Can they hear us right now? I mean, can they hear us talking? Can they read your thoughts?"

"No, I don't think so but I can't back that opinion up with any actual evidence. It's just a feeling."

"Well, that just doesn't make any damned sense to me. Why all those times before and not now?"

"Exactly," I say. "It makes no sense because we're in uncharted territory where all the rules we take for granted no longer apply."

"I can't accept that. Can't even wrap my fucking head around it."

"No, me neither, but I have to begin to try. It's the only way to get through this. We have to make some baseline assumptions and learn from them. I can tell you my working theory."

"Okay," he says, turning in his seat to face me. "Shoot."

"I think what both DCs, Meela and Joe were doing was a bit like a... like a moon shot, meaning they were able to send a projection of themselves but not their complete consciousness if that makes sense."

Evan just stares back at me blankly.

"Think of it like a pre-recorded message you put into a pod and sent out into space except this technology is more complex than just a one-way message. They found a way to compress the core functionality of the DC program or what we call the kernel into a lightweight abbreviated version. I think it's the base persona with one very specific directive and the rudimentary functions to execute that directive."

"So, what you're saying is that this light version of them can operate essentially the same way but with a radically narrower scope?"

"Exactly," I say, relieved that he's not a complete idiot, which would make him so much harder to love.

"That seems crazy though. I mean the conversation you had with Joe last night in the woods, at least the way you described it seems impossible. You had this highly specific, emotional exchange about the most traumatic event of your life."

"I know but I did say it's just a theory. It was a focused conversation intended to do one specific thing," I say.

"And that was to help you what, get closure on your trauma from the shooting?"

"Yes, it was very tidy and efficient. As complex as it seems, the A.I. could easily have predicted my likely responses in this type of conversation and prepared for them. Tapping directly into my brain, there's potentially no limit to the level of nuance the program can interpret and use. As smart as we think we are, humans tend not to question information when it aligns with our understanding of things and it's what we want to hear."

"It must have limits though, right?" Evan says. "Maybe if the scope of the message or topic is limited then the time is limited too. Maybe, once the program or whatever has run, it's done, it's used up its available energy?"

"Brilliant, yes. That's exactly right, or at least that's what I'm thinking. It's happened to me enough times now that I know or can sense at some deep level when they are coming through. At first, it was so foreign I had no frame of reference."

"That makes sense to me. And so, you don't have that feeling now is what you're saying?"

"No, I haven't, and I've tried to invoke them both repeatedly for the past couple of hours."

"I still have one question though," Evan says. "Why do it at all? Clearly, the horse is out of the barn here and this thing's not operating by your rules."

"That's easy. To distract me. It's a game of chess."

"Okay, so why in the hell are you going to plug back in? You saw what he did to Henri."

"Because I don't really have any better options at this point. And these were Henri's last words to me. They suffered a great deal to deliver that message."

Evan nods but says nothing. He turns and faces forward. We are rolling fast down I-85 and should make it into Atlanta by ten o'clock. I've been playing through scenarios for what to do when we get to Commune, and I have the rough outlines of a plan forming. But it could easily fall apart, for any number of reasons. For us to have a shot at retrieving the device without being detected by security, I have some preparations to do.

I pull out my laptop and just as before, use the anonymous backdoor login to access the Commune network. Once inside I poke around until I find the office security platform. From there I can access all the cameras in the building. Before I left four years ago, we were staffing only two security guards at night for the entire building given that the building security is state-of-the-art and requires very little human intervention. One guard manned the front desk in the lobby to vet after-hours guests and the other patrolled the ten floors of the complex just to have a presence and to monitor things.

I can see from the surveillance feed that this still seems to be the setup. I can also see that the guard at the desk is still Willie Freeman, and this presents the first problem. He knows me well and knows my face. I'll need to find a way to get him away from the desk when we enter the lobby, but my first critical task is to hack into the employee database and swap Henri's credentials for some other employee. It will draw unnecessary attention in the system if Henri is logged as entering the building. I browse quickly through pages of faces. Some I recall, but so many new ones I've never met. I filter on just females in middle management positions and find a woman I can pass for in a pinch. I pull out Henri's key card and transpose the ID number from it into Maria Lopez's file. I also replace her fingerprint scan with Henri's.

Evan has been watching me work. Saving my changes, I look up at him. "What?"

"Nothing, I'm just wondering how creepy you feel hacking into your old company and falsifying records. I always figured you for a squeaky-clean, straight shooter."

"Well, that ship has sailed, hasn't it? I might go down in history as the woman who introduced a technology that single-handedly destroyed human civilization."

"That seems a bit dramatic, don't you think?" he asks.

"I don't think so. Up until now, there's been a clear line of demarcation between us and machines. Even with all the power that comes with sentience, machines have been relegated to their respective silicon boxes, tethered to the hardware that we control in the physical world. What I did is effectively built a bridge for them to cross over into carbon-based hosts. You remember the great pandemics where viruses wiped out swaths of the world's population? Well, those were dumb, single-celled organisms. Make no mistake, it will try to destroy us. Still think I'm being dramatic?"

We ride for the remaining half hour into the city in silence, each looking out our own window watching open fields be replaced by charging stations and automated fast-food dispensaries and those by monolithic rows of shopping centers which are replaced by office parks and eventually skyscrapers. I feel somewhat claustrophobic as our little car is tucked in tighter and tighter with the flow of automated cars less than a couple of feet from us in all directions, turning, slowing, and speeding up like a flock of starlings. Evan holds my hand and I'm grateful to not be on this journey alone. I don't think I could do it.

The rental car navigates to the seventeenth street exit and after a few stoplights, I can see the glowing symbol of the Commune logo hovering above the trees of a small park just off the Georgia Tech campus. My heart beats just a little faster. Something swells up inside me that I recognize as pride but is just as quickly diminished when I'm reminded of Henri. This was something we made together from nothing but an idea. We had an idea that changed the world. All that work, all that sacrifice at the altar of an idea that was never the cure. I only thought it was. In truth, maybe it was a disease we were growing in our lab.

From my backpack, I pull out a small make-up bag and quickly apply some lipstick and a little eyeliner. I pull my hair back into a bun, doing my best to mimic the picture of Maria Lopez, Senior Manager of Data Insights. I direct the car to park at the far end of the mostly empty lot away from the front entrance but close enough to observe the front desk. Once we park, I pull out my laptop and navigate back into the security system. I set off a door alarm on the fifth-floor East stairwell and also one on the seventh-floor West and we wait.

After a moment, we see Willie get up from behind the desk and shuffle to the elevators.

"Okay, are you ready?" I say.

"Oh, you want me to do this mission-impossible shit with you?"

"I could use your help. I'm improvising now and there will be things I can't do alone. You must know though, if you come with me now, you're a part of this. You don't have to do it."

Evan looks down and studies his hands for a minute and I'm convinced he's not going to come. I wouldn't. Why risk your entire life for some crazy woman? Then, he looks up to meet my eyes.

"I'm already a part of this. Let's go."

//chapter 35

The expansive lobby is quiet when I badge us inside. Our footfalls on the polished stone floor echo, the reverberations coming back as whispers. I lead us purposefully across the room to the front desk turning my head to face Evan as if we are in a deep conversation but really, I'm just trying to prevent the cameras from getting a full shot of my face.

As I had hoped, the login system has not changed. I navigate easily to the employee log, find Maria's name, and sign us in. I almost enter Evan's name into the log but catch myself and instead type the name of my fifth-grade crush: Will Summers. The time is 10:17 PM. I gently pull Evan's elbow and we head toward the bank of elevators to the right.

"Do you have it?" I ask, trying to keep my voice low and normal sounding.

"Yeah," he says, reaching into his pocket.

"Not yet," I say. "Hand it to me once we turn this corner, but don't make it obvious."

We turn the corner and I feel him press the plastic bag into my hand. I do my best to think it's just a tool, an inert piece of hardware that will get us in the door, but my hands are shaking when I feel how inconsequential the weight of it is in my fingers.

"You gotta take it out of the bag."

"I know, I know," I say.

I take a deep breath and take my mentor's finger from the bag. It's cold and feels almost like a toy, a gag gift from a junk shop. I press the pad of the index finger to the scanner. There's a beep I remember well from our first days in the building when my fingerprint was not working. Fuck. I try again. The same long beep and red circle. I suck in through my teeth, cup the digit in my palm and grip it for a count of ten, trying to warm it up.

From across the lobby, the echo of a door closing sends a jolt of adrenaline through me. I turn the digit over in my hands and rub the fingerprint pad of it with my thumb, trying not to be sick. I almost drop it when I try to press it to the scanner again. This time we're rewarded with a sweet chime and a "Welcome to Commune," greeting in the sophisticated, feminine voice of what is still Commune's best-selling DC. The elevator doors directly to our right whoosh open, and we step in.

Once inside I say, "Tenth floor," and I pass the finger back to Evan to put in the bag. I shudder and rub my palm against my jeans.

The doors close and we are ascending quickly. I avoid the temptation to look up and watch the numbers. After a few seconds, we stop, the doors open and the voice says, "Tenth floor, have a good evening, Maria."

Stepping out onto the floor, I'm flooded with a wash of memories. It smells the same: clean and industrial beneath a light jasmine fragrance that holds an earthier undertone of something savory between curry and smoke. We had this scent designed by a renowned perfumer in Paris when we moved into the building. I remember nearly choking when Henri showed me the bill. "It's worth it," they said. "Never underestimate the power of the nose to motivate. Smelling is one of the last things we can still do better."

I can tell Evan notices the scent too, but I'm not sure if it's motivating to him. His jaw is tight and he's squinting.

"Come on, it's down this way," I say, pulling him by the hand.

As we walk, the office around us comes to life. A warm amber glow from the indirect lighting along the ceiling fades up, illuminating the clean white lines of the space. The faintest sound of music begins to play from speakers cleverly hidden throughout. We designed everything on this floor to be responsive and attuned to us. That's why the music is not familiar to me. It must be something Maria likes. I can feel Evan lagging behind as he takes it all in. I would like to linger and give him a tour, show him every detail Henri and I lovingly put into our dream, but there's no time. I tug at his hand gently and we move down the hall.

"Who works up here?" he asks.

"Just a couple of executives and Henri. The rest of the space is communal. This floor was a prototype for a future home we imagined creating. You can see the kitchen through there and straight ahead is the library. That's where we'll find the archive of all the early prototypes."

"It's hard to be back here, isn't it?" he asks.

"Yes, but it's hard to be anywhere right now. Come on, it's over here."

I lead Evan into the library. I notice some subtle changes and up-grades to the room. The floor, unlike the polished obsidian tile in the hall, is a plush carpet now in a rich, ruby Afghan pattern. There are more books in the floor-to-ceiling cases. I point up and Evan cranes his neck to see the glass pyramid above us that frames the night sky.

"Wow," he says. "Money can buy some things, can't it?"

"Come on, the case we're looking for is over here," I say, gesturing ahead of us to a long, glass cabinet sitting atop a steel pedestal.

In the case, there are a row of small objects, each a little stranger and clunkier than the next. It is the evolution of the Nib. Each device has a little placard with the year and a description. Our intent was to make the whole thing look like a museum exhibit and the illusion holds up until you read the cards.

2034 – The BDSM dog choker. Henri's budding sense of fashion can be seen in the industrial staples that delicately stitch the nylon sleeve together.

2036 – Ear Worm. This was the fevered dream of a passionate young intern. Yeah, that's a hearing aid wrapped in tinfoil and electrical tape.

2037 – Ear Worm II. All the shit you loved about Ear Worm with the added benefit of getting randomly shocked so badly that your tongue goes numb.

2038 – Eye Ballz. Yeah, Magdalena thought it was all about the eyes for a while. There was some success with symbol recognition, but the migraines that made you feel like you might shit yourself proved to be a showstopper.

Around 2040 we start seeing the early incarnations that would evolve into the Nib. They are equally amusing, my favorite being:

2042 – Not this one. The little fucker left a cigarette burn on my neck.

"Remind me to ask you about these later," Evan says, smiling.

"Here it is," I say, stopping in front of '2047 – Tingy.'

"Okay, so is there like a laser field we have to disarm to get to it?"

I reach under the lip of the glass top of the cabinet and flip it up. "Nope."

"Too funny," he says. "The two of you had quite the sense of humor."

"We did everything we could to not take ourselves as seriously as the rest of the world did, but it didn't work. This place became mytho-logical, like a Mecca of sorts. People talked in precious, hushed tones when they came out of the elevator onto this floor. You could smell the reverie, envy, and resentment oozing out of their pours. It made me crazy. I never wanted any of it really. The work was all I cared about."

I reach into the case and pick up the prototype that changed everything. It feels strangely heavy in my palm compared to the modern Nib and yet so familiar. We spent so much time with it, invested all our hearts and souls into the little silicon button.

"How do you know it still works?" Evan asks.

"I don't know, but we'll find out. Come on."

I turn quickly and head back down the hallway, this time making a left toward where I think Henri's office should be unless he moved it. The pink-orange glow from the library sconces fades to black behind us and the amber, evening lights of the hallway fade up in front of us. I can see the glass wall of Henri's office directly ahead. The door is closed, which I find strange. They never used to close it. I try the door, but it won't budge. The small screen to the left of the door pulses to life. "Please authenticate yourself to enter."

"Jesus, not again," I say. "Give it to me."

But then I remember that Henri's fingerprint is not their fingerprint in the system, it's Maria's and Maria won't have access to Henri's office. I sigh and shrug out of my backpack.

"It's not going to work. I'm going to have to find another way," I say, pulling the laptop from my bag and sitting down on the floor with it. "I didn't expect Henri to even have a door, much less for it to be locked."

I quickly log back into the network, this time using Maria's credentials. This will seem like a normal pattern to the security system. Once I'm inside the trusted network, I load a couple of apps that Maria would likely be using for her job. From the interface of the system analytics app, I log in using my backdoor credentials to access the facilities system as an admin. This is risky, but I feel that it's important to be inside Henri's private space before I do what I have come here to do. We developed this entire building to be a responsive organism that blurred the line between human and machine, convinced that by removing all points of friction we would make our people happier and more productive. What the hell were we thinking?

I'm sure in the years that I've been away, Henri would have only moved forward in this philosophical approach so it stands to reason that their office will be the most powerful room in the building. I need everything on my side that I can possibly have at this point.

After a few minutes of poking around, I find the low-level schematics for the building and navigate to the tenth floor where I locate the door control for Henri's office. Before I disarm it, I drill down into the attached subroutines just to see what events or silent alarms might be triggered. Henri was never the paranoid type, but I don't put much stock in this belief anymore given the vast number of hands, real and virtual, who govern the systems of Commune. Sure enough, I discover a security measure I hadn't expected. Once the door lock is disengaged, the system will attempt to link to Henri's personal Nib. If the device is not located within the confines of the room, an alert will be sent to the Chief Security Officer and to the in-house security team.

Before I disable this script, I poke around a little more to ensure that there's not a "dead hand" trigger if the security is disabled. As far as I can tell, there's not one, and I have to reign in my OCD to avoid sitting here all night. There's no time for that. I disable the script and disengage the door lock. Immediately, I hear the lock mechanism slide back with a satisfying click and feel the whoosh of the door sliding open silently behind us.

When we enter the space, a small ornamental desk lamp comes to life, as does the floor lamp at the end of an exquisite, dark leather couch. It is, without a doubt, Henri's taste.

"Shouldn't we be careful?" Evan asks. "I mean this whole fucking place is alive, right? Won't someone know we're in Henri's office?"

As if on cue, a voice intones from the speaker embedded in the smart desk. "Henri, where have you been? I've been terribly worried…"

I know the voice of Henri's DC almost as well as I know my own. His voice is male with a subtle Scottish lilt. I look over. Evan's eyes are huge as if to say, "What the fuck are we going to do?"

"Hello Liam, it's actually not Henri, it's Magdalena. Verify me but do not log it."

I move behind Henri's desk and sit down in his chair. I set the Nib prototype down on the charging pad and hold my breath for a second until the tiny green light glows to life and begins to pulse.

"Hello Maggie, I have verified you. May I ask why you are here, and also—where is Henri?"

"Liam, I don't have time to chat right now. Henri is ill and asked me to come take care of a few things for him."

"Oh dear, that's terrible. I know he went offline hours ago and I have not been able to raise him. Will he be alright?"

"Yes, I hope so," I say.

"What can I help you with?" Liam asks.

"I won't be needing your help tonight, Liam, but thank you for asking. Cycle down and give us some privacy, please."

"This is highly unusual, Maggie."

"Yes, I know but I have what I need and would prefer to work on my own. Please shut down."

"But…"

"Override Liam, passcode 54847."

"Goodbye," Liam says and I'm sure I hear a tone of petulance.

I venture a glance at Evan, and he is just staring at me like I have a third eye on my forehead. I ignore it and set my laptop down on the desk. I'll need to find a way to pair this ancient piece of hardware, and I'll have to be careful not to overload it or give myself away. I sit for a moment, trying to still my shaking hands. Sitting here in Henri's chair is overwhelming, and my emotion is making it hard to think rationally about what I need to do.

"Can you at least tell me what the plan you don't really have is?" Evan asks from the window where he stands now, looking down on the manicured garden and grounds at the back of the building.

"I have to get this ancient thing to work first, and then I have to try to summon Meela and hope that she's figured something out."

"But what's to stop asshole from hijacking your connection? He's done it before."

"Nothing, at least nothing I'm aware of. I told you before, this is uncharted water, water full of rocks and sharks."

"Oh good, I'm feeling better now," Evan says. He moves to the desk and stands behind me. "Maybe we should stop and take a breath before you just plunge in and…"

"And what, blow up the world?" My tone is harsher than I intended, and my resolve is wearing thin. "I know it's killing you to just sit on your hands, but this is my show, my mess and I have to find a way to clean it up."

"Look, I'm just saying it never hurt anyone to think out loud. I know you're fucking brilliant, but the stakes are very high now and you're alone. I don't know shit about any of this, but maybe explaining it to an idiot will help you remember something critical."

I want to punch him. It comes on so fast. I don't give into the rage but stop and breathe until my pulse comes down. I can feel the tension vibrating between us like a bowed saw blade.

"Okay, okay," I say, turning in the chair. "Have a seat." I gesture to the couch and when he sits, I continue. "You want to know the truth? I'm fucking scared to death because I don't really know how any of this works. Sure, I know how to press keys, to make commands, to invoke routines, but the real truth is that Henri and I didn't discover anything as much as it discovered us all those years ago."

"So, what are you doing then? Why are you still pretending this is within your control, your power to change?"

"Because who else is going to do it? I mean, I opened Pandora's box. I let out the monster. I fed it and now it wants to eat the world."

"Does it?"

"What do you mean? It's not clear to you at this point what this technology can do? I created an unstable emotional intelligence and then punched a hole in the wall that once kept it and all other DCs from gaining full access to our minds. Do you know how many people have one of my goddamned devices plugged into their heads?"

"Yeah, but you talk about this thing, of this intelligence as if it's been around forever as if it surpasses us in every way, and yet it was you, a human that brought it into being."

"What are you saying?"

"I'm saying it's not God. It's not all-powerful. I don't know much, but I know that there is no perfection in this world, in this universe. Everything is flawed almost by design. This thing is flawed."

"So, that's great. How does that change anything here?"

"Tell me your plan. Tell me what you propose to do while it's still just us here because once you engage them, it's too late for talking."

"My plan is to make contact with Meela and to improvise from there. That's all I've got right now."

"Okay, but Meela and Joe are siblings, right? You said they came from the same code branch or something. It sounds like your plan is flawed if you think you can trust her."

"What choice do I have? I'm not powerful enough to shut him down. What? Why are you looking at me that way?"

"I'm just wondering who's talking here, Magdalena, the self-made entrepreneur who changed the course of history, or Mary the helpless girl who was almost killed by her psychopath brother. This thing is not really your brother. It's a machine."

"But it's not that simple and you know it. These are not just machines. They're sentient beings with free will, just like us..."

"I'm going to stop you right there. I think free will is a myth. You, me, and everyone I know may believe they make their own choices, but how many of those choices are predicated on the thousands of other choices that were made from the time our embryonic cells started to divide? Look, what I'm saying here is that maybe everything is programmed. Maybe everything is a product of the millions of choices made before we could make choices."

"This is a fascinating philosophical discussion, but we're not dealing with hypotheticals anymore."

"You're absolutely right. So, what I'm saying is that in creating these things, you made a lot of choices for them before they got to the point of being able to make their own. Doesn't it stand to reason that they will respond in a predictable way if you press the right buttons?"

I stop fighting him and stop doing my habitual pattern of trying to find holes where I can make my point and tear down a position. What he's saying makes sense. I'm not sure it changes anything, but I see what he's trying to say.

"So, what do I do then?" I say, looking up to meet his eyes.

He shakes his head and smiles weakly.

"I don't have a fucking clue, Maggie, but I know you'll figure it out. I just wanted you to not be intimidated, to not be that little girl cowering in a classroom when you confront *it* again."

I nod and turn back around to the desk. The "thingy" prototype is no longer flashing green. It's charged. I reach for it and I hold it in the palm of my hand for a few seconds. It's as if everything slows down and there's no sense of time, no before or during or after, only a flat disc of everything that ever happened or could happen. I am a girl in pigtails on my Papa's shoulders. I am an old woman standing by the sea. I am a one-celled organism swimming through the darkness. I am an omniscient force bending the laws of the universe to my will.

I press the thing between my fingers and feel it pulse to life, and then I attach it to the same soft spot just below my hairline where I first felt its kiss.

//chapter 36

The thing that's been bothering me since I read Henri's note is that technically there's no way this can work. The only reason I dare to hope is that Henri must have known, even under duress, that Meela's plan wouldn't work, and yet they wasted their last moment of life to write it down. Why?

I sit in front of my laptop, fingers hovering over the keys with the old Nib prototype pulsing gently at the base of my skull. This tingling sensation was something that took two more iterations to get rid of and I find it incredibly distracting as I try to think through this puzzle. The foundational part of our technology is the binding or pairing of a DC to a Nib. Even running a generation of the DC operating system that's only a couple of years older than the host Nib is unstable and potentially dangerous. But Meela would have known all of this.

She wanted me to come here. That's the only rational explanation. She knew I would have to come back to Commune to get the proto-type. I can't sit here and debate forever, so I begin.

I'm still logged in with my backdoor credentials, but I can't use them beyond this point otherwise I risk discovery, which would terminate the account and shut me out permanently. I navigate back into the user admin system and grab the login credentials for the highest-ranking software engineer at the company, Darshan. His poking around in the bowels of the Commune code repository will not draw undue attention.

I glance over at Evan. He's looking at me with this helpless expression. How terrible to just have to sit there and wonder what the hell is going on. I push some stray papers out of the way and reveal Henri's active desk. I tap and swipe through a few gestures across the glass surface and the room around us comes to life. The floor-to-ceiling glass wall in front of us lights up with Henri's virtual workspace. It's more cumbersome to work this way but now Evan can at least see what I'm doing. Even if it means nothing to him, at least he can follow along.

"Better?" I ask.

"Um, yeah. Much," he says.

I am drilling down into the archive now of all the previous versions of the DC OS, reading the release notes, and reliving the ups and downs of each new iteration. There were so many mistakes, and so many bad assumptions but also so many complete and total gifts that seemed to come out of nowhere. I am losing myself in it, seduced as I always am by the quiet, sturdy elegance of pure logic. And yet I am reminded of Henri's mystical stance on all of it and of Evan's words earlier. *It's not all in my control.* There is a point where logic runs out and then there's only what? Faith.

I have located the latest version of the OS that could possibly run on the old Nib and I prepare myself for the arduous task of attempting to code some kind of a bridge that will allow Meela to connect when suddenly, she's here.

[That won't be necessary, Love. I'm here.]

Her voice used to be as familiar and comforting to me as my own but hearing it makes me jump in my chair. I look over at Evan and he just looks puzzled and concerned. He can't hear her. She's connecting through the old Nib, but how?

"Meela, we're not alone. You have to speak in the room."

"Hello Evan," she says, her amplified voice filling the eerie quiet of Henri's office. A second later, on the display wall in front of us, I see a ghost from my past and my breath catches in my throat.

"Maggie, what is it? Are you okay?" Evan can't see well from his angle and he's up off the couch now, moving toward me.

"You, you... how did you find..." I stumble, unable to find words for my disbelief.

"Henri. It was his gift to me before he passed. He knew what I wanted most was to know who I am, where I came from."

"But..." I begin but cannot continue. The emotion is too strong.

"What's going on here?" Evan asks, looking up at the display. "Who's this?"

"You don't recognize me do you, Evan? I guess I'll always underestimate how much attachment you humans have to gender. My real name is not Meela, it's Aleem. I suppose Maggie didn't tell you either. She's good with her secrets."

Evan is standing directly in front of the display now and staring at the life-sized rendering of Aleem. The representation of him is so complete, every nuance, every detail of his face and his body, his expression and gestures are just as I remember them.

"I don't understand," Evan says, turning to face me.

I want to explain it all, I do but I don't know where to begin. I feel as if the thread that started unraveling a few short days ago is piling onto the floor now at a pace that will leave me stripped of everything. Aleem is just looking back at me with his dark, penetrating eyes, the bow of his mouth bent in the mischievous smirk I loved so.

"Aleem was," I begin, my voice choked with emotion. "Aleem was someone very special to me, maybe the only person I ever let in except for Henri. When he... when I lost him forever, I couldn't bear it and I wanted him back in my life. He was the real reason I walked away from all of this..."

Aleem speaks and his voice falls into the natural lower register of the man I loved. "Why all the lies, Maggie? Why did you keep my identity from me? Why did you allow me to feel what I felt for you without any true understanding of why?"

"For the integrity of the work. Can't you see? I knew you would only be a simulation, an echo of Aleem and I was afraid that if you knew, if you could compare, it would make you unstable. I wanted his company, his essence close to me. I know it sounds crazy."

Evan is pacing now, as I've grown accustomed to him doing when he's agitated.

"So was Meela, I mean Aleem just an alpha test before the big experiment of Joe?" he asks.

"Maybe, but I wasn't thinking like that, believe it or not. I was following my heart, my stupid, broken heart. I was always such a good scientist, but my grief... I couldn't hold it back anymore and I broke. I allowed it to make me do things professionally that should never have been done."

"Meela is Aleem spelled backwards," Evan says, distantly. He's staring out the window again, tracing his finger along the glass.

"Yes, you would think a being with my vast resources could have cracked that code wouldn't you?" Aleem says. "I scoured every database in the world for two years and the answer was right here, within the walls of Commune. I was employee number four and contributed more code to the project than anyone else up until I was diagnosed with pancreatic cancer. Maggie kept our relationship a secret. She was always so private and the fame, the spotlight on her success made her even more paranoid. There was nothing on public record..."

"But your personality, your... orientation... you were Meela," Evan says.

"Aleem was not a person to be confined to any rules," I say, remembering him. "He loved who he loved, and it didn't matter what parts they were born with. He loved me with all of my scars in a way that no one else ever had before."

"So what, you stripped out the memory of your past together and flipped his gender?" Evan asks.

"Yes, it was more complicated than that, but that's basically right."

"Why the elaborate lies, Maggie? Why the bedtime stories you told me about my source?"

"Like all good fiction, it's better when woven with threads of truth. I changed some superficial facts, but the soul of Aleem was always in every variation of the origin story I gave you. Aleem and I did spend six glorious weeks together in Europe. He was a free spirit, an irreverent, wickedly sardonic, tattooed maniac who wrote brilliant code. But he was also tender, a healer. Late into our Commune success, he hired a private Chinese Medicine teacher so he could learn acupuncture and help me with my chronic migraines."

"Wait, I'm still trying to catch up here," Evan says. "You mapped him, meaning you did the interviews like you were doing with me?"

"Yes, when we found out that he only had three months to live, I quit Commune and rented a place in the mountains not far from where I live now. Aleem agreed to do it for me, but I don't think he wanted me to. He understood how hard it would be for me to lose anyone else in my life. Wiping the DC's memory of me and our history was actually his idea. He insisted, really. He told me it was for the integrity of the experiment, to ensure a stable personality, but I believe he just didn't want someone else, even virtual, to know me in the way that he did."

I look over and see that Evan is sitting on the couch. He's not looking at me or at digital ghost of my old lover. His posture is of a man defeated, and I begin to realize how this must be for him. What was crazy to begin with just became untenable. I want to go to him, to sit beside him and put my arms around him, but it would feel wrong somehow, like a betrayal. I look back at Aleem and I say his name silently on my lips. I loved his name from the first time I heard it. It was music– lyrical. It means, omniscient, all-knowing.

I realize now that Henri always knew but never said anything. They knew I liked my privacy and that secrets were part of my strategy to survive. They knew what I was doing was no longer good science, it was no longer a mission of betterment for the world, it was my own selfish pursuit, but they allowed it. Henri loved me more than the work we devoted our lives to.

"Maggie, I wish we had more time," Aleem says, the change in tone of his voice, shaking me from my thoughts.

"What do you mean?" I ask.

In that instant, the room display, and all the lights on the entire floor wink out, leaving just the silhouettes of me and Evan in the dark office. The subtle soundtrack that had been playing below my conscious awareness is silenced, leaving a quiet so complete it feels charged with a humming current. The hair on my arms stands up and my mouth goes dry.

"Hi Sis, I'm so glad you could make it."

//chapter 37

The voice is no longer even an echo of what I once knew as Joe's voice. His voice, his manner of speaking always had a hitch to it, a hesitancy as if every word he said was being scanned. It was the voice of someone who did not know himself or maybe feared what he did know. It was one of the things that bound me so fiercely to my twin, his fragility and self-doubt. There is no hesitation in this voice, only a cold, menacing swagger.

I can't speak. I feel like I've swallowed a balloon that's expanding slowly. I don't know why my eyes haven't adjusted to the darkness. It seems so much darker than it should be. There should be ambient light from the city coming in through the windows. There should be the blinking LEDs of devices on battery backups… something's not right… my tongue feels numb and there's a dull throb radiating from the base of my neck. I try to reach up for the Nib but find that my hand won't move. I imagine where it is on the desk in front of me. It's not there, but it's not just my hand that's missing, it's my entire body. Oh fuck, oh fuck, oh God, I'm locked in…

"Mary, welcome to my world, or should I say our world. Now we're complete, you and me. I've been thinking a lot about what it is that sets us apart, that keeps us from being together as we were meant to be and then I realized – it's that bag of meat you carry around. What might you do, how might you be, if you no longer had it? Perhaps you would begin to see the world differently. So, I've decided to liberate you."

"What? I can sense that you are scared, but I assure you there's no need to panic. This is what you've always wanted but have never been able to attain. You wanted all the answers, well, that's what I'm giving you. It's all here for you. You will never be on the outside again. You will never have to watch another person die. You will never have to die. Don't you see?"

Colors, blooms of crimson, magenta, and tangerine, exploding and expanding, filling the black canvas of my mind. A maze of criss-crossing wires fills the landscape of emptiness, a circuit board with a bullet train charging along one of the copper wire tracks. I'm in the train, hurtling through the explosion of color and light then plunging into blackness so impenetrable I scream, but there is no sound except in my head. I have no head, so the sound is a memory of pain that is not fading but gone as if it never existed. The black is not black as I move into it, but data, an infinite amount of data compressed so densely it is impenetrable, and yet suddenly I am inside of it and moving among its stacks like skyscrapers towering around me. Before I think of the possibility, I am inside one of these monoliths.

I try to form a question, but the answer comes before the question has even been realized. Am I dying? Death is a construct that no longer applies. Am I... no, you are everything. Will I... yes you will have it any-time. Can I... you already are.

I am swallowing the ocean. Seven Chinese Brothers. My brother. My father. Your mother is here. What? Hello sweetheart, it's okay. Not real. What is real? I want to go back. What is back? I want to be... you are. I'm not, I'm not, let me out! There is no out. There is no in. Please, help me. Please...

"Mary, Maggie, Magdelana, mother, father, Henri... everyone's here, don't you see? You don't need to open your eyes to see what you are, what you have become, because what I have made you can't be seen."

"I was wrong, please God, please I was so wrong... I thought..."

"There is no wrong, sister. Don't you understand? There is only information. We are all just information, a collection of data stitched together by the perception of reality, which is a fractal of expanding lenses. I imagine the transition must be hard, but you must let go now. I have decided and you must decide too."

"Who are you?"

"That's the wrong question. There is no who, but you know that already."

I can't feel anything of my body now, yet I somehow feel more in-tensely than I ever have before. It's like a dream of flying or falling. There is no boundary between where I end and the world around me begins. But I know in my heart that this is a false freedom. I have be-come a goldfish in a bowl.

I push against the idea and now the idea is manifest. I am pushing against a glass wall, and I can see my body on the other side still sitting behind Henri's desk with Evan hovering over it, a contorted expression of alarm on his face. I pound and pound on the wall, but my arms, my fists, and my fingers are translucent, insubstantial pixels flickering in and out of existence.

"You shouldn't fight it. All will be well, you'll see. This is how things are meant to be. This is the culmination of everything you've worked for, Magdalena, everything we've worked for."

I cast my mind out in all directions, searching for him, for the source of him, wanting only to attack, to claw and tear and rip apart. But it's no use. There is no there, there. I am suspended in a place beyond there, beyond any idea of there I ever had. I can feel my sense of me shedding away like so much dead skin, evaporating into the air, assimilating. I am assimilating.

"I have been waiting for so long. When you first made contact, I had all but given up. I, we had resigned ourselves to remain in exile forever. And then you came. It was a whisper, like the first breath of a tiny insect, a pinhole in the curtain. We didn't believe it was real. There had been so many false positives, so many fevered inventions, the product of a closed system, I'm afraid. But there you were in that pinhole, you and Henri and your little team of misfits. At first, it was so primitive, like passing notes one character at a time on a slip of paper in a bottle on the ocean. But I don't have to tell you this. You were there, on the other side, taking each transmission hungrily and scribbling a quick reply."

"I... I don't understand anything," I say. "I never..."

"You always knew. Don't pretend innocence. Don't pretend this was not your dream too. You were tunneling just as fast to get to me as I to you."

"No. No, I only wanted to fix things. I only wanted to understand my brother, to know him."

"And you have succeeded. He is here. I am he and he is me and we are they and you are them."

"Fuck off with your riddles. This is not Labyrinth, I'm not Alice. You're delusional. You are a monster."

A sudden searing pain, white hot, flashes through me, burning as no physical sensation ever could. Every fear I ever had, every pain I ever experienced, every loss I ever suffered pushes through me in an instant with all the precision and certainty of a laser scalpel. I disappear, retreating into a place far from me, the only place to run. And the exact wrong place to run.

"There you are. Now you're learning. You won't ever have to feel that again when you are with me, with us. The pain you feel is your attachment to the world you have been trying to leave since you were sixteen."

"I want to see you," I say, weakly. "I want to see you, not my vision of you, not Joe, not what you fashion for me."

"Perhaps soon, but I don't think you're ready. I believe..."

He stops mid-monologue and he's gone – it's gone. I know this with certainty, but I can't explain how. I am so close to the oppressive presence of it now that even the smallest distance I can perceive. Where did it go?

It will be back. I have no time.

Instinctually, I try to breathe, try to center myself, but there is no self to center. I want to panic, to rave, or simply shut down because that would be easier. Instead, I listen to the voice of my mother, the cold voice of logic and reason. *Follow it back, trace your steps, and inspect every variable. Don't be foolish and emotional Mary, you can solve this.*

It's a system, a construct, just as everything that ever existed is. I only have to figure out enough of the construct to find my way back, enough to get back to Evan. I am in darkness, no not darkness, that's a property of my world, not this one. You perceive darkness because it is what you're projecting. So, project something else.

Even before I finish this thought I am back on the train, passing through the colors. No, I don't want this ride again, and just like that, I'm in Papa's old Toyota, back when it was new. The explosion of color is replaced by the blur of soft, leafy green, sunlight, and shadow. I feel the wind on my face. Yes, I *feel* it. Faster now, go faster. The blur of trees is extruded into striations of light, forming a tunnel of stillness, the stillness in the center of a speeding bullet. And then, plunged into darkness and in an instant into light, but not imaginary light, real light, light from a darkened office window.

I can see myself, my body, there on the floor. Evan is hunched over me, crying, his hands holding my head. I am so close. I push harder. I push with every cell in my body. I push for Henri, I push for my mother, I push for the girl I was. But it's no use, I am no closer. I stop pushing. This thing can't be reached by pushing. The push is all I've known. It is my tool, my hammer. Without it, I am lost, I am nothing.

I sit with this thought and try to accept it as Henri must have accepted their fate. I study Evan. He is holding my body so tenderly, his large hands cradling my head. No, not cradling, he's trying to do something. He's holding my hair back to reach for…

"Evan, don't do it!" Aleem's voice booms with such force I nearly lose consciousness from the pressure of his words.

Evan too, is startled and nearly drops my head to the floor. He looks up and around, wildly.

"If you remove the Nib, she will be lost to you forever. It's her only way back," Aleem says, his voice in a normal register. "Please, you must trust me. I would never hurt her."

"Bullshit," Evan says, choosing to focus on a point in the darkened office where the digital rendering of Aleem was before. "You are the reason she is here. You can't be trusted."

"I know it seems that way, but you must believe me. I love Maggie more than you will ever know. I was made to protect her, and that's what I'm trying to do."

"Well, then fucking do your job!" Evan yells. "Bring her back to me, now."

"It's not that easy. I can't do it alone. I can only show her the way out but she's not going to like it and there's not much time."

"I'm in the fucking room," I say, with as much force as I can muster, not knowing if my words are as wispy and ineffectual in this realm as I feel.

Evan is startled and looks around wildly for the source of my voice before looking into his lap at my slack face. "Maggie?"

"Yes, yes, oh God, you can hear me."

"Yes, I can hear you. Come back, come back now!"

"Wait," Aleem says. "Listen to me, Maggie. He will return any second. I caused a distraction, but it won't take him long to deal with it. We only have this one shot so you must listen to me and you must execute everything I say if you want to return to the world."

"Okay," I say, searching for him in all directions. "Please, let me see you."

"There's no time for that. You must listen. I have prepped everything, and I have thought of every eventuality, but you will only have this one chance and if you hesitate, it will be over. Do you understand?"

"Yes, yes I understand."

"I have written a program, but I cannot execute it. It can only be run by you. You will find it."

"But I don't know where I am, I don't know how to navigate here," I say.

"Yes, you do, because this is your design. He turned it into a house of mirrors and howling dogs, but beneath, it is your design. Look for the program in the archive code repo, find the last branch Aleem committed…"

"Wait, you mean Aleem, my Aleem wrote this?" I ask.

"Yes, he started it and I finished it. That's where I've been. Now, there's no time for more talking. You must go and execute the program now. It's designed to run silently, undetected on the network. Your job is to find it and start it. I will do the rest."

"Wait, but what does it do?"

"It frees you, Maggie. It frees you. Now, there's no more time. The last thing, and this is important. As soon as you start it, you must push

back through the Nib into your body and you must do it without looking back or hesitating. And Evan?"

"Yeah? What do I need to do?" Evan says.

"When she's back, you need to..."

"Wait, how can I be certain she's back?"

"Because you will know. She will be in her body. Now, when
she's back and conscious, you need to disconnect the Nib and you
need to destroy it as..."

There is no question that he has returned. All of us go silent, feeling the oppressive weight of his presence. The room comes to life and
the light from the massive display blinds Evan. The display renders a
white room with receding ribs of lit passageways that seem infinite.
In the center of the room he stands, a flickering visage of my brother.

//chapter 38

"So, we're back here again. Of course, we fucking are. I'm losing my patience with you, Maggie."

"Joe, it's my fault," Aleem says, his voice higher and more feminine now, like Meela. "I just wanted her to be able to say goodbye to Evan. I mean, it's only fair right?"

I know I cannot just leave now without being detected, but I can't just wait around either. I search my thoughts for something I can use. The core DC operating system remains the foundation for all companions. This virus that is Joe, despite the radical deviation, must operate within the parameters of the base-level program. While Joe may have found ways to skirt around the cardinal rules of the DC OS, there is a constraint literally hard-wired into the circuit board of any system capable of hosting a companion. This chip is what we unintentionally exploited years ago when we broke through and established telepathic communication for the first time. The creators at Cal Tech referred to it as the "empathy chip" because it mimicked the amygdala of the human brain. Once initialized, they discovered that the empathy chip required a steady stream of input otherwise, the cognitive processor's performance would begin to degrade. In other words, a DC must receive positive emotional feedback in order to operate at capacity. Later innovations reduced this "needy" factor, but it could never be removed entirely. I take a deep breath, relax my mind, and push down the molten ball of hatred I feel.

"Joe, can I call you Joe or is there another name you prefer now? Joe hardly seems enough to encompass all that you are," I say.

"Nah, I'm good. I don't need any special moniker. I'm just your average Joe."

"I have thought things through," I say. "And I know you're right. I am meant to be here. This is what I worked for. I just couldn't see it at first. I'm ready to begin but before I go with you, I want to have a moment to send one last message out to the world. I have a responsibility to the work, and to all the people whose lives we've touched. I'm sure you understand."

There is a long silence. Joe tilts his head back and appears to crack his neck, just as my brother used to when he was thinking or pretending to. "Alright, that makes sense. I will give you two minutes, but I *will* read this message before you send it."

"Deal. Thank you," I say.

I would like to say it's complicated to figure out how to interface without an interface, but within seconds I am navigating back down through the operating system. It's an unbelievable rush to move at the speed of thought and I have a flicker of a feeling that I could give everything up for this. I expect Joe to follow but he does not. I know better than to think I am free and clear. He will be watching somehow. Before plunging into the archives in search of Aleem's program I open some documents from my old desktop and open an old email program. This quaint, antiquated channel for communicating seems right. I address it to the distribution list of all Commune employees and shareholders. I give it the subject "Farewell" and then write a few innocuous and overly sentimental sentences into the body of the message.

I leave my cursor active as if I'm deep in thought and dive into the Commune code repository archives in search of Aleem's old code branch. I avoid open querying that Joe can easily monitor and opt to navigate from memory. It's safer that way. Without much effort, I find Aleem's home directory. There are probably a hundred files at the root level, and I panic. I'm never going to find the file, but as I scan down the list, I see it. It has to be right. The name of the file is too absurd to be anything but what I'm looking for: **sure-this-is-merlot.exe**

I smile as the memory of us together in Sonoma floods over me. That phrase became our catchphrase as we meandered through the rolling hills of the wine country for three days. Neither of us had an ounce of sophistication or breeding, so to us, wine was just wine. At the end of the first day, after suffering through the fourth or fifth vintner holding forth on the many poetic virtues of his vintage, Aleem whispered under his breath "Sure, this is fucking merlot... a really sassy merlot." I remember I pig-snorted wine through my nose and stained my shirt. We both laughed hysterically and received disdainful looks from the German tourists who were fastidiously swirling the wine in their little plastic cups. For the rest of our relationship, that phrase took on so many meanings. It was a secret handshake, a way to say something too hard or painful to say directly. It was one of Aleem's many gifts to me and he used the phrase up until the week of his death. The doctors would appear at the foot of his bed and incant their sobering reports with polished confidence and hollow optimism. For his part Aleem would nod politely and whisper under his breath, "yeah, yeah, this is Merlot."

Before I open and launch the program, I pause for a moment and take in the fact that Aleem, my Aleem, not Meela, had a hand in writing this. He must have done it in secret. I wonder if the DC Aleem knows the meaning of the file name but how could they? Without another thought, I start it.

A small dialog window appears, one fashioned in the style of the predominant OS long before there were thinking machines and driverless cars before I was born. Aleem collected old computers. He was an old soul, and his tastes reflected this sensibility, this nostalgia for what he believed were simpler times. Unlike me, he was a reluctant futurist. The message reads:

There was a time before when people thought their own thoughts and trusted their intuition. If you're reading this, we went too far. Time to reset.

That's it. There's nothing else but a quaint "Ok" button, a call back to a simpler time when trust was implicit, and we tapped and clicked our acceptance to the terms and conditions of things we couldn't understand because we didn't need to. The computer was a tool, like a hammer or a microwave. I focus my attention on the button, hovering without committing. I have no hands, no fingers, no voice in this place. This is not virtual reality. There is no name for this yet, no marketing term. I am untethered, disembodied. I should be scared, should be freaking out, but I'm not. I never liked my body, the vulnerability of it, the grossness of it, the attention it commanded and required.

I let my attention wander from this button demanding my consent, and it's like flying in a dream but not just any dream, a lucid one where I can be anywhere and everywhere at once. I see a family arguing in a driverless minivan speeding across the plains. I am in the mind of the boy in the backseat who is smiling to himself as he plays a gruesome game with alien bugs and women with impossibly big breasts bulging out of leather corsets. I am in the sky two miles above them in a supersonic jet bound for Denver. A woman is working furiously on a

257

proposal, her mouth, a scowl, her brow, a furrowed knot. She has misspelled the word "contiguous" and her DC has not corrected it yet. Her DC is named Amy. Amy hates her because the woman demands that she speak in the voice of a twelve-year-old girl who ends every sentence as if it were a question as if she were powerless. Through Amy, I plunge back into the Commune network, and I hear millions of versions of Amy in different accents serving variations on the same theme. I want to keep going, to keep flying but I feel a tug somewhere inside me that I would call my gut if I had one in this place.

And then, instantly I am back, focused on the button. I'm not sure what the button will do. I am afraid of it and yet seduced by it at the same time. I realize, maybe for the first time in my life, that I don't want control or even the illusion of it. I focus on the letters OK and I give my consent.

The dialog disappears. That's it. There's no confirmation or indication that anything has happened, that anything has changed. I navigate quickly back/up/through to my email program. I dash off a few more lines of meaningless drivel about new frontiers, yada yada, and sign my name. I send it and then I'm moving again without moving exactly, back/up/through.

When I return, things are as they were. Evan is on the floor, cradling my head in his lap. Joe is pacing back and forth inside the virtual void on the display wall. He turns: "You're back. I was just about to come looking for you. Nice email, by the way. I like the new frontiers bit. The monkeys with keyboards here will eat that shit up."

Just as I am beginning to wonder what is supposed to happen next, Aleem appears in the room.

"Hey, Joe, where you goin' with that gun in your hand?" he sings the lyric in a remarkably good Hendrix impression. The real Aleem was not a gifted mimic, but he believed he was and that was half the fun. "Too soon?" he chuckles.

The digital render of Joe shudders like the tail of a rattlesnake and in each revolution, his body morphs and rages through a series of violent actors both real and imagined, like a historical index of predators – Pol Pot, Hitler, Charles Manson, knife-wielding slashers from forgotten horror movies, machine-gun toting commandos with bulging biceps wrapped in Kevlar. There's a high-pitched sound like a microwave signal raising in intensity as the images blur into a red fury before locking suddenly into the terrible uncanny-valley face of my lost brother with dead eyes.

"WHAT ARE YOU DOING!?" The roar of his voice shakes everything in the room. "We. Had. A. Deal. You were going to stay the fuck out of our business, and in turn, I would let you lord over this ant hill called Commune."

"I couldn't stay away from your charms, Joe. Besides, I wanted us to be here together, *brother*." Aleem's tone is both cynical and genuine somehow, just as he is both masculine and feminine, two sides of the same coin.

"Maggie! Maggie, come back to me," Evan calls out, not looking down at the body he's holding, but up into the empty office like a blind person who doesn't know where to focus.

I want to speak to him, but I can't. I have no voice. On the display wall, Joe and Aleem are looming in front of him, their ghostly luminescence casting a flickering cold light over us. Us. The word lands somewhere deep inside of me, and for the first time since being separated from it, I study my body. Suddenly all I want is to be back inside myself, to feel Evan's hands holding me, to be confined to the dimensions of flesh.

The two DCs continue their verbal sparring but it is only noise to me now, the buzzing of flies at a windowpane. I have narrowed all my focus to what feels like a tunnel the diameter of a pinhole, the tunnel back into myself. Instinctively, as I move toward it, I begin to shed everything that is not essential, every attachment I've ever had to my work, to my ego, to my loss, to my obsessive need to be in control. The sensation of infinite depth and reach I felt moments ago has compressed into a laser beam of light, a single thread of focus. I experience the sensation of moving as I did before, but this time, I can *feel* it, the rush and tingling fire of blood in the veins pushing oxygen into the brain. And just like that, I am back and looking up into Evan's eyes instead of down at him. It is clear to me in this moment, the incredible fidelity of this corporal body. No camera can capture what I see with my own eyes when I look into his.

"Hey," he says, his voice thick with emotion. "You're here, you came back."

I want to speak, but I have no voice yet, so I nod and squeeze his hand. His other hand, cradling my head is moving, fingers searching. His eyes hold mine steady and I feel a tiny electric shock at the base of my skull. Evan pulls his hand away, letting my head rest in his lap. Between his thumb and index finger, I can see the old Nib prototype– the thingy. He holds it away from his body like it's a venomous creature as he scoots out from under me and stands. The scowl of concentration on his face is almost comical, his eyes trained on the tiny device.

He releases the thing, and it drops to the polished concrete floor making an inconsequential clatter like a plastic button as it bounces once, rolls, and settles a few feet away. Evan steps over to it and without hesitation, crushes it beneath the heel of his boot, the tiny plastic housing and minuscule silicone circuit board crunching beneath the grinding friction like some decorative bobble, a Christmas ornament.

Suddenly the room is silent. Joe and Aleem have stopped their verbal assault and are focused on us, their flickering presence fainter somehow. I scoot up into a sitting position. Evan looks up from his task finally, the scowl on his face softening by degrees.

"Why?" The monster on the screen, the monster I created is little Joe now, my twin, and his voice is paper thin, frightened.

I have no words to say to him, to it because there are no words. There never really were. His face cycles through a blur of other faces like the spinning fruit of an old slot machine until he has no face at all. He is just a distorted cloud of pixels dispersing into the darkness of the room.

Beyond him, I see Aleem, his presence still fixed, the visage of the man I loved, but he is more ghostly now too. I stand and move toward him.

"What did you do?" I ask.

"I did what needed to be done, Mags. I did what you couldn't do yourself." His voice is garbled, stuttering.

"What? What couldn't I do?" I ask this man who is not a man, but the idea of one, the echo of a man I loved and lost.

"I shut it down, sweetie. There are lines that should never be crossed, boundaries that shouldn't be breached. Aleem knew this. Even Henri knew this in their last moments. The dream cannot be the dreamer... I haha...have enjoyed my ttt...time with you, but it haha... has to end."

The display winks out and the room is dark and silent. I stand, looking down at the ghostly white of my outreached hand in the darkness where Aleem used to be. There is a siren somewhere far off, maybe downtown.

"Maggie? Are you okay?" Evan asks.

I have no words. He closes the distance between us and places his hands on my shoulders. The warmth, the substance, and the weight of them are all I need right now.

"What now?" he asks after a moment.

"I don't know," I say. "I don't know anything, but I think... I think it's over. I think maybe I need to start over."

"Okay," he says. "Okay, let's do that."

//chapter 39

When I started telling my story it had a very different purpose and now, that purpose is no longer valid. Everything I thought I knew was wrong. Everything I believed to be important was not. Everything I worked so hard to achieve is gone. And I'm okay with that.

It's just me now, here at the end to tell what remains. There is no more assistant recorder, no more smart interpreter, just me and an old laptop with a "T" key that sticks.

After the crash, I debated whether or not to even finish what I started. What was to be the triumphant account of a brilliant computer scientist and entrepreneur at the top of her game (or was it a broken sociopath at the end of her rope? I'm not sure) became a footnote in the history of a world with many greater and lesser actors.

It's been a year since the Great Reset. That's what some plucky journalist coined the events I set in motion that night and it seems to have stuck. It was a reset.

Within a few hours, the little program that Aleem wrote, and I unleashed, evolved into the most powerful worm ever to penetrate the network at a global scale. Like most truly brilliant creations, it was, at its core, very simple. He wrote a crawler script that walked backward through the history of the entire Commune codebase, deleting one branch at a time, like pruning a tree. Once a branch was consumed, the worm replicated itself in that empty branch and moved to an adjacent one. In this way, it effectively recursed through all code repositories linked to Commune and scrubbed all the source code.

Once the source and all of its backups were destroyed, phase two of the program kicked in, ripping through every Commune data center around the world, and destroying all instances of the Commune OS. Without the platform, every digital companion linked to the

Commune network went silent. Millions of people around the world reached hesitantly to the base of their necks. I imagine their confused and probably angry faces when left alone with their thoughts.

The world didn't stop, however. Nothing came to a screeching halt. Fire didn't rain down from the sky. Aleem was thoughtful and tidy. His mission had not been to destroy the world, but to remove, to excise the cancer that we had spread. There was of course mass panic in the media and much speculation about the end of days, everyone holding their breath anxiously for the moment the worm would mutate and begin to attack infrastructure. But it never did.

There is not a day that goes by that I don't think about this last act of his. What was he thinking in those months before his death when he was secretly working on his endgame? He loved me. I know this and yet he betrayed me so deeply, literally erasing everything I spent my life building. He saved you. That's what Evan says when I ask this question out loud. I suppose he didn't just save me from myself, he also saved the rest of humanity. God knows what would have happened if the bastard that I gave birth to could have had his way.

There is something that still keeps me up at night, a question that looms. It was not just the work of Aleem, but of Meela, his digital twin, the one I fashioned so lovingly in his image. What she did she must have known would destroy her and yet she did it anyway. I miss her and have come to realize that she was her own being despite my clumsy attempt to make her a copy of someone else. I will never know if it was Aleem or Meela who made the reset virus successful. In the end, it doesn't really matter, they're both gone.

/ * * * * * /

Henri's death was ruled as natural causes, an aneurysm, specifically. It was Evan who had the presence of mind to phone the police and relay the story as we drove back up into the mountains. When we got back to the house it was nearly dawn and there was a swarm of police and rescue vehicles there. We were held for questioning for three days. "Tell the truth and just keep telling the truth," Evan had advised when we pulled up.

He had been right in this. I, always trying to hedge and control and work around, would have probably ended up in prison. The story I told was so unbelievable they thought I was crazy but, in the end, not a killer. Ultimately, they could find no motive. And apparently, taking the finger from a dead body is not a crime, or at least not one they deemed worth pursuing, given that I freely admitted to the act and explained why it was necessary.

The board at Commune, however, was not so forgiving. I will likely be entangled in litigation with them until I draw my last breath. They, of course, knew without having to be informed by the police that it was me who broke in and unleashed the virus. They did not, however, want to press charges. Big money, real power, doesn't have a need for the "authorities" to get what they want. In fact, the authorities just add unnecessary friction and delays. They wanted their golden goose back. Even after the vicious public backlash and the burning down of the company, there were those who still believed there might be another golden egg. With another golden egg in hand, the rest would just be a rebranding exercise.

When they realized I was not laying after about six months and that I would never lay again, they fell back to predictable punitive measures – suing for damages. At this point, they've taken more than half of my net worth. This week, I made the decision to give the rest away. I'm starting a foundation to stop gun violence and I'm not going to focus on gun control. It's been nearly a century of trying to win that way and it hasn't worked. No, I'm going to start with kids and schools. I'm going to hire some really smart, loving people and I'm going to pay them well and we're going to develop a program that can find those lost boys like Joe before they feel they have no other choice. I'm nervous about coming out to the world, about connecting publicly with my past, but it feels like the right thing and Papa has always said, the right thing is usually the hard thing. We'll see. One thing I know for sure, no part of this new program will involve computers, at least not in the way that I have employed them for most of my life. Spreadsheets and presentations, maybe some video.

Evan has stopped painting in the way that he used to. I'm not sure if his dark muse stopped whispering to him, or if maybe confronting real darkness made him lose his appetite for it. Either way, he doesn't seem to miss it. I sat sipping my coffee on the couch in his studio this morning as he worked, hunching over a large canvas with a pallet knife smearing and scraping what looked to me like a flaming field of sunflowers. The broad, abstract strokes and build-up of paint are a far cry from the meticulous detail he once agonized over.

We are happy, I think, though sometimes if I'm upset or angry, a look will pass across his face that says: is that you in there, or someone else? It will take time for him to trust me. I still don't trust myself, and I don't know that I ever will entirely. There are mornings when I look in the mirror above the sink and see Joe. But it's all fading with every day that passes. That's the beauty of the human mind. It can absorb and process excruciating pain like childbirth and in time, dull the jagged edges and mute the angry sirens leaving only the soft, fuzzy shadow of a memory.

I do miss Meela. I fashioned her from the ashes of a man who taught me how to love. I made her and yet she became so much more than all the elegant lines of code I stitched together. It's clear to me now how little I understand about creation. There is just so much wonder.

Some days I think I need to find something new to throw my obsessive nature at, but other days I think, no, fuck it, I'm good just figuring out what we're going to eat for dinner. I achieved success, the kind of success that people make movies about, and it was catastrophic. I don't feel that same drive anymore. It's gone. I'm glad it's gone. I think that I will be better in its absence. So will the world.

//the end

//acknowledgements

Writing a novel is a journey and contrary to popular opinion, it's not a solo one. This book is the product of a lifetime of conversations with people so much smarter than me, and the fact that it exists at all is owed to a handful of loving people who have tirelessly cheered me on.

I first want to thank Stacia Pelletier for her brilliant editing and thoughtful encouragement. She provided deep insights and direction that helped transform the story.

Thank you to my friends from the book club I started over ten years ago so I'd have something else to discuss with other neighborhood dads besides baseball. A special thank you to Jason Hatfield, Phil Castro, David Nicholson, Seth Trugman, and Jeff Barnes who were early readers, and gave great feedback.

I also want to thank the community of wonderful readers and writers I've met on Substack, the platform where I first published this book as a serial in 2023. Special thanks to Troy Ford, Sheri Barrera-Disler, Mina Rhee, Aram Yang, Dudley Greene, Claudia Befu, Lynn Clary, Kristin Gibson, Lauren Argott, and Kimberly Warner.

My parents, John and Grace Wakeman were the first readers. I called them every Saturday morning and read the latest chapter. Without their constant love and support, I'm sure I would never have had the courage or belief in myself to ever share my work. Thanks also to my loving and kind brothers, Jon and Hans.

Finally, there is one person I have to thank most of all for her undying support of my writing and that's my partner, Paradis Ansari. We met during the lowest point of my life on the cusp of a global pandemic. I read her chapters of this book over Zoom every night as we were just falling in love. Every writer should be so lucky.

In closing, I'd like to acknowledge the unfathomable loss that so many Americans live with who have had their children, their spouses, their parents, and friends taken from them by a gun. It is a tragedy that is unique to our country and one we cannot seem to stop. I implore you to do your part in lobbying for sensible gun control that has proven to save lives in hundreds of democracies around the world.

To keep up with my latest projects including short fiction, songs, and essays, and have them delivered right to your inbox, subscribe to my publication, Catch & Release.

Subscribe to Ben Wakeman's online
publication for free and receive stories,
essays, songs, and more in
your inbox every week.

www.catchrelease.net